#1

SUPERIOR'S JEWEL

BARB DIMICH

Keith —
I hope you
enjoy the story!
Barb
Dimich

REPRINTED

ISBN:1539073238
ISBN-13:9781539073239

DEDICATION

For Nancy Wedding

We may not be the "buzzin' cousins", but your Chicken Soup always soothes my soul. Uff-da!

"Barb Dimich has succeeded where few authors can—she's woven an intriguing tale of murder mystery and intense personal relationships into three, edge-of-your seat stories that fiction and nonfiction readers alike will relish. You'll catch yourself making excuses to get back to The Apostle Islands Trilogy."
Joany Haag, End of the Road Radio Morning show Host, WELY Radio

"Superior's Jewel a good read!" (Starred Review)
Arm Chair Interviews, Minneapolis, Minnesota

"Praise for Dimich's dialogue and the suspense that keeps you up all night long reading."
The Daily Tribune, Hibbing, Minnesota

ACKNOWLEDGMENTS

The origin of the Apostle Islands Trilogy came long after my first visit to La Pointe and Bayfield, Wisconsin. With a desire to put many ideas into one simple story, this trilogy came into focus after a phone call to Lori Hinrichsen of Madeline Island's Chamber of Commerce. Best friends Katharine, Michelle and Nicole emerged as three heroines. Lori without your knowledge and guidance of the area and people, I could not have finished the Apostle Islands Trilogy.

To George Toman of the La Pointe Police Department, after chasing you around fourteen miles of rock, I can't thank you enough for filling in the gaps on Wisconsin law, crime scene investigation, the tours and the intriguing 'inside info'. In many ways, our chat iced the cake for an amazing finish.

I am especially grateful to Nori Newago, President of Madeline Island Historic Preservation Association, for your assistance in locating the owner of "Song of The Pioneers" by Elvera Myhre. A special thank you to Elvera's granddaughter, Virginia Lofrano, for permission to use the song that your grandmother wrote. As the story emerged, each verse in Song of the Pioneers became an integral part of the trilogy.

A gracious thank you to the Reiman Family and their friends for bailing my car out of one muddy mess then inviting me into your magnificent retreat overlooking 'the big lake'.

Special thanks to Alice Cadotte for the historical facts and reference materials, and to Linda Ohlandt who shared more cultural tidbits.

Thank you to Roger Lenz for your gun expertise and the patient explanations, and to Rudy Sterbenk for detailing the necessary boat info. Your help was extremely useful and your friendships will always be invaluable.

Barb Dimich

Prologue

Sergeant Kat LeNoir peered through the curtainless window. She recognized the white woman slumped over on the floor in a pool of blood. Her name was Loralela Edwards. Drawing her weapon, Kat aired into portable, "Four-o-six, I got one down inside and need back-up ambulance code three."

"Four-o-six, starting ambulance and back-up."

Red flashing lights swirling in the dogwatch sky was her backup and they'd arrive shortly. Standing to the side of the paint-chipped door, Kat fisted it, waited a beat before pounding a second time when a scream cut through the night stillness. Her adrenaline went into overdrive as she looked up at an open, second-floor window over her head. Dead silence followed the frantic scream that she thought had come from a kid. Her decision to go inside without backup might be suicidal but the kids came first. Maybe a burden, but protecting the children had ownership of her soul. She tried the door and discovered it unlocked. Her nine-millimeter aimed, Kat scanned the inside for other humans and visible weapons. Seeing neither, she moved slowly inward. A pungent stench reeked of day-old boiled cabbage. In one corner of the living room, a tipped lamp gave off buttery rays of light that cast bulky shadows around broken furniture. Loralela was lying in the middle of it. Blood bubbled out of her chest in wheezing gurgles. No doubt, the eruption had come from a domestic battle.

Kat listened for a sec with her ear angled upward before climbing the stairs directly in front of her. The old staircase creaked sharply from the stress of her weight. The sound kept her on full alert. She paused at the top scanning the semi-dark hallway. Light from one room wasn't enough to illuminate the spooky shadows in the hall's unlit corners. Her sweaty, two-handed grip tightened around the butt of her Smith and Wesson. Her muscles tensed, her heart pumped harder, perspiration trickled down her forehead in nervous energy. Taking slow deliberate steps and ready to confront attackers, Kat peered into each darkened room. At the third lit bedroom, she quick-peeked through the doorway, flinched backward then looked in again at Donte *Mad Dog* Johnson kneeling on a double bed. A pile of bedding was drenched in crimson red. Shirtless, Mad Dog repeatedly rammed a butcher knife into the bundle with savage thrusts. His dreadlock hair was short and sticking out of his head in tangled frazzles. A doughnut-like glaze coated his enlarged-to-silver-dollar eyes. She'd seen the haughtiness and crazed facial expressions before. Cranked up on cocaine again, the drug controlled Donte with as much savageness as his thrusting knife.

"Police! Drop it! Drop the knife, Mad Dog! Drop it now!"

Mad Dog ignored her, just kept stabbing away at the bloodstained heap.

"Drop the knife, Mad Dog!"

Suddenly the rhythmic swing of his arm stopped, the knife hanging midair in his hand. Mad Dog looked up, shifting ever so slightly. When he focused on her, a sneaky visual passed between them like slow forward advance on a video remote. He jerked abruptly, scrambled off the bed with his left hand raised in attack mode. Blood covered his body and jeans.

"Drop the knife! Drop it, Mad Dog!"

Prepared, trained, her finger on the trigger, Donte lunged.

Shit!

He flinched with each hit from the discharged rounds and dropped to the floor with a thud three feet from her. The knife fell out of his hand hitting the hardwood floor with a clunk. His mink-colored eyes looked at her with a bewilderment and confusion that replaced his earlier condescending expression. Then, of all things, Kat swore *"thanks"* whispered of his lips.

Officers invaded the lower level storming the upstairs as Kat moved quickly, kicking the blade across the room with the toe of her boot. She pat-searched Donte's pants for other weapons then rushed to the child marinated in blood. Her vain attempts to restore life into the three-year old blew up. She stared at the lifeless Mad Dog lying on the floor. *Damn you, Mad Dog! You wanted your life to end.*

Keying her radio, Kat aired, "Four-o-six. Have Four-o-two go to channel three with me."

Carl, her lieutenant, answered up and was en route as she relived the shoot in her mind. She'd ordered Donte to drop the knife at least three times. She had to remember the exact details as she stared at blood trails covering the walls with stains stretched and splayed offensively toward the ceiling. She'd arrived too late and the outcome was another failed attempt to protect and serve.

With ten years of service to the citizens of Minneapolis, eight on the Northside, their dying attempts to reduce the crime was an epidemic. She'd never shot anyone until now, thought about how they'd been told homicides were down, that major crime was declining. Those declining numbers opposed the distorted statistics. There'd been too many domestic-related calls to this address and Kat knew Donte. She knew them all. Donte's nickname, Mad Dog, came from his over indulgence in the cheap three-dollar wine. At twenty-three, the black male was a pharmaceutically gifted crank user. Each day Kat had watched the payoff of mixing drugs and alcohol. Citizens pumped themselves up with dope and liquor for the payoff of energy and stamina. Gloomy desperation followed extended use. They called it the cocaine blues. The grisly combination was the making of street life and ended by stealing away the life of another.

As officers navigated around Mad Dog's body, one commented four slugs had punctured his chest. Another said Loralela had two stab wounds in her chest. She was barely breathing and paramedics were working on her. Jermaine ... Kat looked at the crumpled and bloody bed. Jermaine was their dead child.

On this early Monday morning, the day after Easter, this was supposed to be the celebration of life.

Song of the Pioneers
By Elvera Myhre

Tho' I wander far away, I always long to return.
To my old home and my loved ones who are
waiting for me there. Where dear mother
and my dear father came to live for many years,
and kept us children all together to work
and play without fear.
O there is no other island so dear to me as thou art.
Mad'line Island, Beautiful Island,
I love the name with all my heart.

CHAPTER 1

Four Months Later

From the upper deck of the Bayfield Island Queen ferry, the engine's monotonous hum rendered a vibrating tickle underfoot. Lake Superior's perky breeze gently caressed Kat's face. She gazed upward at the delicate wisps of whitish clouds painting the sky like an angel's luminous halo. *Their* transparency cast no shadows or doubts, she thought. Not like the tormenting screams and cries inside her mind. Try as she might, she needed to force her thoughts into something positive. But she couldn't. She had plenty of talent and vision now blurred by inner turmoil. She'd been good at her job. She just couldn't find it in herself to care anymore.

What *would* she do with the rest of her life?

Kat glanced over her shoulder for the umpteenth time since boarding the ferry. No one paid her attention, and she sucked down a sharp breath of air. Her efforts to loosen up and relax since leaving the Twin Cities early this morning were futile. It was impossible to clear her mind of the past tragedies but she needed to find a way to release the internal torture. And the only way she knew how to do it was to return to the place she once called home. The more she thought about her need for isolation, the more she realized Madeline Island's privacy would cut her off from the personal defeat. Lake Superior's crystalline blue waters would stop the silent tears that wept inside of her. The big lake's magical charm, archaic magnificence, and La Pointe's quiet peacefulness would provide her with instant relief. She felt positive coming home was the answer to eliminating all her doubts. As the ferry neared the island, she wondered if it was too much to expect liberation.

All of a sudden, there was a feeling of evil in the air. Kat's mind went on full alert. She could smell it, feel it, almost reach out and touch it. She spun around to look. Her pulse racing erratically, the familiar prickle in the pit of her stomach warning her to react cautiously was all trained behavior she took seriously. The threat was there.

The threat she felt stood across the top deck with deep-set eyes fixed pointedly upon her. His eyes were sinister-looking, and for whatever reason tunneling a hole the size of a spent hollow point right through her. Kat took mental inventory of the stranger, a lone white male, thirty-something. He was a skinny one at six-two, about a hundred seventy pounds. His brown hair appeared dyed red at one time. A plain white t-shirt and jeans didn't make him stand out from the others and his arms were free of visible scars and tattoos. His tanned face lacked facial hair exposing a dominating cleft in a square chin. Sunlight reflected a sparkle off a diamond stud in his right ear. But as their eyes connected, his Adam's apple rippled with a rapid gulp.

Kat readied to draw her nine, another automatic habit, when the guy stumbled backward. He pivoted and collided with the skipper before stumbling like a drunk downward to the lower deck. Her right hand on her hip jittered restlessly in support of her troubled thoughts. With her gun belt and shield retired, she was unarmed and hadn't learned how not to react. Though anxiety dominated her life, it was painfully embarrassing to grab for a weapon no longer strapped to her waist. How much time would pass before her observations and reflexes quit reacting? How long until the constant anxiety vacated her being?

When will my composure return and I no longer feel under attack?

Kat shifted awkwardly then did a double take as the skipper ambled toward her. She couldn't remember the last time she'd seen Sully Tanner. His soft, yellowish-brown eyes still reminded her of a fawn. A steel-looking, woolly beard surrounded his mouth where a battered pipe hung from the corner. The saturation of gray was a sign of time but Sully was obviously still a tourist guide on the Bayfield Island Princess. She recalled how he sometimes worked the Island Queen and wondered if the visionary remember her as she recollected the ghost story he told to gullible passengers. Thinking about his entertaining tale, another eerie current swept through Kat's bones. Never believing in the three crying ghosts, she never forgot the way Sully's legend gave her the creeps.

Madeline Cadotte, daughter of Chief White Crane, had three exquisite daughters, Katrina, Nicolina and Mikala, by a French fur trader named Michel Cadotte. Jeweled eyes graced each child, and all of Chief White Crane's people adored the exquisite daughters. For as long as Kat could remember, the skipper bombarded islanders and tourists with legends of each daughter's murder by medicine men the night before their wedding vows. Sully told that some medicine man's divine creator wanted the girl's jeweled eyes for a sacramental pledge. According to Sully, after the death of her third daughter, the Cadotte wife went into seclusion on the largest of the Apostle Islands. Some said the Native American woman disappeared after her third daughter's death. Others said Mother Madeline died within a year of Nicolina's murder.

Kat didn't believe the story though the skipper had a sure-fire way of conning tourists into believing the daughter's ghosts had been crying for centuries throughout the Apostle Islands. He added intrigue with the telling of jeweled bridal gifts Michel had for his daughters, but during his mourning, Michel buried the jewels somewhere on Madeline Island. Throughout the years, tourists had twisted the largess from jewels into gold medallions and coins the French fur trader brought with him from France. Kat wondered if tourists still came to Madeline Island in search of the nonexistent buried treasure. It didn't matter. The rest of Sully's tale spoke to the murdered daughter's three ghosts weeping and haunting the Apostle Islands until the lost dowries were located and three island women united in marriage to their soul mates. Only then, according to Sully Tanner, would the Cadotte ghosts go away peacefully.

Kat smirked. Sully had forever tagged her and her two best friends, Nicole and Michelle, as the three women who must exchange those sacred vows. He always said *they* possessed the jeweled eyes of Madeline's three daughters and were the only women capable of calming the Cadotte ghosts with the promise of love. Kat knew that Madeline and Michel Cadotte were real people, who did have children, but the rest of the tall tale was hogwash. She hadn't permitted herself to fall under Sully's spell years ago though she figured he'd pick up where they left off. Besides, she thought, Michelle had already proved the falsity of his claim with little success at her own marital attempt.

How odd that her dysfunctional life was reconnecting her to the past with charged-up feelings of the skipper's story.

Sully came to a stop in front of her. Swirls of gray-blue smoke from his pipe curled and floated above his head in the gentle breeze. She always thought the fragrant tobacco smelled like cloves. Strangely, that familiar aroma was grabbing at a part of her soul that Kat thought she'd lost forever. Oddly though, sympathy, for what Kat had no idea, filled the gleam in Sully's golden eyes.

"You don't remember me, do you, Sully?"

"Aye, lassie," he said relighting his pipe. "I shan't forget the eyes that twin Superior's crystal blue on a sunny day. But I'm fearful right now."

"Why's that?"

"'Tis overcast and somber shadows hiding yer need to change a cruel world. Tell an old geezer what's shipwrecked such optimism?"

She had never understood the depth of his wisdom and perception. The mystique of it used to surprise her. Today it only clouded her with more discomfort. "Nothing to tell," Kat lied. "How are you, Sully? Still conning tourists with murder mysteries and tales of lost jewels?"

"Aye. Tisn't a tale. Tis true stories of lost love, not jewels. And tis yerself who favors Madeline's daughter Katrina. You have her lucid-blue eyes, Katharine. The jewels of the largest Great Lake." Then as if he had a front row seat into her life, said, "You've never married."

"How would you know that?"

"Yer eyes tell all, lass. They weep openly the way Katrina does."

"The story is a crock, Sully. You know as well as everyone

within a hundred miles there's never been any proof Madeline's daughters were murdered or that ghosts haunt the islands."

"Ahh, Katharine, indeed still too rational. Yer needing proof beyond any shadowed doubt. Tis my own ears are proving all I need to know. Just last week, Katrina wailed up a storm over at Raspberry Island."

"Next you're gonna tell me she talks to you."

"Nay," he chuckled at her sarcasm. "Only cries waitin' for the promise of sacred nuptials between two lost souls. You and yours, Katharine Regina."

She tossed him a slanted look. With a need to know more about the stranger and less about ghosts, she asked, "Who was the guy that just bulldozed his way around you?"

"The Island's mystery man. Been here a couple months before the tourist season picked up. Speaks to no one and like yerself seems to hide a great deal. Josh Cannon's his name."

"You mean he's hiding on the island?"

"Perhaps," Sully said, inhaling deeply on his pipe.

"What's he do for a living?"

"Has the appearance of a tourist. I can't be sure. Nobody knows a thing 'bout the man who carries a purse."

An afterthought, the color was black and Kat smirked again. "That purse is called a fannypak, Sully."

"Tis a sad day I've lived when a man carries a lady's bag."

An explanation seemed pointless. "I can't believe no one knows a bloody thing about this guy. They always know what's going on around here."

"Tis true and I see you still have yer father's strong opinions, Katharine."

She'd forgotten that people in La Pointe once called her Katharine. Her Minneapolis crime-fighting partners kidded her quick moves were cat-like and gave her a nickname that stuck. She supposed folks on the Island would keep their ways.

"Tell me. How is it no one's talked of yer coming back?"

"I didn't tell anyone."

As a trained observer, Kat knew the eyes were nothing more than physiological dead ends. The eyes were not capable of emotion in themselves though they could transmit the most subtle nuances because of their use and the use of the face around them. The most important technique of eye management was the look, or the stare. And right now, Sully was imploring every muscle in his face to break her down into a confession.

Kat looked away and shoving her fists into her jacket pockets. She looked back when he chortled. "What?"

"It was time for you to come back. Katrina's been callin' fer you."

"What ever."

"Tis gonna be hell once you reunite with Nicole and Michelle. I bet the ferry under us their squeals will reach beyond Outer Island when they learn of yer return. You want me to radio ahead? Have someone meet you?"

She shook her head, shuffled her feet anxiously and gazed across the water without speaking.

"I've gotta go, lass. You know where I am when yer needing to cast them woeful eyes overboard."

Pivoting, Sully sauntered away.

A nice old man, but as bat-shit crazy as his ghost story. Kat had other problems to deal with. Sully with his invisible ghosts was not one of them. Pulling her hands free, she propped her elbows on the life rail. Blue water glistened around twenty-one solitary islands, baptized the Apostle Islands National Park. Various boats, kayaks and fishing buoys speckled the surface. A swap of paled clouds floated carelessly overhead. Gulls sailed between the varying blue colors of sky and water. Gentle, tranquil waves rolled in honor of the old girl's spirit that had claimed souls many times over the centuries. Superior could abruptly turn rugged and merciless—*very much like the city streets.* Kat had promised herself not to dwell on it.

She still had to face her family and debated how to handle the inevitable. Thankful for the ferry's leisurely pace across the water's imposing glitter, she honestly didn't know what she would tell them. She inhaled deeply, let it out slowly and tried to settle down. The pulsing knot in her stomach and her pumping heart each demanded more energy than she had to give. And then she saw it.

Madeline Island … with all its beauty and splendor.

The twenty-second island sat prim and precious giving families their claimed privacy from the outside world. *Precious Jewel of the Apostles* folks called the land mass nuzzled quaintly into Lake Superior's South Shore. Kat had been counting on her long-forgotten rock to replace everything lost to her. Confidence and courage for starters. In less than twenty minutes, she'd set foot in her hometown of La Pointe, Wisconsin for the second time in fourteen years, and sighed with relief.

But as though someone still watched her, Kat glanced over her shoulder once more. The stranger had not returned. Was she nervous from the anxiety of returning home for good? More like from the criticism she was bound to receive from family and friends for her decision. They would all have something to say about her quitting a job they all knew meant everything to her. She would invent excuses in her defense, purposely hadn't told her parents, Gage, or Nicole and Michelle. She couldn't tell them the move was permanent. She couldn't tell anyone she had failed. The standard three-day administrative leave, de-stressing, debriefing, the grand jury's finding of justifiable homicide—*a second near death mishap*—there'd been no recant. She made the decision to quit the MPD with little concern of what her comrades thought either. The lack of discussion with them had been ruled her own doing, but her choice had been forced by fate's doing.

A sharp tug of guilt plucked at the edges of her heart and she took another deep breath and let it out slowly. Since her teenage years, she'd wanted to escape this place of sheer boredom. She'd always detested aging here without first exploring the world. With her enormous sights set on big goals, she fled after graduation. Kat suddenly realized how chained events made her run again. Made her run back to the same world she'd abandoned, never wanting to remember the sordid work of a big city cop. What *would* her family and friends think about her lack of willpower and defeated courage?

Her serious-minded older sibling, with his stability, used to be fair and understanding. She had always worshipped Gage. Her only brother had the gift to put everyone at ease. She needed his strength to comfort her wretched soul. Her mother, loving to all, never turned away from someone in need either. Gage and their mother were similar. Neither would denounce her decision.

Nicole and Michelle would be overjoyed she'd finally come back. They'd also be angry with her for not calling to tell them. Maybe that's what Sully meant about having to pay with hell. Nicole the congenial social butterfly of the three best friends had learned early to accept defeats and downfalls. Michelle was the meticulous and levelheaded one with a detailed business sense. She always prepared herself for life that left no room for failure. Each of them loved and cherished the island solitude. Kat was the odd one in the trio and the most rebellious. She couldn't wait to leave their rock and wondered if fourteen years had changed the sisterhood the three of them once had.

Shifting nervously, the last stretch of the trip neared, she dwelled on the strained relationship she had with her father. He would be the hardest on her. A fifteen-year-old nasty argument had strained their relationship. Sure, they had the occasional phone conversation but that fight really had severed the closeness between father and daughter. She feared her father's wrath most—*oh hell* she didn't care what anyone thought. None of them had to live with that death-filled night or deal with the after effects chasing her mind in hot pursuit. If such a thing were possible, she was ricocheting like a misguided bullet in search of *hermithood*, if such a word even existed.

La Pointe came into view and Kat took it all in with mixed emotions. Such a tranquil view greeting visitors coming over on the ferry from Bayfield. The post office, a white two-story structure was a distinguished historical site sitting at the end of the ferry dock. The Beach Club restaurant, Conoco station—Kat perked up. The red and white Conoco sign was gone and she studied the scene for other changes. Several of Madeline's inns stood out as did masts from the distant marina. A backdrop of green strapping pines framed the historical town. Could an insignificant town on an island of solitude soothe her soul? Whether it did or didn't nothing else mattered. She needed to come home.

The ferry neared the docks and Kat returned to the lower deck where she'd parked her beater. Different from her crime-fighting cohorts, her big concern with transportation was in getting from here to there. Her entire life had been crammed into a debt-free, ninety-two Buick. A car's age and appearance had never mattered to her, but her instincts did. Her neck hair stood on end and still feeling eyes upon her, Kat torpedoed another glance over her shoulder. Several people were engaged in random conversations. Some hugged the rail in awe of the scenery. They all looked suspicious to her. Dealing with city slime had trained her well. Too well, she thought. She trusted no one.

Josh Cannon had disappeared and Kat decided Sully was responsible for adding to the uncertainty in her mind. Sully, the old fool, hadn't changed. She had. She had turned into a cynical bitch.

When someone tapped her on the shoulder, Kat swung around full force. A man with carbon dark eyes stood waiting, inspecting her. He didn't speak, but studied her with fugacious eyes as though he needed to borrow energy to replace the strain of some unknown pressure. Six feet plus, raven hair added to his obtrusive height. Straight and styled, his hair was as inky as his eyes. After her own silent examination, Kat blurted, "Do I know you?"

"Doubt it. Name's Mac Dobarchon."

Her street training said to go easy around this glassy-eyed intruder, but stripped of patience to deal with him or anyone else, she threw the man an impassively cold look. Crossed arms and police stance followed. His colorless flesh reminded her of a paroled felon just out of lock-up. She smirked, thinking convicts didn't scare her nearly as much as failure did. Sarcasm would send him on his way.

"Mac Dobarchon, do I look like a people person? What do you want?"

"For starters, a name would be nice."

"What makes you think I want to start anything with you let alone tell you my name?"

"Name exchange is a common gesture when two people meet."

"Not interested. Take your common gestures and use them on someone else."

The ferry kicked the dock and Kat turned and fled to her vehicle. Short cutting through the cars, she entered her trustworthy GM. Once seated, she glanced around looking for Josh Cannon. Mac Dobarchon hadn't moved but continued to stare at her from where she had left him standing. After a moment, he sauntered over to a souped up 4x4. The vehicle was black, like his hair and eyes.

"The guy probably is a felon," she muttered, starting her car. The vehicles in front of hers moved faster than the ones in front of his. She shifted gears and gunned the engine, turning the corner onto the dock and driving onto Madeline Island.

CHAPTER 2

To face her parents, especially her father, made Kat squirrelly. Though a justified excuse had forced her to quit a job she loved, her father would never understand the weight of her decision. Considering past circumstances, she knew what his reaction would be and contemplated whether to tell her parents the truth, deciding the shock of her return was enough for now. Split-second panic finished her off. Instead of turning left to head home, Kat went straight, to the police station. Gage would have his clodhoppers propped up on the old desk the way their dad used to do. She remembered clearly the way Dad kicked back in his chair filling his gut with sturdy caffeine and reading stuff everyone already knew before the Island Blazer had time to print it. She bet herself Gage would be doing the same.

Kat drove onto the tarred lot of the historic Town Hall and parked. She glanced in the rear-view mirror while tapping out a repetitive beat on the steering wheel. La Pointe, the only town on any of the islands, dated back to the early 1700's, maybe further. She couldn't recall. What she did know was that fourteen miles of plush wilderness maintained a year-round population of a couple hundred residents. The yearly inhabitants of the largest island bragged about the beauty and the peace of the great water encircling their island. They also gloated about their solitude, but always catered to the additional twenty-five hundred summer tourists each retreating from the tedium of their lives.

She supposed her reaction was also a retreat. After weeks of debate, through many sleepless days and nights, it felt more like running full speed to escape the torture and pain of defeat, escape from her exploding world following a second occurrence of another death-defying incident. And here she sat in front of La Pointe's police station with the constant embedded feelings of neuroses.

Just get on with it the voice inside her head ordered.

Kat checked her surroundings and rolled out of the overstuffed Buick. She locked the doors from habit. A Catholic Church built in the 1800's with a rising steeple sat peaceful and white across the street. She shuffled toward the backdoor of the station. A wave of heat unfamiliar to the area made sweat ooze from her pores. She wavered some more, twisting her fingers together, chewing on her bottom lip before she entered the small office. She inhaled a couple of deep breaths, forced herself to relax then turned to reach for the door handle. The door swung open unexpectedly and she was shoved backward, falling harshly to the asphalt.

"Lady, you all right?"

The palm of her hands smarted and her backside felt worse. Except for her pride, she was fine and recognized genuine concern in her brother's voice. He picked her up with strong hands.

"I'm sorry. We've been meaning to get a doorbell—"

"Gage, you always did remind me of a bull in a China closet," Kat said, shoving the mass of long hair out of her face so he could see her.

He stepped back. "Pipsqueak? When—how—do Mom and Dad know you're here?"

She despised the nametag he'd donned her with, but the excitement in her brother's voice elevated her spirits. "Ten minutes ago, drove and—"

He pulled her into a tight hug, lifting her feet off the ground. In brotherly fashion, he swung her in a circle. "Damn, Sis! It's good to see you!"

Then he planted a scratchy smack resembling a kiss on her cheek. Placing her feet back on the ground, he held her at arm's length.

"You look great! Why the surprise visit? How long you

staying?"

Righting herself, Kat rubbed the mild whisker burn on her face and took a long look at her brother. Broad shoulders sufficiently filled a white police shirt he'd tucked inside uniformed pants. Those same shoulders were once her tower of power through high school difficulties and teenage dilemmas. She needed him now the same way he needed to rid his face of the stubble. His rumpled hair had lightened to the color of a tarnished sunset the way it always did in the summer. She'd missed Gage way too much.

"You got time to talk?" she asked.

"For you, Pipsqueak? Always. On the other hand, maybe I should call you Sarge. I was just leaving to go fishing for the afternoon, but come on in."

His roguish grin hadn't changed either, and she asked, "You sure you can spare a few minutes?"

"You bet," he said, unlocking the bolted door and ushering her into the station. "The fish can wait while I visit with my favorite sister."

"I'm your only sister," Kat said as an agitated voice on the police radio interrupted.

She waited for Gage to answer up. Except for the scent of a recent paint job, the Island's station remained as plain and confined as she recalled. One large and one small desk took up the floor space while wanteds, police info and mug shots of the FBI's top ten hung on clipboards nailed to the walls.

The door swung open. Kat gawked in disbelief when Mac Dobarchon entered the office. He stood equal to her brother's authoritative stature. His inky-black hair, which gleamed in sunlight on the ferry, gave him a sinister appearance indoors. The color matched a pair of rather arousing eyes. Neither did a thing for his pale skin. An open shirt collar revealed the same crisp black hair beneath his Adam's apple. Kat hated to admit that she actually found the sinister appearance attractive. Inadvertently licking her lips, she gulped when the glowing blackness of those fascinating eyes connected with her own misery. She recognized the pain and quickly figured out she wasn't the only vulnerable one standing in this office. Wondering who he was, she suddenly realized this guy was following her and before she could interrogate him, Gage interrupted her thoughts.

"Can I help you, sir?"

"Um, yeah. I'm spending some time here. Does your department provide a safe service for valuables?"

"A safe service? For valuables?"

"Yeah, Chief. You know jewelry, stuff like that?"

"It's Gage. Gage LeNoir."

"Mac Dobarchon," he said, and they shook hands.

"This is my sister Katharine."

Cringing at her brother's friendliness, Kat shoved her hands into the pockets of her baggy windbreaker. "We've already met," she muttered, wondering how a civilian recognized the pendant on Gage's crisp white collar to address him by title.

"Not exactly," Mac said, facing her. "Katharine, my pleasure. I admit I saw your car in the parking lot—"

"You are following me!"

"Well, yeah, I guess I am. Didn't mean to make you nervous."

"*You* do not make me nervous," she snapped, curling her concealed fingers tightly into fists. "I told you I wasn't interested."

"I believe," he countered, "what you said was I could take my common gestures and use them on someone who *is* interested. You can't blame a guy for trying to engage in a friendly conversation with a beautiful woman."

The cockiness that blossomed out of those disturbing black eyes ticked Kat off. She eyed him critically for a long moment then said, "Flattery won't work, Dobarchon."

"Then what will?"

"You're a pushy man."

"Very. What'll work?"

"If I throw you a stick, will you leave?

"Probably not."

"What part of *I'm not interested* don't you understand?"

"Mac," Gage interrupted, "we don't provide that service. Where you staying?"

"The Carriage House," he answered. "Mind telling me how to find the place?"

Attentively, Kat watched and listened. Dobarchon was alone on the ferry when he hit on her. The Carriage House used to be the honeymoon suite. She assumed it still was. Gage gave him directions but when Mac Dobarchon left, Kat realized she'd been briefly distracted from personal misery by this aggressive man. Pushy people were controlling and she had no interest in controlling men. Besides, his black eyes spelled danger and she didn't like the way they examined her either. His eyes seemed to penetrate her soul—a place she kept a list of failures never to be revealed to anyone. Glancing at her brother when Dobarchon left, Gage watched her curiously. "What?"

"That was interesting."

"Interesting my ass. It was irritating!"

He grinned. "Maybe. But you gave him a look that only means one thing."

"I did not!"

"I might not be big city, Sis, but my observation skills are razor sharp."

Heat matching the outside temp flooded her cheeks. "They can't be too sharp. He said he was staying in the honeymoon cottage. And the last place tourists go when they're on vacation or a honeymoon is the police station. What do you think he really wanted with La Pointe's finest?"

"Miss City Girl always thinking there's an ulterior motive. Seems to me he answered that and was just being friendly." Gage grinned again. "Am I gonna have to keep my eye on you?"

"I must be in penisville where men don't comprehend English," she grumbled, "I said, I wasn't interested."

Now he laughed. "Sis, your actions speak louder."

Annoyed by the transparency of her feelings, Kat changed the subject. "So tell me big brother. How's it feel filling Dad's shoes as police chief? What's it like not being under the iron thumb of arrogance?"

"Not much difference. The last couple of years Dad had retirement planned. More or less let me handle things."

"You mean there's actually something to handle around here?"

"Adeline Girard's got a new dog with a bark bigger than his bite."

"What happened to Smoky?"

"Passed on from old age. She missed the pet and got herself

another pup when Jim Berger's bitch had a litter. A golden lab. Named him Secunda. The name's Latin for second child."

"I didn't know Mrs. Girard knew Latin."

"She doesn't. Some tourist told her. You remember Jesop Merryweather?"

"Yeah."

"He's still alive and kicking. Calls daily about bear trampling his flowers at night and deer eating vegetables from his garden. Yet old Jesop made one of them deer his pet. Tied a blue scarf around the deer's neck. No one can shoot it during hunting season."

"Really?"

"Remember the Stewart's?" She nodded and he told her, "Those three barfly's have graduated from brew-ha to idiot oil over at the Tavern. Several nights a week Nikki calls needing me to break up another fight or argument between the Islands's designated drunks. So far, they only knock each other's brains around. But the cool part about being chief is I get to boss around Joe Hamlin—"

"Little Joey Hamlin?" Kat wanted to ask about Nicole and Michelle but the news about Joey surprised her more. "The kid I used to babysit is a cop?"

"Joe's not so little anymore. That was him on the air but I doubt he'll like you calling him Little Joey. He needs me to see something. Told him it'd be a few. Tell me. The big city been keeping you busy?"

"Not anymore," she mumbled.

"You still a diehard about keeping your body a temple? Or you want some coffee?"

"Yes, no," she replied, expecting some kind of reaction about her response. Gage replaced the station's coffee carafe on the hotplate, which she doubted was still hot, plopped into the desk chair and slurped from a battered mug. Over the brim of a badly stained cup, he studied her. "What?"

"Has the prodigal and determined daughter finally come to her senses?"

His casual interest didn't hide an understanding she observed in his eyes. Their mother had employed the same look on them as kids even if she didn't like the choices they made. "Aren't you even gonna ask me why?"

"Katharine. You know I'll support anything you decide. I gave you my blessing even when I disagreed with your leaving here. When you're ready to talk, you'll come to me wanting big brother to fix whatever mess you've gotten into. You know I'll do whatever I can. You also know I'm not the one who's gonna send you on a guilt trip because you quit. With that ruling free spirit of yours, I'm assuming you did in fact quit."

In the cramped space, Kat paced figure eights on the tiled floor.

"You still wiggle and jiggle when you're nervous."

On one fly-by, Kat grabbed the stapler off the desk and began smacking her hand with it. "Yeah, I quit. Will you go home and tell Dad for me?"

"You haven't lost those large pleading eyes either. How is it you held your own in a big city police department as long as you did?"

Kat stopped in front of him, stapler midair. "What's that supposed to mean?"

Shrugging, he sat up. "I'll go home with you, but you'll have to tell Mom and Dad yourself."

"Please, Gage. Tell them for me. I'll pay you back with anything."

"Pipsqueak, I love ya, but your paybacks have exceeded the national debt."

"This will be the last time I ever ask you for something—promise. Just this one last time."

"Been awhile since you've asked me for anything," he said. "What gives?"

"Please, do this for me," Kat begged, pacing some more. "I swear I'll never ask you for anything ever again."

He watched her with tongue in cheek. When she unconsciously whacked her hand harder, his restraint gave way and he cut loose with hard-core laughter. "Didn't hurt yourself, did ya?"

"You think this is funny?"

"Pipsqueak, you should see yourself right now. I said I'd go home with you, but you'll have to tell Dad whatever secret you're keeping. Besides, I'm not sure what to tell him. What happened? Why you really here?"

The door to the office swung open a second time and a woman

entered talking a blue streak.

"Gage, I know I'm late with your lunch order. Had myself a pickle of a situation at the Tavern. Hayden forgot to reorder for the bar. Neither of us is used to all the business starting so early. Gypsy called in sick and—"

Halting abruptly, Nicole squealed, "Great balls of fire! Katharine Regina LeNoir!"

"Hey, Nicole."

"Don't you hey me! I want a hug."

Practically tossing the food onto Gage's lap, Nicole grabbed Katharine in a tight squeeze, held on for several moments before examining her at arm's length.

"When did you get back? You never called!" Facing Gage, Nicole accused, "You've got some explaining to do. Honestly, what were you thinking not telling us our best friend was coming home?"

"Nikki, she just showed up here. Didn't tell anyone, just like I forgot to tell you I was taking the afternoon off to go fishing."

Disappointment flooded Nicole's liquid brown eyes, and Katharine spoke in Gage's defense. "Nicole, I know it's rare when I side with Gage, but he's right. Nobody knew I was coming back."

"Great balls of fire! How could you not call and tell your parents you were coming home?"

Guilt waves pulsed through Katharine's veins. Shuffling her feet, she explained, "I was trying to con Gage into telling Mom and Dad I'm back when you barged in here."

"Tell them what?" she asked, spinning Katharine to look her over. "Good god woman! What have you been doing to yourself? You've lost weight! You get home right now and say hi to your folks. Later the two of us will go shake up Michelle's meticulous day. I have a few things to take care of at the Tavern, but afterwards the three of us will catch up on your life, Katharine. We'll relive our rite of passage the way we did the first time we stayed up the entire night. And Gage. Go home with your sister and give her whatever support she needs. Katharine, I'll be by the house around five to pick you up."

"Whirl in, whirl out. Nicole, you haven't changed."

"Five o'clock. Be ready. I have to get back to the Tavern. Besides, this office has less space than a shot glass. Jiminy, it's good to see you! Enjoy your lunch, Gage."

Nicole whooshed out as fast as she had entered as Gage clicked the mic attached to his shoulder to answer the dispatcher.

"Your partner needs you at his location ASAP."

"Ten-four," he responded, and switched channels. "Joe, you on the air?"

"Yeah, Chief. I got somethin' you need to see."

"What is it?"

"Ah ...'bout seven miles in on the dirt road from the County Road. I need you here. Right now!"

"What have you got?"

"You need to get out here—now!"

"Can it wait? I'm in the middle of something."

"That's a negative, Chief."

"On my way," Gage huffed into his H-T. "Sorry, Sis."

"You mind if I tag along?" she asked, following him outside.

"Not at all," he said, exiting the station. "But avoidance won't change the inevitable. *You* have to tell Dad why you quit your job."

Seeing Nicole and thinking about Michelle as they got into the squad car, Katharine asked, "Did you ever hear the reason why Michelle divorced Derek?"

"Nope. Figured she decided she'd made a mistake. Why?" he asked, pulling out of the parking lot.

"I can't believe the way everybody knows what's going on around here that no one knew what Derek did to her."

"Know what? Pipsqueak, she stayed married to the man less than a year."

Jerking her head sideways, Katharine asked, "Didn't it ever occur to you why?"

Gage veered the squad onto a dirt road. He slowed minutes later coming upon the Crown Vic. "Yeah it occurred to me. Just figured she found out marriage isn't what it's cracked up to be."

Gage stopped, parked and both exited. Katharine said, "I don't know the details yet but he was abusive to her and she's one person who didn't deserve it."

Her brother looked at her across the car's roof with contorted brows and an agonized expression. His mouth tightened as he glanced toward Joey's empty squad, telling Kat that he had no clue what Michelle's had done to her.

"Joe, where the hell are ya?" Gage yelled impatiently, muttering, "Fish won't wait forever."

"Over here, Chief."

Several yards into a stand of timber and overgrowth Joey popped his head up and waved. "Over here!"

"What's he doing in the woods?"

"Drinking coffee and eating donuts."

"Funny, Pipsqueak. They'd have to be mighty potent considering the way he's covering his mouth."

It was automatic for Kat to inhale. As quickly as she caught the whiff of the rank air, her feet stopped moving near the squad's front bumper. Clammy moisture seeped out of her flesh as her heart pumped out beats to an old cadence. "I-I'll wait here," she said.

"You okay?"

Kat nodded, her fingers starting to tremble. Gage jaunted through the ditch toward Joey. Tagging along with her brother had been a mistake. Unable to dispute the sickly pungent odor, Kat leaned against the squad car, scanning her surroundings warily—once a cop, always a cop. Since that night, she'd acquired a twitchy spasm in the corner of her eye along with a host of other symptoms. She squeezed her eyes shut and swallowed back the dread forcing its way up her throat like vomit. She felt certain of Joey's discovery.

"Get a grip, Kat. Just calm down. Inhale. Exhale. Nice and slow. It isn't what you think."

An uncivilized groan from Gage countered her pep talk. She straightened and waited as he wended his way back through the brush. A dichotomy of emotions saturated the gentle blue of his eyes. The ease with which he moved was gone as her brother approached her, half in anticipation, half in dread.

"Katharine ...,"

The strain in his voice wilted hers to a whisper. "Gage, what is it?"

"When you made sergeant, didn't you work homicide for a

while?"

Stiffening, Kat glanced down the dirt road. A verdant forest blocked Lake Superior's fortifying water. The peace she'd come looking for was destroyed by that simple question. Biting her lip, she said, "Two years. Why?"

"Joe's found something out of my league. I could use your help."

The desperation in his voice told her to walk away, leave right now. Kat crossed her arms tightly to halt her trembling as the familiar shakes started. She forced herself to look back at her brother. "W-What kind of help?"

"Joe's found a body. A kid, I think."

No! Not another child!

CHAPTER 3

An uneasiness steadily grew inside of Katharine with ferocious energy. She wanted to bury her head in the sand like an ostrich. If she couldn't see the situation, didn't have to be part of it, it couldn't hurt her. Losing her icy surface calm, her arms came undone like a volcano spewing fire and rock and her shoulders retracted. Clinching her fists until her fingernails dug into her palms, she took out the anger she felt with herself on Gage. "What in blue blazes do you mean *think*?"

"It's hard to tell ... she looks young," he said with pleading eyes. "Weather's been extremely hot."

Sidestepping him, Katharine stomped off and navigated the same path he'd taken. It was reflexive training and conditioning that compelled her to face what she knew was gruesome. Swatting angrily at hoarding flies, she nodded curtly upon reaching the man she once babysat then stopped suddenly, gaping at the ghastly form. Yanking her shirtfront across her mouth and nose, her heart rate sped up and felt like a massacre inside of her chest. Sweat beads molded themselves across her brow and nape of her neck. Her mouth watered, her stomach contracted and turning abruptly away, she heaved. One of them tugged back her hair and held it until she'd finished tossing this morning's breakfast.

"Chief, there's some water in my squad."

Katharine wanted to cuss and swear but instead she straightened, and swiped at her mouth with the back of her hand.

Joey offered her a sympathetic smile. Gage hustled over with the bottled water he'd retrieved and handed it to her. Her fingers were shaky as she took the bottle, guzzled then spit out the warmed liquid.

"Katharine, I'm sorry I made you do this. I'll call Dad—"

"You didn't make me! And Dad's not gonna know what to do since neither one of you has ever seen a corpse like this." Katharine spit again. "What's the temp?"

"High eighties."

Mad as hell at herself, the well-grounded instincts kicked in and took control. She studied the body for s moment then said, "Your *kid* appears to be a teenage girl. I'm guessing she's been dead about twenty-four, maybe thirty-some hours. Beetles are having a feast on dried skin near the greenish-red coloring of her head and neck."

Both men nodded with innate programming though their unfamiliarity with this color of death kept them from speaking.

"I'm pretty sure those bugs signify death occurred at least twenty-four hours ago. The coloring hasn't spread to her chest and thighs but it'll tell the medical examiner more about the time of death. Since I'm not a scientist, I'd guess decomposing's been accelerated by the weather, and that factor will distort rigor along with a possible struggle she had against her attacker."

"First, Katharine. There's no way she's been *here* that long. Critters of the forest would've found her," Gage said. "Second. How do you know she struggled?"

"You're right. Someone dumped her. Dried blood around the fingernails indicates she may have scratched her attacker. Use yellow tape and enclose the crime scene in a wide circumference. Since there's no crime lab to speak of, Gage, you'll need a camera. You'll also need to call the medical examiner over from the mainland."

"Excuse me, ma'am. How wide? Do we close the road to summer tourists?"

Katharine choked on Joey's polite address. He looked as green as she felt and probably went through digestive reflex long before he ever contacted Gage.

"You don't remember me do you, Squirt?"

His fresh face colored fiercely. Joey had grown up into a trim, lean young man. A shaggy bob remained as corn yellow as ever. "Joey, you use to love ladybugs and called me Katybug because you couldn't say Katharine."

"Geez, yeah! Now I remember. You teased me and called my freckles ginger speckles."

Both men followed her when Katharine moved away from the corpse. "That I did. And if I didn't know better, I'd swear you've acquired more."

"Don't know about that but it's sure good to see you again, Katybug."

"You too. Um, yeah, the road needs to closing until you and Gage process the area. Use yellow police tape. I'm assuming you do have police tape?" Gage nodded as she asked, "Do you have a camera?"

"Back at the office."

"Someone needs to stay here until the M.E. arrives. The scene has to be photo'd extensively and examined. You'll have to mark and take measurements. Distances from body to road, stuff like that. You should also do a sketch of the crime scene."

"I'm debating if I should call the crime lab in from Ashland. On the other hand, the death scent will attract critters quickly. Can we remove the corpse as fast as possible?"

"No! You're gonna need photos of the entire area surrounding the corpse. You better mark her outline too, and photo the victim from every direction facing the woods and the road."

"We really need your help," Gage told her.

Ignoring his plea, she said, "There's hints of another trail from the road over there and where each of us has walked onto the crime scene. You'll have to identify Joey's entry, yours and mine to figure out where the body was dragged in. Examine each trail for trace evidence and snap off pictures of anything you discover before you touch it."

"What specifically are we looking for?"

Feeling drained, hollow, and lifeless, her reply was still automatic. "Torn clothing which may or may not match the victim's. Blood to be analyzed for comparison to the victim's. Anything you find, no matter how insignificant it appears, needs to be noted in detail. Joey, you'll have to give a statement on your discovery. What prompted you to look here in the woods?"

"That's easy. I was driving with my window down and caught the putrid smell on a breeze. I stopped, thinking it was a dead deer or some other animal. My nose guided me. What're we gonna find within the area you want roped off?"

"I think my sister's big-city experience is telling us the girl didn't die here but somewhere else. The area has to be checked for evidence."

"Gage is right. The girl was dragged in since none of us made a wide path like the one I see over there," she said, waving her hand at the dirt road. "Doesn't appear to have rained in the past forty-eight hours and the area around the body might expose something. Keep to the same trails you already made."

"How do you think she died?" Gage asked.

Refusing to look back, Katharine inched further away. She needed hot salsa to reduce the olfactory discomfort. Gage and Joey followed.

"I didn't see any blood from obvious entry wounds to indicate stabbing or shooting. An autopsy will tell you the cause of death. Either of you have any idea who she is?"

The two men glanced at each other, frowning. "Probably a tourist's kid," Joe finally said.

"I'll request the M.E.," Gage said. "Joe. Go to the station and get the camera. See if you can get a hold of both seasonal officers. They can help us here."

The English language contained no word to describe the fetid odor, but Katharine stayed put, waiting until Joey walked away. "Gage, you do not want inexperience trampling through your crime scene. You need to keep everyone out. Have the other two close the road."

"Joe, wait a minute," Gage yelled. "You're thc boss, Sis."

"No I'm not! I can't ... I'm not carrying and I don't have my badge anymore."

"Katharine, I really need your help. I'll swear you in. You're right. We've never had a murder. And somewhere on this Island, there's a parent waiting and wondering. They'll want an explanation why their teenage daughter is dead. For which I don't have the answer. I'm asking. Please. You've handled homicides by the dozen. This should be easy for you."

Totally unfair. She *had* worked murder investigations, but not anymore. Katharine groped for the words knowing her brother would never flaunt how much she did owe him. But his request was impossible. Staring off, she whispered, "Gage, I can't help you ... I can't do this."

Tears formed in the corners of her eyes. The eternal agony would kill her. When the watery streams threaded down her cheeks, Gage tugged her in with a hug and held on.

"Pipsqueak, what's wrong? Talk to me. What happened to you?"

She swallowed hard, squared her shoulders and brushed him away. Crying was unacceptable. A sign of weakness her dad always said. Katharine swiped at her eyes and took a deep breath. Death was everywhere. Escaping its control was abject. Her self-doubts confirmed her inadequacy and instability. The unmerciful backlash was unforgettable. "I'm okay," she muttered, and started scrounging the area surrounding the dead girl.

She didn't hear the next thing Gage said to Joey. Didn't care either. Unable to explain failure to her brother, she'd always despised the way Mr. Born Efficient was successful at everything. Too automatic to stay, too unwilling to leave, it took about three minutes for her nose to adjust, then thirty silent minutes passed while she helped Gage tape off the perimeter around the body. When Joey returned, he and Gage snapped off several rolls of film with an antiquated Pentax 35mm. They measured and marked the trails for identification purposes and cautiously examined each one for blood and clothing threads. Katharine continued a search of the area as far away from the victim as possible.

"Chief, I left messages with Pete and Alesha to call in. You still wanna close the road?"

"I need you here. We'll wing it for now."

"I never knew Katharine was a cop. She really knows a lot about forensic anthropology."

Gage stopped what he was doing. "Knows what?"

"You know. The study of physical anthropology. Techniques used to determine the sex, age and genetics of biological materials for civil and criminal law. Forensics."

"Jesus, Joe," he muttered, staring at his deputy in open-mouth wonder. "You sound like a forensic Webster's."

Shrugging, Joe asked, "Where's she work?"

"Street sergeant for Minneapolis ... worked homicide for a couple years after getting her gold shield."

"Well. Now I understand."

"What's that?"

"Why you let her see this. When I found the girl, I didn't know what to tell you or dispatch on the air. Damn near had a cow when she got out of the squad. I really didn't know who she was."

"You did just fine, Joe and let's just do the best we can."

"Is she gonna be okay, Chief?"

Gage glanced over his shoulder at his sister. "I'll make sure she is. How you holding up?"

"Rough at first, but I'm hanging in."

He didn't respond as he looked over at his sister a second time.

"Chief, she's been avoiding this spot and hunting the area like a beach bum. I'm kinda worried about her."

Katharine wondered if they knew she could hear them. Both mentally and physically, she wasn't prepared for this. She always tied her back when she worked but now it hung long and loose and she flipped it back over her shoulder. Continuing her foray through the thick wooded mass, she hunted for indications and traces of evidence within the crime scene tape. Gut instincts had never terrified her. Traumatic cases never did either until *that* second incident.

"Don't think about it," she whispered, and concentrated on a nagging thought she had about the body instead. An annoying voice in her head kept telling her she'd missed something. It came from the lack of the forensic experience Joey thought she had. Katharine stopped and looked back. With her thoughts spinning, she swatted hungry flies and slued sharply, tripping over a fallen tree. Scraping thicket and undergrowth on the way down, she let cut loose a whole bunch of liberated curses landing face down. Sharp pain pierced her arm as Katharine heard Gage yell in a voice filled with angst. She sputtered a second mouthful of four-letter words as she rolled off the heartless tree branches. Both men had rushed over to her as she spotted the culprit—broken glass—causing the injury to her arm. She pushed her hair out of her face then caught a flicker of laughter in Gage's eyes. If she'd been on her feet, she definitely would have slugged him. Joey's sympathetic face stopped her from spouting another round of profanities.

"Gage, don't even think it! And quit standing there like a couple of dipsticks. Get me out of this damn tree!"

They overstepped the enemy, lifting her to her feet effortlessly.

Brushing off, she fumed, "Wipe that smirk—"

"Sis, you're bleeding! Lemme take a look at your arm."

"I just scratched it on some broken glass. I'm fine."

"Hey! Anybody out here?"

Shifting, Gage muttered, "That'll be the coroner."

Joey and Gage went to head him off. Katharine looked down and recognized the black label on a broken whiskey bottle lying in soft duff. After a difficult shift, some of her x-partners randomly rejoiced in Johnnie Walker Black during male rituals. They said the smooth blend of scotch and whiskey was a legal painkiller. It helped them to forget the street evil.

Liquid sitting in the crook at the bottom and an unbleached label set the wheels in her mind in motion. The heat would have dried up the alcohol remnants. Weather elements would have faded the label's color if the bottle had been here for any amount of time. Latents on the glass would also identify the bottle's owner.

Squatting, Katharine cleared away dead leaves from the shards. Mentally noting the locale, she rose and traipsed through thicket to retrieve an evidence bag, cursing flies and mosquitoes all the way. Approaching the three men, the foul odor had intensified under the sun's blaze.

"Katharine, this is Del Cadavor, the medical examiner."

"Howdy, ma'am. Cadavor, *with an o's,* my name, bodies are my game."

Gawking in disbelief at the thin-stature M.E., the man with a dry sense of humor carried fewer years than his thick graying hair told. A whimsical twinkle in mist-blue eyes was a dead giveaway of the desire he had to perform his job.

"Mr., um, Del," she settled on, "I'm guessing the vic's been dead about twenty-four hours, maybe longer. There's signs of dragging, but no evidence of clothing threads in the brush."

"Cause?"

"That's your job. Blood in her fingernails indicates a possible struggle."

"Uh-huh," he uttered casually. "Did you know the opening up of a corpse is called autopsy from the Latin word autopsia, meaning self-seeing? As early as 1800, doc's wanted firsthand knowledge about the human body's innards."

They all gaped at the medical examiner.

"It's true," he said. "Most were superstitiously horrified of corpses. Threatened violence to any doctor who dared dissect the dead. Bet you didn't know autopsies used to take place behind locked doors."

"Fascinating," Katharine scoffed. "Just fricking fascinating. You think we can speed this up before maggots consume what's left of the corpse?"

"The man speaks the truth."

All four swung round to look. Katharine blinked. *What's he doing here? How'd he find us?* Mac Dobarchon approached from the ditch. He'd parked his black jeep behind the squads and the coroners van.

"Back in 1827 the notorious William Burke murdered at least fifteen paupers so he could supply doctors with subjects for dissection."

"Del Cadavor, with an o," Gage said, "Mac Dobarchon. This is Joe Hamlin and you already know my sister, Katharine."

Their nonchalance shocked Katharine and she stepped back when they swapped handshakes and wisecracks about the M.E.'s name. It irked her more to watch them bond over a dead body. It also confirmed her belief that all men were four short of a six-pack. Not to mention, how these idiots were obstructing an active crime scene.

"Beginning in Edinburgh," Dell went on, "studies began producing info that shifted public opinion and made anatomy a major branch of modern medicine."

"That's right," Mac said. "The concept created an essential turn for criminal investigations. The once illegal self-seeing by experts became standard practice in murder cases. And it certainly appears you've got yourselves a murder here."

That got Katharine's attention and she inched closer. How would an outsider, one bordering on stalking charges, who should've been forbidden to enter the crime scene, know the victim was murdered?

"Island's first," Gage replied. "I'm soliciting my sister's help since she worked homicide in Minneapolis."

And so did that! Katharine tossed a ferocious glare at Gage at the same time Dobarchon gave her an astonished look. Unable to digest anymore, she ripped out the words impatiently. "Gage! I need gloves and an evidence bag!"

Her outburst induced unwanted attention, placing her frail composure under more attack. Withdrawing herself was lost when Dobarchon stepped up to play paramedic. He lifted her arm to observe her wound.

"This has to be cleaned out. You can't risk an infection."

"It's a scratch," Katharine huffed, yanking her arm away from him.

"It's a deep scratch and needs peroxide."

"Pipsqueak, what do you need an evidence bag for?"

Dobarchon's inquisitive gaze pulled on her soul with intense emotion until she was forced to look away. Elaborately casual, she explained the discovered bottle to her brother.

"Johnnie Black?" Gage questioned. "As in Johnnie Walker Black?"

"You wanted my help! The bottle's evidence. Yes, I said Johnnie Walker Black. Why? What's the problem?"

"I hope like hell I'm wrong, Katharine."

"About what?"

"It'd have to be extremely potent alcohol to produce ulcers in her mouth," Del told them.

The M.E.'s preliminary wasn't nearly as unexpected as watching Dobarchon go from ashen gray to chalky sick. He stiffened right up. The expression in his eyes mutated from pure agony to an inexplicable look of rage.

"Death came slowly yet she hasn't been here long," Del said. "There's a bracelet on her left wrist I'll bag and return to you. I found camouflage-colored threads underneath the body. Could be from a tarp used to drag her in here."

"How long you think she's been here?" Gage asked.

"There's no bullet or stab wounds. The blood in the nails is from digging them into her own flesh, not necessarily a struggle with her attacker. Gouging occurs during the throes of death. I'll know more after closer examination. There's ligature markings on both wrists indicating she was held against her will. Fellas, she definitely fermented some place else. The greenish-red coloring in her skin indicates lividity."

Swatting flies, Gage questioned, "Telling us what?"

"Lividity forms at the lowest point of the body. Her coloring tells me the body was positioned with her head downhill during death. She's lying flat now."

Lividity was the critical point Katharine missed earlier.

"The fact other nature scavengers haven't gotten to her is what tells me the body hasn't been here long. Maybe a couple of hours, judging by the ants. I'll have a full report for you tomorrow, Chief."

A hot afternoon sun magnified the situation. Katharine imagined a hundred places in the Apostles where one could be placed in a downward position while death tediously consumed them. The cliffs came to mind. Too public she thought, peeking at the girl's ankles and noting they were clean of markings. Several tourists drove by slowly to gawk while the others bagged and loaded the body. A day filled with stressful anticipation nose-dived. Then Dobarchon left hurriedly. This road wasn't the most direct route to his rented abode and Katharine's level of suspicion skyrocketed. She would learn the real reason Dobarchon was here, but right now, she needed to get home, face her parents and shower before Nicole picked her up.

CHAPTER 4

The wood-framed screen door slammed behind Katharine when she and Gage stepped into their mother's kitchen. There'd been little conversation between them since leaving the crime scene. Though Gage's admitted lack of knowledge didn't deplete his obvious confidence, she wondered if he would tell their parents about the dead kid. How and what would he tell them after four hours of crime-scene processing? He sent Joey back to the station and told him he'd be there shortly.

"Anybody home?"

"Hi, honey," his mother said, entering the kitchen from the living room. "Are you hungry?"

"Ma, look what wandered into the station," Gage said, brushing a kiss across her forehead.

Gage towered over their mother's pleasantly full, small-framed body and blocked Katharine's view and she had to inch around him.

"Lord, have mercy! Katharine Regina! My baby you've come home!"

Flapping her arms, her mother locked Katharine in a tight embrace. "Hi, Mom," she said, returning the hug for a drawn-out moment.

"Oh, Lord!" Paula declared, holding Katharine close. "I'm going to cry." Then she escorted her to the kitchenette size table.

"Mom, don't start or I will, too."

"I can't help it, honey. It's been too many years. When did you get here? Just look at you. You're prettier than you ever were. It's wonderful to have you home. Why didn't you call?"

Tears streaming down her mother's cheeks incited mist in Katharine's eyes. Big brother grabbed a box of Kleenex, tossed it at her and Katharine caught it. The caffeine junky then helped himself to a cup of coffee. In the midst of her mother's chatter and tissue yanking, Katharine wondered again if Gage would say anything about the body.

"Are you hungry? You've lost weight. Let me fix you something to eat. I haven't started supper but I'll get on it right away."

Her mother's auburn hair had faded and her undersized physique had filled out with age. Those tender facial features, prominently engrained, were the ones Katharine always looked to for encouragement. "I'm fine, Mom. It's good to just come home. Please don't go to any trouble."

Plucking another tissue from the box, Paula wiped her eyes. "Katharine, you should have called. I would've baked. Oh, it doesn't matter. I'm so happy to see you," she repeated, giving her daughter another affectionate squeeze.

"What's all the ruckus—"

The familiar voice boomed. Katharine shifted and their eyes met for the first time in fourteen years. Her father halted abruptly this side of the kitchen threshold. He gave her a wide-eye gape. With her own drawn out stare, Katharine couldn't do much more than gawk herself. Her father's top was bald. It shocked her more than the leftover clumps that had aged into silver along the sides of his head. Gage's height now soared above their father's stunted bulk. The once statuesque and ascetic-looking police chief had withered in size. She wondered when his power and robustness had been extinguished as she observed the deterioration of bright blue in his eyes. Katharine then realized, with sadness, that her father had grown old. When she returned two years ago for Michelle's wedding, pride had kept her from coming home to see him. What could she say to him now and after several long moments of stares whispered, "Hi, Dad."

"For crying out loud, Frank. Close your mouth and say hello to your daughter."

"Katharine."

The cool disapproving tone of his voice pierced her heart. He had stiffened, dismissed her like an annoying mosquito. So much, that she believed he still hated her for her own stubbornness.

"What'd Joe need, son? That boy's too shaky. He'll never get the hang of the radio and talk the way a man's supposed to talk."

Miserably, Katharine watched Frank LeNoir do that familiar foot shuffle and turn his attention to her brother. He still brooded over the stupid quarrel they had years ago. She couldn't believe his unjustified attitude had continued throughout fifteen years. She supposed it was too late for forgiveness. His heart would remain conventional and unbending.

"Son. I asked you a question."

"Dad, let's go outside."

As they headed toward the door and exited together, a vision of childhood darted through Katharine's mind. Picking her up from kindergarten in a squad car, her dad would buckle her into the oversized front passenger seat that swallowed up her pint-size body. She'd learned to love the scent of new leather during those one-on-ones with him.

Occasionally, a woman's voice squawked out of a dashboard black box with several child-interesting controls. When it did, the miniature blinking light on the front lit up solid red while the woman rattled off words. When the voice stopped, the red light repeatedly blinked some secret code. So secret, Katharine made a game of it. At the age of five, she had discovered the police radio to be the most fascinating object in life.

Grunting, her father would stuff his colossal body into the driver's seat, wink at her tenderly, and say, *"Well, Pumpkin,"*—he always called her Pumpkin—*"looks like Mrs. Girard's dog is bothering folks again. You wanna go with your old man to check it out?"*

Her heart soared with excitement each time he asked. And every day she anxiously rushed through kindergarten to spend the afternoon with her dad. It became daily routine. They'd drive over and give Smoky several attentive pats alongside a mindful talk. Then stuffing himself back inside the squad, the top cop said, *"Old Smoky just wanted to say hi."* Then off they'd go to Frosty Blue's to sneak their favorite ice cream. Didn't matter that it might be twenty below outside. The day's standard operation was to slurp down a mint chocolate-chip ice cream cone. It was as secret as the blinking code on the radio.

They'd return to his office where he allowed her to play hide and seek under the largest desk. It was the only place on the planet, Katharine recalled, where she could spy on the world and anyone who might enter her dad's police station. She loved the confined area. Not only was it a second home, but it added to the security she'd always felt with him. The hidden surveillance provided her with feelings of invincible power. She could monopolize any situation with supreme responsibility.

The telephone, rather than the clock, set the dinner hour, too, she remembered. Every day, the phone rang at exactly five PM. She'd hear Dad say, *"Okay Ma, we're on our way."* He'd hang up and pretend he couldn't find her. Then Madeline Island's police chief would sing those stupid lyrics, *"Oh where oh where can my Pumpkin be."* He'd open desk drawers looking before he'd nudge her with his feet under the desk—

Her mother's voice brought Katharine back from the past. "He's still furious with me, isn't he?"

"Oh, honey, it's not anger as much as it is the hurt of losing his little girl."

Just then, Gage and their father returned inside. When Gage glanced her way, Katharine signaled with a quick headshake to indicate she hadn't revealed anything to their mother.

"This is so wonderful having both my children home at the same time," Paula piped. "It's been lonely around here."

Their mother's little frame contradicted her huge and constant love. Katharine realized their mom and Gage were more alike than memory had served. Like Mom, her brother enjoyed the security of a home, children and the casual island lifestyle. Though Gage would never carelessly admit it, Katharine always believed he wanted his own family. She'd never doubted for a minute he'd make a fair, understanding parent, and wondered why he never settled down with anyone. Most women might kill for a man of his easy-going charm.

Katharine sighed inwardly knowing her brother was right. She had to be the one to tell her parents she'd quit her job. As always,

Gage's presence made doing it a little easier.

"Um, Mom, Dad ...," best way to say things, was to just spit it out her dad taught her. "I quit my job."

"Oh, Lord, Katharine! Why? You loved that job!"

Looking past her mom's concerned face, her father grunted before he stalked out of the kitchen. Her sense of loss went beyond words or tears. She'd stopped guessing years ago how Frank LeNoir could stay angry with her when *his* commitment to law enforcement made her become what she had.

CHAPTER 5

"Gaaawd, Katharine. How much more boyish can you dress?"

"I'll take comfort over what you're wearing, Nicole."

Katharine looked at her own attire. She didn't think she was that badly dressed. She'd slapped on a maize striped toggle shirt and baggie drawstring pants, tied back her hair, left her face plain, stuffed cash into her pocket and slipped bare feet into a pair of flats. She shifted her eyes from Michelle's neighbor lady stealing a peek through a window. Her very slender friend was overly dressed in a short flimsy skirt that exposed long gorgeous legs and an hourglass shape. Since Nicole never had a need to exercise, Katharine felt cheated. She also hoped word of the murder hadn't spread. She needed to forget the awful afternoon for a night of catching up with her two best friends.

"Hon, do you realize how frumpish and unattractive you look to the male eye?"

"Do you realize you're beyond the age of wearing spandex tubes and miniskirts? How the hell do you keep your balance in high heels that are prescription for pain?"

"They make me feel powerful, more or less."

"A contradiction," Katharine muttered.

Nicole opened Michelle's front door, and shouted. "Michelle, we're coming in and you'd better be decent. Look what I found hanging around the halls of—"

"Nicole!"

Before Katharine could stop her, Nicole had pranced inside Michelle's house.

"You can't just barge in there!"

"Watch me."

"And if she's amusing some hunk in hot sex?"

"There's a joke and a hopeless cause if I ever heard one. Michelle's been a dried up prune since the big D. Won't give the male species a first glance let alone a second one. Can't blame her after what happened. Unlike me, who can't live without being the object of male worship, I don't know how she does it."

Nicole moved with a graceful glide, stabbing Katharine with pangs of jealousy for the first time. Out of spite for that, she grumbled, "Still desperately seeking love."

"What'd you say?"

"Was the divorce really hard on Michelle?"

"That's putting it mildly. The marriage was harder." Nicole whirled around. "In your words, he was one drunken bad ass."

Katharine stopped abruptly. *Drunken badass* was shoptalk implying cruel assaultive behavior. "How could Michelle let him abuse her? She was always the one with her head screwed on the tightest?"

"Katharine, Michelle didn't *let* anything happen, but you have to hear from her what she went through with Derek."

Checking each room, Nicole said, "Now where is that woman? She has moves as predictable as a mechanical bull. She's always home on Friday's at five. Come on, hon. Let's check the backyard. You aren't gonna believe what she's done out there. It became her sanctuary after the divorce."

Katharine followed Nicole through the house, taking in everything. Mismatched used furniture filled the simple, well-kept space. Sturdy green vines and healthy ferns overflowed hanging baskets for limited window covers. She thought it okay if she avoided looking at the naked glass. Michelle was still a heavy-duty reader. One wall lined with hundreds of paperbacks and hardcovers backed up fact. The absence of pictures, family photos and personal stuff contradicted Michelle's domestic needs. Was Michelle's marriage as bad as this room implied? Her faithful-writing mother said Michelle bought the house after a short marriage and quick divorce. She didn't pass along detailed reasons for the break up. Said she wouldn't spread gossip and scoffed at those who did. The reality hit Katharine hard with increasing guilt. Would her long absence exclude her from a loyalty pact the trio had sworn out with finger pricks at the age of nine? Katharine jumped when a streaking, black furball darted around furniture and ducked behind the couch seeking refuge from intruders.

"That's Keeker, the newest member of Michelle's family," Nicole told her. "I think the girl's traded in male companionship for that of an arrogant pussy. Michelle, you out here?"

Katharine trailed Nicole outside and stopped suddenly at a white trellis entrance. She was gaping at paradise. Full of color and life, the backyard challenged the inside of Michelle's house. A frothy crabapple tree centered the fenced-in backyard. Honeysuckle and vibrant burgundy peonies laced a white picket fence. Old fashion lilacs had ownership of the back property line. Michelle had created—no, Michelle had meticulously designed individual gardens. Sweet pansies and petunias mingled with vibrant grape-colored lilies. Frail, white daisies socialized with tulips already blossomed. Away from the shade of the crabapple tree grew an ample supply of raspberries, tomatoes and carrots, rhubarb and cukes. Herbs flourished near patches of assorted vegetables.

"*Omigod!*" Michelle shrieked, and stood. "Katharine! You never called and told us you were coming home!"

Michelle's physical appearance added more alarm than Keeker the cat crossing her path had. She was shocked to see Michelle's once trustful eyes hollowed and distrusting. Pinched lines encased both. An artificial smirk had replaced a once infectious beam. Any trained eye would quickly see Michelle's mask of pain and grief.

"Why are those, the first words out of everyone's mouth?" Katharine asked.

Mud covered with flowers in one gloved hand and florist sheers in the other, Michelle ran to Katharine and tightly hugged her.

"Omigod, I've missed you! It's been so many years. When did you get here? How long are you staying? And now I think I'm gonna cry."

"Don't you dare start." Katharine paused. "How are you? And

what have you done to your long beautiful hair?"

"Too much work," Michelle muttered, brushing it away with the back of a hand. "I cut it off awhile back."

Katharine merely studied her when a fearful twinge flickered through Michelle's green eyes. Tongue-tied by her friend's lie, she re-hugged her to hide a new worry. Michelle was a victim of abuse and that thought pained Katharine. "You both look great," she finally said.

"Oh, blast it," Nicole exhaled. "Now, I'm gonna start crying. I told myself I wouldn't."

Breaking the embrace, Katharine said, "Ah, geez, don't you start, too. Get over here and join us you saucy twit."

Moisture formed in Katharine's eyes with another startling revelation. She'd been lonely without her two best friends in her life. And no matter how much masking she did of her own inner turmoil, she needed them both.

Additional hugs and squeezes out of the way, Nicole dabbed her eyes. "I can't believe you just called me a saucy twit."

Giggling, Michelle said, "Nicole, you are a saucy twit the way you prance around the Island with that fashion flare of yours. What in god's name are you wearing now?"

"Something I picked up in Ashland last week. You like it?"

"Yeah, whatever," Michelle said.

"Get your fanny inside and clean the mud off your face. We're going out to celebrate Katharine's homecoming. We've got a ton of catching up to do."

"We can sit right here and play catch-up without the effects of the Tavern."

"Not a chance, Michelle Callihan."

"Nicole. Don't even think about starting this argument with me again. You know how I feel about bar hopping."

"Michelle, you never go out anymore and one night sitting in the Tavern won't kill you."

"But you'll twist my arm until I drink myself sick. Like the last time I listened to your nonsense. And I won't be much good at work tomorrow with a hangover."

"You're gonna manipulate yourself right into old age if you keep working seven days a week."

Katharine didn't know which shocked her more, the rising tension in Michelle's voice, or the fact her detailed life had forced her to become a workaholic. "You're not really working seven days a week, are you?"

"I am not going to a stinking bar where men and women drink too much and ogle each other for lack of better entertainment on a Friday night."

"It's not a stinking bar," Nicole shot back. "I'm proud of what I've done with the Tavern!"

"Let's not forget what you do with those who frequent the joint, Nicole."

"You're jealous!" she yelled back.

"You *stupid* twit! The last thing I am is jealous! You better than anyone knows that."

"Yeah, Michelle. I know quite well how you wallow in self pity on a daily basis."

"How dare you!"

The blows just kept coming. Listening and watching the falling out between the only two people Katharine trusted tied her stomach into stretched-to-breaking knots. Michelle's emerald green eyes narrowed fiercely. Nicole vice gripped her own hips with both hands ready to erupt in response. Katharine had heard enough. Even Keeker the cat who'd been watching from afar ran and hid.

"Alright you two, knock it off."

"Shut-up!" they spouted in unison.

Their outburst forced Katharine back a step.

"What do you care, Katharine? You never call or come home anymore. You can't possibly think you can parade in here unannounced expecting us to pick up where we left off fourteen years ago."

Clutching what little self-control she had left, Katharine declared, "That works two ways, Callihan! The last time I heard from you was when you called and announced you were getting married!"

"And my wedding is the only time we've seen you since graduation!"

Michelle bit down hard to stop her bottom lip from quivering.

Tears welled up in her eyes, and oh God, how Katharine hated those kinds of tears. *That kind* always followed the administering of pain, the torture of being hurt. She'd seen it plenty in the job and mostly wanted to cry alongside the victims.

"Do you have any idea how much I needed you when my entire life went to hell right in front of my eyes?"

"Thanks for nothing," Nicole screeched.

"No you don't, Katharine! You were too engrossed with doing whatever to think about us. As kids growing up, we always came second with you."

"How can you say that?" That knot in her stomach tightened. "You guys always came first. You're my only friends. I need you. Both of you."

"Omigod!" Michelle cried, slapping a hand to her mouth. "I'm sorry. I'm sorry. My divorce was finalized a year ago today. It's hard. I'm sorry."

Tears seeped into Katharine's eyes and stung harder. The growing anger that rumbled around inside of her on low boil wasn't because of this argument. "Michelle, I'm sorry. I didn't know. Neither of you told me. I heard about your divorce from my mother. I'm sorrier for what you went through."

"You brushed us off a long time ago. We just figured you didn't care anymore."

Shuddering inwardly, a knob swelled in her throat, matching the knot in her stomach. Katharine didn't want to believe the fault hers. Instinctively, she did the only thing she knew. She pulled Michelle into her arms and hugged her tightly. "I'm so sorry I wasn't here for you. I'm home to stay now."

Nicole stepped over and wrapped her arms around each of them. "I love you both so much. My tongue is always in motion before it checks in with my brain. Katharine, we've seen you once since high school and here we stand and fight. Michelle, I'm sorry, too. I didn't forget. I just didn't think you wanted a reminder. I thought it'd be good if you weren't alone tonight."

"The Tavern is where I met the son-of-a-bitch. I hate going in there."

"Oh, hon, I'd forgotten that. I'm sooo sorry."

"Everything okay here?" a male voice interrupted from behind.

The three women turned and stood teary-eyed as Gage and Joey walked into the garden.

"We got a call of, and I quote, a cat-fight."

Giggles consumed their tears. Nicole and Michelle exchanged looks. In unison, they said, "Mrs. Hardy!"

"Mrs. *B. B.* Hardy?" Katharine asked, recalling the nickname they'd given Michelle's now neighbor in their younger years. "She was sneaking peeks through the window when we got here."

"That'd be the one," Michelle said. "Evelyn Hardy is still the Island's *Busy Body.*"

"Some things never change," Katharine came back. "Gage, we're fine and just getting reacquainted."

"Joe and I thought we had a cock fight on our hands when we came around the house."

"We're fine," Katharine repeated. "We'll take care of the problem. Won't we ladies?"

"Just like we used to," Nicole teased.

"Pipsqueak, if you pull any tricks closely related to your high school days, I'll toss you all in a cell for the night."

"Bro, you don't have a jail cell," Katharine chirped.

With the moves of a jungle cat, Nicole rolled her hips toward the two uniformed men. She had *the look* in her eye as she brushed a finger along Gage's chin.

"You promise to keep your eye on us too, big boy?"

Gage never flinched, just maintained his police stance while facing Nicole with a studious look of his own. He was probably more po'd about being pulled away from the paperwork that went along with a murder than he was with Nicole's hip action.

"Joe, this situation is worse than quicksand. The more you struggle with it, the more you're sure to sink."

Katharine grasped the change in her brother immediately. He *did* have a vulnerable side. His expression was a mixture of hurt and some kind of obvious longing. She quickly realized Gage really wanted to be oozing in that muck before he turned abruptly. Joe followed, and they disappeared around the corner of the house.

"That man's piston is standard issue and looks mighty damn slick in your average anything," Nicole sighed.

"I can't believe you just said that about my brother!"

When Nicole turned and faced them, arousal poured out of her big brown eyes. *Oh*, this was all too curious Katharine thought. Those two were destined from childhood to fight and argue viciously with each other. What was going on between them now? Yep. She'd definitely been gone way too long.

"I swear the woman is one giant hormone with a twenty-four hour orgasm," Michelle said, stuffing the flowers into a galvanized can filled with water.

"Well. That's more than I wanted to know," Katharine said.

"You're both envious of the fact I have an incredible body and know how to use it. Got us out of another mess, didn't it?"

"Flaunting is by far more accurate. And as I recall, it was your body that got us into a lot of trouble," Katharine reminded her.

"I've got an idea," she said, ignoring the sarcasm. "I'll get a couple of pizzas, a bottle at the Tavern and we can indulge ourselves with fantasies."

"I'm game," Michelle said. "You with us, Katharine?"

"Iced tea and salad for me."

"No way!"

At their simultaneous disagreement, Katharine studied them for a moment. Their eyes were eager in anticipation of renewed acquaintances. "What the hell. One slice and one glass of wine then."

"Good," Nicole said, headed for the house. "But it's gonna take more than one slice of pizza to put weight back on your scrawny behind."

"It is not scrawny! It's firm. And tell me why you keep looking at it?"

Michelle grabbed her arm before Katharine could think twice about chasing after Nicole.

"I gotta tell you, this is one time I agree with the saucy twit. Are you puking up your meals and starving yourself to death?"

"Michelle! That's more disgusting than what comes out of the saucy twit's mouth. No! I am not puking after I eat."

Washing off the mud with a garden hose, Michelle asked, "Then what?"

"I work out and I eat healthy. What's wrong with that?"

"Nothing. It's just ... you look all balmy. And marmy."

"Marmy?"

"I know Nicole missed your comment. The one where you told me you were home to stay. What gives?"

She exhaled. The thought of telling her best friends the truth tore at her insides and she settled for the half-truth. "You're gonna hear about it sooner or later. I quit my job, Michelle."

"Omigod! Why?"

She shrugged.

"You loved that job." Michelle eyed her momentarily. "Katharine, you're not sick, are you?"

"No. It was just time for a change."

She focused elsewhere when Michelle tossed her an I-don't-believe-you look. The day had already turned into more than she bargained for and so was this conversation.

"What really happened? You weren't fired were you?"

"No! Nothing happened. Let's talk about what your ex did to you."

Stunned, Michelle dropped the hose.

"Well?"

"Derek didn't do anything that I didn't let him get away with."

"That's not the way Nicole tells it."

Michelle grabbed the hose, but not before Katharine observed her brows drawn together in an agonized expression.

"Nicole couldn't keep her big mouth shut if her sex life depended on it. She had no right telling you about the indignity I suffered."

Another round of *those* tears, trembling, shakes. Katharine knew abuse very well. "I'd say it was more than indignity. Michelle, Nicole refused to tell me anything. How bad did he beat you?"

"I forgot how nothing ever escaped you."

Moving closer, Katharine gingerly wrapped an arm around Michelle. "Why didn't you call me? Why didn't you call Gage or my dad? In fact, I can't believe Gage didn't drop kick the bastard into Superior."

Pulling away and wiping her nose with a dirty garden glove, Michelle said, "No one but Nicole knew what Derek did to me. You were too far away."

Katharine reigned in the familiar steed named anger. "You

mean you never had him arrested?"

"I just wanted him gone."

"How long before it started?" she asked, embalming her own rage.

"A week after the honeymoon. I filed for divorce seven months later."

"And Derek left? Just like that?"

Michelle nodded. "I'm sorry for blaming you. I didn't want you to know how I failed."

Now there's a word! "Michelle, just because he used you for a punching bag doesn't mean you did anything wrong. And you're certainly not a failure because some s-o-b doesn't know how to treat women."

"I was as much to blame."

Bullshit! A telling moment, Katharine made a silent promise. If the ex ever set foot on *their* island again, he'd be singing soprano dissonance for the rest of his life. The front screen door slammed and both women looked.

"I'm back and need some help," Nicole called out. "Wait til you see what I've got."

Swapping shrewd looks with Michelle, Katharine said, "Do we dare ask?"

"I've gotta start locking my doors. That woman thinks every unlocked door is a personal invitation to enter."

They went inside and met Nicole re-entering the front door with three boxes of large pizzas.

"Great balls of fire! Did you guys hear?"

"Hear what?" Michelle asked.

"Joe found a dead girl in the woods on the old dirt road just off the County Road.

"Omigod! Who was she?"

"No one knows, but we've just had our first murder ever."

"How'd it happen? When did it happen?"

"Don't know. Hayden heard about it and told me. This is awful—I can't believe it! No wonder Gage had his shorts twisted in knots. Did he say anything to you about it, Katharine?"

Unprepared to answer, she half shrugged.

"Like brother, like sister. I called our order in before I left and I have something for everyone from veggie to meat lovers. I need help carrying in the booze."

A silent prayer of thanks the saucy twit never took a breath, Katharine asked, "You need help with one bottle of wine?"

"Nicole manages the Tavern, Katharine. I'm sure she brought home everything *but* wine."

"Not quite. Now get out here and help me."

They did, with Katharine successfully avoiding the conversation about La Pointe's homicide. Couldn't possibly discuss it, let alone with these two, and keep her turmoil buried.

"What the ...," Katharine said, gawking into the trunk at several bottles of ambiguous labels and coke.

"The case of Miller Light is Michelle's because all she drinks is beer. Katharine, we get the hard stuff."

"The saucy twit *did* buy out the Tavern."

"You actually believe she paid for this," Michelle groaned, trying to lift the case of beer.

"Lemme get that you lightweight."

"Lightweight?"

"Michelle, you are a lightweight." Nicole flashed a grin and flipped her long golden hair over her shoulder. "Paybacks are such a bitch aren't they, sweetie."

"I am not a lightweight. I haul dirt for my gardens."

"Yeah, in a little red wagon. I'll make the drinks. Michelle, get the plates and napkins. Katharine, tell us what you meant about coming home."

"Thought you said she didn't hear me," Katharine muttered, glancing sideways at Michelle.

"I was wrong. Sue me. But before you do, tell us why you quit your job."

"Great balls of fire! She did what?"

"It's true, Nicole."

"No way! I don't believe it."

"Well, try," Katharine blasted.

"Why would you quit the best job in the world? That is what you called it."

"How are your parents, Nicole? What country are they in this week?"

Nicole just stared at her. Her lack of response said Katharine had hit a chord. Flipping open a pizza box, she then asked, "What's really on a veggie pizza?"

"Not meat. It was the closest thing to healthy I could get and still classify it as sinfully delicious."

"I watch my weight. I'm not a bloody vegetarian."

"I'll share mine," Michelle offered, wrinkling her nose at the veggies.

"I don't think so. I want what she's having. If I'm indulging in vices for one night, I'm making it worth my while."

"Here's a Long Island iced tea. Now quit avoiding the question and tell us why you quit the M-P-D," Nicole demanded.

Grabbing a slice of meat-lovers pizza, Katharine stuffed a huge bite into her mouth.

"While you were gone, she said it was time for a change," Michelle answered. "Won't say why she needed that change."

"We'll have it out of her by morning," Nicole hummed, sipping her seven-seven.

Katharine swallowed as both women stared at her. She finally exclaimed, "There's nothing to tell! I've been gone since graduation and it was just—it was time to come home."

"Yeah, right. When hell freezes over. Michelle, how 'bout some music? You can skip the classical crap and go straight to *Love of My Life* on Santana's soundtrack *Super Natural.* Then the Rolling Stones, *You Can't Always Get What You Want* would wrap it up mighty fine."

"Since my player accommodates three CD's, I choose Jon Secada."

"Breakdown, by Melissa Etheridge," Katharine said, relieved the subject had changed.

"Can't always get what we want," Nicole told her.

"If I didn't know better, I'd think you were each describing your love life," Michelle said.

"You fell in love and he dumped you," Nicole blurted. "That's why you left Minneapolis."

"Jarvis, give it up!"

"Can't blame us for trying to find out why our best friend quit something that meant everything to her. So, if you aren't going to tell us why you quit, tell us about all those good-looking hunks you worked with and how many you did."

"Jesus, Nicole."

"Well, how many?"

"This tea from New York tastes pretty good," Katharine said instead. "What's in it?"

"You know what I'm thinking, Michelle."

"Sex. That's all you ever think about, Nicole."

"I think we should treat Katharine's face to some color."

"Over my dead body!"

"Hon, that can be arranged."

"Nicole Louise Jarvis, you try and I'll take you down in a choke hold!"

"I'm getting myself another drink," Nicole said, laughing. "You ladies ready yet?"

Both nodded, grabbing a slice of pizza.

"I wanna know," she yelled from the kitchen, "if the two of you were marooned on a desert island and had your choice of one movie star, who would the lucky man be?"

"Steven Seagal," Katharine replied.

Returning, Nicole handed each their drink and sat. "It's a toss up for me. Mel Gibson or Pierce Brosnan."

"Wimps against Seagal," Katharine taunted.

"They are not."

"Mel's too old and who can tolerate Pierce Brosnan?"

"Talk about old. Seagal could be your father."

"He could not."

"Could too!"

"Not!

"Too."

"Cary Grant."

Their mouths dropped open as they both gaped at Michelle.

"What? Cary Grant was so debonair with those large brown eyes and long dark lashes," Michelle defended with a sigh.

"I think the operative word is *was*. As in Cary Grant is so dead."

"You didn't say he had to be living."

"Well, hon, he should at least swing your style," Nicole threw back.

"That wasn't Cary Grant," Michelle scoffed, knowing full well what she meant. "That was Rock Hudson."

Laughter rolled out of Katharine as Nicole shrugged off her innocent mistake.

* * *

When Katharine opened her eyes the next morning, body and mind had separated. Her head felt like it'd been smacked with the butt end of a twelve-gauge. Her tongue had enlarged to three sizes too big for her mouth. On the other hand, maybe it was cotton-balls wadded up inside. It took a moment for her to focus then she recalled the previous evening. Why would anyone habitually rape themselves with alcohol? Slowly, Katharine rolled to her side, forced herself up off the floor. Her stomach flip-flopped, and her first hangover worsened when she tripped over Michelle.

"Sorry, Callihan."

"Oh my God, my splitting head. I need caffeine and aspirin," Michelle groaned, then shrieked, "*It's eleven*! I was supposed to be at Mrs. Chernak's at eight this morning!"

Peeking out of the kitchen, Nicole informed her, "I called and told her you were sick and would reschedule."

"You didn't!"

"I tried to wake you. Besides. You're working too hard with all the landscaping contracts and the Town Board. I made breakfast for the two of you. Love you both. Bye gotta run," and out the door Nicole flew.

"How come she looks better than we feel?" Katharine wanted to know.

"Good question. I've gotta call Mrs. Chernak and get over to Town Hall."

"Michelle, you can't be serious?"

"Afraid I am."

"Why on Saturday?"

"Today, it's called Baines, Inc."

"What's that?"

"Baines Incorporated is a world renowned architectural firm. The owner is Travis Baines. He originally wanted to build a mall here on Madeline Island, but we said no. Anyway, I've been in a fax fight with him ever since he sent his goons here to scope out land."

"What land?"

"Over between Millet Street and the burned down café bordering the County Road. He thought we needed a junior Mall of America. There's no way I'd let that happen."

"Michelle, you're right. A mall that size would never fit there."

"That's not the point. Carter Taylor and I told him we'd never allow commercials on the Island. It didn't take him long to catch our drift. Then the weasel got on Ted Evans good side. Ted made a deal with him to design and build a ballroom attached to the Tavern."

"What does Nicole think about it?"

"She's thrilled. Says it'll improve business."

"So, what's the problem?"

"This guy's determined to build here. He's already given us a list of contractors they want to work with and shown us drawings. With a reasonable bid, the Town Board voted in favor of the deal. Baines told us he'd keep everything the same ... I suppose a ballroom could be good for business."

"You've had him checked out, haven't you?"

"Yes, but I don't trust his motive. I mean, why is this old coot so persistent to build here? What's the big deal about our Island?"

"Have you met him or the contractors?"

"Not yet. It's almost like he doesn't exist. He keeps sending in his second team. Some guy named Abbott."

"Michelle, when did you start working full time on the Board?"

"I'm not. This is just using up a lot of my spare time."

"How many hours are you putting in a week?"

"A few," she lied. "I've gotta take a shower and get going." Michelle paused. "Katharine?"

"What?" Waiting for her to say something, she repeated, "What?"

"Whatever your reasons are, I'm glad you're home to stay. I've missed you more than I realized."

CHAPTER 6

Colorful street terminology accompanied Katharine's grueling efforts to peel the grease paint off her face. Sometime during their juvenile ritual last night, the saucy twit—Katharine doubted Michelle's involvement—painted her face. She then went for a jog as she did most mornings after dogwatch because running relieved her after-shift despair. This morning, working up an admirable sweat helped dissolve the alcohol and fat she'd wrongly put into her system last night.

She hated to admit Nicole had put one over on her, but the intoxicant had freeze-dried her emotions. She'd actually mellowed under the influence and by so doing, briefly forgot La Pointe's first homicide and her own messed up life. A cool shower and reliable Visine disposed of the red streams in her eyes.

Ready to greet the rest of the day, Katharine moseyed downstairs to the smell of freshly baked cinnamon rolls. The familiar aroma permeated the 1960's style kitchen. Her mother, a superb pastry chef in Katharine's younger years, probably had a compulsion to feed the entire neighborhood as she once did. She and Gage knew the homemade goods were what drove kids to play at the LeNoir house when they were younger.

"Katharine, you left in such a hurry yesterday. We didn't have a chance to talk. Gage mentioned you went with him when poor Joe found that girl."

So Gage had told them. "I ran into Nicole at the station. We'd already made plans, and, well ...,"

"You want a buttered cinnamon roll and something to drink?"

"Iced tea if you have any. Without sugar."

"Honey, don't you want something to eat? You're so thin."

"No thanks. Where's Dad?"

"Was going to take the boat out and go fishing, but this murder has him hot under the collar. I'm sure he wants to work the case with your brother."

"Let's sit and talk, but please not about that. I've missed you lots, Mom. How have you been?"

"Same old. What are you going to do with the stuff in your car?"

"Haven't given it much thought. It can stay there for now. I have something for you as soon as I dig it out."

Removing the last rolls from a pan, Paula said, "Katharine, you didn't have to buy me anything."

"I know. I couldn't resist."

Carrying glasses of iced tea to the table, they sat down.

"Dear daughter, it's positively wonderful having you home. It's been too many years. I know how much your work meant to you, but Lord knows I'm selfish. I'm glad I don't have to worry about you down in that big city anymore."

Because of the job or the big city, Katharine wondered, studying her mother's face. Paula's pale blue eyes hinted at worry only a mother's eyes could reveal. A straight line replaced the easy smile on her mom's face. Supposedly, parents always know when their children are hurt and confused. Sipping the lemon-flavored tea, she figured her mother's thought for the day would be worried curiosity. Her mother rambled and generally asked questions instead of answering the ones asked when other thoughts were floating through her mind.

Katharine set her glass on the table. "Mom," she began and stopped when her mother's eyes filled with moisture. "Why are you crying?"

"I'm concerned about you," she said, wiping her tears. "Katharine, you were always so confident. Just like your father."

No she wasn't. "Mom—"

"You're both stubborn, but you always had to be in charge,

leading the pack into adventure."

"I remember the adventure part when we played hide-and-seek," Katharine said, leaning her elbows on the table. "I loved hunting for the bad guys."

"Indeed you did. Now your brother, unlike yourself, was born efficient and easy-going. But you also had a strong desire to care for the needy. Though it was difficult for you to express your feelings verbally, your passion came out in your drawings. You had a natural gift for spontaneous creativity. It was the one thing you didn't acquire from your father."

Katharine sat up. "My sketching! I forgot! I used to sit on the beach and draw for hours when I was a kid."

"I put away your supplies if you want to try your hand at it again."

"You did?"

"You bet I did."

Had her mother always known she'd return home needing to draw? *Can I draw away the internal fear of my failure?*

"They're in the attic. I'll have Gage bring everything down for you."

"No need. I can get it myself if I decide to try. I wasn't very good at it." Katharine avoided the delicious smell of cinnamon as long as possible. Helping herself to a roll, she smeared it with butter and thought, so much for jogging.

"Oh, dear. Along with your immense confidence, you were always your own worst critic."

"I'm not as confident as you seem to recall." She bit into the freshly baked roll and the sweet dough melted in her mouth. More tears welled in her mother's eyes and rolled down her cheeks. "What's wrong?"

"Honey." Paula reached over and touched the top of her daughter's hand. "I can see the misery in your eyes. Something has happened to you, but I know whatever it is, you won't explain it until you're ready."

She reads me like a classic novel. "Mom, don't worry. And please don't cry. I'll be okay."

"Katharine, some day when you have your own babies, and I hope you do soon, you'll see a look in their eyes. I see that look in yours and Gage's eyes. When it happens to you, you'll worry, too. You'll agonize over your children's sorrow and pain, loves and losses, and your heart will ache when you realize you can't stop your children from falling down."

"I need to work this out myself."

"I know you do, honey. Just remember that sometimes sharing our troubles helps us to understand them. When you're ready, I'm here to listen."

Biting her lip, Katharine looked away. Her words came out quietly. "It's Dad I feel weird around."

"Oh, honey."

"He still hates me for what I did. I saw the same resentment yesterday. I just wish I understood how he can hate me as much as he does."

"Katharine Regina! Your father does not hate you. You're the apple of his eye. That man just refused to accept the fact that someday you would leave. It didn't matter for what. I kept telling him the day would come when you'd marry and go away. But in the end, you left for all the wrong reasons. And he has his own logic system. Always thought he'd keep you tucked away safe and sound."

"He was never prepared for my announcement to become a cop," she muttered.

"No, he wasn't. Even I didn't see that one coming. Guess I should've known from the way you tagged along with him all those years. You always preferred your dad's company to young men and your girlfriends."

"Mom, how can you say that? Nicole, Michelle and I spent hours together."

"True, but Dad always came first with you. There were many times when you dumped them to spend a day ...,"

Katharine studied her mother as her words trailed off. "What else were you going to say?"

"He wasn't prepared to lose you the way he did. That fight you two had broke his heart."

"What do you think it did to me?"

"Your relationship was severed. Neither one of you has been the same since. Katharine, you need to talk to your father."

"How can I? His actions speak loudly."

"Not any louder than yours, honey."

Beginning to recognize her own needs, Katharine knew she couldn't postpone the showdown with her father. "Mom, do you think I made a mistake with the career I chose?"

"Honey, what I think doesn't matter."

"Yes it does. You never have voiced what you thought."

"Well, you certainly can't use me as a barometer for the decisions you make."

Thinking about Michelle's accusations yesterday, Katharine recalled her childhood behavior. It boiled down to the things she and her ex-boyfriend, Steven had argued over frequently. Spoiled rotten. Always doing what she wanted he said. In her short-lived relationship, he misunderstood the quietness she required after a shift. He thought it was disinterest and aloofness in their relationship. Eventually, jogging after work replaced their morning routine. It was the only way to avoid the arguments. Finally, Steven ended what little they had together.

"Mom," Katharine said, thinking of another memory. "How much do I love you?"

The game they once played produced a prolific smile on her mother's face. "This much, Katharine Regina."

Her mother opened her arms and Katharine leaned over and hugged her. "Think I will dig out my sketchpad and hit the beach for the rest of the afternoon."

"Will you be home for supper?"

"I'll let you know. How's that?"

"I've got whist tonight. I'll leave something warming in the oven. There's a big dresser up in the attic. The whole thing is filled with your art supplies."

Her mother left the kitchen and Katharine indulged in another buttered roll before she climbed the stairs to the attic. It didn't take long to dig out a spiral bound sketchpad, box of charcoal pencils and florescent chalk.

She needed downtime, particularly outdoors and away from people. To think. She loved the open air, which was another reason for the choice to follow her father's example. Contrary to a stuffy office, the outdoors gave her a clear perspective and healthy insights. *The best kind of therapy.*

Headed for the cliffs, and God willing, she'd figure out why the past was playing catch-up with her life. Sketching had once been a diversion for doing exactly that, especially out on the cliffs. The way Superior swelled, rippled and surged into the rock always helped her cope with pressure. She loved Madeline's wild kingdom, too, the occasional raccoon and beaver, abundant blue cranes, gulls and egrets, deer and fox. Even black bear roamed the island, but she seldom saw one.

As her memories of an almost perfect childhood flowed back, Katharine recalled telling her dad on many of their one-on-ones, how someday she would live in the forest caring for the animals. He'd look at her and tell her she could do whatever she wanted. She didn't know that doing what she wanted excluded becoming a police officer.

Katharine approached her favorite spot near the cliffs and suddenly felt stark fear. Maybe it was the Island's first homicide adding to her quirky doubts. A murder was the last thing she needed or expected upon returning home. Yesterday, standing over that body, her chest felt as if it would burst. Today, the tight knot tangled inside of her still begged for release. Taking a deep breath, Katharine shook off the feelings and headed in the direction of a secluded low-lying shoreline.

Her thoughts were all over the place. She didn't know why she'd thought about Steven at all. She hadn't thought about him since the relationship ended and she moved out. When he said she'd failed at loving him and called it off, he hadn't understood anything about her. Oddly, his words didn't bite as hard as his timing. It was three days before that Easter night. But how could he know? How could anyone know? It didn't really matter anymore. Not like Michelle telling her she didn't care about her friends. Or Nicole calling her a first-class nag. And Gage saying her paybacks exceeded the national debt. Their words all hurt more than Steven's words had. Deep down she'd never really loved Steven. She'd given him what she could. But she loved her family and her friends—once loved her job. And what she needed right now was for everyone to understand her.

Her thoughts shifted again to the breakfast conversation.

'It broke his heart.'

The fight she and her dad had had destroyed her on the inside, too. All her life he'd taught her to be the best she could be. He'd taught her downfalls were unacceptable. Failure was the ultimate downfall. How could she have failed her dad? The one man who'd been her idol. The one man she'd trusted and loved more than anyone. Had her father actually hung that much hope on her? To do what? All she ever wanted was for him to feel pride in her accomplishments. Maybe it was a mistake to go against his wishes and become a cop. She never would've had to kill a man. Never suffered the aftermath. But she desperately wanted to be like her dad. To do—to *have* his job.

The argument they had came back in blazing color. The hurt ran deep and cut like a knife. They'd been going at it for a half an hour.

"Women aren't cops!"

"But, Dad, that's what I want to do," Katharine mewled, pacing the office floor.

"That's the end of this discussion," Frank bellowed, slamming the desk drawer shut. "If you want my financial support for college you will not become a cop. That's my final word, Katharine."

"Then when you said I could be whatever I wanted you were lying to me? Or were you just patronizing me?"

"That's enough, young lady!" he shouted, stood and stalked around the desk.

He'd launched the chair with such force it hit the back wall, but Katharine refused to be intimidated. "No, Dad, it isn't enough. I wanna know. You're paying Gage's college tuition so he can be a cop to replace you some day. Why won't you help me with mine?"

"That's not the point."

"Why can he be a cop and I can't? Why don't you want me to be a cop?"

"It doesn't matter why."

"Yes it does! It matters to me what you think."

Heaving out his words, he shouted louder, "What I think is if you want me to pay for your college education, you'll do what I tell you!"

"Well, Dad, that's where you haven't got a clue. I'll never become something I don't want to be just because you think it's what I should do. What you're saying to me this moment tells me you've been lying to me all my

life. What else have you lied to me about?"

That's when he slapped her across the face. She stood there stunned in that small office space, silent and much shaken. She heard his quick intake of breath over the drone in her ears. A muscle quivered near his jaw. Then he stepped back, shocked by his own actions. They gawked at each other for the longest time.

She refused to break down, and finally spoke with quiet, but desperate firmness. "All I ever wanted was to be like you."

Katharine never forgot it. It had been the first and only time he'd slapped her. She didn't know which had hurt her more. His refusal to believe in her, the patronizing talk or the slap. Regardless, the look on his face said she'd sucked the life right out of him with that last comment. He walked out and left her standing there. She didn't see him again that day or night. And the rest of her senior year turned into a nightmare.

Had she known the outcome of the days, weeks, years to follow, would she have chosen a career she hated just to appease her father? Would she intentionally have abandoned Michelle during the loss of her brother, or thoughtlessly forgotten Nicole through the years? Had she prematurely abandoned her career? She didn't have the answers, but knew her life had turned to dog puke. This moment she had no clue what she'd do with the rest of it either, and exhaled loudly.

Her feet were wandering like her thoughts. Katharine finally stopped and looked around. The only sounds were the soothing hypnotic cadence of rolling waves and the caterwauling, gray-backed gulls. She picked a spot and burrowed into the creamy-colored sand. It took little time for a lost hobby to flow again from her eye to chalk to pad. Kinda like riding a bike. Once you learned you never unlearned. And the lost hobby came back quickly. The perception of edge and space, light and shadow flowed from her fingertips onto the cotton fiber paper. She glanced up several times to absorb the sky, water and passionate colors of ballooned out sails.

Several sailboats moved across the waves as if they were weightless. Watching, one in particular became the focal point of her first drawing. A bright red sail exploded against smaller white sails and the boat's planing hull. Only the colors made it appropriate to name this one American Hero. Holding it up and examining the chalky lines, she added gulls flying overhead and touched up the splashing waves. It wasn't her best, nor were there any heroes. Yet, ardor and fervor of her appreciation of the scene had flowed faithfully onto the parchment.

Separating the sketch from the pad, Katharine placed it in the sand carefully. Utilizing her subdominant visual right brain, she shaped her next drawing with a charcoal pencil. Contour drawings of shapes and spaces rendered the use of value to light and shadows. Perception of relationships in the art world made drawing simple. Without that concept, any sketch lacked reality. Color enhanced value for someone who wanted to paint. Painting didn't interest her as much as charcoal and chalk. She hadn't known she had a natural gift either until college. Her mother was right.

As the afternoon slipped away, Katharine blocked out the grumble of motor boats and screeching gulls diving for dinner. She always drew what she saw without realization of or regard for her artistic skill. It didn't matter she decided, placing another drawing in the sand. The hobby made her relax and she wondered when she'd given it up.

Probably about the same time she'd given up on her dad. How could she confront him now? What would she say? *"I'm sorry I loved and respected you so much that I wanted to be just like you."*

It almost was what she said the day of their fight. What would he think of her now if she confessed the real reason that she quit her job? Would he give her the understanding essential to her being? She'd always been daddy's girl. Before their life-altering fight, he always provided her with the love she needed. Without his love, she felt empty, drained.

Looking back at the fateful experience, Katharine admitted the sad truth graciously. Her father meant everything to her. "So, who's the real fool here? I lost him. I quit my job and here I am bouncing around with nowhere to go and nothing to do."

Chapter 7

God, he loved sailing! Didn't matter where he sailed there was never enough time for the water sport. The minute he set foot onto the deck of a boat, tension dissolved. The excitement of the excursion provided personal enjoyment, comfort and solitude. His favorite outdoor activity also curbed the angst of his stress. After yesterday, he definitely needed to release the growing pressure. He never should have stopped to see what the locals were doing in the woods. *I must have been insane*, Mac thought. Though he was curious when he saw the squads, he supposed it was his fate.

The wind on his port side, Mac changed course tacking to starboard to clear the right of way to the oncoming motorboat. The sailboats he'd been watching appeared to be involved in a race now. He was a closet racer. He raced everyone on the water but was the only one who knew it. Today he wasn't doing so well. But he also had bigger ambitions and dreams than to race. When retirement rolled around, he'd get himself a thirty-foot cutter and become a blue-water sailor. His rig choice leaned toward the cutter's smaller sails. The mast moved farther aft occupied forty percent of the boat's length from the bow. It allowed for two headsails in front of the upright pole and provided greater flexibility. The cutter was also easier to handle in hardcore weather. It was perfect for a one-man team. Perfect for a loner with plans to head to the East Coast by way of the Great Lakes system someday.

The other sailors glided out of sight and Mac drifted aimlessly until the breeze hooked his mainsail. It was then he spotted Katharine, couldn't miss that vibrant sunrise-colored hair against the sandy white beach the way it stuck out like road kill. Though she'd tied back the fiery mane in a ponytail today, the same breeze that sated his sail breathed life into her hair. He grabbed his Nikon, aimed and focused the zoom lens, snapping off many shots. She was working some task while she sat in the sand and he replaced the camera with a pair of binoculars. After a moment, he realized she was drawing. He also realized he couldn't take his eyes off her. That alone set alarm bells ringing simply because other than one life-altering exception, emotions never swayed his judgment. He'd always been completely devoid of sentimentality until last December. Yesterday, while on the ferry from Bayfield to Madeline his emotions were once more tossed about. He'd been watching Katharine then, too, from the stern. Actually, he had stared rudely at her bright red hair—couldn't stop himself, just like now. Completely untamed, vibrant, natural and long, that hair of hers cemented his attention the way it tumbled carelessly, *erotically*, down her back. His insides quivered with hints of a second, life-altering force. And he never suspected a woman's hair color to control him in the same way narcotics controlled the addict's mind and body.

He didn't know her name, but she did intrigue the voyeur. The disturbing moment left him with weird internal feelings. While he examined every move she made, then and now, he recognized nervousness the way she kept checking over her shoulder. He knew the defensive reactions to threat when she whipped around like a fearless hero in a standoff gesture. It reminded him of a warrior princess, one readied to do battle. Then she flinched and so had he. He thought her energy odd and followed the direction she looked for her potential aggressor. Her eyes were molded on the ferry's skipper sauntering toward her. The closer the skipper moved toward her, the more she physically challenged the old man with an authoritative stance. Mac's curiosity was piqued and he studied her body language more than he'd ever studied anyone. Body signals were an engrained language. Hers changed several times, from power to defiance to agony to meekness. She communicated with physical action and taut expressions, contradicting her carelessly clothed diminutive figure. At first, he'd thought *his* staring had caused her reactions. But with her guard that intense on the skipper, she never saw him standing at the ferry's stern. Even if he had missed her reaction to the skipper, there was no disputing her self-defensiveness.

Then it happened. She turned. The skipper walked away and Mac's heart did a kick bang inside his chest to a pair of the most magnificent blue eyes he had ever seen. Big, topaz blue the color was a mixture of the universal stone and the body of water beneath the ferry with a sparkle as vibrant as polished diamonds. He swallowed hard, actually choked as he continued to examine her. She was so unrefined yet so lovely that his own awareness of her reduced him to a sap.

It was automatic for him to follow her when she went below. He had to, and tapped her on the shoulder. She whipped around ferociously to face him and *whammo!* Her apricot milky skin beckoned to him. A chin of iron determination challenged him. Intense energy bounced off her and bagged him. It sent more hot quivers into his gut until he took a closer look at those astounding eyes. Pure agony poured out of them. He'd seen the look many times. It reflected his own personal catastrophe that he couldn't walk away from. The secrets in her eyes struck him square in the core of his soul and in that gripping moment, he lost his breath. The longer he stood there like a mute bozo the more he sensed she'd once known harmony. She tried hard to conceal her suffering, but prominent grief shone through in betrayal to her. He suspected some tragic devastation had caused her torment.

The sailboat rocking brought Mac alertly back to the present scene. His lungs were heaving now. His palms were sticky with moisture. Katharine looked stiff sitting in the sand. Her rigidity reminded him of more than he wanted to think about. Seeing *that* dead girl yesterday reminded him of more than he wanted to think about. Swallowing back dry spit, the mass of his misery was permanently stuck in his throat. Many times, he'd see his own anger reflecting back from mirrors and glass panes. Tried to drown it but misery was timeless and had turned him into a goddamn floor pacer. He actually held ranting conversations with the bare walls, started carousing into the wee hours with alcohol inducement only to awaken and remember every miniscule detail of his torture.

Curses fell out of Mac's mouth. It was difficult to watch people fall into victimhood, but to watch himself crumble was his own personal hell. Doing his job had always been the point. He once avoided emotional entanglement and certainly never revealed any imperfections or mistakes ... until last December. Another lifetime ago, that unseasonably warm night turned into his bitter demise. Too late for the right choice, his first career mistake had altered his life forever. In the days that followed, he tried to bury the rage. It just sneaked up on him, resurfacing anywhere it damn well felt.

The killing had started again—yesterday was positive proof of that. The thought of it made Mac groan. How could it have started again? What had he missed? Why had there been a delay to the sequence? Could this death really be unrelated? Hell no!

Stop thinking about it!

He continued to watch Katharine through the binoculars as a distraction to his thoughts. Deep down, his gut said he almost wished he'd never spotted her on the ferry. He wouldn't have followed her to the station. He didn't need this kind of commotion. Not now. And he never should've stopped to see what the cops were doing in the woods yesterday. It was a judgment call that fell into job curiosity. After all, he *was* site-seeing.

What is it about that blazing red hair? And those striking blue eyes? He felt captured—more like manipulated the way she looked at him. It filled him with a driving sense of urgency. He recognized her feigned indifference. But his heart still turned over in response to her eyes. He despised the eyes. Victims always beckoned with their eyes for help. The eyes always got to him. Let him not forget Katharine's pretentious smirk either.

Damn his urgent hunger. *Screw* his compelling pity. He refused to help this time. He didn't want to rescue anyone. Regardless, her obvious suffering made it impossible for him to ignore his inborn compulsion to reach out and at least try to end her torment. His own vitality had been revived by the claim she'd levied on him. Wasn't that reason enough to save her from her own demons? If he didn't help Katharine—his adrenaline was rushing through him like a bull—ill fortune would always prevail. The relentless power of failure would overshadow him forever.

"Shit," he muttered. "I shouldn't do this."

Instinctively moving, Mac thought, *this* could be misconstrued as stalking. Didn't matter. The excitement escalated inside of him as he began steering his friend's sailboat toward the beach. Approaching the island, he chose his spot and maneuvered the rudder with the tiller. The wind did more guiding of the rig than he did, but finally lowering the jib, Mac dropped anchor securely. He jumped into the waist-high water and approached the shore.

Katharine still hadn't noticed him. She was lost in her own energy. He stayed back for a moment not wanting to disturb anything or drip water on the sketches. Exhilaration consumed him more, watching her draw. Her strokes were quick and fast. The movement of her hand sent waves of renewed power jolting through him. The very air around her felt electrified to the point it cut off his own supply. The intensity of her strokes was tied to the way her eyes danced. It evoked persistent yearning in her. Mac wondered for what and glanced down at the sketches in the sand. His heart flip-flopped more. Mourning crammed every drawing. Was the grief for a lost love? For a different, happier time in her life?

After several moments of standing there, he said, "You have a rare God-given talent, Katharine."

Her head came up. Her eyes were big, as blue as the water and pierced an intrusive hole right through him.

"Where'd you come from?"

"Those are good," he said, gesturing to the drawings.

"Thank you. It's a hobby of mine. Where'd you come from?"

"It's a very good one."

She cocked her head sideways and glanced at the sailboat in the water. "That was yours? You swam to shore?"

"Nope. Walked. Water only came to here." He indicated on his shirt.

Katharine picked up one sketch and held it up to him. "I guess you should know I've named this one American Hero."

He stared at the sketch as his heart pumped his blood harder.

He saw no heroes but a desperate man worrying to extreme. "I'm no hero nor do I own the boat. The sailboat belongs to a friend of mine. She's a sloop. I prefer the cutter."

"She's a what, and you prefer a what?"

"It's a sloop. I prefer a cutter. Sailing is my hobby. Someday I'm gonna own a thirty-footer and sail out to the Atlantic."

Those bewitching eyes did it to him again. Analyzed him with suspicious caution. It sent those hot quivers surging through him like lava flow. "Would you like to go sailing with me right now?"

"Dobarchon, I'm positive your wife will object."

Caught unaware, he blurted, "My what?"

"You said you were staying in the Carriage House. That's the honeymoon cottage."

"Honeymoon cottage," Mac repeated. "I didn't know. Either way, I doubt my reputation will be worse for wear. I don't have a wife."

"You're obviously a man on the prowl. Staying in the Carriage House won't help your cause."

She said it so matter-of-factly he let out a short laugh. "The Carriage House was the only place available on short notice. I assure you marriage is not a possibility with my lifestyle."

"You referring to your career or personal lifestyle?"

She went back to drawing and Mac realized she could care less what he did for a living. As she'd already said, she wasn't interested in him. Nevertheless, he had a desire to know what she thought so he answered, "Career. I'm a street sweeper for the City of Green Bay."

Her stunned look was brief because she knew what he meant. "You haven't been home for a while judging by your brother's reaction to seeing you yesterday?"

"Once, since—how'd you know that? You didn't show up until we were inside."

Mac laughed. "You said it yourself. I followed you and saw the reunion outside the station. How long are you home for?"

Her police-trained eyes cautiously picked him apart. It drove him crazy to the point he believed those striking eyes were probing the detailed thoughts of his mind, heart and soul. When she didn't respond again, he thought his efforts were a lost cause. He'd come this far and he wasn't about to give up and opted for what he thought she might discuss. "You ever considered selling your sketches on the side? They really are exceptional."

"Nope."

"For starters you might frame one and put it in one of the gift shops here on the island. You'd be surprised by what tourists will buy. Especially if they're interested in island scenery."

"They'd have to be stupidly rich to throw away money on these."

He selected a black and white etching of an old man working a fishing boat. Another lonely soul he silently mused. "I myself appreciate sketch art and would be willing to pay a fair price for this one. Just look at the detail, the accuracy, the passion. It shows a man's dedication to his work."

"Dobarchon, its charcoal on paper."

He gazed down on her curiously. Her attitude was prepared. So prepared it drastically contradicted the emotion he saw in her drawings. "Katharine, it may be charcoal on paper to you, but there's a lot of spirit here. How much would you charge for this one?"

"You just won't quit, will you?"

He grinned now.

"Forget the pay. You can keep it, if you'll just go away."

"Can't do that. I have to give something back in return. Since you're uncomfortable with sailing, how 'bout dinner tonight?"

"You're a determined little sucker," she said with a short laugh. "But I like that. If I agree, will you back off and leave me alone? Dinner for the picture?"

"How's seven sound?"

"Seven is fine."

"Great. Since you know what's best around here, I'll let you decide where we go. Where can I pick you up?"

"My best friend manages the Red Rock Tavern. She'd never let me forget it if I went elsewhere. I'll meet you there."

"Red Rock Tavern at seven. Is it casual or formal?"

"Casual. You won't catch me putting either foot in heels."

"A woman after my own heart." He smiled spontaneously. "I'll see you this evening. Bring the sketch."

Mac strolled back into the water before she could renege. He climbed into the boat, raised sail and drifted away. When he looked back, she was watching him and his heart did that little flipping thing. He just smiled and waved.

While his sailboat maneuvered waves from the wake of a spirited motorboat, Mac thought about the picture she'd drawn. Nothing had ever stirred his blood as much as the artist had. She had an incredible flair to put on paper what most never noticed. Her freehand skill was indeed a natural gift. He wondered if she knew how much emotion she exposed in her sketches. He also sensed a dominance to control her surroundings. Cops did it with feigned coolness and prudence. Unfortunately, there were dark secrets in her eyes. They told him something ate away at her the same way his insides had been chewed raw. Her pain went beyond a lost love. She also failed to ask him about yesterday. Instinct told him she wanted to, but held back. Why *didn't* she ask him what he was doing at that crime scene? And on that point, Mac presumed he was at the top of their list of suspects. He laughed wholeheartedly at that one.

CHAPTER 8

Walking to the Tavern, Katharine's emotional state reminded her of an aroused teenager. It made her think of the soaring anticipation she felt the day they handed her a college diploma. It was identical to the thrill she had experienced the day she hit the Minneapolis streets for the first time. All because of a simple dinner date. *Payment,* not a date. Or was it? The drawing she held in her moist palm said payment. Her heart and mind weren't convinced. Dobarchon was as slick as his onyx-colored eyes. She couldn't believe she'd agreed to this.

Little shocked her, but when he told her his vocation, her face gave her away. His eyes gave her another answer she knew too well. Watching him was like staring into a mirror and seeing her own distressing face. So, if Dobarchon was a cop, as she now believed, why did he look as if he'd seen a ghost when the M.E. gave his preliminary on the dead girl?

Katharine entered the Tavern and stopped just inside the doorway. She wondered why Michelle thought this was a stinking bar. With a full service lounge dead ahead, and a restaurant to the right, the Tavern and its waitresses provided welcoming and friendly hospitality. The casual ambience sufficiently mellowed everyone. Maybe the liquor, too, but whatever Nicole had done with the place worked. Adding a ballroom to the current coziness could only enhance the atmosphere. She completely understood Nicole's verbal defense last night and again, jealousy over Nicole's obvious success swallowed Katharine up.

"I like it."

She shifted about, recognizing his voice. "Like what?"

"Your hair," Mac said. "Hanging long and loose gives you an innocent aura."

He produced a single rose then twisted a strand of her hair around his finger. "What's this for?" she asked, slapping his hand away.

"Look but don't touch," he teased. "The flower is for you."

"In exchange for what?"

"An evening of conversation without ulterior motives. Hope you haven't been waiting long."

"No. I was admiring how Nicole manages the place. Here's your sketch. I covered it so it wouldn't smear."

"Nicole's the best friend you mentioned?" he asked, accepting the drawing.

"Since birth."

"Katharine?"

"And here she comes now."

"I never expected to see you out after last night. How's your head feeling? You're not still angry with me are you, hon?

"The way my head felt didn't tick me off as much as what you did to my face. Nicole Jarvis, Mac Dobarchon."

"Nicole, good to meet you," Mac responded, offering a hand.

"Welcome to the Red Rock Tavern. Dobarchon? That's French, isn't it? Are you from around here?"

"Yes, it is. I'm visiting from Green Bay. Heard a lot about the Cadotte treasure and thought I'd check it out."

Nicole believed less in ghosts than Katharine did, but she at least conversed on the subject with Mac. Katharine had learned long ago that she and Nicole were opposites. It was obvious Nicole utilized her natural gift of gab to stimulate conversations with the patrons whether she agreed with them or not.

"It was nice meeting you, Mr. Dobarchon," Nicole said. "Enjoy your stay on our Island, and your meal."

"Thank you. I'm sure I will."

Leaning into Katharine, she whispered, "Where did you find this incredibly handsome hunk? I want all the details tomorrow."

Nicole walked away and Mac grinned, angled his head and hummed into Katharine's ear. "Never been given that title. Tell me. What did she do to your face?"

"Something I'd never tolerate if she hadn't blitzed me with tea from New York."

On Nicole's instructions, a waitress approached and led them to a table. Mac steered Katharine to a chair and waited until she sat.

"Tea from New York?" he asked, sitting across from her.

"Something like that."

"Do you mean Long Island Iced Teas?"

Sitting where she couldn't see who came and went, Katharine suddenly felt jittery. It was a legit feeling. Cops didn't sit with their backs to doors. She glanced effortlessly over her shoulder, responding, "I guess that's what Nicole called them."

"Those are potent. How many did you drink?"

"I don't generally drink and need no reminder on potency. I lost count after three."

"If you're not a drinker, I'm surprised you made it past your first one."

"Maybe I didn't." Katharine cringed, thinking about it. "What makes them so powerful?"

"Vodka, gin, rum and tequila."

"Mixed all together!" she squawked.

He nodded. "How did your head feel this morning?"

Recalling the half-full bottles left on Michelle's counter, she looked across the table for the first time at him. "Like I'd been beaten with a baseball bat."

"Who else was there?"

"Michelle Callihan. Another friend. The three of us were born and bred here."

"Would either of you care for a before dinner drink?" the waitress interrupted politely.

"Katharine, you don't strike me as a coffee drinker."

"You're right. Iced tea with a twist of lemon."

"I'll have a tap, light beer," Mac told the uniformed woman who acknowledged the order before walking away. "Now, tell me about island life. Why the lack of fast food joints and entertainment?"

"There's not much to tell. La Pointe has strict zoning and the consensus is no commercialization. Year-round residents pride themselves on the privacy the island offers."

"It sounds like you don't like it here."

"Growing up on fourteen miles of rock, I couldn't fathom living and dying here. I wanted to see what the rest of the world had to offer."

"Then you left in search of challenging experiences never to return until now?"

"Yeah, something like that."

"What did you do? Where'd you go?"

"Went looking for something big to happen. College."

When the server returned with their drinks, Katharine grabbed hers, drank and scanned her surroundings.

"Did you become someone who made a difference in the world?"

God no! She had malfunctioned! Recalling his conversation with Nicole, Katharine said, "I suppose hearing about fairytales and fantasies all my life blinded me to the reality of human greed."

"I assume your reference to fairytales is the famous missing Cadotte treasure of gold?"

"Well, the story is famous. But missing gold? No way. There's no truth or proof that gold ever existed. Besides, as the fairytale goes, it wasn't gold, it was jewels."

"Then you know the story?"

"Yeah, I know it. What's your interest?"

"Desire for richness," he said with a grin.

"You're a first-class liar."

Letting out a laugh, Mac said, "Tell me the story of the Cadotte ghosts anyway."

With an exasperated sigh, she began. "The skipper, who's a tour guide on the Island Princess, swears Nicole, Michelle and I are the three women who can stop the Cadotte ghosts from crying."

"Wailing ghosts, hidden jewels, intriguing. Tell me more."

She studied him for a long moment then asked, "Are you here on a scavenger hunt in search of something that doesn't exist?"

"Would it matter if I were?"

"Probably not. But I might have to resort to my first opinion of you."

"Katharine, you flatter me. But I already know your first opinion. What's your second?"

"You might be surprised."

"Not much surprises—"

As quickly as he'd made the declaration, he'd stopped and it was automatic for her to scan the dining room looking for trouble. Seeing nothing unusual, Katharine asked, "What's wrong?"

"Has anyone ever told you how beautiful your eyes are? They're hypnotic to this man and that stunning blue color has pierced my soul."

The waitress returned saving him from her flippant retort. With the interruption, she also realized this man had intrigued her. The street sweeper's seductively rich voice had mesmerized her so much she'd forgotten to look over the menu.

"Would you mind if I ordered for both of us?"

Shaking her head, Katharine waited while he rattled off several unappealing items. Food was the furthest thought from her mind. The fact that he held her interest longer than she expected dominated her thoughts. His profile strong, his voice confident, his personality was a winner. She hadn't wallowed in pity muck since arriving at the tavern. When the waitress left, Mac again faced her with those rich black eyes a second time.

"Tell me about the illustrious ghosts that inhabit the Apostle Islands and how the Cadotte fortune changed from jewels to gold."

For his persistence, she met his irresistible grin with a smile. His eyes grew openly curious. She resisted less this time. "The truth is Madeline and Michel Cadotte had at least three daughters who were real people. I'd imagine in a parent's eyes all their children were graced with jeweled eyes. But Sully, the skipper on the Island Princess, swears otherwise. His claim is that medicine men murdered each one of the three daughters the night before they spoke their wedding vows. He tells people that medicine men sacrificed the daughter's lives in a ceremonial dedication to their divine creator."

"Why?"

"For their eyes."

"Are you saying the women were murdered for their eyes then the eyes were offered as gifts to this phony divine creator?"

She nodded. "According to Sully, it's more along the lines of a sacrifice to their beliefs. He says that after the death of her third daughter Madeline Cadotte turned into a recluse on this island. Most think that's why the Island was named after her. The truth is the naming of the island, Madeline, was a dedication to her life. Her real name, Esquaysayway was Native American. She was the daughter to Chief White Crane and christened *Madeleine* by the priest in Sault Ste. Marie when he officiated at her wedding to Michel Cadotte. When she and Michel returned to La Pointe, Madeline presented her christened name to the island. Chief White Crane decided this island would bare her name in his daughter's honor. The rest is all fictitious."

"Interesting."

"How so?" she asked, curiously.

"Interesting that you know as much as you do about the wedding and the family, but the ghost story eludes you."

"It doesn't elude me. I choose to deal with facts. Ghosts aren't real. I can't begin to tell you all the details of what Madeline did. Michelle's the history buff. But I guarantee there's no proof any of their children were murdered or that ghosts haunt us waiting for the nuptials of three women. There's also no truth that a dowry Michel gave his daughters was in the form of jewels, or that it ever existed."

"You've left out why this Sully person thinks you and your friends can stop their ghosts from crying."

The amusement she observed earlier in his eyes glimmered brighter. Her insides shifted uneasily before she told him, "He thinks all three of us have the eyes of the so-called murdered daughters. Because of that, each one of us has to marry our soul mate before the ghosts will stop haunting the Apostles."

"People can actually see these ghosts?

"No."

"Then what?"

"Sully says they cry waiting for lost love. I don't know why he thinks what he does. Never cared enough to find out."

"And you don't believe in true love."

"I don't believe in ghosts or fluffy concepts."

"Ahh, Katharine. Every now and then it's good to put your faith in fairytales."

"Do you believe in ghosts or happily ever after?"

"I see what is, and unfortunately it's not always happy." After taking a sip of beer, Mac added, "You're right about one thing. The concept of love being happy-ever-after is fluffy and sadly overrated."

An appetizer served, Katharine asked, "What are these?"

"Sautéed Portobello mushrooms with garlic toast. Try them."

Katharine took a slice of toast, forked and tasted a mushroom. "Wow! These are good."

"I hoped you might like them."

Before they finished, the waitress delivered a side salad with dressing. When the main course arrived, Katharine again asked, "What's this?"

"Mediterranean Chicken."

The aroma tingled her senses. Throughout the meal, their conversation continued conservatively. He was relentless with the questions and she answered cautiously. *Fantastic* described the meal. With no opinion about the rest of the evening, Katharine surprised herself by sneaking a few long looks at the man sitting across from her. He had masked over the pain she first saw rooted in his eyes. Intrigue, and occasionally when he let tenderness through, filled them now. It almost looked like Mac Dobarchon kept a front to hide his secrets. Didn't matter, she thought. Her interest had risen in the street sweeper. She was also sorry she'd been rude to him. She actually had a desire to learn more about this man, as well as what his interest was in the dead girl yesterday. The sad part was she didn't know how to ask, but police work had trained her how to find out.

"Mac, this was one of the best meals I've had in a long time and well worth the trade. Thank you."

"Then it's been a fair exchange. Dessert?"

"Um, no thanks. I'm stuffed."

"How 'bout a walking tour of La Pointe?"

"I don't recall that being part of the deal." Regretting her snappy response, she said, "Why not."

"Great. Let me take care of the bill and check out the men's room."

"I'll meet you at the front door," she told him.

Picking up her rose and Mac's sketch, it dawned on Katharine that she hadn't looked over her shoulder since dinner was served. He'd diverted her thoughts with crafty charm. No matter how smooth he used it, the technique was called interrogation. She smiled to herself, thinking about his tactics—*no way did he work for the street department.*

A shimmer of light fell upon her pathetic life. She thought about Steven again. They never had two-way conversations. Steven told and demanded, never asked. Maybe the difference between Mac and Steven came with experience, but then she'd never asked about Steven's previous conquests either—didn't know if he had notches, didn't care. *Good God! What made her wonder about Mac's?* Did she care? This entire evening was payment for the drawing she held in her hand. It was just dinner, but near ten PM, they'd talked for almost three hours. That had to be some kind of record.

She made her way to the front door to wait for him. How experienced was Mac Dobarchon? He gave her confidence—

"I'll be damned! Katie LeNoir! You're sexier than I remember."

Her shoulders went rock hard. Katharine didn't need to look. The boisterous voice was an old classmate with illicit intentions. She turned and faced the Stewart brother. "It's Katharine. Been awhile, Kevin."

"Too damn long, Katie. How 'bout a drink with an old friend? Curt and Mark are here but they'd never miss me."

Reeking of stale cigarettes and day-old beer, he slobbered his words in her face. Kevin always harassed the girls in high school, especially her. He used lecherous catcalls to get her attention. She expected them to start any minute. His assumption was that heckling filled a date card. Gage had nailed it—this Stewart was a drunk. "No, thanks. I'm waiting for someone."

"Still think you're too damn good for me?"

"Frankly, I've never thought about it."

The hair on her neck rose when he deposited his stubby fingers on her shoulder and slid them along her arm. She nailed him with a pointed glare, which he ignored or missed then squeezed her arm.

"Maybe you should give me some thought, Katie-doll."

"Remove it," she demanded.

"I'll make you so dizzy you'll forget your own name."

"Not in this life time. Get your hand off me. Now."

"Or what? You'll call big brother to save you."

His grip tightened. With quick, furtive moves, she had him in a chokehold. "Back off, dirtbag! I wasn't interested in your pick-up truck sex in high school and I'm not interested now!"

Unable to breathe, Kevin went limp in her arm. Nicole was approaching rapidly and Katharine dropped him. Kevin hit the floor with a thud. That's when she saw Mac sizing up her talent. Her cheeks flamed.

"Kevin Stewart! You're outta here!"

"Kiss my ass bitch," Kevin wheezed out.

"Out! Now!" Nicole ordered.

"When I'm damn good and ready," he panted short of breath.

Mac inserted himself between the women and Kevin. Towering menacingly over the Stewart brother, he spoke in a low growl, which Katharine couldn't hear. Whatever he said was effective. Kevin Stewart found his breath, stood and took the direct route through the exit.

"Are you two okay?" Mac asked, turning to face them.

"Thanks for the help, Mr. Dobarchon."

"It's Mac. No problem."

"This is a nightly routine with him and his brothers." Nicole smoothed her skirt as though she'd just tossed Kevin out herself. "Did you enjoy your meal?"

"Very much. Thank you."

"I hope you'll come back real soon."

"I'm sure we will. Katharine, are you ready?"

"Yeah," she said, leading Mac outside.

"Pick-up truck sex? Dirtbag?"

At least the semi-darkness hid the flush in her cheeks. "Kevin Stewart is a loser with a dishrag smile. Gage said Nicole calls frequently when the three of them are raising Caine in the

Tavern."

"Three?"

"He has two brothers."

"Who on God's green earth would have the courage to procreate more than one of those?"

"What did you say to him? I've never known any of the Stewart's to fear anyone."

"It's a man thing. Not every day do I get to see a woman handle herself the way you just did."

"It's a girl thing," she tossed back. "And you already know how and where I learned it."

They walked in silence as dusk settled under a midnight blue sky. The first sign of stars winked obscurely. Katharine looked up at the vast sky unaware of how much she'd missed the after-dark radiance of Lake Superior's spell. City lights and towering buildings had always swallowed and masked the heavens in Minneapolis.

In that same moment, she also decided Dobarchon was definitely interesting and wished she knew how to carry on a conversation with him. Maybe it fell into the category of fantasy. In the end, it might prove disappointing.

CHAPTER 9

Knowledge of Madeline Island's first murder spread across fourteen miles of charm and beauty quicker than wildfire. Nervous gossip and sub-rosa murmurs spread faster. Folks began locking their homes for the first time. A few skittish tourists packed up, ending their vacations prematurely. Nobody knew the teenager, which didn't change the facts. Scandal and terror had frozen an enchanted island like a good Nor'easter.

Frank LeNoir bellied himself up to the kitchen table at six AM. The newspaper clutched in his hands held no interest. Slurping morning coffee, he brooded over the missus' concern. She tossed and turned all night, which disputed her verbal reassurance that Gage would capture the killer. Around four AM, Frank got up and took his place in the rocker by the window. In the hush of early morning, he sat there listening to his wife's familiar breathing. Amidst his meandering thoughts, he finally dragged himself downstairs.

He never should have retired. Islanders would allow his reappointment. They'd want this homicide resolved quickly, efficiently. Islanders were uneasy with his son's unpolished skills. That much he knew. The boy had rough edges and callow behavior that betrayed him to the public. The wife called him efficient when the truth was Gage lacked zeal for the status of his job. His son lacked other things Frank mused disappointedly, but that was another matter. Solving La Pointe's first homicide had priority. Spoiled, naive Island residents needed pacifying. When he was the police chief, he constantly took calls just to smooth ruffled feathers. All weighty issues, petty disturbances were part of a boring job. He welcomed barking dogs and loud music complaints over Jesop Merryweather worrying about his precious gardens. Most days Frank figured Jesop just wanted conversation. In his day, it was plain good P-R to appease Islanders, but this murder was big. When Gage entered the kitchen, Frank figured he'd start slowly.

"Morning, Gage."

"Morning, Dad."

"Coffee's on." Frank paused. He just couldn't start slowly. His mouth ran ahead of his best intentions. "This murder's got everyone riled up."

Filling a mug, Gage plopped down opposite his father. Taking his first swallow, he said, "I know."

"How'd the medical examiner list the cause of death?"

"Poison."

"What kind of poison?" he asked through the paper that separated them.

"According to Del, one of nature's most toxic. Something called abrin."

"Abrin?"

"Yeah. I'm wondering with Joe's increased marijuana arrests if someone's mixing abrin with marijuana and selling it."

"Abrin comes from the protein lectin. It binds to carbohydrates like an antibody and is generally extracted from plants."

"Dad, we both know you're not reading that paper. What's really on your mind?"

"Commonly comes in the form of a pea. It'd have to be broken and digested for it to have full effect."

"Now you're startin' to sound like Joe."

Dropping the newspaper, Frank scowled. "Have you identified the dead girl yet?"

"Sixteen year old runaway from Ashland. The only evidence is a bracelet the girl wore, and a liquor bottle Katharine found."

Lifting his coffee cup, Frank studied his son over the rim. "Why's your flighty sister involved in this?"

"She's not, yet." Standing, Gage poured himself a second cup. "I'm working on her to help."

"You're wasting your time. That girl abandons everything she ever starts."

Gage leaned against the sink. "Katharine's not giving anyone a valid reason why she quit her job. Nikki's tried to get it out of her, but nothing doing. Until Katharine does tell us, I can't judge her. You shouldn't either."

"Your sister's always lived on the edge waiting for excitement to come to her. When things get boring, she gives up and moves on."

"You're wrong! Ten years in one job is not giving up and it's damn hard to believe Minneapolis was boring. Something happened to her."

"Katharine's a quitter," Frank sputtered. "Especially when she doesn't get what she wants."

"You do not spend ten years working large city streets and quit because of boredom, Dad. I know what she saw and I know you're not getting a Minneapolis paper to read the want ads. Are you too busy wallowing in ignorance and anger not to notice her panic attacks?"

"Your sister panics because she knows she failed all of us and herself again."

"*Failed*," Gage blew out. "She was on the honor roll every year in high school, graduated from Stout U with the same and made sergeant in a large city police department. How do you see that as failure? Better yet, I wanna know how you see it as failure to us?"

"This discussion's over! Your sister's downfalls are none of your business. We should be concerned with who killed that girl."

"And there's another mistake you're making, Dad. It's not *we* anymore! *You* are retired. This case belongs to Joe and me."

Gage dropped his cup in the sink and stalked out through the kitchen door.

Neither man aware of her presence, Katharine held her breath. Coming downstairs, she'd heard their voices and listened from the living room. The conversation grated on her like a heel blister. More outrageous were her father's words. They were an act of groundless cruelty.

She eighty-sixed her sketching plans. Her dad's assumption she was a flighty failure filled her with desperate ache. She needed to restore his affection. The fact she'd killed a man and the anxiety it caused weren't the issues anymore. Restoring his opinion of her became top priority. Later, she'd figure out a way to deal with the past and the fierce control it had on her.

Tossing the art supplies on the couch, Katharine bolted out the front door to catch Gage. He'd already driven away. Removing car keys from her pocket she tugged the car door open, slid in and was in pursuit. Catching up with him at the station, she called out, "Gage."

"Pipsqueak," he said, looking up. "You're up and out early."

"You still want my help?"

When he stopped at the open threshold, she explained, "I overheard you and Dad just now."

"Everything?"

She nodded as he steered her inside.

"He's wrong about you, Sis."

Gage headed for the coffeepot then left the room with the empty carafe and returned moments later with it filled with water. She waited, watching him dump five scoops of grounds into the basket. "You got any orange juice around here?"

"Fridge in the conference room. Help yourself."

"Gage, I appreciate you sticking up for me, but it's not about being right or wrong. It's about what Dad thinks of me."

"I meant what I said. Katharine, I've never thought of you as a failure. I'm proud of what you've done, but I'm also concerned about you. You've changed."

She toppled onto a chair too lazy to get the orange juice. She felt some of her anxiety drop from her shoulders. How she appreciated Gage. She especially loved the way his lofty stature filled her with assurance and security. His presence and caring softened her doubts. A kind of tenderness reflected from his pale blue eyes. *He really is worried about me* she realized her heart swelled inside her chest. Though she needed his support, she couldn't explain herself to him. He didn't wait for the coffee to finish and stole a cup.

"Are you gonna tell me what happened to you?" he asked,

plopping into the chair behind the desk.

"How can one man keep his mind closed and hold a grudge for fifteen years? Did you know Dad was waiting up Saturday night after I had dinner with Mac? He met me with his fatherly scowl when I walked into the house. Felt like I was back in high school."

"Mac Dobarchon? Thought you decided his staying in the Carriage House made him a married man."

Katharine stood and began pacing circles on the station's tiled floor. "It was the only rental available. He's not married."

"Then the Y chromosome comment *was* a disguise for your interest?"

"Why is Dad being such a jerk?"

"Pipsqueak," Gage said, leaning back to watch her. "You're gonna hate me for saying this, but you and Dad are identical."

Jerking around, Katharine's icy glare pierced the conventional calm.

"You're both control freaks. And stubborn, rigid thinkers."

"You can stop with the compliments any time, Bro."

"You have no idea how low Dad's tolerance of me has been since you left. I've never been good enough for the standards he demanded from either one of us. Bet you didn't know he held off retiring an extra year because he didn't trust me to do the job."

"That's crap! He favored you all through high school, grooming you to replace him."

"Only because I did everything he expected. Can't you see that?"

Mystified, Katharine pondered his words. She read pure dejection in his face. "I thought this job was what you wanted."

"Don't misunderstand," Gage said. "I'm pleased with who I am and what I've become. But your leaving zapped the vitality right out of Dad. No matter what I did, it never came back—"

"You're wrong about that."

"No I'm not."

Katharine applied her standard tactics. "Gage, you're more like Mom, loving and giving. You've always been there when I needed you."

"Yeah," he exhaled, "reliability at its miserable best. You've been gone a long time, Sis. I've become an imitation of Dad. Set in my ways. And though he's too fricking ornery to admit it, I watched some of his lost spark return when he saw you Friday."

The anger in his voice had heightened making her counter with, "Yeah right. That's why he had so much to say to me after all these years."

"Pipsqueak, that works both ways."

Well, now, she'd certainly heard those familiar words a bit too much. Katharine didn't know whether to penetrate the deep hurt she observed in his eyes or argue her defense. Wavering, she finally asked, "How come you've never married? I think Nicole's got her eye on you."

"Not the marrying kind, Pipsqueak. Besides, Nikki has both eyes on every man who sets foot on Madeline and then some."

"Bro, you've always loved kids. Deep down I know you'd love to settle down with a family. How come you haven't?"

He leaned back, rocking the swivel-tilter. "Thought you had a degree in criminal justice instead of psychology."

"I majored in political science, minor'd in art. But any idiot can see you're definitely marriage material."

"Pipsqueak, I know what you're doing."

Feigning innocence, she rippled, "I'm not doing anything."

"You're avoiding my question."

"I'll make you a deal," she countered, coyly. "If you don't ask what happened to me, I'll give you my expertise on this murder case. If nothing else, it'll raise Dad's opinion of you. His doubts about both of us are crystal clear."

"You realize it'll only take a couple of calls to find out what I wanna know," Gage replied.

"Yeah, but I'd rather you make another call instead."

"To whom?"

"City of Green Bay."

"Green Bay? Why?"

"I wanna find out if what Mac told me is true."

"I'll call on one condition. Tell me why you're dating someone you suspect of murder."

"I don't suspect Mac of murder! Whatever gave you that idea?"

"I saw your reaction to him when he showed up the day Joe found the girl. I'm still wondering what he was doing there. But I'd really like to know how he knew that girl had been murdered."

"Good question. So, tell me. Why *did* you let him enter the crime scene? You know better than that."

"His interest. It's too coincidental he'd just show up." After a moment, Gage added, "*Your* interest in him is questionable, too."

"I had dinner with him once for payment of one of my sketches. He told me he was a street sweeper for the city. I think he's a cop."

Sitting up, Gage set his mug on the desk. "Sis, I'd feel a lot better about Mac Dobarchon if what you say is true. I'll call right now."

"You didn't really suspect him, did you?"

"When he showed up, I wasn't sure what to think. If he is a cop, it might make sense. But what's his interest?"

Locating the phone number in the police directory, Gage dialed. Katharine went to retrieve the orange juice from the conference room fridge. When she returned moments later, Gage had completed his call.

"Pipsqueak, you're right. Mac Dobarchon is a homicide detective. How did you know?"

"An intense cop look."

"That ain't the only look he's got."

Ignoring his comment, she addressed several questions to herself. What was Mac's interest in this murder? Was he running away from something? If so, from what? Was his reason for running the same as hers?

"You gonna tell me what happened to you?" When she didn't respond, Gage said, "Fine, Sis. I won't ask you that question anymore. But I need a guarantee that you can handle working this homicide. I do not need another I-told-you-so from Dad."

"I have to do this," she finally spoke. "I need to prove to Dad and myself that I'm not a failure."

"All right. I'll swear you in and give you a badge."

"I don't want to be lead on this. You'll have to treat my help as guidance."

"No problem."

"I heard you tell Dad the girl is a runaway and she died of poisoning."

"Yeah," Gage said, unlocking the desk and pulling a file. "Here, tell me what you make of the M.E.'s report."

Katharine took it and began reading. "You find anything on the liquor bottle?"

"Not yet. They're still putting the broken pieces together."

Death resulted from heart failure brought on by poisoning from the highly toxic chemical abrin. The teenager, named Sherry, was way too young to die Katharine mused. She looked at Gage. "We need to learn more about this chemical abrin. Where does it come from?"

"You sure you want to do this?"

She nodded.

"You always did jump into everything with both feet first. Dad said it comes from lectin. Damned if I know what that is."

Katharine chuckled. "Neither do I."

"Bet me a ten, Joe will know."

"Pass. I think you know something that'll certainly cause me to lose."

"Smart woman."

"When you gonna have the crime scene photos back?"

"Tomorrow. What do you think they're gonna tell us?"

She shrugged trying to forget the scene of the dead girl. "Have you interviewed anyone yet?"

"No. Don't even know where to begin."

"Morning, Chief, Katharine."

"Hey, Joe. Grab your coffee and pull up a chair. Katharine's agreed to help. And since you've verbalized your interest in science, explain to us what lectin is."

Joe filled a Packer's mug and sat at the smaller desk. "Technically, lectin is a protein that binds carbohydrates together in the manner of an antibody usually extracted from plants."

"That's exactly what Dad said," Katharine responded. "Glad I didn't make that bet."

Gage flashed her a smug smile, asking Joe, "What kind of plants?"

"Since lectin isn't what actually killed her, I think we should concentrate on the poison itself, which was abrin. That comes from a houseplant called abrus precatorius."

"How do you know this, Joe?"

"I wanna know what an abus prick is," Katharine said.

"Abrus precatorius," Joe repeated. "It took me awhile but I found it online last night. It originates from a twisting perennial vine grown in tropical climates. Florida for one. The poisonous seed is also called a rosary pea and comes out of a pod about an inch long. The pod harbors several poison beans or seeds. The outside shell of the bean is bright red with black spots."

"You said tropical climates?"

"Yeah, Chief. I found info that says Canada ships them, too, but no website I plugged told me much other than they can be imported. Most info alluded to if your pet ate or swallowed the pea. If a pet ingests the pea, it doesn't necessarily mean death. The curious part about the whole thing is that rosary peas have been used for centuries to ward off evil spirits."

"Why wouldn't an animal die if it ate the pea?"

"The shell, which harbors the poison, might not dissolve or crack. The pea's shell has to be opened to expose the poisonous seed inside."

"Joe, you've been making a few more arrests involving marijuana. Is it possible marijuana could be laced with this poison?"

"Possibly. The seeds would have to be ground up finely and mixed with the marijuana leaves then rolled. But I'm not sure just inhaling it will kill. I think it has to actually be digested."

Listening, Katharine was formulating an investigative plan. "Okay. Here's what you're going to do. Joey, uncover whatever you can about mixing this poison with illegal drugs. One of you has to find out the name of every guest on the island up to a week before the girl died. Then interview all of them."

"Are you nuts?" Gage exploded. "There's three thousand people here with the celebration of the Island's homecoming in another week."

Familiar with the annual festivities, Katharine said, "And it's imperative you find out where they all came from. Compare the info with what Joey discovers on the origins of this plant. Since the M.E. has determined the time of death, you need to find out where they all were at that time."

"What makes you so sure the murderer is a tourist?"

"I'm not sure, Joey. I wasn't excluding Island residents from the list. The hot trail factor has already been lost with delays. You can't overlook anything or anyone. Gage. Find out as much as you can on the victim. Her habits will tell us how she made it from Ashland to Madeline Island. I'm very interested to learn why a runaway came here versus running to a large city where no one would notice her. It makes me think she knew someone up this way."

"Joe, I'm promoting you to sergeant since your probation's almost up. Work with Pete and Alesha. Call all the inn's owners and get those lists."

"Thanks, Chief. I'll get on it immediately."

"Katharine, will you do the interviewing?"

"We'll do them together. The sooner the better. They need to be recorded. Have you got the equipment?"

"I'll get it."

* * *

Mac stared catatonically through the bungalow window at the aquamarine-colored water. Three days of deliberation over the latest dead girl left him disinterested in the beauty and thrill of sailing.

He and Green Bay's finest had spent the better part of the last two years looking for the murderer in a wave of serial killings—six to be exact. He felt deep-fried when the killings stopped in December last year, the same way they did the year before. The sixth victim's death had preceded several thousand arguments over a never-ending search to find the murdering parasite. Then his captain insisted he take a leave. But he couldn't. With no murder on the same date this month as the previous two years, he finally conceded. He was told to, or else. Now a seventh victim had surfaced.

It *had* to be David Patriot who killed this girl. When the M.E. pointed out the ulcers in her mouth, it was like a bomb going off in his brain. It was just one fact of several similar facts between the six teenage girls murdered in Green Bay. The bracelet was another. The first six girls had died as the result of a deadly chemical. Had this one died the same way?

An FBI profile on their killer revealed a ton of info accurately describing the unknown suspect. Unknown, Mac thought, until one piece of evidence exposed a name and proved the profiler's accuracy. The killer started decompensating and turned sloppy. David Patriot made a mistake at the scene of his sixth victim. The one victim Mac would never forget and where guilt would forever haunt him. Many nights he blamed himself as if he'd killed Clarissa himself. Following Clarissa's death, Patriot disappeared and nobody knew why, but his departure did contradict the profiler's reason for sloppiness—*"he wants to be caught"* she had told the Task Force.

With the exception of dinner with Katharine the other night, Mac had been on the sailboat vacillating instead of enjoying the activity. He couldn't shirk his responsibility any longer. He had to get involved in this case and grabbed his keys, exiting the Carriage House. As he locked the door of the bungalow, he heard a woman crying. He stopped, looked around, but saw no one. The woman's cry ended as quickly as it began. The only sounds came from the slap of water on the shore and long-legged, blue cranes. The ghost conversation with Katharine at dinner came back to him—Mac shook his head and exhaled. The towering pines had probably trapped a Lake Superior wind.

He slid onto the seat of his Jeep, started and raced the vehicle along Bay Road toward the police station. His adrenaline rushed with the tune of the engine's hum. Going too fast, he swerved erratically into the station's lot, slammed the brakes and shifted gears abruptly. Mac jumped out, hoping to find Gage inside. He didn't expect an empty office when he yanked the back door open. Then he heard voices. Trotting into the hallway, he followed the sound and stopped at the conference room door. Peeking inside the room, two other uniformed officers sat with Gage and Joe. Katharine leaned against a wall reading paperwork. Gage looked up absent-mindedly then quickly stiffened.

"Detective. What do you need? Or have you come to volunteer your services?"

Rarely caught off guard, Gage's question surprised him. The others shifted and looked his way. Katharine glanced up and did a double take. A light of excitement was vivid in her eyes. He exchanged a smile with her and moved into the room. "You found out."

Gage stood and walked around the table. "Yeah. My sister took an active interest in your career. She suggested I call Green Bay. Frankly, I was already suspicious the way you marched onto our homicide scene."

"Understood." As the others went back to work, Mac erased his original thoughts about the Island's police chief. He'd had serious doubts regarding Gage LeNoir's capabilities as well. "I figured you for a greenhorn myself when you let me walk in there the other day."

"Gage is a greenhorn," Katharine said, sending her brother a smirk. "He hasn't learned you never volunteer info."

"Is an out-of-work sergeant going to teach him the ins and outs?"

She stiffened at the question then stood motionless. Her shocked expression was completely unexpected, and Mac regretted asking the question. Shifting, he told Gage, "I stopped by because I may have info about your homicide."

"Well, now. My sister is right about my experience, but what's your interest in this murder?"

"Gage, we've all had a first in this business. I've been working ...,"

Their words blurred together as Katharine's pulse roared in her ears. Shrinking away, in need of fresh air, she sneaked outside. The sweat that formed across her brow could buy stock in her twitching muscles. Inhaling a deep breath, she marched the back lot's asphalt until her pace turned frantic. How did Mac find out? The department didn't release officer info. The look in his eyes told her he'd discovered *the truth*. She paced anxiously wondering who had told him.

"Katharine."

She swung around. "What right did you have to call and check on me?"

He dodged a dagger-filled glare from her, and said, "I might ask you the same thing."

"You were suspicious to us!" Crossing her arms, Katharine whirled away from him. "You had no right," she muttered.

"You haven't told anyone why you quit, have you?"

She spun around. "I want to know who told you!"

"Your lieutenant."

Katharine stumbled back a step. "Carl would never do that."

"Maybe not under normal circumstances, but he owed me. He also said it was a huge loss when you resigned."

"How do you know Carl? What did he tell you?"

"College. After graduation, he went to Minneapolis. I went to Green—"

"What exactly did he tell you? When did you talk to him?"

"It took a day before we finally connected. He said you were cleared of a justified homicide then quit. Katharine, I'm sorry. I had no idea you hadn't told Gage."

"You're a cop," she retorted. "Would you disclose the fact you killed someone?"

"Gage is a cop and I might talk to another cop. I just assumed ... you know, since the two of you seem close."

She gripped her torso to stop the trembling. *Thankfully*, Carl hadn't divulged everything. "I don't wanna talk about this. There's nothing to discuss."

"You have to talk about it."

He assumed the shooting had caused her defeat. The man had no idea there was more to it. "Why do you even care?"

"Let's just say it's an inbred need I have and let it go at that." Placing a supportive hand on her shoulder, he reassured her. "Katharine, I won't say a word. I promise."

The mere contact made her shake more. Looking up at him, his unfathomable eyes were compelling and magnetic. She couldn't deal with this.

"How long have you been avoiding facing this head on?"

"I'm not avoiding anything!"

"Yes you are."

"Do not assume anything about me, especially my weakness," she replied angrily.

"What you did in the line of duty is not a sign of weakness. When you're ready to talk, I'll be here to listen," he said somberly. "And, Katharine, you do need to get the demons out of your system."

Tensed up, she kicked a rock to free the grating tautness inside of her. She'd already talked about the shooting in a mandated debriefing. Talking about it wasn't the problem, but she'd be damned to hell before she'd tell Mac Dobarchon anything. And as far as her friends and family went, they didn't need to know either. Lifting her head to the brilliant blue sky, Katharine exhaled. "You realize if Gage knew, he never would have asked for my help."

"Under the circumstances, I wouldn't have asked you either. In the meantime, let's get back. I don't think Gage and Joe like the way I watch you."

She suppressed a grin now. "Frick and Frack have a macho need to protect."

"I doubt either will appreciate those nicknames. Come on. I'll explain why I need to be involved in this homicide."

"Mac, how come you never said anything at dinner the other night?"

"At the time, I didn't know you'd resigned but I have my own demons to deal with and I didn't want to believe what I Gage stumbled upon. I've been on the boat ever since our meal together debating what to do."

When her eyebrows rose in curiosity, he said, "Katharine, it's a long story and it's ugly. Ever heard of the Green Bay serial killer?"

CHAPTER 10

"Mac, you were supposed to be on leave from this case!"

"I know, Captain, but Patriot's left his mark here in the Apostle Islands. The locals found another sixteen-year-old runaway. She's from Ashland and it's identical to the others. I need you to fax the entire case file to La Pointe PD."

"Eight months of waiting and the sonovabitch started over the *end* of July."

"Uh-huh, with one difference, He's switched from paraquat to abrin. The results are the same."

"Then what makes you think its Patriot?"

"First clue was the victim's mouth ulcers. It's the same M-O, Native American female, sixteen, bracelet, liquor and the wrist ligatures. I'm working with La Pointe's Chief, Gage LeNoir. It'll be faster than driving back to Green Bay if you fax the entire report here."

"I'll send it with your partner."

"Cap, let's keep a lid on this for now. If Cole comes up here, it'll raise bureaucratic suspicion."

"Agreed. Have you told Linda?"

He heard the whine again and glanced out a bungalow window. He saw nothing but sailors, which he truly envied. "Uh, no," he answered, thinking about his sister. "I can't raise her hopes in any way."

"Mac, I'll back you a hundred percent, but I don't want another ass tattoo from our Chief's boot. That stunt you pulled still hasn't been resolved."

His fist tightened around the mug he held. "Captain, you know as well as I do those hypocrites were wrong."

"Those hypocrites rule the roost and you committed political homicide."

"Cap—"

"Dammit, Mac! You're a good cop! And what I know is this; you let your emotions cloud your judgment."

"What would you have done?" he shouted into the mouthpiece. His anger grew within him, and Mac didn't wait. "That scrawny bearded bastard had no right talking to the media!"

"Alright," Sanders sighed. "You'll have the report by the end of the day. Pinch this guy before he kills again. And keep me informed!"

"Guarantee it."

When the phone call terminated, Captain Dick Sander's words from another dispute replayed in Mac's head. He was not blunt and forceful in his dealings with people. He did an insane job some would never consider. If he started showing tact and understanding, it would provide additional errors in his work. It would serve him up another platter of punishment. Besides, hadn't he proven himself many times over with his ability to concentrate and work intently on closing cases by arrest?

Fury consumed him. The City's bureaucratic obstinacy was kindred to chronic constipation. After seven long months of fighting off authority, he finally gave up and cashed in his stacked up time. What the hell, he decided. Why not check out the Apostle's? He'd been hearing about the islands all his life. Born and bred in the cheesehead state, with two Great Lakes bordering it, he had never taken full advantage of Superior or Michigan. He drove from Green Bay to Bayfield, boarded the ferry and continued on to Madeline Island.

Maybe his coming here really was destiny. Regardless, he now understood why another murder hadn't taken place in Green Bay at the beginning of July. He just never expected to find it here. Why had Patriot moved from Green Bay to La Pointe he wondered? *Because the media aired his photo.* Though the Task Force hadn't connected the months and dates of the murders to anything, two of the six victims turned sixteen just before dying. The FBI Profiler said their dates of birth were flukes and not related to Patriot's reason for killing. He disagreed. The age of the victims seemed important, but the significance for the killing had baffled everyone on the Task Force.

A knock broke his concentration and Mac walked over and opened the door. He drew in a breath. All he could do was stare at her. Katharine looked terrific in faded jean shorts, a baggy Packers t-shirt and a pair of Reeboks that had seen better days. She also looked as rugged and wild as the first day he laid eyes on her.

"Well," he finally managed. "This is a nice surprise. Come in."

"Am I the only cop who doesn't drink coffee? Dobarchon, that caffeine will kill you."

"You stop by to criticize my habits?" he asked, drinking from the mug he still held.

"I came by to see if you wanted to take a run around the island."

He choked on the coffee. "Are you nuts? I don't run down suspects. Why would I run around an island for no reason?"

"Just thought you might like to spend some time with me."

Mac grabbed her wrist before Katharine slipped away. "Never said I didn't want to spend time with you."

"Then let's go. Running is good healthy exercise."

"So are sailing and sex." He grinned now. "Spend the day on a boat with me and I'll prove it."

She yanked her hand free. "You actually believe you can make me squirm by mentioning sex?"

"Apparently not."

"Besides, sitting on a boat isn't exercise."

"Trust me. You won't sit much if you spend the day sailing with me."

"I suppose not if I'm lying on the boat deck like your proposal suggests."

Oh yeah, he indeed liked the spunk. He accepted the challenge and turned up his smile a notch. "Whaddaya say. Are you game?"

"You're pretty sure of yourself, Dobarchon."

She'd given him the once-over several times and he leaned

forward. "Very when a beautiful woman gives me a certain look, Princess."

"Princess?"

"Yeah. As in warrior. Come inside where I will convince you to spend the day sailing with me."

"You're one confident little sucker and downright positive you can entice me into anything. Bet you've never had an insecure moment in your life."

"You catch on quick, Princess."

"Let's hope you do the same. I'm meeting Gage to go over the interview process when I'm done jogging."

"Speaking to that, I just got off the phone with my Captain. He's faxing Green Bay's report to the station. It's a couple hundred pages and will take a while. Come in."

She finally accepted the invitation and Mac closed the door. As she roamed the room, he tugged on a t-shirt. He'd decided instantly upon seeing the rental, the Carriage House contained all the comforts of a modern home. A dazzling view of the beach and the sound of Superior's waves probably added romance and passion for those on their honeymoon, but he cared little about romantic getaways right now.

"Dobarchon, if I didn't know better, I'd think you were hiding."

He looked at her for a long moment. "Why's that?"

"It's too neat in here. There's nothing personal lying around. It's like you're keeping some deep dark secret."

"You implying I should be a slob or you just being nosey?"

She shrugged. "Tell me why you're so sure this murder was committed by Green Bay's serial killer?"

"Have a seat. What can I get you since you don't drink coffee?"

"Ice water is fine."

"Will bottled do? How 'bout breakfast? I'm cooking."

"No breakfast. Bottled is fine."

Cocking his head sideways, he studied her some more. Extremely practiced with short answers, she had the ability to irritate him if he allowed her to do so. He supposed it would fall into one category or another of the disguises she wore.

"Why do you keep looking at me like that?"

"Didn't know I was looking at you in a certain way," he said, and moved into the kitchen.

"You do it all the time." She pulled out a chair and sat. "Now, tell me again why you think this murder is related to your serial killings."

Once more of the million times he'd analyzed the case, Mac went over the evidence in his mind. He removed bacon and the ingredients for French toast from the fridge.

"Exactly two years ago Patriot started his killing spree in July. The next was October then December. He waited eight months, and killed three more the same dates the following year. With the exception of the poison he used on the first six, and the dates he killed, everything is identical right down to the Johnnie Walker bottle. Here we are eight months later, but at the end of July with the seventh victim in a new location."

"What do you mean the end of July?"

"He's done his killing the first weeks of July and October and the week between Christmas and New Years."

"That bacon's gonna kill you with all the caffeine you drink."

"Turkey bacon is good and healthy. You should try it." He seasoned and whipped the egg mixture. Personal frustration mingled with renewed hope, and he told her, "I have to find him, Katharine. I have to stop the bastard before he kills again. He's sick. He'll keep killing until I can throw him into a cell. He deserves the death penalty."

He wondered if the physical signs were obvious to her. His relentless pursuit of a criminal vibrated through his tightening muscles and clenched jaw. His emotions stirred by fear and uncertainties had put his composure under attack but brittle silence dredged on before he continued. After several minutes, he asked, "How long did you work homicide in Minneapolis before you went back on the street?"

"Two years but it barely qualifies me as experienced."

"You don't classify yourself as an expert?"

"Well, no, not really. Why?"

"Your crime ratio is higher than Green Bay. You had a lotta practice when you first made Sergeant a few years back."

"I remember. We hit an all-time high but I find it odd you keep tabs on Minneapolis homicides."

"I don't generally. Carl," he told her.

"I'm gonna call and chew him out for telling you so much."

"Carl'll quake in his boots when you do."

"He's afraid of me."

"Darlin', with that red hair and those sexy eyes, I'm scared, too. The combination is bewitching enough to drive any sensible man insane."

"Are you a sensible man, Dobarchon?"

Hun-uh, he wasn't going there! Green Bay's police chief had called his obsession to bring in Patriot a fixation. This case was his only priority. It was directly responsible for his current leave of absence. "I'm as crazy as they come," he muttered.

"Tell me more about Patriot."

"His behavior reflects his personality." Setting two plates on the table, he said, "Patriot doesn't kill for greed, jealousy or profit. His victims aren't close to him, but strangers. With each one, he becomes more ritualized. The rituals have meaning to him."

"And that meaning would be?"

"He lives in a fantasy. Murdering is his attempt to fulfill whatever his fantasy is."

Katharine soaked the French toast with syrup and forked a piece, putting it in her mouth. "You're a good cook, Dobarchon. Tell me about Patriot's physical and emotional state of being."

"Before we knew who we were dealing with, the profiler told us he most likely had a history of child abuse. He's probably a loner filled with rage and feelings of inadequacy. The report's completely accurate. We learned Patriot's father abused him at a young age. That's the factor leading to his rage and violence. According to his mother, who still lives in Green Bay, Patriot's father believed David couldn't do anything right. In fact, the father called him devil spawn."

"Is the father still alive?"

"No."

"How'd you find out it was Patriot?"

"The killer starts to feel out of control, which is psycho mumbo-jumbo for he wants to be caught. After the last victim, he left ...,"

When he didn't go on, Katharine reached over and touched his hand. "Who was she, Mac?"

He heaved himself upward, tipping the chair to the floor and stomped toward the coffeepot to refill his cup. "Dammit, Katharine! He lures them in with drugs and kills them with paraquat. He ties 'em up and obtains some sort of sick thrill off of watching them die a slow painful death!"

"Paraquat? Our victim died from abrin poisoning. Where's the connection?"

"It's the only evidence that's different. Everything else is a match. Paraquat kills by skin contact, ingestion or inhalation. We know it wasn't absorbed through the skin since a severe rash would've developed. Initial symptoms in the first two to five days of ingestion are burning mouth and throat, along with tongue ulceration. The victims suffer abdominal pain, diarrhea and fever. Days five through eight are final with tachycardia, respiratory distress, cyanosis and fatal lung damage. Not that it's significant, but paraquat also turns the urine blue."

"Are you telling me all the victims suffered horribly for that many days before actually dying?"

He nodded as if he were re-living each victim's final days.

"And you still believe this murder has Patriot's mark?"

"I'd stake my life on it."

"What's the connection to the Johnnie Black?"

"We don't know. It might be part of a ceremony while he watches death consume his victim. Odds are on he uses the liquor as a formal dousing over the body. I think he mixes the paraquat and whiskey and forces the victim to drink it. The autopsy revealed both whiskey and paraquat in each victim."

"Maybe both ways are right and he does it like a sacrament."

"Maybe."

"But you don't know why?"

"Nor have we been able to get past the fact that marijuana was also found in each victim."

"What's that got to do with anything?"

"In the late sixties and early seventies the Government inadvertently caused numerous poisonings by spraying illegal marijuana fields with paraquat in an attempt to kill the weed. The fields were harvested and the weed smoked, killing many."

"Mac. Gage has Joey checking to see if abrin can be mixed with marijuana. He says it's become prevalent on the island. I see why you're convinced. Maybe Patriot has his own plants and is dousing them with the abrin."

"Could be. The problem with that theory is we didn't find any plants at his place in Green Bay."

"I don't think Gage had the remnants analyzed from the bottle I found. But the more I think about my idea, the less I'm convinced it's any good."

"Why?"

"We don't know if abrin is soluble and can be mixed with liquid or marijuana. Joey doesn't think so. This poison seed is also known as a rosary pea and is used by some to ward off evil spirits."

"Like the Catholic Rosary is used. So why switch from paraquat to abrin?" he asked.

"I dunno. I also can't recall if the autopsy revealed whiskey in our victim."

"Let's get the remnants tested and recheck the autopsy report. I need to know if the La Pointe victim had marijuana in her system."

"You got a photo of this dirtbag? So we at least have some idea who to look for?"

He nodded, took another swig of coffee. "Katharine, I'm sorry. I didn't mean to vent my anger toward you."

"Mac, how did you know the sixth victim?"

Breakfast was a lost cause. He made his way to a window that faced the Great Lake. No matter how many times he tried to forget, the facts brought his emotion to life. "Her name was Clarissa Noma."

"Noma? That's Michelle's middle name. Do you think there's a connection?"

"No. The bastard zeroes in on naïve, helpless and troubled sixteen year olds. Clarissa had just turned sixteen the second of last December. Little did we know she wouldn't live to see her seventeenth birthday. She had problems, minor at first, then escalating. I fell into the trap—it won't happen to me or mine. I really thought it was a phase and Clarissa would outgrow it until she ran right after her birthday."

Rotating his cup and watching the coffee swirl, Mac relived his fatal mistakes. "Clarissa was my niece, Katharine. She was my sister's only child. Linda begged me for help with her. I really thought my sister was overreacting after Clarissa swore to me up one side and down the other, she wasn't using. The two of them had typical mother daughter quarrels I chalked up to the trials of parenting. I made the first of the two biggest mistakes in my career when I blew off my sister's plea for help."

Katharine stood and moved toward him. "It's not your fault. You can't blame yourself."

He turned to face her. Compassion overflowed in her eyes. Seeing the tenderness for the first time caught him off guard. She did that a lot to him. He didn't know why, but the control she had narcotized him. With her hair being the main attraction, the untamed energy in her mouth went unnoticed until now. Mac fingered her lips and Katharine twitched slightly. He was stunned when their eyes connected in passionate arousal. She was pulling him into the electric air that surrounded her.

"This isn't good, Princess."

Standing on tiptoe, she touched her lips to his. He didn't resist. He couldn't. Her lips were warm. They invited him to indulge some more. The moment heating up, his fantasies expanding, her body molded itself to him. He wrapped his arms around her. She overflowed with tender persuasiveness and he lost himself in her mouth. Surely, he thought, she was letting go. All he had to do was take.

A dizzying current raced through Katharine. Her senses were spinning. Her spirit was soaring. It all came to a screeching halt. Her brain took over in cop fashion. Breathing hard, she pulled away. With the peaking energy waned, Mac radiated a vitality that could draw her in like a magnet. Katharine cleared her throat. "I'll see you at the station in thirty minutes. We can go to work on arresting Patriot."

She turned and sprinted out of the bungalow leaving the door wide open as if nothing had happened. Confused, Mac wandered restlessly around the room. Katharine had kissed him so quick and hard it left him panting and blinded by lust. His urges were strong and not entirely of his doing. If she hadn't backed away, he would have pursued, and conquered. He let go a deep breath and disposed of the food on the plates.

He went upstairs, stripped and stepped into a cold shower. They'd be treading on dangerous emotional ground if he and Katharine went forward with the obvious. Patriot's arrest was his priority. *Damn! He wanted her.*

* * *

Katharine bolted from the Carriage House in the direction of her parent's place. She needed to shake off the arousal. When it came to charming the opposite sex, boldness wasn't in her vocabulary. Nor was she wanton with men, but Dobarchon challenged all her logic. Unable to discover the origination of this new energy, she slowed down to catch her breath. She fingered her mouth. The intensity of the moment seemed to fuel her actions. The kiss she initiated, and a very good kiss at that, sent mixed feelings rolling through her. The silent sadness in his face had absorbed her into involvement. Nevertheless, she took pride in self-control. Others who fraternized within the troops triggered job distraction.

She did not intend to fall under this spell and sprinted down the road silently verbalizing, *I won't do that again*, then remembered Mac had said he'd made two mistakes. What was the second? She made a mental note to ask him later.

A blowing horn sent her off to the edge of the dirt road. She looked over her shoulder as a pick-up truck pulled up alongside. Katharine stopped running and jogged in place.

"Hey, Katharine. How's it goin'?"

"Fine," she panted.

"I heard about the trouble Kevin gave you the other night at the Tavern."

She stared at the man inside the blue Dodge Ram sitting in the middle of the road.

"You don't remember me, do you?"

"Curt Stewart, right?"

He nodded. "Sorry about Kevin the other night. Gage mentioned it since he heard about it from Nicole."

Katharine stopped jogging. "I don't hold you responsible for Kevin's actions. Besides, no harm done."

"That's good to hear. I know the three of us tend to get a little rowdy. I just wanted to apologize."

"Accepted."

"Aren't you a cop somewhere?"

She nodded, unsure if Gage swearing her in qualified as her being a police officer anymore. Bullnecked, Curt had a friendly face to go with his meaty, teddybear body. His butterscotch-colored hair was lighter than Kevin's was. "Curt, what are you doing these days?"

"Married Josie Hanson. We got a kid, Clyde."

"Oh? I thought Josie married what's his name?"

"Terry Hunter. They broke up. We got together and, well, you do the math. Clyde is fourteen. You should stop over. I know Josie would like to see you."

The trio of best friends titled Josie a rich bitch in high school. Though she'd earned it, Katharine strongly doubted Josie wanted to see her now. "What's she doing these days besides raising a family?"

"She helps out at her dad's inn on occasion."

An envious twinge pummeled Katharine's insides. Raised on a gold platter, Josie rarely suffered financial woes. "Where you working?"

"Road construction for the county under old man Dupre."

"On the mainland?"

"Yep."

"Listen, it's good to see you. I was on my way to see Gage and I really have to get going."

"Gage have any leads on the murder of that poor kid? Josie's nervous as a wet cat. She won't rest until the killer is caught."

"Couldn't say."

"Where'd you say you were a cop?"

"I didn't." Katharine hesitated before deciding a white lie wouldn't harm anyone. "Minneapolis."

"You here to help Gage?"

"Gage is very capable. As one cop to another it's automatic we help each other if asked."

"Tell Gage if there's anything I can do to assist, all he has to do is ask any of us. Folks are worried."

"I'll let him know."

As he drove away, Katharine thought it very odd that he'd stop to chat. She also thought it unusual that Curt hadn't heard from someone of her coming home for good.

CHAPTER 11

Several hours slipped away while Frank sat in the darkness. Around three in the morning, he got out of bed and hunkered into the ancient rocker his wife discovered at a blasted flea market. She wanted to get off the island she'd told him. *It'd be nice to spend the day together* she claimed, dragging him over to Ashland. She always said that when she heard about a sale. Though Frank habitually balked at her whims, he also habitually gave in to his wife. He had no idea the day he lugged the rocker into the house that he'd be the one spending time in it. He'd hauled this piece of junk home years ago then recalled Paula's gratification that night.

The worn wood on the armrests was smooth to touch now. The tapestry seat had changed many times and Paula always wanted him to refinish the wood, but he didn't think it worth his effort. Besides, what he thought about the rocker didn't matter. For thirty-five years, Paula had been his entire life. None of what she enticed him into made any difference to him. He'd always loved her. He'd never forget the first time he laid eyes on her. He fell hard. What a tough catch, but he did catch her. Because he'd never let her go, of course, he'd do anything for her. Had he known back then about her shrewd ways, he still would have chosen Paula. Maybe he should consider refinishing the rocker for her.

He glanced over at his wife. Most nights her restless stirring kept him awake, but tonight he found comfort in the sound of her rhythmic breathing. Listening to her purring breath in the dark hours had depleted the charged up thoughts in his mind.

The downstairs door opened and Frank tottered forward in the rocker. An awaking sun had consumed the silent night. He peeked through the bedroom window as his daughter stepped outside. It always amazed him how much Katharine favored her mother's looks. Her petite frame and copper red hair were identical to Paula's. That's where it stopped. Paula was serene while Katharine was dynamic. All her life, his only daughter did exactly what she wanted to do. He supposed he was responsible for that. Parenting was complex. Their worries were genuine. Regardless, his baby girl had been gone too long and the lost years grieved away inside his heart. While he realized it too late—his heart wasn't what was important, it still throbbed painfully inside his chest—he had chased Katharine away.

How could he accept that his Pumpkin wasn't his little girl anymore? How would he deal with the grief he saw in her eyes when he didn't know the reason for that grief? Did his son really think he was blind? Her slumped posture and the defeat in her intense blue eyes stopped him dead in his tracks the day she re-entered the house. The despair in her child-like face shocked him so much that it just about killed him. His baby girl had suffered some awful devastation and that hurt him more than he'd ever admit to anyone. He couldn't admit how much he wanted to shuffle downstairs right now and bundle his Pumpkin into his arms either. He wanted to soothe away whatever troubled her the way he used to do.

Frank resented himself for that, too, and let the curtain fall. He rocked back and forth, occupied with many thoughts. Paula was dead wrong about his rigid opinions and closed mind. His little girl grew up and just didn't need him anymore. Swiping the back of his hand against his cheek, he swallowed hard. *Gage was right*, which also irritated him. His wife and son had forced him to think long and hard about many things.

* * *

Katharine sat on the porch step, stretched, yawned and mulled over the case. The interviews from the lists Joey put together were proving to be ineffectual. They hadn't discovered Patriot's name at any island rental. Mac had returned to Green Bay to get the photo of David Markus Patriot. Each time his department faxed the mugshot, it came out charcoal gray and unclear. Up late the last three nights, she finally finished reading the three-hundred page police report a few hours ago. Forensics had identified one fingerprint at the scene of the sixth victim, Mac's niece.

Guilt consumed Katharine. Nearly losing her life had left her powerless on the streets, left her feeling insecure and weighted down. Propping her elbows atop her knees under the morning sunlight, the more she thought about it the more she realized life had been drained from her soul. She was going through the motions of helping her brother while her heart and mind quietly rebelled against everything she stood for. She couldn't muster any more energy to give. No matter how hard she tried to forget, she couldn't erase the bloody image of Easter Sunday or the serious mistake that followed the fatal shooting of Donte Johnson. She became incapable of performing her job safely or satisfactorily in those trying weeks.

Sighing, her own life going amuck was sickening, but Clarissa had lost her life. And the more she thought about that the more she realized her agony didn't hold a lighted candle to Mac's torment. The sad part was she now needed to prove her father's opinion of her wrong. If she didn't, the gamut of perplexing emotions would never go away. Sheathing pride and inner feelings would be difficult, but she'd make determination the driving force to win her father's love back.

A gentle wind rustled the leaves of trees while feathered friends hid within and jabbered endlessly. Her parent's house was roosted on a craggy bluff. Leafy trees hid the nook well. Lake Superior's rolling waves slapped rhythmically unseen beyond the ledge rock where a once shiny red swing-set she and Gage, along with friends, had played on as kids sat at the property's back. Katharine assumed her mother kept the rusted set with hopes that grandchildren would one day play there, too.

Gazing over the naked yard, a new coat of stain revived a wood picnic table. *Dad must be spending hours out here since retirement* she mused. The weedless grass never looked more immaculately manicured. Oddly, the otherwise barren parcel of land reminded her of her father's life, plain and simple with no contradicting conflict. She once associated the backyard as belonging to her mother. Today, it had her father's badge imprinted all over it.

She glanced upward at a ruckus from birds in the neighbor's pine. A gentle breeze curled around her body. The cloudless sky indicated another warm day. Perhaps another hard run and a day at the beach sketching would eliminate her mounting dread. Maybe she'd call Nicole and Michelle, see if they wanted to do something—anything to distract her from her past memories.

Jittery as a wet cat, physical exertion helped to deplete some of her anxiety and she unloaded her car several days ago. Her mother loved the music box she purchased at a craft show in the Cities. The animated tune *The Entertainer* was her mother's favorite from the movie, *Butch Cassidy and the Sundance Kid.* Katharine stood and went inside the house. She smiled, recalling the way her mother oo'ed and ahh'ed over the hand-carved box. Her father hadn't come down for morning coffee and she grabbed the ringing phone.

"Okay, I'm taking yours and Nicole's advice. I've got the day off if you guys want to get together."

"You must be psychic. I was gonna call you two and see if you wanted to do something today."

"Nicole will want to shop. That's the last thing I'm doing," Michelle said

"Me either. Let's get a boat and go out."

"What time? I'll call Nicole and tell her what she always tells us."

"I'll pick you up in about thirty minutes and we can roust her outta bed together."

"Girlfriend, you're just as devious as she is."

Smiling as if Michelle could see her, Katharine said, "I owe her."

When she disconnected, her smile rapidly dissipated. Katharine gulped hard. Her dad stood in the kitchen entry, watching her. "I'm sorry. Did the phone wake you?"

He shook his head and shuffled over to the coffeepot to start a morning routine he could probably do in his sleep. Her internal energy said take flight.

"If you girls wanna go water skiing, you can use the runabout. It's gassed up."

Katharine shifted abruptly. She stared at her father's back as he filled the coffee carafe. She didn't know how to respond to his generosity.

"How's Michelle?" he asked.

"She's goo—" her words broke off when his question hit like a rock. Unusual concern had altered the tone of his voice. "You knew!" she accused.

He poured the water into the reservoir and glanced over his shoulder at her. When he averted his eyes back to the task of filling the basket with grounds, she exploded, "Dad, how could you let that s-o-b do it to Michelle?"

Frank flipped the *on* switch and faced her. "I tried to help, but she refused. Best I could do was give her advice."

"Wait a minute. Michelle said Nicole was the only one who knew."

"True, she didn't tell anyone. Ran into her one day. She'd tried concealing her bruises with makeup. I told her she could have him charged with domestic assault. She wouldn't hear of it and swore me to secrecy. I gave her the usual confidential referrals."

"Michelle doesn't have a mean bone in her body! She didn't deserve it!"

"I know. None of us deserves it, Katharine. From time to time fate forces us into situations we never dreamed possible. When it happens, the choice we make is sometimes the only choice we have. We do the best we can."

Staring at him, wordless of response, she wondered if there was a hidden meaning. Had he lost control of his tongue and thoughts? She looked closer and noticed he'd dropped the arrogant shield, decided there was no hidden meaning. She wished he would give her the same concern he gave Michelle as he shifted nervously and dug into the pocket of his khaki knee-length shorts.

"Here's the key for the runabout. You girls be careful."

She didn't know how to respond to the charity or the fact that he spoke to her in a civilized manner.

"Here, take 'em. Go on and have fun."

"You aren't going fishing?"

"You keep stalling and I might change my mind."

Though he fought back a smile, it had touched the corners of his mouth, and he forced himself to maintain detachment. That was his struggle with obstinacy, she thought, taking the keys. As she turned to go, she said, "The backyard looks good."

Just great! That's as bad as men bonding over a dead body. She stopped, turned and surprised herself when she gave him a squeezing hug. "Thanks," she said quietly and escaped quickly.

* * *

Michelle pounded on the door, and Katharine yelled, "Jarvis get that tight little butt of yours out of bed!"

Turning the handle, Katharine discovered the door open. "Idiot. Doesn't she lock her doors?"

"I'm not going in there while she's still sleeping. She'll kill us both."

"You think she'd give it a second thought if the situation were reversed?"

"Good point," Michelle said, and grinned. "Jarvis! We're coming in."

Nicole's décor consisted of newfangled leather furniture and metal-tube lights. The flawlessly clean rooms felt cold and impersonal. Katharine thought it lacked cozy comfort. Glancing around the room, regretful twinges ran icy in her veins. Nicole never had a family, and Katharine understood for the first time how siblings and parents were the nucleus of hearth and home. Michelle led the way to Nicole's bedroom and flipped on the light switch in the semi-darkened room.

"Just look at her. She actually sleeps wearing one of them eye masks."

"Working dogwatch, I always said I was gonna get myself one of those. Never did get around to buying one."

"You think she plugs her ears?"

"Either that or she's deaf as a doorknob." Katharine inched closer to the canopy lace-covered bed wondering why it challenged the living room décor.

"Can you believe it, Katharine?"

"What's that?"

"Even in her sleep she looks hot to trot. I've never seen anyone look that good."

"It's the honey-gold hair. Wish I had her hair."

"Why? You have gorgeous hair."

"Yeah, right," she rebutted. "Just what we all need is hair with a fricking mind of its own."

"And you think my mop of fine drab brown is so much better?"

"Michelle, at least yours has a healthy shine. You should never have cut it off."

Fear flitted through Michelle's eyes and Katharine could only imagine the worst possible scenario. "You wanna wake her up or should I?"

"You can."

"I'm strangling you both for waking me up!"

Michelle screamed and Katharine jumped when Nicole sprang upright and pushed back her eye mask.

"What are you two doing in here?"

"You always sleep naked?"

"You jealous of my chest, LeNoir?"

"Answer a question with a question," Katharine muttered.

"What are you two doing in my bedroom?"

"Dad's letting us use the runabout. We're going out on Superior for the day."

"What time is it?"

"Almost ten," Katharine said, and yanked the covers back.

"Omigod!" Michelle shrieked. "She's buck naked!"

"I didn't get to bed until four and you're waking me up before noon?"

Averting her eyes, Michelle scanned the bedroom, grabbed a robe and tossed it at Nicole.

"Up and att'em," Katharine said.

"I need a shower first."

"No shower, no makeup. We brought food. We're going to Raspberry Island to do some water skiing."

"I'm not going anywhere without my first cup of coffee. Michelle, put on a pot and don't let Katharine touch it."

"I won't, but she's right. There's no time for primping. You get ten minutes, Nicole."

They headed out when Katharine stopped in the bedroom threshold. "Nicole, you really do need to lock your doors at night."

"Yes, officer. Get out!"

By the time the three women made it to the marina, they'd argued over which island to visit, who would steer the boat and who would ski first, changed their minds many times and finally agreed on Michigan Island and to let the day run its course.

"All right you two, I have to be back by four this afternoon."

"For what?" Michelle yelled over the motor.

"Work."

"I called and told them you were sick and wouldn't be coming in tonight." Nicole's tightly drawn brows imbibed Michelle's added taunting. "Paybacks are such a bitch. Aren't they, *sweetie*."

On the big lake, they headed north. Halfway to Michigan Island, Katharine slowed the speed and shut off the I/O. "Guess who I ran into the other day?"

Both women shrugged, removing their life jackets to protect their bodies with sunscreen.

"Curt Stewart. I never knew he married Josie Hanson. What ever happened to her and Terry?"

Sliding on her Rayban sunglasses, Nicole said, "The bleach-blond bitch with basketball breasts was told Terry couldn't pave her way financially."

"And Curt Stewart can? He's no prize bull either," Michelle said.

"I had to bite my tongue when Curt told me they had to get married. Was she really pregnant with his kid?"

"What a crock. Nobody has to get married, but yeah she was pregnant all right." Leaning backward in the seat, Nicole propped her bare feet up on the brightwork. "You think for one minute Josie didn't plan the pregnancy? Especially after her father made her dump Terry our senior year. Poor Curt never saw what hit him until it was too late."

"Josie's an idiot who expected someone to wait on her all her life." Michelle grabbed Pepsi's from the cooler for her and Nicole, bottled water for Katharine. "Old thunder thighs had to find marriage material for that reason alone. I doubt Terry ever gave matrimony a second thought back then. Nor do I believe Clyde belongs to Curt."

Katharine sat upright. "What?"

"The kid doesn't look anything like Curt."

"You think he belongs to Terry and because her father made her break up with him, she went looking for Curt?"

Michelle shrugged. "You want this water or don't you?"

Taking the bottle, Katharine picked up her sketchbook and charcoal pencil, drawing what she saw. Two friends sitting in her dad's runabout. "I've never understood why any woman thinks the only way to marriage is through pregnancy."

"I'll never marry a second time," Michelle said. "The single lane looks damn good to me."

Nicole repositioned herself directly into the sun. "I'll never give up my independence."

"What a crock," Michelle hooted. "You're so desperately in need of male attention it's pathetic."

"*That* has nothing to do with independence."

"Bet me."

"Men have always been your focus," Katharine told her.

"I'm not arguing that point. At least I acknowledge my needs and desires."

"Oh please," Katharine countered.

"It's true. I have a need to kick you both where the sun doesn't shine and a deep desire it hurts like hell."

"You can try," Katharine said, cutting loose with laughter.

"Hey! Do either of you remember the name of that awful camp our parents forced us to go to the summer we were sixteen? Remember what we did to Josie," Michelle asked.

Katharine stopped drawing. "Camp Ojibwe. The old feather and toothpaste trick."

"One of our better ideas." Michelle giggled. "Remember how we squeezed toothpaste into her hand and tickled her nose with a duck feather."

"Yeah and the bimbo used the other hand to scratch her itch," Nicole added.

"We got her good when we filled that hand, tickled her nose and watched her use both to smear her face with Colgate."

"My Colgate," Nicole flouted.

"You think we were too mean to her?" Katharine asked.

Tying her hair back, Nicole said, "They waged a war first with us when she and Margie put honey in our shampoo."

Katharine looked up from her sketch a second time. "What ever happened to Margie?"

"Married and divorced three times. Right, Michelle?"

"Has a kid from each," she answered. "Lives in Bayfield now and last I heard, she's a waitress somewhere. Remember how we stole Margie's clothes in gym class when she went to take her shower?"

"We didn't steal her clothes. We just sorta moved them."

Giggling some more, Michelle said, "Throwing them in the boy's locker room is not sorta moving them, Nicole."

Katharine held up her sketchpad to compare the faces of her best friends to her drawings. It had been too long since she'd relaxed or laughed. She felt human again even if it was at someone else's expense. Recalling Margie without clothes and screaming, she said, "Is it any wonder my brother doesn't trust us?"

"Gage lost trust in us our sophomore year when he witnessed the fight we had with the brats. Good God, we were so juvenile back then."

"Omigod! I forgot about that."

"Wow, Katharine. Those are an amazing likeness to us. Look, Michelle. She drew us perfectly."

Removing her sunglasses Michelle looked at the tablet. "Katharine, if you want a job, I know the gift shops would be thrilled to sell your sketches."

"No offense, but I doubt anyone would buy your portraits."

"Probably not, but you excelled at art in high school. You obviously haven't lost your gift and should start drawing again. Go talk to Iola Tibbs. Arrange some kind of deal with her."

"Mac told me the same thing."

Keyed up, both women sat forward. "Tell us about your date!"

"Ran into him on the beach while I was sketching. He wanted to buy one but I gave it to him in exchange for dinner. That's all it was. Other than both of us helping Gage with this homicide, there's nothing going on between us."

"Michelle, have you seen Mac Dobarchon?"

"No," she answered, shifting into a relaxed pose. "Why's a tourist helping Gage with the murder?"

"Let me tell you. Mac is not just a tourist. He's a tall, dark cop. And a mighty good-looking piece of meat."

Katharine's eyebrow arched believing it pointless to discuss the male body or any part of it. "How'd you find out Mac's a cop?"

"Hon, you forget where we live and how we spend our lives being nosey. Everyone knows about the murder and Mac Dobarchon. Does Gage have any clues as to who killed that poor girl?"

"Couldn't say."

"Can't, or won't? You were with Gage when Joe found her body. I can't get that ornery son-of-a-gun to spill his guts."

"Katharine, you were there! And saw it? I heard it was ghastly. How come you never said anything Friday night?"

Shifting uncomfortably, Katharine gazed out over the water. "All I'm saying is we're working on it."

"Figures you'd help. It's in your blood. What I can't figure out is why you quit your job," Nicole persisted.

"None of this is on the table for discussion. I'm hungry."

Shifting, she stood and raised anchor then revved up the runabout and made straight for Michigan Island. As the boat's motor drowned out further conversation, she saw the exchange of looks between her two friends. When sweat formed across her forehead, she raced the boat harder. She wasn't sorry she'd squelched the discussion. Feeling both their eyes upon her, queasiness rooted in her belly. She continued steering toward the miniature island. If she hadn't had a grip on the boat's wheel, she would have paced the deck. The panic attacks were increasing and half the reason for her lack of sleep. Overly active muscles increased her bodily ache. Hot flashes, which could pass for menopause, had turned into a standard operating procedure. And she'd become a victim of her own negative self-talk.

Focusing on the Michigan lighthouse as it came into view, she settled down just a bit. The last thing she needed was to wreck her dad's boat. Slowing the runabout to spot jagged rocks, Katharine shut off the I/O in three feet of water. Restarting the engine in any less would toss sand into the propeller and seriously harm the engine's cooling system.

Dropping anchor a second time, a thin cry pierced the air. "Did you hear that?" Katharine asked.

"Hear what?" each asked simultaneously.

"A woman. I heard a woman crying."

Michelle frowned at Katharine while Nicole scanned the area. "I think it's that fat little gull scurrying along the beach over there."

They'd think her crazy if she carried on, but she heard Sully's ghost as clearly as her well-toned ear deciphered the difference between emergency vehicle sirens. She'd been hearing the cry since returning home.

When Nicole hurdled the boat side, Katharine tossed her sketchbook and supplies into the cooler and handed it over then jumped into the water. Michelle followed.

"Water's warm," Nicole said. "I'm going for a swim before I eat."

"Think I will too," Michelle decided.

"I've been thinking about income. I'm gonna do some sketching of the lighthouse. I think it'll make a fascinating scene."

"Go for it," Michelle told her as they waded to shore.

Katharine sauntered away. She wasn't hungry anymore. Instead, she found a spot and squatted in long grass and four-petal blooms she thought might be buttercups. Her personal knowledge on flowers didn't fill a thimble. Horticulture was Michelle's area of expertise. Nevertheless, she liked the lazy-yellow blossoms.

Gazing upward at the ancient lighthouse, it was one of six built in the Apostle Islands. After carefully drawing the outline of the light's stucco edge, she etched in the black trim on each window and the door all the way up to the walkway, lantern and lightening rod. Next, she shaded in the house's aging roof and perfected the background pines. She drew the grassy field of wildflowers then held up the book to admire her artwork.

With exception of Nicole and Michelle's chatter in the background, serenity had encompassed her under the sun's warmth. Though engulfed in tides of weariness and despair, drawing had calmed her into wisps of sleepiness. Katharine lay down, but her mind returned to its tortured thinking. She was so tired her nerves throbbed. Exhaustion and trouble fed off her stress. Sleep was the cure—if she could just get some—just five minutes. The memories burned vividly in her mind—*Shots rang out. The commotion and screams blared in Kat's ears. Her brain repeatedly ordered her to draw her nine, but her hand was frozen on her belted weapon. Icy fear twisted around her palpitating heart. Sheer black fright as dark as the unlit city sky swelled within her body. She'd been shot! Nicole screamed the moment it happened. She was going down, panic rioted within her and Kat fell hard, hitting asphalt. Nicole kept crying.* 'Stop crying!' *she yelled. But those tears just kept rolling out of her like a heavy drowning waterfall. Kat screamed again.* 'Stop crying, Nicole!'

Michelle could pacify Nicole. But when the cries switched to the blood-curdling scream embedded deeply within Kat's memory, she attempted to breathe life back into the three-year-old. She was too late. Two were dead and she had killed one of them.

Katharine's eyes flew open. The sun had shifted measurably. She jumped to her feet and checked her body for blood. Sweat beaded her forehead and all she could do was gasp for air. New screams rang out. She shook as horrific images grew in her mind. The shouts were real and she bolted toward the shore of the anchored boat scanning and searching the area frantically.

"*Katharine! Katharine!*" Michelle screamed her name.

"Where the hell are they?"

Running along the sandy beach, Katharine searched the water and shore. "Nicole! Michelle! Where are you?"

The familiar clump of anxiety settled deep in her gut. She continued searching as her mind jumped on with terror. "Michelle! Where are you?"

"We're over here! Omigod! Hurry, Katharine!"

Michelle was halfway down the shoreline. Nicole was out of sight. With her heart thumping madly, Katharine ran at high-speed and came to a jerky halt where each woman stood. Inhaling the ungodly smell, she gasped, choked. She didn't have to see what her nose knew well. Her body stiffened unmercifully.

Death was there, lying in the grass and rocks.

CHAPTER 12

"The wind shifted," Nicole blustered.

They held their breath and covered their noses to block the putrid odor floating by on the wind's tail. Katharine used Nicole's cell phone to contact Gage, and now they waited. Sitting cross-legged in the sand, Michelle tossed agates into the water one right after another. Her face turned ashen and stayed that way after she puked her guts out from the rank fumes that kept shoving them further down the shoreline.

"How much longer until Gage gets here?"

"Soon, Nicole. He has to wait for the medical examiner to come over from the mainland," Katharine told her. "Michelle, you okay? You're kinda quiet."

With her arm hung midair, she gaped at Katharine. "How did you do this every day of your life?"

"I'm really sorry you two had to see this."

"*Omigod!* You say that like this was an everyday occurrence. It's no longer a mystery why you quit, Katharine. I can't believe you lasted ten years."

"I can't believe she became a cop in the first place," Nicole muttered.

Sitting between them, Katharine pulled her knees up and hugged them to her chest. "What else was I supposed to do with my life when I once believed I could save the world?"

"Katharine, your reactions haven't gone without notice."

Nicole rubbed her shoulder. "Hon, what really happened to you in Minneapolis?"

Squeezing her knees tighter to her chest, her eyes filled with moisture. Swallowing with difficulty, she couldn't hold it in any longer. She spoke in a whisper. "I shot and killed a man."

Both women gaped at her. An electrifying shudder reverberated through Katharine and she wondered what made her tell her friends the half-truth. Motionless, she mused, *now I know I've really lost it.* The long brittle silence broke with the revved up sound of an outboard motor approaching. It was Gage. In lightning-fast motion, Katharine was on her feet. She waved to him and he waved back.

"It was ruled a justified homicide. Gage doesn't need to know. Don't ever think of telling him or anyone else," she said, walking toward the shore.

"I can't believe I called her a nag. Next time I spout off, beat me, Michelle."

"What about me? I accused her of filling us in on bullshit. It's no wonder she lost touch with us."

Katharine ignored their muted dialogue and stopped at the water's edge. Her emotions turned to relief, and excitement, seeing the man with jet-black hair and a raw-boned physique alongside her brother. Mac must have just returned from Green Bay. She waited for Gage to cut the engine and float ashore. He lifted the drive out of the water then tossed the boat's rope to her. She grabbed it and pulled in the twelve-footer. Both men jumped out, rushing toward her.

"Are you okay?" they asked in unison.

"We're fine," she told them. "Where's the M.E.?"

"Joe's meeting him. They'll be here shortly with the Park Rangers."

"Park Rangers?"

"Yeah, like I explained to Mac after you called, this one's out of my jurisdiction. National Park Service handles the other twenty-one islands, including a quarter mile offshore of those islands."

"Body's down the shore that way," Katharine pointed. "I'll show you." Mac followed her and Gage went to Nicole and Michelle.

"Are you really okay?" Mac asked.

"My father actually had a conversation with me this morning for the first time in fourteen years. I've only had two panic attacks today, discovered one corpse and just informed my two best friends I shot and killed a man. It's better than most days. Did you get the photo?"

"It's back at the station. You don't have to do this. Just tell me where she is."

"His M-O has changed."

"I said," Mac insisted, impatiently, "you don't have to do this."

"Mac—"

"Don't do this to yourself!"

His expression a stone mask, she recognized the rough-with-anxiety voice. "Gage has never asked me for anything. We have to pinch this scumbag."

"Not at the expense of your health," he blew out in exasperation.

His words were loaded with ridicule and his frankness was unwelcome. "You still think its Patriot?"

"I spoke to the profiler before I left. She said the possibility exists, as he feels less and less adequate, Patriot will kill more. She's been accurate so far."

A swirling breeze off Lake Superior carried the corpse's odor and Katharine choked back a cough.

"Stay put! I can find the girl myself."

"Mac, the results came back on the liquor. There's no trace of poison. And I spoke to the M.E. He said there wasn't any pot or drugs in her system."

She articulated her words so seriously he wondered when she relaxed last. Rigid posture opposed her wind-blown hair. He knew of one way to distract her, and said, "I missed you, Princess."

When her lips parted in surprise, he turned, letting his nose guide him to the eighth victim.

"Now why'd the jerk have to go and say that?" she muttered.

Mac chuckled to himself and kept walking. Gage caught up to him, and both stopped a few feet from the corpse.

"This is unfucking believable! If those three hadn't come over here today, we never would have discovered this one."

"Eventually, someone would have." Mac spoke somberly as he analyzed the scene. "Makes me wonder if there are others."

"The Park Rangers don't have the manpower to do a ground search of twenty-one islands."

Still stewing over jurisdictional lines, Mac didn't need anymore agencies involved in this case. "Gage, what're the odds she was killed here?"

"You've got more experience at this than I do."

"There's the Johnnie Walker Black bottle," Mac said, pointing. "The bracelet and ligature marks are identical. She was dragged in from the shore. She also looks about sixteen and Native American."

Gage shifted slightly then circled the body. "Everything's identical except the broken bottle."

"What do you mean?"

"The first one *was* broken. That's how Katharine cut her arm. Come to think of it, the bottle wasn't found near our first victim either."

"The first six were in one piece and near each victim. Gage, we may have a copycat."

"If you don't go there, I'll wager we get jurisdiction on this one. How long you think she's been dead?"

"Not my area of expertise, but I'd guess a few days."

"Critters would've found her if she had been here long."

"She didn't die here, Gage. I want this one. We have to prove this one's ours."

"Let's get this secured."

Together they taped a wide circumference around the body. They carefully examined the surrounding area and, once more, discovered tarp threads along a trail from the waterline to the body. Late afternoon, the humidity and blazing sun intensified the emanating smells of the decaying body. Tourists hadn't invaded the area, but waiting in silence increased everyone's internal dread. The lack of discussions was a disguise for anger and defeat. Katharine sat on a rock hugging her knees. She stared out over the water until two more uniformed men arrived in a twenty-five footer and disembarked. Gage assisted them with beaching the boat. He introduced Mac to Tom Coville, head of the Park

Rangers. Tom introduced Gus Rankin from Ashland County's Criminal Investigations. Gage then briefed the newcomers on La Pointe's murder victim.

"There's two dead girls?" Tom asked. "One's an Ashland runner and neither of you have any idea where either murder was actually committed?"

"We have eight dead girls," Mac said. "And we don't know the actual murder location of any of them."

"Has the FBI been called in?"

"We had them do a profile after the third Green Bay victim. They stepped back since the first six all died within a limited locale. I'm convinced the last two killings took place somewhere else and Patriot dumped them later. Every victim has Native American background and is sixteen. Each scene is identical with the only clues being a bracelet, a liquor bottle and ligature markings on their wrists. Autopsies reveal a long slow death from abrin or paraquat poisoning. The profile indicates his reason is ceremonious."

"Let's get started with processing before the coroner arrives for his walk-through. I know Gus will do everything he can to throw this case back at ya. Right, Gus?"

"You bet. The corpse looks like it's been disrupted."

"Nikki Jarvis discovered the body by tripping over it," Gage told them. "They found her," he said, indicating to the women.

Mac, Gage and Tom stayed put when Gus stepped under the yellow tape and opened his kit. He offered up a jar of peppermint camphor for their nasal discomfort.

Subsequent to an extensive examination, Gus said, "This guy is squeaky clean. Thorough. Except for camouflage threads I found on the trail from dragging the body, there's no evidence beyond what you mentioned. Except for this."

"What?" Mac asked.

"What're the odds your suspect was wearing hot pink?"

"I doubt he's a drag queen," Mac retorted.

"We've got clothing fibers here that don't match what the victim's wearing."

"Nikki's wearing pink shorts," Gage offered.

"Let's check her out. See if we have a match."

Gus and Gage went to where the women waited while Mac and Tom remained with the victim.

"Mac, my wife's got a bracelet just like this one."

"Really? We know the beads are hand strung not manufactured, but we haven't been able to run down the source yet."

"I think she told me she bought it in a local gift shop. I'll find out and let you know."

Joe arrived with Del Cadavor, the medical examiner, while Gus confirmed the pink fibers came from Nicole's shorts. After a walk-through, the M.E took custody of the body. With help, she was bagged and placed in the boat Joe brought over from Madeline Island. Nicole and Michelle returned with Gage, and Mac went back with Katharine.

Docking and securing the boats in the marina, Joe went with the medical examiner to the mainland. Gawkers looked on with hushed murmurs and questions. Del advised he'd have the autopsy report in the morning. But it was agreed by all, they'd work together until jurisdiction was established.

"Mac, I'm taking Nikki and Michelle home. I'll meet you and Katharine back at the station."

"Dad will be worried about the runabout," Katharine told her brother.

"Gi'me the key and I'll drop it off with him on my way. Here, take the station's keys."

"Mac and I will start the reports."

When Gage left, Mac asked, "Your friends gonna be okay?"

"Michelle and Nicole are tougher than they look, but nobody should see what we see."

Mac slid into the front seat of her car. "No one ever deserves to see anything that morbid. Shit happens, Princess. We have to move on."

"Mac, I'm not very good at this, but I really am sorry you've had to deal with the loss of your niece."

He shrugged. "At least we caught a break. Before that night, we had nothing. We're always sucking wind backwards behind this dirtbag."

"You think this is a hate crime against Native Americans?"

"Considered it immediately. The ages and sex would vary in a bias crime. He targets sixteen-year-old girls. The age and the way he kills them has specific meaning to him."

"None of the victims are sexually assaulted, are they?"

"Nope. The profiler's analysis leans toward schizophrenic tendencies."

"Which means what? How does it vary from a psychotic serial killer's tendencies?"

"You've read the reports?"

She nodded.

"He's out of touch with reality, Katharine. He might hear voices in his head telling him to kill. His motive could involve a belief he's someone else or that he has a job to do and needs to avenge someone or something. He might even believe an evil force is pursuing him and murder is the only way out of danger. Though similar characteristics exist between the two, one difference between a sexual and psychotic killer is that Patriot didn't live anywhere near where the bodies were found."

"Meaning what?"

"His reason for killing has nothing to do with sexual inadequacy."

"Mac, what if he's been killing them here on the island all along and taking the bodies back to Green Bay? If he knows he left a print, wouldn't that make him change the location of discovery?"

Arriving at the station, they exited her car.

"A possibility, but we never released the info on how we discovered Patriot was our prime suspect. Besides, Green Bay is a long ways from here. It's impractical."

They stopped in front of the door and Mac took the keys from Katharine to unlock it. "But then to a sane mind anything he does is senseless."

"True. There is another way of looking at this, and I'm afraid it's not good."

"What's that?" he asked, ushering her inside.

"He either has help as in a cult, or we've got a copycat."

"I mentioned the copycat idea to Gage, but I don't buy my own theory. If a cult is involved, that means we're dealing with the domination of one group thought. The leader has a seduced spirit or misused faith."

"And membership requires complete acceptance of the leader's beliefs," Katharine added. "Obeying the rules through loyalty to the leader. Unless you were hot on their trail, a cult membership wouldn't change the location of the kill either."

"I hope like hell we're wrong on both counts."

When Mac headed for the empty coffeepot, Katharine slid in behind Gage's desk and sat. "Where's the photo of Patriot? I wanna take a look at it while you make coffee."

"You know, Princess, I was beginning to think you were afraid of the water the way you've avoided sailing with me."

"Not the water. I was leery of you."

"Why?"

"Because," she shrugged. "Oddly enough, being a cop, you never asked what my first impression was of you at dinner the other night."

A colorless, baggy t-shirt with rolled up sleeves devoured a pair of cutoffs. Mac decided she probably wore whatever was convenient. "Didn't have to. The look on your face told me you thought I was a felon. It didn't make sense then, but it does now. What I can't understand is why you thought that way about me."

"Well, you're half right. You remember the day we met?"

"Can't forget it. Actually, I first saw you on the top deck of the ferry."

"Really?"

He nodded. "You were preoccupied. Looked lost and in pain."

"I felt someone staring at me. When I turned to look, there was this man. He jumped backward and almost knocked Sully down the stairs."

"You reacted defensively. I didn't know it then, but later realized you had readied to draw your weapon. I thought your jitters were from my secretly watching you. I was standing at the stern. Tell me now. What was your opinion of me?"

Katharine grimaced, recalling her automatic reaction to draw her retired nine.

"That crimped expression can't be good. I saw the same look on your face when I tapped you on the shoulder that day. Was I that repulsive to you?"

"I'm actually recalling what an idiot I was to go for a weapon that wasn't there. Not thinking about my first opinion of you. Remember, I wasn't interested."

He'd never let Katharine know how much her statement had zinged him. When she located and picked up the envelope with Green Bay's logo, he asked, "Are you interested now?"

"The fact that you followed me to the police station lessened my interest. When you drummed up that ridiculous excuse why you came here then shortly afterward showed up at the first crime scene, my suspicion of you skyrocketed."

"Oddly being a cop, you'd already drawn your conclusions? I was guilty of anything you could drum up until proven innocent?"

"I don't think you're guilty of anything now."

"*Now!*"

Katharine flinched from his quick erupting voice. "What's the matter with you? Why are you angry with me?"

"Just answer the question."

"I already did."

"I'd like an answer to the one about your interest in me."

"I can't give you an answer to that one."

"Why not? It seems simple enough. Either you are or you aren't."

"Don't push me on this."

"Most of us deal with the hand we're dealt then we get on with our life, Katharine."

She stiffened. "What happens to me or my life is none of your business!"

"You became my business when we joined forces to capture Patriot."

"Screw you!"

"Hear me loud and clear. I won't risk additional mistakes or victims because you're stuck groveling in the poor me syndrome! And I'm not gonna wait forever for you to decide how you feel about *us* either."

Katharine slapped the envelope on the desk and sprang out of the chair. "There is no *us*, Steven! There never was!"

Mac stepped back as if to amputate himself from her. Intense anger overflowed in her face. It matched her expression from the day he watched her drawing on the beach. When she snatched her car keys and bolted for the door, he yelled, "You can't keep running from your problems or continue to avoid the obvious. Who's Steven?"

Hand on the doorknob, Katharine stopped. With a silent groan, she yanked the door open and fled, plowing through Gage and Joe.

"Pipsqueak?" Gage looked at Mac. "What were you two yelling about?"

Mac stood with the coffeepot in-hand while both men waited for a response. He thought his vexation with Katharine was evident, and asked, "Did you get statements from Nicole and Michelle?"

Gage nodded. "What's wrong with Katharine?"

"You'll have to ask her."

"I'm asking *you*!"

"I'm not telling you."

Caring less who he offended, Mac wasn't losing Patriot again. This case was as personal as it was professional, and one dirty scumbag was going down for eight murders.

CHAPTER 13

Exiting Iola Tibbs' gift shop, Katharine's heart pumped as radiantly and as brightly as the daffodil sunshine. Her sketches 'aroused feelings' Iola had told her. Embarrassingly pleased with people's mushy reaction to a natural talent, Katharine had a new job. Iola agreed to sell the drawings then in afterthought offered her a manager's position in the shop as well. Aging, the sixtyish Islander was contemplating selling her business. Said her husband Wilbur wanted to travel, but making the decision to end a life-long passion was difficult for her.

During their conversation, Iola recalled several pranks the trio of girlfriends had traded with Josie and Margie years ago. Katharine's flamed face triggered more memories from the spunky woman with dove gray hair and crinkly hazel eyes. The shop owner's ribbing was friendly and Katharine decided she liked Iola Tibbs.

Headed for the marina, she needed to think through a strategy to make her new career work. Her father always said success came with preparation. At the age of thirteen, she'd devised a thriving blueprint to get a college education. Working full time summer jobs and after school during the winter months she saved every check. Living with a cop's salary and hearing repetitiously, money doesn't grow on trees, she had to earn her own income. Unfortunately, it hadn't been enough just to pass up teenage indulgences. In the midst of trying to save, she also dealt with

Nicole and Michelle's displeasure of her career decision. She gave into their shopping sprees with a silent promise to work part time jobs through four years of college. When her first real job came with MPD, the paychecks made her feel wealthy while doing something she loved. She passed the sergeant's exam three years later, received a promotional raise, her stripes and gold shield. She had achieved her blueprint for success.

Today a similar feeling of gratitude encompassed her. It was a genuine response to her dilemma of what to do with the rest of her life. Monday she'd start a new job and a new life managing Iola's gift shop. It didn't sound like much, but today it meant everything.

Stepping onto Gage's high-speed Chris-Craft, sketchpad, beach bag and mini cooler in hand, Katharine secured a personal flotation device around her upper body. She started and maneuvered the speedboat out of the slip then headed for Raspberry Island. Gage's rich mahogany boat, with glistening chrome and exceptional craftsmanship, served its purpose for adventures and rescuing spirits. Releasing a large barrette to free her hair, the wind whipped at her face and heap of red strands. Regardless of Superior' busy highway on a Saturday, Katharine harbored secret desires to do some surfing. She increased the speed of the boat.

Shifting into forward gear, she went for it and shoved the throttle wide open. The high-powered runabout sped faster. The stunt boosted the boat's speed by pushing the craft up over the bow wave onto a larger crest. It surfed wave planes that progressed upward from behind the boat. Although extremely dangerous, Gage had taught her well in their teens. Water splashed up as her hair flew wildly, and Lord! It felt exhilarating to release pent-up frustration.

As much as she tried to forget the homicides and the cries and screams, her mind wouldn't let her. July had passed and almost two weeks into August, there hadn't been a ninth murder. Nor should there be according to Mac. But Gage. What could she say about him? He was irritated with her last Sunday for giving up resolve of La Pointe's two murders. She just couldn't do it and blew her brother off by convincing him Mac had more experience.

Gage's face displayed outright disappointment. His soft blue eyes exposed worry. How could she explain the Michigan Island victim had done her in when Nicole and Michelle discovered the body? She had no other choice than to abandon him in his hour of need. Consumed with more guilt, she couldn't help it when she'd lost her ability to protect and serve. The argument with Mac proved her decision was right. Her mental state *would* jeopardize his case.

Each water droplet splashing her face felt like reoccurring twinges of shame. Her father wasn't wrong. She was a quitter. Mac, like Steven, wasn't wrong either. He had her pegged. He called her self-pity a poor me syndrome. In the heat of the moment, calling him Steven was a stupid mistake, a slip of the tongue. Their argument provoked her internal rage and her words rifled out of her mouth faster than fired rounds. Steven always started their arguments, but she also realized too late, Mac wasn't Steven. *Thank God.* Steven always complained she floundered in emotions and chewed on her feelings. An afterthought, maybe the two men were alike.

Her stomach knotted up tighter and Katharine increased the boat's speed. Her insides had died a thousand deaths because she'd given up on herself—on everything—they were all right. Why didn't they understand her dilemma? Her strength and energy to render protection to Nicole and Michelle or help Gage solve a murder had vanished. With attempts to squash the demoralizing emotions, she needed to break free of the verbal self-abuse. She increased the boat's speed more. Her dad would have to live with his beliefs regarding her imperfections. Mac wasn't exactly right. She *was* dealing with the problem the only way she knew. Humbly, she thought, she probably did owe him an apology, but she did not owe him an answer to his question about her interest in him. How could she maintain a relationship when her emotions were out of control?

With the wind whipping at her face and hair, Raspberry Island came into view. It was still her favorite spot in the Apostles. Between the speedboat and Raspberry Island, a man started flapping his arms from a utility boat powered by an outboard motor. *Idiot was gonna flip his damn boat!* Katharine eased down on the speed, allowing her wake to catch up gradually. Once it did, she reduced power further coming off the plane she'd been surfing. With a long stretch, and plenty of time, her watercraft eventually zipped on by the man's boat. She smiled and waved to him. He didn't applaud her wake or the uproar she had caused to his denizen of the deep. He flipped her off instead.

Katharine arrived at Raspberry and shut down the engine then moored her water hotrod. Sunscreen applied, she reached for a bottle of water from the cooler. Opening her drawing pad, she drew what she saw. The lighthouse built high atop a reddish crater-like cliff, Katharine always favored this island the most. Primarily woodland, the hunk of rock continually fascinated her the way big ol' honkin' trees grew out of the rust-colored sides. The excitement of a brand new venture in the gift shop ruled her thoughts as chalk filled the paper. She would sketch in her free time and learn the business ins and outs while earning a paycheck. If she could just get her body to cooperate with her mind, maybe she'd find the peace she once owned.

Her lips pursed disgustedly at the etchings. She stopped, shook her hands to dispose of the jitters, but couldn't calm her trembling fingers. If she didn't come to terms with her failure, she'd turn into a nutcase. Sleepless nights had permanently invaded her life. Hard runs around Madeline helped, but she'd dropped more weight. Nothing seemed to erase the events of her city life. Feeling locked and loaded like a premo weapon ready to fire, she mulled over her self-expectations of personal and professional perfection. Why was it so important?

Inhaling deeply, Katharine ripped out another disastrous sketch, crumbled the paper and started fresh—six times! Numerous drawings later, some started to meet with her approval. After a few more rejections, she began drawing different angles of the lighthouse. One storm scene with high rolling waves pleased her enough to draw another. She completed several more good pieces as the hours slipped away with her frustration. She squinted into the bright sunlight at the sound of a woman's cry. The whimper was faint but clear and the same one she'd heard at Michigan Island. Had it not been for a windless day, Katharine would have blamed the disturbance on Lake Superior's blustering breezes.

Setting the tablet on the seat beside her, she scanned Raspberry Island then slowly stood. An eagle flew proudly, soaring under a blue sky. The noble bird was the source of the woman's cry. Watching it soar, she decided it would make a great drawing and grabbed the sketchpad.

"Ahoy, lassie. Did ya hear Katrina?"

Shifting about, Sully motored up in a fishing boat alongside her racer. She hadn't heard the putter of his outboard, but quickly observed a stimulating challenge in his eyes. "Sully, it was an eagle."

"Nay, lassie. America's bird doesn't cry, she screeches arrogantly. That sound is Katrina's ghost crying out to you."

"Sully, this is nuts! You're nuts! The Cadotte ghost story is an exploited fairytale."

"Ah, lassie, I see in yer eyes you've heard Katrina but are afraid to believe the inevitable."

What was the point of arguing when she couldn't deny his claim? "All right, I heard it. I also heard it on Michigan Island, but I doubt it's a ghost."

"She's not an *it*, lassie. The old girl's got you."

"How do you know *that sound* is Katrina?" she demanded in her police-inquiring tone.

"Already told you. She cries here at the Raspberry light."

"Then why'd I hear her at Michigan Island?"

"Katrina's got a hold on yer broken spirit. She'll follow yer jeweled eyes wherever ya go now."

"Ridiculous," she huffed, crossing her arms.

"Lassie, you've already encountered yer soul mate. And yer ready for love. When ya let it happen, you'll finally put Katrina to rest. Tis all the old girl wants."

"Sully, there has to be two willing participants in the game of love."

"Aye, lassie," he said, grinning. "In time you'll see love tis not a game. First yer heart must be open to receive the notion. When it is, you'll be rid of that shipwrecked optimism. Open yer heart, Katharine. Let Superior's magic fix yer tired soul."

Sully tipped his head upward and she tilted hers up, too.

"Listen. Katrina's callin'. You hear her?"

The chanting cry of a woman floated on the air. This time the crying didn't sound sorrowful. Chills spiraled down Katharine's spine when she heard Katrina's joyful song. It was as though the ghost was an affirmation to Sully's foolish words. Katharine swore she felt moisture forming in her eyes. Touching them, she discovered both were dry.

* * *

Mac huddled over both autopsy reports. Sherry Martin, the seventh victim, ran with the eighth victim ID'd as Jennifer Wicket, also a runaway from Ashland, Wisconsin. The Green Bay victims along with Wicket were dead from the chemical paraquat. How could two teens run together and one use drugs when the other didn't? Why was Sherry Martin the only one of eight victims to die of abrin poisoning? The questions engulfed and drowned him. And the changed M.O. was loosening up everything in the case.

Tom Coville had called to inform them that his wife did own an identical bracelet to the one found on all eight victims. The problem was Native American women in the area hand-strung the wrist jewelry and sold them to gift shops throughout Ashland and Bayfield counties. Anyone could purchase bundles of the inexpensive trinket.

The station door swung open and Mac looked up. He'd been waiting for Gage to return from Bayfield. Instead, an old man hobbled inside with support from a bamboo cane. Patches of sweaty, graying hair plastered his forehead like flypaper. He huffed and wheezed until he inched himself inside and shoved the door shut.

"Can I help you?"

"Who're you? I need a talk with the Chief."

"Not here," Mac told him.

"Where's that youngster, Sergeant Hamlin? Need to tell 'em about black bear and deer bloody destroying my gardens."

"Not here either. Leave your name. I'll have one of 'em get back to you."

"Why you got yourself behind the Chief's desk?"

Mac met the old man's hawkish stare. With deliberate leaning on his carved-wood cane, Mac realized *he* was the interfering outsider on this island.

"Yer that deetective from Green Bay, ain't ya? When you gonna solve these murders? Folks are terrified. Been locking doors for the first time."

"We're working on it. If you wanna leave your name, I'll have Gage call you."

"Youngsters," he scoffed. "You tell the Chief, Jesop Merryweather needs a talk with him."

Merryweather turned to leave, and Mac muttered, "I'll do that."

With the speed of a tortoise, old Jesop turned around and shuffled toward the door. Mac scribbled out a note as the old man went out and he went back to reports. Five minutes later, the door swung open a second time. He glanced up at a hefty woman who strutted into the cramped office. She marched past the desk, turned and stood stoutly in front of him.

"I was expecting the Chief. You must be that copper from Green Bay who gives advice on the murders of them poor girls. Land sakes! When are we gonna be able to relax again and not have to worry about more killing?"

"Gage isn't here. Leave your name and I'll have him call you."

"You tell the Chief my kid's missing and I need his help again."

That nailed his attention and Mac sat upright. His first thought was they had their ninth victim. "What's your kid's name?"

"Secunda Girard. Wandered off sometime during the night."

Scratching out the name on a tablet, Mac looked at her. "Secunda? Is that Native American?"

Giggling, she sung, "No sir, sonny. It's Latin. Means second born. Decided the name fitful when I got my second honey from Jim Berger's bitch who had a litter awhile back."

"Secunda is a goddamn mutt!"

"That's right. A golden lab. Whaddaya gettin' so hot and bothered about? This here's routine with the bitch."

"What's your name?"

"Tell the Chief Adeline Girard's gonna need help roundin' up Secunda. Fool critter thinks he rules Madeline. Don't quite understand he can't be chasing other bitches whenever he wants."

"Fine," Mac grunted, making notation beneath Jesop's message.

Adeline opened the door. A thick-bodied man, years younger than Jesop Merryweather attempted entry around her. The poor sap should've ducked when Girard snarled and toasted him with a menacing glare. They danced around each other until the man finally stepped back. This place imitated a three-ring circus Mac mused.

"Can I help you?"

"I'm looking for Gage. You must be that homicide detective here to help crack the murders of those young ladies."

"There's obviously no need for a newspaper in this town."

"Got that right," the man said, with a snort. "Nothing gets by us. Name's Curt Stewart."

He extended his hand, and Mac rose to return the gesture. "What can I do for you?"

"I stopped by to offer my help. Gage and I went to high school together."

"You related to Kevin Stewart?"

"I am. How'd you know that?"

"Your brother gets cheap thrills out of harassing women."

"The night you and Katharine had dinner at the Tavern. Yeah, I remember," Curt said. "I apologized to Katharine for Kevin's behavior after Gage mentioned it. He's always been overly protective of his sister."

"Wouldn't you be if she were your sister?"

Scratching his head, Curt said, "Guess so, if I had a sister. Know I wouldn't take kindly to any guy treating my Josie that way."

"Listen, Curt, I'll tell Gage you stopped. Don't mean to be rude, but I've got work here."

"Sure, sorry for the interruption."

As Stewart lumbered out of the station, Mac shook his head. Simplistic is what they all were. Positioning himself in the chair, he refocused on the paperwork in front of him. As he deliberated possibilities of Patriot's change in M-O, the door swung open again.

"Gage, I swear to god if one more person comes in here whining over stupid—"

"Well excuse me! I was just bringing you lunch."

Shooting out of the chair, Mac blew out, "Nicole! I'm sorry. Half the island's residents have been in here. Can't tell if they're more curious about me or the homicides."

"Don't worry about it. Everyone's nervous. Well, you understand. Folks just aren't used to dealing with fear much less murder."

"How you and Michelle holding up?"

"We'll be okay. We're more worried about Katharine. She hasn't really been herself since coming back. Did you hear? Both Michelle and I are delighted she started managing Iola's gift shop today."

"That right?"

"The one on Main Street across from the ferry dock. It's open from nine to six-thirty. I thought for sure she'd have told you."

"Nicole, I'm sure you and Michelle are both aware Katharine and I haven't seen each other or spoken since last Saturday. And I'd bet you know why."

"You're half right. But she didn't tell us the reason you're not talking. Mac, give her a break. Katharine's trying to work things out. Being bred into a family of cops, she's always been protector of the three of us. Besides a bad circumstance, she and her dad don't see eye-to-eye on several things."

He poured himself coffee and listened.

"Don't get me wrong, I love Katharine. But Frank can be very controlling and stubborn, which is where Katharine gets it. Both have high expectations of themselves and everyone around them. Other than the fact Frank is old fashioned and not artistically gifted, there's no mistaking those two are related. You can't begin to imagine his anger when his only daughter announced her decision to become a big city cop. They argued until she left home after graduation."

Mac nudged his butt cheek onto the corner of the smaller desk and drank from the Styrofoam cup.

"You see, Katharine loved and cherished her father and I'm sure she still does. He was always the most important person in her life. For as long as we can remember she dreamed of being Frank's successor here and following in his tracks until she discovered Frank was prepping Gage to take over. We were in seventh grade and the news broke her heart. She still wanted to be a cop like her dad and her uncle over in Bayfield. So one day she fabricated this silly notion of discovering the world and decided she'd leave the Island. Shocked the shit out of Michelle and me. We tried to talk her out of it. So did Gage. She wouldn't hear of it. Our senior year was when she got up the guts to announce her decision to Frank and Paula. The entire year she and Frank fought bitterly about her decision. Then she left."

"And she's only been back once?"

"Twice now that she's home to stay. Once for Michelle's wedding which proved a waste of time, but that's not the issue. Katharine spent the weekend with me, wouldn't go home to see Frank. Paula had to come over to my place to see her. After the incident in ...,"

When Nicole stopped, Mac supplied, "Minneapolis."

"You know?"

Her big brown eyes grew huge and Mac nodded. "I also know she told you and Michelle about it."

"What incident in Minneapolis? Told you what?"

Mac rose. Nicole gasped. Gage and Joe were standing in the open doorway to Town Hall's corridor.

"Gage LeNoir! Why you sneaking in here quiet as a pair of bedroom slippers? How long have you been standing there eves dropping?"

"*Nicole!* Don't toy with me! What happened to Katharine?"

Nicole narrowed her eyes and wrench-gripped both hips with her hands. The rage that flowed through Gage's steel blue eyes reminded Mac of Katharine. And he was stuck between the two of them when Nicole cut loose.

"Gage Andrew LeNoir! You settle down right now and don't you ever speak to me in that wicked tongue again or you'll find yourself regretting the day you were born!"

Gage catapulted into the office, planting himself in front of Nicole. The two of them tossed hateful glares at each other. Gage stepped closer, towering over Nicole menacingly.

"Don't say it, Gage!"

"Damn you, Nikki! The only regret I have is how you yap pointlessly at me and flaunt yourself in front of me every chance you get! You'll have your own regrets if you don't tell me what happened to my sister!"

"Go to hell!"

Nicole sidestepped Gage then sashayed out of the station with the snappy click of her heels on tile exploiting her rage. Mac had heard Nicole cried easily then wondered if Gage had ever been the cause of the tears that had wormed into her eyes like a computer virus. The distraught look on Gage's face gave him the answer, and he quickly surmised Nicole didn't have a clue how right she was about regrets.

"Nikki—shit!"

The door slammed shut and Gage shoveled a hand through his hair then punched the wall with his fist. With a quick visual in Joe's direction, Mac realized days ago that Gage kept his eye on Nicole more than any man should allow. *Poor sap.* Fear of a need for companionship was an emotion all men refused to accept. Made them less of a man if they needed anyone. Mac also understood what a promise meant. Katharine had vowed Nicole and Michelle to secrecy, but he didn't see the point since she wasn't working the case anymore.

"Mac!" Gage exploded, whipping around. "I'm in no mood for the way you dodge answers about what's going on between you and my sister!"

"Gage, your sister and I made a deal."

"She has some bullshit hype for not telling me what happened to her. I wanna know right now what you and Nikki were talking about!"

"You'll have to ask Katharine yourself."

Lurching forward, Gage grabbed Mac by the shirt collar. "Does this deal include sleeping with my sister?"

"That's none of your damn business," Mac growled.

"I'm making it mine! If you hurt my sister, I swear you'll regret the day you locked eyes with her!"

Mac shoved Gage aside. Since the discovery of the second murdered victim, tempers were flaring rapidly. Normally, Mac didn't hunt up trouble, but his own pent-up frustration added to his already foul mood. A promise was a promise and Katharine wasn't fulfilling her end of the deal.

"There's a couple of messages for you on the desk. I'll be back later."

Mac exited the station as Gage erupted, "What the hell you looking at, Hamlin?"

CHAPTER 14

Mac cared little what Gage thought. The only need he had was to capture David Patriot. *He'd* never fall into the manipulation trap of the feminine mystique as Gage had. It scared the hell out of him. Besides, one screw-up had already cost him dearly. The second screw-up, with a pending outcome, stressed him almost to breaking point. He couldn't afford additional judgment errors when it backed up his personal theory—emotional entanglement caused mistakes.

Because of that, he told Katharine to get on with her life. He made it crystal clear to her, he didn't need her help with his case. *Whom was he kidding?* She consumed his thoughts twenty-four hours a day. Her compelling beauty annoyed him. The claim she had on independence drove him nuts. Her paladin attitude confused him way too much. So then, why was he about to meddle in an area where he had no business, especially when he didn't want to be involved with her life? *It was an itch.* In truth, he hid ambitions to scratch that itch. He hungered for an ounce of accuracy to Gage's accusation. He wanted Katharine ever since spotting her on the ferry.

Mac found Iola's gift shop with no problem. Stepping inside, he lingered in the small store to check things out while he waited for Katharine to finish with one of several customers. With his back to the counter, he spotted several of her pictures already framed. The drawings amazed him. Intense emotions emerged from each one. Deep feelings reached out to him and clutched at his throat. He felt sympathy for an unsuccessful fisherman. A storm scene vented anger. Simple wild flowers depicted tenderness. That one really got to him. He wondered how black and white illustrations could consume him with wind-swept passion. But they did, and the weeklong buildup of hostility disintegrated.

"Hello. Is there something I can help you find?"

The melodic sound of her voice, a lavender scent he'd noticed upon entering the shop—*Linda and Clarissa both used lavender fragrance*—and the drawings aroused Mac beyond self-control. He continued to stare at the sketches because he knew his voice would betray him. After several seconds, he managed, "I wonder if the artist would sign my sketch."

"Mac?"

Shifting, he produced a noble smile then stumbled backward in absolute awe. A quick intake of air into his lungs felt like he was sucking wind in a wild storm. She'd pushed her hair up. Wisps of silky, reddish-gold loops framed her face. Insignificant makeup made her skin radiant. A bluish summer dress revealed a shape that seduced him. The diamond sparkle in her eyes alluded to an undisciplined wild beauty. Quivers, equivalent to the first day he'd laid eyes on her pulsed through his body with a dangerous urge to tame her.

"What's the matter?"

The abrupt tone of her voice righted his sappy heart. Mac cleared his throat. "You look good. Working here seems to agree with you."

"How can it when this is my first day? How'd you know I was working here—never mind. What do you want?"

He *wanted* to touch her *everywhere*. Could he get past that cold, proud glare boring into him? Then he observed a deeper meaning to their visual interchange. The spark of some indefinable emotion contradicted a scowl. Prolonged anticipation? This desire he hadn't noticed before was attraction. And it ricocheted between them. Speaking again, his voice had warmed. "Katharine, we need to talk."

"Did something happen to Gage? Is he all right?"

Her eyes filled with familiar fear and Mac touched her shoulder to calm her. "Gage is fine. Is there somewhere we can talk privately?"

She looked away, watching several customers. The door opened and two more entered.

"No. I can't leave the shop unattended. Iola will be back later. What do you want?"

"Have dinner with me tonight. I'll pick you up here at six-thirty."

Removing his hand, his heartbeat continued to manipulate his feelings. It devoured his purpose for coming here. The moment prolonged, Katharine adjusted and straightened shot glasses with hand-painted lighthouses on a nearby shelf.

"Excuse me, Miss. Do you work here?"

"Yes. How may I help you?"

"Six-thirty," Mac interjected, before exiting the shop.

Rushing outside, he inhaled fresh air then ground his teeth in pure frustration. He came here with one intention. To tell Katharine her selfishness would cost her two good friends. He left with a dinner date instead. He despised his own weakness. The warrior princess had turned him into a wanting wuss. Nearness to her felt like a miserable spell she cast upon him. Since their argument last weekend, guilt had consumed him, but he also believed she'd come back to him needing help with her ruptured past. It bothered him to realize she didn't. It pissed him off more that she had no interest in the capture of Patriot.

Mac slid in behind the wheel of his 4x4, whipped a reckless U-turn and drove uphill toward the station. Parking, he slid out of the 4x4. Gage exited the police station and stomped toward him. Anger crammed his face. Before Mac could thwart off attack, he caught Gage's fist in the jaw and fell backward.

"You son-of-a-bitch! You knew! It's my job to protect Katharine, not yours!"

"She's too damn stubborn and won't let me help her you idiot!"

Gage rushed him a second time and Mac scrambled up, landing a blow in his midsection. The gunshot punch stunned Gage enough to make him short of breath for a second.

"That's my sister you're calling stubborn!"

"Seems it runs in the family."

A second hard cuff connected with Mac's chin and he drove his body into Gage's belly. Both men stumbled to the ground. Mac clipped Gage in the eye with a right before each scrambled to their feet with clenched fists and circling each other.

"What the hell do you think we were arguing about last Saturday? Told her I didn't need her wallowing in self-pity causing mistakes in my case."

Swinging, missing, Gage stumbled. "This isn't your case you horny bastard!"

"It was mine first! Your sister was pissed off and called me Steven. That's when she stormed out of the station. I've seen her once since and for crissake I'm not sleeping with her!"

"You're not gonna either!"

Gage wound up and rammed his fist into Mac's jaw a third time.

"Sonovabitch," Mac snarled, spitting blood then nailed Gage with another wheezing blow to his stomach. "It's not me you're mad at. Now back off!"

Panting, Gage leaned over alongside Mac. The frothy head of stupidity had been boiling all week. Joe was propped against the outside wall of the station, thumbs hooked atop his gun belt and ankles crossed. A mile-wide smirk plastered his face, which told them he'd received a great deal of pleasure watching them pound the crap out of each other.

"Feel better?" Mac asked.

Nodding, Gage inhaled deep breaths. "Christ. I can't believe she didn't tell me ... she shot and killed a man. She always had enthusiasm for life. I could see it was gone from her eyes. I figured eventually she'd come to me like she did when we were kids. I'd fix whatever broke her. I don't know how to fix this."

"Nobody can. I figured eventually she'd come to me." Mac spit more blood. "Katharine is stronger than we've given her credit for. All we can do is be there when she's ready to talk. I just came from the gift shop where she's working. I think she found her own way of dealing with the stress through her drawings."

Gage rose and peered sideways. "Who's Steven?"

"Damned if I know."

"You've had your eye on my sister since you hit the island. You mess with her, Mac, and my fist will punctuate any further discussions we have."

Mac dabbed at his bloody lip, felt his jaw swelling. "We're having dinner tonight. Deal with it."

Rubbing his stomach, Gage reiterated, "Maybe I'm not making myself clear."

"Obstinate essob. I'm dating your sister with or without your approval. Now we can stand here and argue or we can catch ourselves a killer."

Grunting, Gage ordered, "Joe, wipe that shit-eating grin off your face before I cram it down your throat!"

The three men re-entered the station. The burgers and fries Nicole brought over still sat in bags on the large desk. Gage tossed one at Mac and Joe.

"We have to move into the conference room," Gage barked. "It's too frickin' crowded in here."

"Fine. Bring the coffee pot," Mac shot back, setting the lunch aside. His mouth was in no condition to chew and he poured a cup of condemned brew. "What'd you find out from Ashland PD about the two runaways?"

Gage eased in behind his desk. "Parents filed the report a week before we found the Martin girl. Both were runners for the past three years and failing in school. They've got a couple of petty's for possession. According to Ashland PD, they had a tendency to hang with a rougher, older crowd."

Joe went and sat behind the smaller desk. Mac took a seat on the only available chair in the middle of the shrinking floor space. "Patriot must be reaching his breaking point. He's never killed a two-for-one special in the same month."

"Makes sense when these two ran together," Gage said, matter-of-factly.

"Assuming that's why he killed both, why use abrin on one and paraquat on the other?"

Joe finished his burger and fries and went to work on Mac's. "Listen, I've done more research on abrin. Actually, the abric acid kills. The outside shell contains a tetanic glycoside drug within the bean. That's what inhibits the digestive process. The plant is grown all over the world, including Florida and Hawaii, and is available in store-bought houseplants. Death occurs anywhere from several hours to three days after ingested."

Gage reached from his chair to fill his coffee mug. "Knowing this helps us how?"

"The plant is available but paraquat isn't because it's a toxic herbicide used to kill weeds. It's not sold in your garden variety stores. When the chemical's ingested and goes untreated, it kills by the eighth day." Between bites, Joe added, "Maybe this guy gets his thrills from the ritual and wants death to last as long as possible."

"So why switch?" Mac asked.

"Possibly liked the concept behind the rosary pea warding off evil spirits but didn't know death came quicker," Joe said, finishing the French fries. "Tried it once then resorted back to paraquat. The second victim's time of actual death was four days after our first."

"Or we have a copycat," Gage muttered.

"Assuming Joe's theory is accurate, and fits with the FBI profile, where is Patriot letting their bodies decompose before he exposes and dumps them for someone to find? Why did he leave Green Bay and come here?"

"You never discovered where he committed the murders in Green Bay?" Gage asked Mac.

"No. I'm also bugged that Martin didn't have any marijuana or whiskey in her system, yet Wicket did. It doesn't make sense since they ran together."

Studying Patriot's photo, Gage said, "I think we need to get this photo out to the Islanders and on the local news. Find out if anyone's seen this guy."

"Gage, doing that had the opposite effect in Green Bay. We think Patriot saw it and fled after the media aired it."

"If we don't let the public know, others could die."

"Believe me I know. I had the same argument with Green Bay's police chief and mayor."

"You're gonna have it again with me."

"For crissake, Gage! Think it over!"

"I've been thinking it over for a week now! I've never seen this blond-haired guy but maybe somebody else has."

"Give it another—"

"Whaddaya need, Pete?" Gage blasted into his portable.

"Chief, Alesha and I think we got a visual on a guy who resembles the photo of our suspect."

"Where ya at?"

"The Marina. He took a boat out headed toward Bayfield. You want us to go after him?"

"Find out who the boat belongs to. Wait for me there!"

"Got it, Chief."

Looking from Mac to Joe, he said, "Let's go."

* * *

Seated behind the gift shop counter, Katharine's feet needed rest. Numerous customers with sales had astounded her to the point she'd spent the entire day stirred up with physical activity, interacting with customers, learning the inventory, and feeling alive. The heart of her emotional arousal came when two of her sketches sold in the morning. Giddiness took over and kept her flying high. In fact, though she'd been less than receptive to Mac, she felt excited now by his invitation to dinner. Iola stepped from the back room and it was reflexive response for Katharine to stand at attention.

"Heavens, relax child. You certainly earned your wages today."

"Is it this busy every day?" Katharine asked, re-sitting.

"Pretty much. Tell me what you think about the business."

"I'm sure my thoughts are slanted since my level of excitement rocketed after two of my drawings sold."

"Speaking of which, I've decided not to take my standard forty percent cut."

"What? Why not?"

"My dear child, having you here giving me a break is worth every penny. This is the first time in years I've been able to relax during the tourist season. I've avoided the agony of standing all day. Wilbur will be thrilled he doesn't have to give me a foot massage tonight."

Katharine smiled. "I can certainly relate. My feet are killing me."

Both looked up when the door's bell jingled.

"Mom, what are you doing here?"

"Paula, how nice of you to stop by."

"Thought I'd come over and see how my youngest is doing on her first day. Besides, I need a birthday gift for Suzanne Saturday night. I can't believe we've pulled off a surprise party for Frank's sister-in-law. That woman knows everything. Land sakes she's been calling me every day since those two girls were murdered. Wants to know if Gage has caught the killer. Guess I can't really blame her. We're all worried which of us that crazy man might get next."

"Let me tell you, Wilbur and I haven't been sleeping very well either."

"At least, I don't have that problem," Paula stated. "Now Frank. He's been up every night, wandering the house. But then, the man doesn't sleep most nights of his life."

Her mother was right. Katharine had met her father a couple of times. She also considered explaining to them that Patriot only targets sixteen-year-old Native American girls, and then decided against it. The two women would play twenty questions with her and she didn't want to ruin her euphoric state of mind.

"Will you be attending the party, Iola? Nicole has worked hard on the arrangements and keeping it secret."

"No way am I missing out on seeing Suzanne in shock. Wilbur's not too excited about going, but I informed him he'd be cut off from his husbandly duties if he didn't."

Katharine chuckled when her mother's cheeks flushed.

"Paula, you should buy one of Katharine's framed sketches for Suzanne."

"Dearie, you read my mind. The woman has everything. She wouldn't dare shun her niece's drawing. Show them to me."

"Mom, Aunt Suzanne won't want a sketch of mine."

"Katharine Regina this isn't your decision. It's mine. If the old bat doesn't like it, well, that's too bad."

"Mother!"

"Honey, there's a lot of things you don't know about Suzanne and me. We go back a long way. Don't we Iola?"

"Indeed. Katharine, your mother and I used to taunt Suzanne the way you and your friends tormented Josie."

Katharine gawked at the two women in utter astonishment.

"Iola, my daughter has the same response her father does most days of his life. Close your mouth, dear. It's true. Iola and I were identical, maybe even worse than you three."

"How come you've never said anything?"

"A parent never confesses their own wrongdoing to their children. Maybe because telling you, you'd have to accept the fact your mother isn't perfect."

Iola brought over three of Katharine's pictures and laid them down for Paula to study. "Your daughter's very good."

"Oh, Iola, I figured that out years ago. I'll take the Raspberry light storm. Suzanne's deathly afraid of Superior's temper and this one will throw us into stitches when she lays eyes on it. Your aunt's fear is the only reason she moved off the rock, Katharine."

"That's right," Iola crowed. "The pansy really believes Madeline will sink."

To her interested amazement, Katharine never knew her mother to speak ill of anyone, let alone Aunt Suzanne. Right now, her mother was whispering something to Iola who laughed. "I can't believe you two."

"Seems your mother's ripened with age, Katharine."

"The only difference between you and me, Iola, is I never got caught red-handed in shenanigans."

"Why was that?"

"Not in front of my daughter."

"Your daughter is an adult and wants to hear more."

"That may be, but you're not going to be the one to shed light on the subject now or ever."

"Oh, pooh. I'll gift-wrap this for you. Katharine, you've done well today. You can go. Shop closes in ten minutes and I'll tally up for the day."

Katharine checked her watch, wondering if Mac would be on time. "Um, someone is picking me up here at six-thirty. I'll wait it out."

"Believe it or not, my daughter has a new beau and thinks she's being coy about it."

"I never said a man was picking me up."

"Forgive her, Paula. Being gone for so many years, she's forgotten nothing escapes us. Word spreads faster than poison ivy.

I heard that detective from Green Bay stopped in here today. What's his name?"

Katharine wouldn't give either the satisfaction of an answer and busied herself dusting and straightening shelves.

"Mac, somebody. Have you seen him? Now there's a man I'd set my cap for if I were younger," Paula said.

"Set your cap for?" Katharine asked.

When they rippled with laughter, she realized getting answers from either woman would be impossible.

"Oh, to be young and innocent, Iola."

"You're not gonna explain are you?"

"Nope," each woman crowed.

"The way she keeps checking the time, you better prepare yourself, Paula. Might just have ourselves a match in the making."

"About bloody damn time!"

"Mother!" Katharine screeched loudly.

"I was starting to think grandchildren were completely out of the picture. Honestly, Iola. I don't know what's wrong with either one of my children."

"The reason I left Madeline is quickly coming back. Gage is older. Go harass him about marriage instead of me."

"But darling, I don't get to plan his wedding."

"I'm not sure why you thought you'd be planning mine. Marriage is out of the question." A few minutes late and Convinced Mac wasn't coming Katharine retrieved her purse and hurried out of the gift shop.

A man she didn't want a dinner date with in the first place had stood her up. A man who was stuck on himself. The way she saw it, she had two choices—he had a lot of nerve standing her up! She could either go over and complain to Nicole and Michelle, or trot over to the station and ream Dobarchon a new hole in his tight little ass. Not that she liked him. It was principle. The jerk didn't even have the decency to call and cancel so she could find something better to do.

Katharine skulked away from the shop en route to the police station. She'd never admit to anyone that she'd been thinking about Dobarchon with excessive frequency. She thought about him so much it made her brain hurt. She circled the corner of

Town Hall and halted near his black Jeep. Marching toward the entrance, Katharine hesitated then pulled hard, yanking the door open and burst into the station. It was empty. She trotted into the conference room and could care less if others were huddled around the table when she cut loose.

"No man stands me up and gets away with it, Dobarchon!"

Heads swung. Mac glanced at his watch, and muttered, "Oh shit."

"Hah," Gage smirked. "Let's see you crawl your way out of this one."

Mac straightened, faced her for the argument she was about to start. Katharine took a deep breath, but instead blew out, "What happened to your face?"

Mac glanced at Gage, looked back at her. Gage had dried blood on his knuckles and one very red, swollen eye. "Gage, what happened?" Katharine demanded.

"Pete, Alesha," Joe said, "come outside with me."

Waiting until they left, Katharine shoved the conference room door shut. "You two beat the crap out of each other. Why? What's going on?"

"Pipsqueak!" Gage heaved. "You've really got nerve!"

"What are you talking about?"

"If you don't tell her, Gage, I will."

"Tell me what?"

"Sis, I know what happened in Minneapolis! Why couldn't you tell me? Why won't you let me help you?"

Katharine reamed Mac with a pointed glare.

"I didn't tell him! But he's right."

"*Right?*" she blasted. "Why do men always pride themselves on handiness? Why are you always seeking out broken women and trying to fix us? Problem with both of you is neither one of you are equipped to fix anything beyond your cars! Listen carefully to me. I do not need rescuing! And I'll just bet you, big brother, you ran straight home and told Dad."

"Dad already knew."

Flinching, Katharine's knees softened to the consistency of green-pea soup. Mac grabbed her arm and guided her to a chair near the table. A bleak wintry feeling consumed her. "Leave me alone," she said, slapping him away.

"Stop trying to be a superhero," Mac ordered. "Let us help you."

"I don't need help. How, Gage? When did Dad find out?"

"Right now your lieutenant is on a first name basis with all of us. Probably thinks commitment papers are in order the way we've all called him to find out what happened to you. Dad's known for the better part of a week."

"Mom doesn't know, does she?"

"Hun-uh."

"Gage, I'm sorry. I just couldn't."

In a sideways glance, the photo lying on the table caught her eye. Grabbing it, Katharine blew out, "I know this guy! He's not blond. His name's Josh Cannon."

"Katharine, that's David Patriot," Mac exclaimed. "How do you know him? Whaddaya mean he's not blond?"

Katharine gathered strength and stood with the photo in hand. "Mac, this is the guy I told you about who was on the ferry and bumped into Sully. Those grizzly bear eyes and that cleft in his chin are impossible to miss. I'm positive this is the same guy. His hair is brown, which I think he probably dyed red at one time."

"Pipsqueak, we spent the afternoon chasing down a blond man who wasn't Patriot."

"We just got back a few minutes ago," Mac told her. "I'm sorry about dinner, but I lost track of time."

His black eyes expressed enough sincerity to back up his apology. Katharine couldn't resist a smile, and told him, "You're forgiven this—"

"Pipsqueak!" Gage interrupted hotly. "Did Sully tell you if this guy was staying on the Island?"

"Yeah, but he didn't say where. Sully told me the day I came home, this man's been here since before the tourists started coming over."

"That'd put him here early spring," Gage said.

"Which explains why there was no murder in Green Bay," Mac replied.

"Sully also thought the guy might be hiding something."

"Princess, this is the best news I've had. I think I love you."

"Your jaw need introduction to my fist again?" Gage asked.

"You can try," Mac retorted.

"Go screw yourself, Dobarchon."

"Gage!"

Before Katharine could reprimand her brother, Mac and Gage exchanged what she always titled idiotic light bulb expressions. Simultaneously, they reached for Joe's tourist lists, studied them and discovered Josh Cannon's name on one list. He'd been renting the Upland Cottage since the end of spring. It was a newer, one-story rental on the northwest corner of the island. Hidden away in the Island's forest, the property belonged to Ben McEvoy.

"I wanna check this place out ASAP," Mac said. "Can we get a search warrant and a judge to sign it right away?"

Gage nodded. "Sis, we really need your help ID'ing this guy."

Her heart jumped inside her chest. "I can't. I'm sorry. I just can't do it!"

Dread welled in her throat. With the start of another panic attack, Katharine fled from the conference room. The unbearable struggle made her too dangerous for society, too unreliable for anyone's good.

CHAPTER 15

A tight knot within her goaded for release. Katharine didn't go home, and ran unrelentingly. She couldn't let her parents see her trembling this way. Panting hard in shallow quick gasps, she came to an abrupt stop. She'd run less than a mile to the beach in a pair of sandals. She swiped the sweat from her brow with the back of her hand and walked off the spasmodic vibration that lived inside of her. Anxiety spurted through her until parents scampering after rebellious children refusing to leave had redirected her attention. She then noticed couples strolling hand-in-hand along the shore while others squatted in the sand. None had noticed her.

Katharine headed for the dock and squatted on the edge. She removed her sandals and let her feet hang lifeless above the water. Dismay filled her as the sun descended below the horizon. The impending darkness was a sure match to the heavy burden she carried. Her life was sinking right in front of her eyes. *How do I stop the chaos and horrid memories that keep racing inside my mind?* Chewing her bottom lip until it throbbed in unison with the beat of heart, hot tears slipped down her cheeks. *I need more time to erase my mistake.*

Feminine giggles distracted her and Katharine looked up. She wiped the tears from her cheeks and half smiled at the three teenage girls at the T end of the dock. They reminded her of the hot summer nights she once spent with Michelle and Nicole. The teenagers had the same contagious gaiety she once had in her life.

One, a blond, with her bikini backfield in motion reminded her of—Katharine sat up. A lone adult male with dark hair approached the girls. Blue sky had changed quickly into night's darkness making it difficult to get a good physical description of the man. He stood a few feet from the girls engaged in small talk with them. He followed the girls when they dove into the water.

One of the girls climbed out and Katharine heard her say, 'he's so cute, let him come with us'. Words and giggles echoed off the metal wharf from the other two still in the water. The dark-haired guy lifted himself onto the dock. He said something inaudible then helped the two girls out of the water. The teens moved away from the man, huddled together and spoke in muffled whispers. Their discussion would center on whether to let the guy go with them. After mere seconds of debate, the girls wiped off with towels left in a pile on the dock, faced the stranger and invited him to join them. The man's wicked smile baring white teeth went unnoticed by the teens, and all four slipped into shorts and t-shirts over their swimsuits.

When they began walking toward Katharine, she choked. Terror twisted her heart. The man was a dead hit for Josh Cannon! He was the same man she observed on the ferry and in the photo. Katharine scrambled to her feet when the four sauntered on by her. She wanted a better look, and said, "Jim, is that you?"

The four stopped and the man turned. "Excuse me?"

Shit! How do I stop him without a weapon or car? Ill equipped to undertake such a task, her words came out in a rush. "I thought you were someone else."

"No problem," he said, and the four continued walking.

He appeared not to remember her. Katharine's muscles tightened when she heard Patriot name the girls. Ginger was the blond, Sadie had dark hair and Jessica was Native American. They headed for a black, older model Chevy parked in the lot. She had to stop those girls from getting into that car, but her feet were frozen in place. Patriot started the car and one climbed in the front seat of the vehicle while the other two scrambled into the back. When Patriot backed the car up, Katharine still couldn't move nor could she read the car's license number on the unlit plate. Her heart was thumping madly, felt as if a hand had closed around her throat as she watched Patriot exit the parking lot and drive east on Main.

"Lady, you all right?"

She blinked and jerked around. *No! She wasn't.* The familiar feelings of inadequacy swept through her, her chest heaved and swelled the same way she'd watched some men suck beer out of a bottle. More would die because she couldn't do her job, because her feet felt cemented to the dock.

"Lady, do you need help?"

She committed to a brief nod that seemed to will her to take the first step and took off running full speed back to the police station.

* * *

There wasn't time for neatness. Mac hand wrote a search warrant for the Upland Cottage. Gage had made prior contact with a judge who agreed to meet Mac in Bayfield to sign the search authorization. Unanimously, they agreed Gage and Joe along with Pete and Alesha would stakeout the rented lodge. With the keys to Gage's speedboat, Mac had completed the legal document and was heading out when he collided with Katharine.

"Katharine!"

He grabbed her shoulders to keep her from falling. Desperation swamped her widened eyes. Terror etched her face more accurately than she'd ever drawn on paper. She was panting in short, frantic breaths.

"Mac, he's got three more! They're in a black Chevy—he's gonna kill three more girls! I saw Patriot at the beach—he's eastbound on Main. I couldn't see the plates and I couldn't stop him. I couldn't stop him, Mac!"

"Slow down. Take a deep breath. What're you talking about? What happened?"

"I went to the beach. I heard the girls laughing. Three. Ginger, Sadie and Jessica. Jessica's Native American. Patriot was with them. They were swimming then left in a black Chevy together. I couldn't stop him! Mac, I couldn't stop Patriot from enticing those girls."

It was hurried. It was rushed, but he got the picture. "Katharine, you're sure it was Patriot?"

She faced him and spoke with complete affirmation. "Yes. It *was* Patriot. He's nurturing a mustache. They got into a four-door, older model black Chevy and drove east on Main from the beach."

"Katharine, get on the air and tell Gage and Joe. They're waiting at the Upland Cottage. I was just leaving to get a warrant signed."

"I can't let him kill again, Mac."

He stopped. "What are you saying?"

"I'm telling you I have to do this. We've got to nail him."

Exasperated, he said, "Katharine, I don't have time for on again-off again decisions in the matter."

"Mac, I need to do this. After you execute the warrant, I'll explain *everything*. But right now I need you to believe in me."

The expression in her eyes pleaded to him. He deliberated shortly then brushed a finger under her chin. "Princess, I never stopped believing in you. I'll be back within the hour. Get a hold of Gage and tell him to get after this guy."

Katharine hesitated when Mac went out the door.

He'd never stopped believing in her?

New excitement replenished the emptiness inside of her. There was still a chance for her to grow whole again. Suddenly, her courage and determination became a rock inside of her. She contacted Gage with the information on Patriot then locked the station and rushed home to change clothes.

At ten-thirty, she tossed her damp dress on the bed, hurriedly threw on in a pair of jeans, t-shirt and tennis shoes then ripped open the box labeled equipment and faltered. Her empty gun belt and police license lay on top of the clutter. Stripped of her nine by her own doing, she had buried the weapon at the bottom. Katharine took the license and pocketed it then removed the gun belt and placed it on the bed.

"Katharine?"

Her father stood in the bedroom threshold. However crucial the moment, she silently assessed his posture. The very way he stood there said his shoulders were a yard wide. *Oh, God, how she needed his support right now.*

"What are you doing?" he asked.

"I saw the killer at the beach, Dad."

Digging deeper into the cardboard box, she yanked a wooden box out from the bottom. "Patriot was seducing three more teenage girls into going somewhere with him. He has to be stopped before he kills again."

"Katharine."

Standing, she couldn't look at him or talk to her father about what he already knew. Instead, she stared at the wooden box that contained her Smith and Wesson. After silent deliberation, Katharine lifted the cover. The stainless steel barrel lay against black velvet. She slid her fingers across the weapon before removing two empty magazines out of the box. Her dad stepped into the room and gestured to the gun.

"You mind?"

Handing him the box, she nervously watched as he removed the firearm.

"Nice weapon," he said, bouncing it in his hand. "Double action. Fourteen rounds in the magazine. Not bad. Not bad at all."

Katharine dug and found a container of cartridges inside the box on the floor. She efficiently loaded both magazines with bullets. Next, she buckled the gun belt to her waist. She'd lost so much weight it was loose around her middle on the last notch. Inserting one magazine on her belt, she held the second and waited for her dad to hand over the nine-millimeter.

"I'd have thought you would have preferred the 3904 model with a smaller grip."

She gave her father a look that lasted an instant. "Nines don't stand up to the heavy duties anymore. I wanted fourteen rounds instead of eight."

"Are you sure you're up for this?" he asked, handing the weapon back to her.

Katharine inserted the magazine into the butt. She dropped the hammer release, pulled the slide back releasing a bullet into the chamber then pushed the hammer release into fire position. Her dad was still watching her, and she muttered, "I'm sure."

"Watch your back, Pumpkin."

Her head came up fast. He hadn't called her Pumpkin in twenty years. Tenderness, worry, *love*, they all flashed in his eyes. An almost hopeful glint replaced all their years of misgivings.

Katharine cleared her throat a second time. She couldn't let emotions affect her now and shoved the pistol into her holster. She grabbed her sketchpad. "I have to go, Dad."

* * *

Patriot had disappeared again.

All six worked into the wee hours Monday night. With a signed warrant in hand, they scoured the premises for traces and leads, but were too late. Patriot had checked out of the Upland Cottage a few days earlier according to the owner, Ben McEvoy. Much to everyone's disappointment, the place squeaked of cleanliness.

Returning to the station, Mac contacted his partner in Green Bay and passed along Patriot's new physical. He advised Cole to keep an eye on Patriot's apartment in Green Bay.

"Katharine, what did you say the names of those three girls were?"

"I only caught their first names," she told Alesha as she kept drawing. "The Native American was Jessica. A blond with short hair and a body all men would slobber over was named Ginger—"

"The third was Sadie Rogers," Alesha finished.

Katharine looked up. "You know them?"

"Yeah, we know them. Caught 'em drinking a couple of times with seniors. Right Pete?"

"That's right. Jessica's last name is Henderson and Ginger Morris is a sweet smelling, hot little number sure to break hearts. Or, as you said, make a man slobber."

"According to the parents," Gage said, hanging up the phone, "Jessica is the only one not home yet. Ginger and Sadie arrived home about fifteen minutes ago. Both said Patriot, or as they know him, Josh Cannon dropped the two of them off at their homes first. They admitted they'd been driving around drinking beer and smoking pot."

"At least we can make a momentary assumption he's still on the island somewhere since the ferries aren't running and the marina's closed until morning." Mac looked up from his hand-written statement. "Any of you have any idea where he might take her?"

When no one responded, Joe said, "Depending on his choice poison, we're under a crucial time frame to find Jessica. Abrin reaction time is several hours to three days. Paraquat is two to five days. Safe side for medical treatment leaves us less than a forty-eight hour window."

"I'm done." Katharine held up the sketchbook showing them an identical of David Patriot with his new hair color and mustache.

Impressed, Mac said, "Katharine, the resemblance is uncanny. That crater in his chin and diamond stud are perfect."

"Sis, give it here. I'll run off copies and fax one over to the Park Rangers and Bayfield PD."

"Gage, we're gonna need all the help we can get," Mac said. "You think the Coast Guard would get involved?"

"Unless something happens in the water, they're not gonna do much for us except transport. Then we'd have to request it. I'll fax them a photo and advise of the situation anyway."

"I'm gonna drive around the island looking for the black Chevy," Mac said.

"I'll go with," Katharine announced. "There's also a possibility Patriot has a boat stashed somewhere and has already left the Island."

"It's three now," Mac said. "If the other two girls were truthful, it's only been thirty minutes since they parted company.

"Alesha and I will start at Jess' house," Pete said, "then we'll check the shoreline for boats."

Gage ran off copies of Katharine's sketch, handing one to everybody. "Joe, we've got the back roads after I make a couple of calls," he said.

Mac stood. "Make sure your portables are working and don't make a move if you spot him. Get on the air. Patriot isn't known to carry or use weapons, but I'm not taking any chances since his M-O has changed. Katharine, you ready?"

"Ready."

They left the station backtracking toward the beach. Mac decided to pursue Main Street the way Katharine saw Patriot travel earlier. The Jeep's whirring engine manipulated the silence of the A.M. hours. Scarce and oily lighting from street lamps filled the main roads now barren of human life. The stillness might easily convince anyone the island was impotent of life if one didn't know better. The sweltering afternoon had transposed into refreshingly cool. Conglomerations of dazzling and dwarf-like stars winked and flickered in the vastness of an ebony sky.

"This reminds me of my childhood," Mac told Katharine. "And that's a place I haven't been in a long time."

"What does?"

"The quiet night-fallen allure. It reminds me of being raised on a llama ranch. Linda and I would sneak out after dark to the llama barn and—"

"You raised llamas? Where?"

"I didn't. My father does. Got a few acres in Cameron, just south of Rice Lake."

"Mac, that's not far from here. What exactly do people do with llamas?"

"They're used for breeding, selling their wool, pets and protection. They can also be trained for animal therapy assistance."

"Wow, all that?"

"Linda and I can vouch for their therapeutic value. We each had our own growing up. I swear General Wickerbee and I had a psychic bond."

"And here I thought most kids had dogs for pets."

Grinning, Mac said, "Linda's older and got hers first. She named him Einstein. I used to tell her he was a worthless degenerate she should have named Halfwit. But that was only because I couldn't have my own llama until I was ten. The year I turned of llama age, I watched his birth. I remember the little guy popping out all slimy-looking. Did you know newborns are called cria?"

Katharine shook her head.

"Mine was scrawny and butt-ugly with these," Mac hand gestured, "floppy, banana-shaped ears. I was mad because I thought I'd been cheated. Didn't know that's the way all llamas looked before they grew up and I refused to have anything to do with the beast."

"Don't tell me you were a llama racist?"

"Einstein had grown up into a stretchy-looking beaut Linda pranced around the ranch like some damn prom king. I was always jealous until one day I was out back of the house sitting in my mom's peacock wicker chair grumbling. Can't even remember about what. The llama I refused to acknowledge came up behind the chair and starts nibbling on it to get my attention. I think he knew Mom would go ballistic. Then he starts honking off an alarm pitch that sounds like a cross between an engine starting and a turkey call. He gives me a solid nudge in the shoulder before he takes off in this three-beat gallop across the fields. As a curious kid, I naturally followed."

In sharing a part of his past with her, Katharine realized it came easy for Mac. She felt his energy, heard the emotion in the sound of his voice. It was one way of overcoming his burden. Many times over the better part of the last several months, she'd dug up her own memories to forget. "Then what happened?" she asked.

"That's the day I named the llama. I figured the lanky beast was crazy but I'm running as fast as I can after the degenerate. It was hard to keep up with him because he's propelling himself through the air in what's called a pronk. To this day, I'll never understand how General Wickerbee knew Linda was in trouble."

"What happened to her?"

"My sister had a hair-brain idea she could teach Einstein to jump fences. When she tried, Einstein fell, knocking Linda to the ground. The llama landed on top of her. When I got there, mine started nudging me hard. I had bruises on my back from it, but he'd sort of point with his front paw and nose, showing me what to do."

"Was Einstein dead or alive?"

"Alive. At the time, I think Einstein also knew if he moved he'd crush and kill Linda who was unconscious. Einstein weighed three hundred plus. After long deliberation by a small kid, General Wickerbee and I got Linda out from underneath him. Then the General starts nudging me back to the house. I swear I ran at warped, pronk speed while Einstein and the General stayed with Linda. I told my Mom and she called 9-1-1."

"Was Linda okay?"

"Yeah, but she had a mild concussion. I've never let her forget she owed the General and me. I also quit calling Einstein Halfwit."

"How'd you get the name General Wickerbee out of all that?"

"General was the highest honor I could give my llama for saving Linda. Wickerbee came from the way he got my attention.

Chewing on my mom's wicker chair. Anyway, noiseless nights remind me of when Linda and I used to sneak out to the llama barn and sleep with them. We'd leave the barn door open and lay under the stars talking about whatever came into our childish minds."

"You're really close to your sister, aren't you?"

"Yeah, I am. And I haven't thought about the General in years." He flashed another smile. "Thanks, I guess I should take my own advice about talking. But I'll never ...,"

"Sometimes, going back helps us to go forward," she replied softly.

"I should have listened to her, Katharine. Clarissa might still be alive."

"Mac, don't do this. You can't think like that or believe the fault—"

"Dammit!"

His explosive voice penetrated the quiet night and Katharine waited.

"I'm younger, but I always took care of Linda. I played protector the same way Gage protects you. I'm responsible for her pain because I wouldn't listen to her. Losing her only child almost killed her."

"Mac, you are not responsible for what that bastard has done. That'd be like me saying Gage is to blame for what happened to me. Have you tried talking to Linda about it?"

"She says she doesn't blame me."

"Then believe her."

When he gestured an impatient shrug, Katharine said, "Your sister is hurting, but deep down she knows what happened isn't your fault. As cops, we all have high expectations. The uniform makes us feel immortal. The need to protect others is ingrained in us."

"Katharine, you know as well as I do that if our expectations weren't high, we couldn't do the job we do."

They drove for several more minutes without speaking. She couldn't stop herself from pondering the same inward questions Mac had. She looked out into the darkness. After a lengthy silence, she asked, "You really think Gage protects me?"

"Princess, how do you think I got this sore jaw?"

"I wanna know why the two of you were fighting over me."

"I know what he's thinking where you're concerned. I treated every guy Linda brought home the same way."

"I hope Linda told you the same thing I'm gonna tell Gage."

"It's none of our business?"

"And then some."

"Can't change what's bred into us, Princess. We're taught early that no man messes with our women. Be it mother, sister, wife or other."

"Do you realize how pathetic you all sound the way you establish dominance over your territory?"

With a sideways glance, he asked, "Do all women think alike? That's real close to what Linda told me before she hauled off and slugged me."

Katharine covered an urge to laugh, and one more time recognized Mac provided her with something Steven never had. Conversation. "I think Linda and I would get along great."

"I know she'd like you."

Turning away a second time, Katharine stared into the shadowy timbers of the night. The dull empty ache still gnawed on her soul. "What's not to like? I'm a first class nag whose let my best friends down. I have a father who won't speak to me because I chose a man's job and failed. My brother thinks I leech on him for favors and, well ...,"

"Well, what?"

She looked at Mac. "I'm sorry I called you Steven. The fight you and I were having was taking on the same tones of something he always said to me. That I flunked out at loving him. Since coming back here, I've been told by everyone how I'm a failure at everything in my life."

"Katharine, you and I weren't fighting. I was setting the record straight. I am not going to lose Patriot this time. Now tell me more about this guy that's torn your world apart?"

"We were living together but he didn't tear my world apart. I did it myself after he ended whatever we had a couple of days before I shot that guy. Steven always did have perfect timing," Katharine muttered.

"What did you mean when you said you couldn't be trusted?"

A gamut of mixed feelings surged through her. Mac's question hammered at her before she began. "I went through the standard debriefing and administrative leave after the shoot. I didn't have a problem talking about it. Though hard to deal with the outcome, I felt confident it would be ruled justified. Where my doubts began was one day after I'd come off a dogwatch. I went to all-day court and couldn't sleep before I had to go back to work that night. After roll call, I hit the streets like I did most nights and that's when it started."

"When what started?"

"Brutal panic attacks. Sweats. Clammy hands so badly I couldn't grip my weapon. My heartbeat slaughtering the inside of my chest. The voice of the screaming child. I took myself off the street and spent the rest of the night working in the office, but it continued to happen."

"Did you ever talk to anyone about it?"

"No. I couldn't. Then one of those humid, sultry nights, we were backed up with five pages of pending calls. You name it, it happened that night. I was in the area of a shots fired and put myself arriving. I'd heard the shots en route but found nothing when I got there. The call stated someone wanted to be seen. One of my squads rolled up behind me as I was getting out."

Reliving the death-defying incident in her mind for a moment, Katharine swallowed hard and continued. "Gunfire rang out loud and clear. Flashes and bullets were flying from both sides of the street. I knew they were gunning for us when bullets hit the back windows of our squads. We'd been set up and were caught in crossfire. I heard shouts coming from neighbors but was stuck where I stood outside my squad. I was hypnotized by the red flash from my lightbar. I could hear people screaming but I couldn't move. Sweat was pouring out of me. My hands were shaking so badly I couldn't get my weapon out of the holster. Then I heard my guys yelling at me to get down after they dove to the pavement. The last thing I remembered was falling and my body smacking the asphalt then the lights went out."

"You thought you'd been shot."

She nodded, re-experiencing the vivid details. "I learned later, one of my officers had tackled me. I hit my head on the way down and was knocked out for a second. I was taken to the hospital, but when the shift was over, I knew I couldn't be counted upon anymore. I turned in my resignation that morning and told Carl to take me off the street my last two weeks. I forbid him to tell the guys."

"Katharine, shooting and killing a man changes your life. It changes the way you look at and what you think about everything. In some ways, you're a hero, but in other ways, there will always be the accusing look from the bastards who don't know any better. If that were all that went with the job you did, it'd be easy. It's when your morally subconscious tells your morally conscious mind that what you did is wrong that it becomes a lethal weapon against you. The argument between the two builds up and tears you into pieces."

"You sound like you've been there, Mac."

"Not me, my partner killed someone. My moral dilemma is with the fact I didn't trust my sister's judgment. Now my niece is dead and the killing continues. At least you stopped one parasite from killing more. Think about that for a while."

What Mac said made sense in a way she had never considered. Since Easter, she had accepted her failure to protect. Though her body rebelled against the immorality of what she did, her only alternative had been to quit a job she loved. She ran away so others wouldn't die under her direction and command. In the end, the trilemma didn't change the finality of death no matter who did the killing. Mac had made her interpret something she'd been ambiguous about since she pulled the trigger. She looked at him across the Jeep. "Thanks, Dobarchon."

He laid his hand on top of hers and gently squeezed. The gesture diminished her defeat and made her spirit soar. The awakening experience left her reeling while they checked every hidden location and driveway for Jessica. The strong passion she once knew within herself was slowly coming back. They drove in silence for some time when Mac instinctively pushed in the clutch, slammed the brakes and shifted into neutral. Katharine slid forward on the seat, bracing both hands on the dash.

"What is it?"

"I heard a girl crying."

Katharine scanned the area and listened. He looked one way, she the other into the woods. Then she heard the distinguished weeping. It came from overhead and Katharine looked to the dawning sky. "It's just Katrina."

"*Who* the hell is Katrina?"

"Sully's ghost. Katrina Cadotte."

"Just fricking great! All I need is a whacked out ghost running interference."

"Mac, can you really hear Katrina?"

"Hear her? She's been wailing since the second day I set foot on the island. I thought I was losing my mind."

CHAPTER 16

The Divine Creator had spoken.

"Take only one at a time," he said.

Hence, the killer did. *Oh, he had pride.* He always did as told. He always performed his obligation with extreme skill.

And the payoff was to admire his beautiful Jess. She belonged to him for four days. Fondling her flawless flesh, he discovered he liked the smooth, silky feel. It made him twittery inside. He gazed for hours at her delicately carved bones and rosy-colored lips. She had hair that shined as black as oil and bronze curvy shoulders beckoning with small budding breasts beginning to fill out. His love for her excited him in ways he never thought possible. But the longer he studied Jess, the more his feelings of misery turned to hatred for her until he mourned inside, grieved over the persistent yearning and the constant lack of self-fulfillment. The only way to carry out his fantasy was through death. He knew that from the beginning. He'd always known that.

And she was his until the end.

Beautiful Jess, he thought, you were so eager and gluttonous for drug inducement, so eager to blossom. The first time he saw Jess, she aroused him with a sense of urgency. She was by no means blind to his attraction to her and the very idea of having her vibrated through his entire body. She eliminated all his weaknesses and provided him with a renewed sense of safety. Lust and greed made it easy to desensitize her. It was his insecure desire that made it difficult for him to hug and keep the pleasure he so desperately needed. Sadly, he could only observe her. Sadly, he couldn't satisfy desire. It came from constant fear buried inside himself. Taking more of them relieved the fear, made him anxious about the pleasure he sought. The Divine Creator preached such needs were covetousness and he must avoid them.

So he turned his greed into a ritual stimulation.

Every time he manipulated one of them into joining him the excitement of his addiction rose many notches. Sedating their mind and bodies was easy for him. He did it with the holy water and the sacred pea. His despair was depleted by the power he had over them. Then he'd watch while their eyes glazed. He'd tolerate the wait as their bodies went limp, waiting for his insides to explode in anticipation of death. And throughout the four-day ceremony, he bathed their exquisite bronze flesh with holy water while he admired them; he whispered soothing words in their ears always lapping up the scent of their sweet-smelling hair. The touch beneath his fingers to their soft fleshy curves made him quiver the same way they shuddered with fright. He didn't neglect them. He never maltreated them. He wasn't cruel or exploitive of them. He loved them. He loved them all because they gave him pleasure as eager and erratic as a summer storm. They made him feel safe. He must feel safe.

He felt his own power and control return when they begged for release. The more their sinful eyes pleaded to him, the more he fed the revered pea and sacred golden water to them. They needed to be nourished. They needed saving.

But he must also be good. *Must obey.* The sacrificial killings furnished him with ultimate supremacy while taking a life replaced the life taken. The ritual made him invincible. He'd never had that before he learned of the Divine Creator. *They* told him he could conquer all with this power. He was surprised when he did triumph over. Although the rules had to be strictly adhered to, none knew how and when to feed the Creator's soul. The offering must always begin at the dawn of new light. The execution must always take place in July, October and December. It was the key he'd been told. He didn't know the importance of it, nor did he care. He wanted to take when he needed to take. And it was time.

The necessity for pleasure poured into him and flowed with the blood in his body.

He began the ritual chanting. The Divine Creator said it destroyed the burden of his acute emotions. Chanting cleansed the dispute between his love and hate. It destroyed his affliction to act out his internal hostility. He acted to escape his cavity—the hole of darkness—the impotence he felt when left alone.

And so he hummed loudly, thriving on the energy and soaring from ground state to charged electricity. He chanted until it became thunderous, until his arousal drowned the voice that cursed him ferociously. Sweat frothed his brow and restored his suffering spirit and soul as he embodied every emotion. Humming, chanting, he panted breathlessly until the feelings of unworthiness dissolved and once more, he had escaped the hand that swung the sword—

"What are you doing?" the grating voice screeched in his head.

"You will do as I *say!"*

She interrupted the Divine Creator. She always did! She called herself the Supreme Being. The killer glanced around, blocked the interference and chanted at full strength.

"Slay your burden again and again!
Relinquish the powers of love and hate.
Look to thyself, take care of thyself,
For nobody cares for thee."

Hot and fervid, his body released fluids that made him quaver with the freedom. He would never forfeit himself to anyone again. He would never be held captive. *Give them all what they want and watch them surrender quickly.* With the revered ornament on the left wrist, the killer chanted volubly to the Divine Creator.

"Slay your burden again and again!
Relinquish the powers of love and hate.
Look to thyself, take care of thyself,
For nobody cares for thee."

The involuntary tremors of arousal began and his entire body vibrated, soaring higher, exploding in the downpour of fiery sensations. The pleasure was pure and explosive. And as his beautiful Jess took her last breath, his chest rose and fell in bitter triumph. It was time to pledge the virgin flesh to the Divine

Creator.

A wicked smile filled the killer's face. Purity finally blended in perfect union and freedom would come to him alas.

And life had ended.

Absolution achieved.

He *must* do this again.

He would do this many times.

* * *

The forty-eight hour window to stop the ninth murder came and went. Apprehension over Jessica Henderson's disappearance defiled the Island worse than any Superior storm. Katharine and the guys worked in shifts. Mac, Gage and Joey were grabbing a few winks on cots they'd setup in a back room of Town Hall. Pete and Alesha were at the marina while La Pointe residents banned together in attempts to rescue one of their own. Under Tom Coville's direction, the Park Rangers beefed up patrols within the Apostle's while Bayfield residents congregated for manhunts on the mainland. Grief merged with worry chiseling fear into faces. Riled up Town folks became impossible and formed their own manhunts.

Personal fatigue paralleled with Katharine's sinking spirit. The plight to find Jessica increased, but the invasion of rain and rough waters left the searches limited to land. Since they had scoured every inch of the rock with persistent frequency, Katharine suspected Patriot had made it off Madeline Island. It was only a matter of time before someone came across the teenager's decaying body. She felt sure the discovery would be here on Madeline. Like a prize, Jessica would be displayed for all to see.

Sheer exhaustion powdered Katharine but she sat hunched over the small desk inside the station re-reading reports. Documented facts and evidence gave no insight to the actual vicinity of the last two murders. She had personally interviewed hysterical Sadie and Ginger, and now scanned their statements for any vital lead. Both girls said the three had met Josh Cannon Monday while water skiing. Initially, headed for Devils Island and the Sea Caves, Josh convinced them the caves at Sand Island were closer. The teenagers then followed him in their boat, docking near Sand lighthouse. They spent the day checking out the caves and hiking.

The girls were kept apart before and during their statements. Katharine vividly recalled Sadie and Ginger's callow declarations. Both girls had cooed what a nice guy Josh was. Out of fear for their safety, he forbade them to consume alcohol until they finished swimming. Josh told them he had a cooler in his trunk and later provided them with beer. He drove them around La Pointe while they drank. They parked down at the Hangout smoking pot as well.

Kids went to the secluded Hangout on the north side of the island when they didn't want to be caught doing things they weren't supposed to do. Smirking about it years later, it was the first place the cops always looked.

Following two hours of questions with each teenager, Katharine discovered she knew more about David Patriot without meeting him than Ginger and Sadie had learned in the course of a day's company with him. Ginger adamantly stated she'd never met any man that shared his attention equally between three girls the way Josh did. When questioned why they left Jessica alone with him, both girls admitted Jessica's parents gave her a later curfew. The fact parents let their teenagers stay out until two A.M. didn't surprise Katharine nearly as much as it enraged her. Rereading Sadie and Ginger's naive statements, Katharine ruminated whether she, Nicole and Michelle had been as simple-minded when they were sixteen.

Looking back, teenage life had been simplistic, bursting with hopes and dreams of an uncomplicated future. Would she have refused then to believe that Josh used a fictitious name the way Ginger and Sadie refused to believe it? Would she have been as naïve?

Knee deep in police reports for several hours, the parched screech of door hinges added to the bleakness that anyone coming into the station might have good news. It was Michelle and Nicole carting in meals as a way to help. Katharine stood and stretched. She moved her head in deliberate sideways motion then stretched her neck muscles side to side.

In unison, both women asked, "Any word yet?"

Depleted of energy and life, she shook her head.

"Great balls of fire! I go to bed every night feeling as if I'm gonna crawl right out of my skin with fear. You guys have any idea where this creep is holed up?"

"Nicole, if she did, do you think for one minute they wouldn't go get him," Michelle said.

"Ladies, I'm in no mood for bickering today. Are they still going through with Aunt Suzanne's party tomorrow?"

"Yes," Nicole answered. "Amazingly, everyone thinks it will keep his or her mind off Jess' disappearance even if short lived. We're going ahead with a three o'clock start time. You're coming, aren't you?"

"Doubt it." Katharine linked her fingers behind her head and performed a brief workout then welcomed the salad Nicole had prepared.

"Nicole convinced me to go," Michelle said. "You sure you guys won't at least make an appearance?"

"We're all working round the clock on little sleep. None of us wanna face an onslaught of questions we can't answer."

"I know. I'm dealing with Baines Inc. who's asking a lot of the same questions."

"Then you've finally met him?" Katharine asked.

"Not yet. He's having a love affair with his fax machine. I'm receiving several a day from him. Or, I should say they have his name on the paper."

"Tell you what. If he's got a problem that's gonna halt the progress of the add-on to the Tavern, have him call me here."

"Anything to get him off my back, even when I want to halt this project myself. Oh, I ran into Iola this morning. As much as she liked having you in the shop, she totally understands your commitment to catching this guy."

"I know. I just felt bad I let her down after one day. I think I'd enjoy working there and hope she'll give me a second chance when this is over."

"Iola definitely wants you back," Michelle told her, reassuringly. "She's holding your job for you."

"Katharine, hon, I've got a ton of work to do at the Tavern for the party. We better get going. Mac's invited. Don't forget to mention it to him."

"Invited to what?"

Their heads turned to Mac standing in the hallway threshold. "I'm sorry," Katharine said, "did we wake you?"

Mac indicated no and headed for the coffeepot.

"We're having a surprise birthday party for Katharine's aunt tomorrow at the Tavern. Michelle and I are trying to convince Katharine and the rest of you to stop by."

"Thanks," he said replacing the carafe and looking at the dark-haired woman. "You must be Michelle. Glad to meet you."

"Likewise," Michelle said, shuffling backward. "I hope all of you can make it to the party for a little while."

Mac took a swig of coffee. "Can't promise anything."

Katharine swallowed the last of her salad, washing it back with iced tea. "We have to get back to work here. Thanks for bringing us something to eat."

"It's the least we can do."

Michelle and Nicole each hugged Katharine then left.

"You get any sleep, Dobarchon?"

"Hun-uh. Sounds like a moto-cross race the way those two are sawing logs back there."

"Eat something while I run down a theory I'm tossing around."

"Princess, I'll hear any ideas you have," he said, sitting at Gage's desk. "You do realize it's unlikely she's still alive?"

Katharine nodded dismally. "Based on the poison's facts, I believe she's near death. I know if we found her this minute, we're too late to save her life."

Mac bit into a hoagie sandwich. "Based on decomposition, we know he doesn't expose the body until after they're dead. It's been four days since her disappearance. Depending on whether he uses paraquat or abrin, we won't find her for several more days."

"Maybe not. I've been reading over the statements I took from Sadie and Ginger. Both said they were going out to Devils Island, which is located quite a distance west of here."

"But they went to Sand Island instead because Patriot told them it was closer. Is it closer?"

"Not by much, depending on which end of Madeline you leave from and the route you take."

"So what's the deal with these two islands?"

"They both have sea caves. You can hike the islands but only access the caves with a small boat or kayak."

"And you're thinking because he persuaded the girls to Sand Island, he's performing his ceremony at Devils?"

"Yeah, I do."

"I'll buy that but it still doesn't fit with the six homicides from Green Bay. And I'll lose jurisdiction if that's true."

"Pipsqueak," Gage said, from the threshold, "there's more-than-normal traffic at Devils Island because they're doing reconstruction on the light."

Looking at her brother, she asked, "Did you get any sleep?"

"A little," he said, removing the pot of day-old coffee. "Sis, if you're thinking remote, Outer Island would be the likely spot. Not many go there because of distance."

"As soon as the rain stops, we can go out with Tom and his men and search the entire island."

Glancing through the window, Mac said, "Looks like it'll be awhile before that happens."

Heads jerked abruptly when all heard a commotion outside. The door was yanked open and Mark Stewart slapdashed into the station wearing glossy yellow rain gear. His hiking boots were steeped with mud and his fox brown hair clung to the sides of flushed cheeks. He panted short of breath.

"We found Jess! She's in our shack on the north end! Curt and Kevin sent me back to get you. Damn, it's grisly, Chief. We're too late. She's already dead."

"Where's the shack?" Mac asked.

"About a mile in behind Upland Cottage. Can't get in with a vehicle. I'll guide you."

"Katharine, get Joey. I'll call Del."

Mark led the way into the saturated forest. The further in they trudged carrying equipment to process the crime scene, the thicker the shadows. Twigs snapped underfoot while they negotiated inclines around plentiful fallen trees and stumps as tall as totem poles. They branded a trail over logs so rotten they'd formed simple mounds while ducking and dodging low hanging trees caused from wind cripple. The further they scaled into the virgin forest the denser vegetation. The going was extremely difficult, and flies and mosquitoes buzzed and attacked hungrily. Pinned beneath a heavy mass of leaden-gray clouds, the rain slowed at times to a dismal drip.

An earthy scent of decaying leaves mingled and hung in the air under fragrant scents of pine and Katharine hoped the heavy woodsy tang would deplete the odor of death. Plush emerald green moss dressed tree trunks. An occasional wind murmured through pines and hemlocks while birds chirped. When more thunder sounded, each looked up as the heavens expelled showers to drench their surroundings. Though thick masses of birch, poplar and aspen blocked their paths, it left little in the way of shelter from the rain.

Organic matter in various stages of rot tiled the forest floor giving new birth to the life of insect homes, various lichens and fungus. With the shortest legs, Katharine had a supreme disadvantage over the men. She had no hankering to lean on a pile of fungus beetles and snails nor did she want an introduction to a bat population burrowed in mold. Almost a mile inward now, she thought the ancient growth and decay was symbolic to their objection. Life was to death as old was to young. Light was to blackness as peace was to discord.

"Not much further," Mark yelled back, interrupting her thoughts.

Her panting, like everyone else, was heavy and she timed it as a distraction with a new patter of rain drips. They reached the shack in just under an hour. Curt and Kevin sat on logs waiting for them. Another cloudburst opened its mouth dumping additional buckets of water onto the crime scene. Faces fell. The downpour had annihilated the hut located in a miniature clearing. All they could see was a foot. Jessica's foot.

"Mac, it's your call," Gage yelled over the rainstorm. "How do you wanna handle this?"

Squinting upward, he shouted, "With this cloud coverage, we haven't got much daylight left. Let's salvage whatever we can and clear the scene faster. Seal all evidence in plastic until we get it inside to dry."

It took ten minutes to uncover Jessica's body and Joey and Del bagged it quickly protecting the lifeless being from further desecration. Katharine scanned the area looking for indications of other trails. She spoke with the Stewart brothers who each confirmed they entered the forest the same way Mark had guided them into the shadowed depths. Thirty minutes slipped away in their haste to collect and salvage the evidence before they began the journey back to town.

* * *

Katharine tossed and turned the entire night. Her father's roaming the house wasn't what kept her from slumber. She certainly didn't understand at a time like this how Gage, or their mother, could sleep soundly.

What kept her alert was her mind. It played ping-pong between many unanswered case questions and the sense of relief Mac gave her when he identified her moral dispute. The fact that he had figure it out astounded her. He'd been the only one to clarify a conflict of ethics she couldn't conceive or grasp alone. Relief merged all night long with her personal web of suspicion. She honestly believed they were dealing with two killers. Copycat? She wasn't as sure of but definitely two killers. Desperately, for Mac's sake, she wanted to be wrong, but the use of two different poisons made it impossible to believe otherwise. A psychotic serial killer didn't switch M.O's mid-stream unless to confuse the chaser. And that truth built an argument with the profiler's report, that the killer wanted to be caught. Mac also told her the profiler said as a killer feels less adequate he would murder more. Katharine didn't dispute that point, just the way the killing was done.

The key, which stumped all of them, seemed to be in *when* he murdered. The first six victims were all reported missing within a week of the same calendar dates. The months of July, October and the end of December. Those months and dates definitely held meaning for the real serial killer. It was victims seven and eight found dead at the *end* of July that implied two killers. Then with the discovery of their ninth victim in August she felt certain they were searching form more than one maniac. With no other way to explain away the reason for the out-of-control homicides, she would have trouble convincing Mac. Her theories would create friction with the man who unquestionably made her shiver eagerly each time she saw him.

At six A.M. sleep was a lost cause and Katharine got up and

showered. Dressed, the familiar cry floated through the bedroom. She pulled the shade to look. Pouring rain continued, like Katrina's frequent wail. When Mac said he'd heard the ghost, new excitement swelled inside of her. Ever since, she'd subconsciously dwelled on Sully's fairytale—the next thought clicked like a self-cocking hammer release. Katharine grabbed her shoulder holster from the cardboard box and strapped it on, removed her weapon from the gun belt and checked it. Through the sleepless hours, she decided to start wearing her nine concealed until they caught Patriot. She grabbed the extra magazine, tugged on a baggie jacket and hurried out. Her mother was in the hallway headed for the bathroom.

"Katharine, where are you going in such a hurry?"

"Morning, Mom. Tell Gage I'll catch up with him later."

"Are the two of you going to Suzanne's party?"

"We'll try," she said, giving her mother a kiss on the cheek. "I gotta go. Don't forget to tell Gage."

* * *

Mac opened one eye and discharged a guttural moan equivalent to the roar of the thunder outside. Returning to his bungalow at four A.M., he never made it past the couch to the loft's bedroom. He pushed himself upward and swung his feet to the floor. Irritable, a yawn duplicating a bear's growl lurched out of him.

Downpours had converted into rabid squalls Friday night before they made it back to the station. The Stewart Brothers said it was an afterthought to check their hunting shack. The only salvation came because that hut established jurisdiction of the last three victims. Rain, however, had destroyed a lot of the evidence and obliterated a solid connection to jurisdiction of the previous six murders.

The victim was tied up and wearing the same bracelet as all the other victims. The hut and the body's position gave them the answer to the question of lividity of the first Madeline Island homicide. With the hut on a hill, Jessica's body slanted downward. Lividity had not yet begun with the Henderson girl since the coroner advised she'd only been dead a few hours. Jennifer Wicket and the six Green Bay victims didn't show the same signs of lividity as Sherri Martin and the latest victim did. That fact would kill their case in court.

He and the others processed what little could be recovered from the crime scene. They discovered a bowl of nuts and Joe identified several bright red seeds from the abrus precatorius plant. The bastard fed her poison mixed with peanuts. A three-quarter-empty Johnny Walker Black bottle left near the victim was sealed in an evidence bag and Gus Rankin took both for analysis and latents. A Ziploc bag of marijuana they uncovered near other drug paraphernalia was also handed over to Gus. The chain of evidence was complete.

But the unanswered questions perplexed Mac. There was no evidence of the deadly paraquat used to kill the first six and the eighth victims. He doubted lab tests would produce the poisonous chemical in the Johnnie Walker this time either.

Why had Patriot switch unless he desired a more expedient death?

"It'd make sense if Patriot knows we're onto him," Mac said aloud.

But why sixteen-year-old Native American girls? That question overwhelmed him the most since the second homicide. Patriot definitely had a fetish for that race of girls since Ginger and Sadie didn't have an ounce of Native American blood in them and were both still alive.

Stocking footed, Mac stumbled into the full kitchen and turned the water faucet with a hard yank. He filled the glass coffeepot, pitched grounds into the basket, thrust the coffee can back into the cupboard with more oomph than necessary, and slammed the cupboard door shut. Mad as hell about it, he didn't blame Gage for exposing Patriot's picture.

Stationing his butt against a counter and crossing his arms, the sound of raindrops splattered against a window. Slithering downward, they vanished and preceded new drops that followed a reprehensible cycle. If he hadn't allowed Katharine to distract him on the ferry that first day, he would have seen Patriot himself. That pissed him off as much as her idea did that they were dealing with a second suspect. She had to be wrong. Or was she? The investigative facts were clear-cut, methodically engrained in his mind.

There's nothing clear-cut about Katharine LeNoir. She was unapproachable and self-protective. She was stubborn as much as she was determined. She was certainly forthright. He liked that. Her vacillating life made sense, but lacked order. Nearness to her made it impossible for him to assemble any facts much less digest the fact that he *wanted* her as much as he *needed* to nail Patriot. He glanced at the window where they stood when she'd kissed him with pliant enticement. She confused the hell out of him. No woman had ever ambushed him with stone-blind lust before. Did he *need* her as much as he *wanted* to arrest Patriot? It didn't change the fact that three more girls were dead because he'd been distracted by her. He screwed up big time again—Patriot had escaped and this case reminded him of the raindrops reprehensible cycle.

Shaking off the dismal thoughts, another one crossed his mind. He couldn't go back to Green Bay when he'd been derelict in duty. Pouring coffee, he meditated over those morbid thoughts now. Was he cut out to do the job anymore? Sanders, his Captain, had notified him of the Department's decision a few days ago. A willful act the police chief called it then rendered a thirty-day suspension. He couldn't argue the willfulness or the intent with which he did what he did. Nevertheless, it also meant he no longer had any authority over the Green Bay homicides. Sanders had also informed him the mayor was deliberating civil charges unless he submitted his resignation.

He owed closing this case to his sister and Clarissa. Patriot would be jailed without parole before he'd ever consider handing over his shield.

CHAPTER 17

Late afternoon, showers dissipated to a fine drizzle. Mac and Gage completed their interview with the last of the Stewart brothers to no avail. Not one had been to their shack since the previous deer hunting season.

"Kevin was nervous around you," Gage said. "How come?"

"I'm sure he didn't know I was a cop the night he decided to harass your sister over at the Tavern. We had a talk."

"I see."

Mac yawned, stood, and stretched. "Didn't Katharine tell you where she was going?"

"I didn't see her this morning, but her car is gone and she took her weapon."

"Where the hell'd she go?"

"You're wrong if you're thinking Katharine bailed on us."

He began pacing. "Has she always been unpredictable?"

"She's got a mind of her own. She's always done what she wanted. Right now, she's determined in her own obstinate way to catch this guy."

Gage stopped what he was doing and stood straight. "A lot like you are, Mac."

Sucking air in through his teeth, Mac grabbed a stapler and slapped it in his hand. "Aren't you the least bit worried about her?"

Gage sized up the significance of Mac's restless manner and

snorted out a laugh. "Your macho image is being reduced to a babbling incoherent idiot over my sister."

"I'm not babbling. I'm concerned Patriot will start targeting all women."

"Whatever you say," Gage muttered. "Katharine probably went over to the party. Let's pack it in for a couple of hours and check out the Tavern. Joe will call us if anything comes up."

* * *

The surprise birthday party was in full swing. Balloons and crepe paper streamers hung from the ceilings and walls. People packed the lounge and banquet room spilling out through sliding doors that opened to an awning-covered patio at the back. Casual conversations carried throughout the Tavern around square tables. Some flocked to a blazing fire at the lounge's floor-to-ceiling rock hearth. Mac figured the need for a fire in the midst of summer fell into the category of crazy islanders.

The chef had prepared hot and cold appetizers and hors d'oeuvres. They were attractive in shape, color and garnish and displayed buffet style in the banquet room. Two elegantly decorated sheet cakes were the work of a professional. Musical instruments for live entertainment throughout the evening sat on a small stage opposite the food. The lounge bar served beverages for all ages.

Discussions went hush when Mac and Gage zigzagged through the crowd. Fear and doubt filled people's eyes. Anger came out in muttered misgivings. Some sat with fisted drinks trying to forget the horrid events by means of alcohol inducement. Still, exhilarated laughter from several who appeared not to care either way filtered through those enraged by the murders. Scanning the tops of heads, Mac didn't spot Katharine's fiery red hair anywhere. His worrying was legitimate.

"This way, Mac. I'll introduce you to my aunt and parents."

"Gage, you made it."

"Hi, Ma," he said, giving her cheek a peck. "This is Mac Dobarchon. Mac, my mother, Paula, and my dad, Frank."

Mrs. LeNoir's eyes were set relatively far apart. Even-tempered and tolerant, they were downright neighborly in an endearing way. Mac wondered if people took advantage of her good sport.

Katharine had her mother's modest frame, but her sharp, stabbing blue eyes belonged to her father. Skepticism to everything and everyone, he thought. "Mrs. LeNoir, it's nice to meet you."

"Mercy," she spoke eagerly, and hooked her arm inside his. "Call me Paula, and this old goat standing with his mouth open, just call him Frank. We're very informal around here."

Mac shook hands with Frank LeNoir. His firm grip reminded Mac of his daughter's need to control. "Good to meet you, sir."

"Likewise, Mac. What're you drinking?"

"Dad, we can't stay. Ma, is Katharine here yet?"

"I haven't seen her since she left this morning. Check with Nicole or Michelle while I introduce Mac to Suzanne."

Paula led him toward a polished woman with a raked back hairstyle. Clearly, the woman went to painstaking efforts to conceal age with grace.

"Suzanne, this is Mac Dobarchon. Mac, this is Suzanne and Frank's brother, Garrett."

Mac and Garrett exchanged handshakes. The LeNoir brothers had similar stone-like firmness of face and flesh. The second Mrs. LeNoir, who eyed him with suspicious curiosity, was enthroned like royalty on her chair. Impeccable attire intensified her prudishness. Down turned lips implied worldly pessimism and the anticipation of unhappy outcomes.

"Happy birthday, Mrs. LeNoir."

"Thank you. You're that young man from Green Bay who's working with Gage on these horrific murders aren't you? Mr. and Mrs. Henderson are terribly distraught over their daughter's death. This is a grave loss for our communities, Mr. Dobarchon, not to mention the rest of us are suffering fright with all this killing."

"Suzanne!" Paula exclaimed. "I told you we were not going to discuss this when I picked you up."

"You also said we were going shopping. How is it that you cleverly kept this party a secret from me? Never mind," Suzanne said, waving off her in-law. "It's my birthday. I will talk about whatever I want with whomever I want. Thank God, I moved to Bayfield. Now appease me young man. Are you, or are you not, working with my nephew to catch the killer?"

"Yes, I am."

"What exactly are you doing to capture him?" she demanded, waving a speared finger at him.

"Oh for God's sake, Suzanne. Garrett was a cop for thirty years. Stop being a ditz when you already know they aren't going to tell you anything."

"She's been acting like a ditz her whole damn life," Iola cooed behind them. "Do you really think she has the will to change this late in life?"

Paula swung around with Mac in tow on her arm as Suzanne hissed under breath.

"Don't start, Iola. I'm lidding this pot before it boils over. This isn't the time or the place and you both know it," Paula said with a sideways glance at her sister-in-law.

Suzanne's posture straightened more. Her superiority reigned with predominance. Iola closed the circle in a standoff and Mac was trapped between them.

"Iola, you still don't know what to do with the sense God gave you," Suzanne spat.

"At least God gave me sense."

Paula exhaled heavily. "Mac, this is Iola Tibbs. I'm afraid you'll have to excuse both of them for their lack of manners."

Iola slid her arm into Mac's free one. "My, oh my, if I were only a few years younger."

"Harlot," Suzanne puffed.

"Strumpet."

"You're—"

"Happy birthday, Aunt Suzanne," Gage said, from behind them. "Sorry about the short visit, but we stopped by for a few minutes and need to get back to the station. Mac, let's grab something to eat."

He bid farewell to the women and followed the police chief.

"Thought you might need rescuing. They've been that way for as long as I can remember."

"Mac, you made it!"

Nicole and Michelle approached.

"We took a breather. Have either of you seen Katharine?"

"No," Nicole said. "In this crowd she could be anywhere."

"Nicole, you did good planning the party."

"Thanks," she said, flashing him a glittering smile.

Scanning the crowd, he saw Katharine enter the room. "I'll be right back."

He picked his way through the growing group toward Katharine. A feigned plastic smile, the concocted one he knew well disguised her exhaustion. When she spotted him, her expression brightened and his heart did that little flipping thing. They met halfway and he told her, "It makes a man feel good when he's greeted with a smile."

"Is that right?"

"Where have you been, Princess?"

"The library and the historical museum. The latter proved a waste of time and I have to talk to you privately."

"You spent the day reading? Why?"

"That's what I need to talk to you about."

"First, you'll wish your aunt a happy birthday," he said, taking her elbow and guiding her. "Gage already introduced me to the entire family."

"You met my parents?"

"Does that bother you?"

"Well, no, it's—"

"Katharine!"

"Great. Just what I need on no sleep," she muttered.

She didn't have to look to know Josie Stewart's voice. But watching, she thought it incredible the way folks cleared a path as Josie be-bopped through them all until she stood in front of them.

"How's it goin', Josie?"

"Couldn't be better. I've been looking for you ever since Curt told me he saw you jogging. You left so soon after graduation. Well, you can just imagine what most of us thought around here."

"No I can't," she spewed out.

"I was shocked when I learned you were helping find Jess' killer. It's so nice that you're Gage's little ole assistant. Honestly, Katharine, you still look the same. It's obvious you still spend as little as possible for clothes."

Katharine inhaled a quick sharp breath as Mac gripped her arm.

"Do you have kids? Are you married?"

Katharine shook her head.

"We should run together some day. But you look like you could put on weight. How is it you never fully developed? I've been working out for several years lifting weights and making dying efforts to keep my shape ...,"

The street taught Katharine to tolerate criticism, but the way Josie was eyeballing Mac, with the same sex-craved eyes she had in school heated her insides. She crossed her arms tightly for self-control and silently suffered through the verbal diarrhea. It was working she observed the way Mac stared at Josie. But who wasn't staring at her breasts popping out of the low cut, sexy, silky, slinky, pathetic dress.

"... let me tell you. Curt and the boys are so upset over these murders. It took every ounce of my energy to convince them to come here today."

The Stewart boys had their paunches shoved against the bar tossing back Tequila shooters. "I can see exactly how concerned the boys are," Katharine snapped.

"With all this killing, I haven't had a decent night's sleep in a coon's age. I'm just so scared that I just hate when Curt goes off to work. Now Katharine, where are your manners? I've been patiently waiting for an introduction to this very fine-looking man."

"And you can keep waiting," she replied, her insides exploding in jealous rage when Josie laid her hand on Mac's arm. She turned sharply and was pulled back.

"Would you excuse us? Katharine and I were just on our way to see the guest of honor."

Guiding her in the opposite direction, Mac teased, "Careful, Princess. Your teeth are showing."

"And you're drooling."

"I am not drooling."

"Assistant my ass! If that rich little bitch had any clue."

"Just keep walking."

"We need to talk," she said hotly.

"So you said. But unless you know Patriot's whereabouts, it can wait. You haven't slept and I'm convinced you haven't eaten since Nicole brought you that rabbit food yesterday. Wait here while I get you a plate and some iced tea."

Further rebuttal was lost in Suzanne's greeting. "Well, Katharine Regina, finally you show up."

"Happy birthday."

"You haven't been over to Bayfield for a visit since you came back. Why is that?"

"We've been busy," she replied, shoving clenched fists into her jacket pockets.

"Too busy to visit?"

"I'm working with Gage on the homicides."

"Young lady you need to stop all this silly nonsense and find yourself a husband. Leave a man's work to men."

The challenge stiffened her. She tossed her hair over her shoulders in a gesture of defiance ready to retaliate when someone tapped her on the shoulder. It was Michelle.

"I need to talk to you for a minute."

They moved through the crowd toward a vacant wall. "What's up?"

"Nothing. I'm familiar with Suzanne's sarcasm. I got the you-should-keep-your-man-happy speech, too. I also saw your reaction to Josie and figured you needed an out after the bombardment. You almost ripped Josie's eyeballs out when she put her hand on Mac."

"Did not," she snapped.

"Josie's not worth showing the anger especially when Mac only has eyes for you."

"The slobber was dribbling out of his mouth and landing on top of the bitch's boobs."

Michelle gaped at her before bursting into laughter. "You forget who you're talking to? He did everything he could to look everywhere but at her boobs."

"You're siding with him."

"Oh, Katharine," Michelle said compassionately. "You've always had good sense about everything except in the area of relationships."

"You mean like recognizing you were abused?"

"Ever since you discovered your dad preparing Gage to replace him, you've shut down your feelings toward men. I think you still believe all men will cause the same pain your dad inflicted on you in seventh grade."

"Michelle, why do they all think I'm not qualified to be a cop?"

"Since when does Katharine Regina LeNoir care what others think? Forget 'em. Find a way to open your heart again."

Though they were each speaking to different subjects, Michelle's comfort sent unexpected warmth surging through her. "Sully told me to open my heart. Do you remember how he always compared the three of us to the Cadotte ghosts?"

"He still does," Michelle said frankly. "Katrina for Katharine, Nicolina for Nicole and Mikala for me."

"I'm starting to think he might be right."

"*Omigod!* Have you gone completely off your rocker from the stress?"

"I dunno. I'm not sleeping, which doesn't help."

"It shows. You look like walking death. You know. Marmy."

"I feel marmy." Katharine half laughed now. "Michelle, I'm hearing Katrina's cry. The first time was at Michigan Island. Remember when I mentioned it?"

"I didn't want to say anything in front of Nicole."

"I heard Katrina again the day I went out to Raspberry. Sully showed up and confirmed it. Then Mac and I heard her the night Jessica disappeared. If it weren't for them, I'd think I was crazy. I heard her again this morning at the house."

"Mac heard Katrina?"

Katharine nodded as she scanned the crowded room of island folks. Still steaming over Josie's criticism of her wardrobe, she glanced down at herself. Was everyone staring at her because of the way she dressed or was she imagining that, too? She thought she heard the murmured words, *'the least she could is dress up for her aunt's party'*.

"Ignore them, I do. They're curious about why you came back the same way they're all dying to find out the juicy details of my divorce."

"How have you kept it from them?"

"It's hasn't been easy. Let's get back to our ghosts. I never told Nicole this because she believes less than you do in ghosts, but after my divorce, Sully asked me if I'd ever heard Mikala crying before I'd taken my vows."

"Had you?"

"Not once. Lately, I swear I can hear her and think I'm losing it. If what Sully told us all our lives is true, it doesn't make any sense since I'll never allow men to be part of my life again. Nicole is right. I won't give them a chance. I can't."

"Believe me I understand what you went through and I feel horrid for not having been here to help you."

"It wasn't your fault and I'm sorry I tried to blame you."

Katharine hugged her. "I'm here if you ever want to talk about it."

"Thanks, but I'm just not ready."

"When you are, girlfriend, I'm here," Katharine said before she ended the squeeze.

"I love Nicole, but some days I don't think she totally understands what I went through."

"Maybe not, but she does care. She'd give her right arm for either one of us. It's awkward for her when she never had parents. She's afraid of saying the wrong thing."

"I know," Michelle sighed.

"Tell you what. I'll try to open my heart if you'll open yours again."

Michelle studied her for a long moment. "Okay. I'll agree to try only because I think this just might be right for you, Katharine."

"You never do what you're told," a male voice interrupted behind them.

Michelle jumped as Katharine swung around to face Mac. A dark shadow on his jaw complimented his scowl. "Excuse me?"

"Thought I told you to stay put. I've been carrying this plate around for ten minutes looking for you." Shoving it into her hand, he ordered, "Here, eat."

She readied to spout off when Michelle flashed a steadfast look. "I'm sorry, Dobarchon. Michelle wanted to talk. Thanks for getting me something. You were right, I'm starving."

"We'll finish this up later," Michelle said, walking away.

"She doesn't like me much, does she?"

Swallowing a barbecue meatball, Katharine asked, "Why would you think that?"

"The way she keeps her distance."

"While I eat, you watch her interact for a while and tell me what you observe."

Mac kept one eye on Michelle and the other on Katharine while she wolfed down everything he put on the plate. After several moments, he had both eyes on Michelle. She nervously jumped three times when people approached her from behind. She stepped back from face-to-face encounters keeping safe distance between her and others. Though she smiled, it came with extreme difficulty and hesitation.

"Who did it to her?"

"It started a week after her honeymoon. She filed for divorce seven months later."

He crossed his arms tightly. "She had him arrested didn't she?"

"I asked the same thing. She didn't tell anyone except Nicole. My father discovered it accidentally, but she refused his help."

"That's not acceptable."

"Mac. Abused victims have already been forced. You just can't push some to do the right thing because the law says so. She did the next best thing and got rid of him."

"Katharine." He took her napkin and wiped barbecue sauce off her chin. "I meant it's not acceptable what he did to her. I abhor men who hurt women and children a great deal more than murderers."

She merely stared wordlessly at him. His eyes were dark with rage. His jaw muscle twitched against already hardened features.

"If I ever meet this guy, he won't have to worry about jail. I'll teach him a lesson he'll never forget."

"Get in line, Dobarchon."

"Not a chance, Princess. He shows up, he's mine."

He meant what he said and the idea of it melted Katharine down quickly while the beat of her heart sped up. His dynamic vitality to protect her friend had disintegrated any previous misgivings she had about him. A persistent warm glow flowed through her so much she had to force herself to settle down. Mac had spoken to her heart's desire.

"You're doing it again, Princess."

The tone of his voice had softened and butterflies flittered inside her stomach. His steady gaze bore into her now with some silent expectation. "Doing what?"

"Hypnotizing me with those sexy eyes. It's supposed to be sunny tomorrow. Go sailing with me."

Feeling the heat rise in her cheeks, she guzzled back her iced tea then tossed everything in a nearby container. "Based on the last time you asked me to go sailing, it sounds like you're inviting me to have sex."

He threw his head back in laughter. People looked and her face heated up more. "Well. Now that we've got their attention, let's really give them something to talk about and leave."

He gave her no time to recant, grabbed her hand, tugged her from the room and ushered her outside. In one circular motion, she was in his arms putting hers around his neck. His mouth came down hard and powerful. Her pulse leaped with excitement as her heart hammered against her chest. Her own eager response shocked her before the kiss changed. His lips softened to touch like a whisper, massaging her tired soul. Completely weakened, she clung to him, hungry for more before they parted mere inches and gazed at each other.

"Princess, I wanna unveil all your secret weapons including the gun you're concealing. But before I do, I need to tell you something."

"That you prefer Josie's company?"

He let out a long, audible breath and pulled her closer to him. "She thrives on scandal. The more sex and lust the better for that one."

"You were looking," Katharine said hastily.

No, Princess, I wasn't. And I do not prefer that kind's company."

The man was just full of surprises and she pulled back to study him.

"I swear," he said.

"That's about the nicest thing a man's ever said to me."

"What kind of men have you been dating?"

"I'd rather not discuss that subject."

"Well, I've got one you'll want to talk about," he said, letting go of her.

She began walking with him. Early evening, the drizzle had

stopped and a stimulating scent of evergreen hung in the humid air. The shroud of gray clouds had trapped the piney aroma. Katharine looked up at Mac. His face had grown dark with pained suffering.

"What is it? What did you want to tell me?"

Taking her hand, they strolled toward her parked car. "Katharine, Green Bay has suspended me."

Coming to a jarring halt, she blurted, "What? Why?"

"It was the second mistake I made in my career. After the last homicide in Green Bay, I had an argument with the police chief and mayor because they wanted to air Patriot's picture. I was trying to cope with my guilt over Clarissa's death. Anyway, the mayor went against the Task Force's better judgment and plastered his picture on every TV station and in the papers. In the heat of the moment, I blew up. Guess you could say I lost control when I tattooed my fist into his face."

Katharine winced. "How bad was it?"

"He's missing a couple of teeth and needed stitches in his forehead. I wouldn't be here now, but Sanders thought it might be good for me to get away for a while."

"Then you had no idea Patriot was here killing again?"

Shaking his head solemnly, Mac told her, "My Captain called to inform me of the outcome of my actions. He said he wasn't gonna let the Chief know he'd made contact with me."

"Then he's backing you?"

Shrugging, he said, "Yes and no. He agrees with me and the Task Force about airing the photo. Given my relation to Clarissa, my actions were still unwarranted."

"How long is the suspension?"

"Thirty days with a condition. The mayor wants my badge or he's gonna file assault charges."

"Technically, you're working without a badge?"

He nodded.

"So we just get Gage to swear you in here. He already swore me in."

"Katharine, I don't want to involve either one of you in my problem on the pretense it might harm the case."

"We're already involved."

"I want this bastard put away for life but I can't voluntarily resign until he is. I won't let Linda down."

"What're you gonna do if they force you to resign?"

"Haven't thought about it. Gimme a lift back to the bungalow."

She drove in silence ruminating over the earlier conversation with Michelle. Her best friend had nailed it. She'd unknowingly carried the painful setback throughout her life and now compared it to the ache in Mac's eyes. It didn't come close. She had an urgent need to toss her own misery and failures into Superior in order to relieve Mac's grief. She just wasn't sure how she planned to do it. Mac also made a valid point about harming the case, but she'd find a way around the problem—she always did. Since he'd lost the most, he had to be the one to receive credit for Patriot's arrest. And that, she realized, brought up her second dilemma. Katharine stopped her car in front of the bungalow. "Yes."

"Yes what?"

She looked up at the clearing sky. "Sun's gonna be out tomorrow. Yes, I'll go sailing with you."

"Princess, come inside with me for a while."

"We're both existing on little or no sleep. Are you sure?"

"I've never been more sure of anything," he confessed.

They exited her beat up car and walked together. Once inside, she took off her jacket as Mac tossed his and traipsed across the room.

"I'm getting myself a scotch. You want anything to drink?"

"Water's fine," she replied, sinking into an overstuffed chair and adjusting her gun from poking her ribs. Mac handed her bottled water and parked himself on the arm of the chair she'd chosen.

"What did you want to talk to me about?"

Katharine looked up and slid her hand into the one he offered. She'd already decided she'd only talk facts. "I spent most of the day at the Island's library reading about Madeline and Michel Cadotte."

Kissing the back of her hand, he said, "I thought you didn't believe in ghosts."

His actions were distracting but she continued. "Madeline and Michel were real people. What I discovered is that the wedding dates of a couple of their daughters match the dates of your first six homicides. I double checked my findings."

Stunned, Mac dropped her hand and stood. He slugged back the scotch. "Katharine, are you sure?"

"Yes. There's no truth that any of the girls were murdered the night preceding their vows. Each of them did marry in real life and lived to ripe old ages."

"What about a hidden treasure?"

"It doesn't exist," she answered matter-of-factly.

"Do you really think because of a made-up story this bastard hears voices telling him to kill young girls?"

His energy now redirected, Katharine stood and faced him. "Could be. An idea came to me this morning when I heard Katrina the ghost crying again. That's why I went over and read up on the history. I wanted to find out for myself where, if any, is the connection."

"Which means the profile is dead accurate and I was right. Our dirtbag's psychotic and probably hears some fairytale medicine man telling him to kill."

"The other fact I verified is that each daughter was half Native American, half French. Three of them were also sixteen when they married, but not when they died."

Her eyes were intense and as blue as he'd ever seen. He set the glass on a nearby table and pulled Katharine into an intimate embrace. "The entire Task Force including the FBI spent two years trying to figure out the reason why he kills. You did it in a matter of weeks because of a moaning wind."

"I wouldn't go so far as to say that. Nor does it prove why he's doing it. There has to be some significance to the dates with something in his life."

His lips slowly descended to meet hers. She sighed, and the lingering kisses coaxed her.

"Thought you said this wasn't a good idea."

"Did I say that? I don't recall."

His breath was warm against her face as he tasted, sampled and caressed her flesh. He played with her hair and explored the hollow of her back, pressing her closer to him. Her spine tingled with excitement but when he buried his face in her neck breathing kisses, her knees caved and she wrapped her arms around him. He held her tight and devoured her mouth with a more urgent kiss. Their tongues tangled in a dance marathon vibrating a chord that chimed inside of her in resounding celebration. Of what, Katharine had no idea.

He raised his mouth and gazed at her. "You've got a look, Princess. It's begging me to satisfy your quenchless thirst."

The accelerated thumping of her heart kept her from a response. He brushed her lips with his, persuading her more.

"It's the ache to be fulfilled."

It was too hard to resist and too easy to lose herself in the slow trail of compelling kisses he placed along her chin and neck.

"Let me show you," he whispered into her hair.

Slight of breath, Katharine leaned back to study his face, silently debating what she really wanted from Mac Dobarchon. He was magnetic and full of vitality. He'd radiated energy into her tired soul, helped her deal with the unforgettable trauma, and untangled her whirling emotions. Her peeking desire and his hardened interest was lust, she thought, though she couldn't resist when he scooped her into his arms and nuzzled his face in her hair. He kissed the palpitating hollow near her throat. Excitement slithered through her when he grazed an earlobe. Her own eager response shocked her.

"I want you, Princess."

He wasn't asking permission and eased to her feet. Rapidly they removed and hung their gun belts. Mac hooked Katharine by the waist, pulling her close and her heart lurched, began hammering inside of her chest. And then his mouth was on hers again, their tongues touched in a kiss that sang through her veins. He really did know how to drive and control her, did it with the urgency of surviving a storm.

"Are you sure?" she asked.

Taking her hand, he kissed the palm, "You're making my mouth water."

He stroked her back and Katharine arched into him ... his hands were everywhere, exploring, caressing, teasing then at her waist, her back and again pressing her close. Literally seconds passed before they began grabbing, ripping and stripping off their clothes.

Katharine gazed at him like a stalking panther. He could do less himself when her naked body summoned him. She took the first step and he kissed her, trailing a string of kisses along her neck, her collarbone, the swell of her breasts. His mouth dropped lower to her belly, her navel ... and lower.

"Mac!"

She was on the brink of going off the deep end but managed to intertwine her fingers in his hair, his breathing was ragged but his kisses were steady.

"I've waited patiently day and night for you."

She matched his urgency with her own lusty needs touching him intimately. He immediately lifted her into his arms easing her onto the bed.

He devoured her mouth in another greedy kiss. Teasing every inch of her flesh, his fingers moved swiftly as steady as his kisses. He slid a thumb up and down her arms and circled the palms of her hands. He traced sensuous circles around the rosy tips of her breasts until they crested and peaked hard.

She was breathing heavy herself trembling everywhere he touched her with the warmth of his tongue. His search for her pleasure points sent shivers up and down her flesh. Unable to reciprocate, she encouraged him with a hip thrust, felt a helluva formation that electrified her. His hands and lips searched hungrily until both their bodies were slick, moist, and hot, until her wall of defense cracked, until her soul had absolved the anger and fear. She rose to meet him, saw his eyes were dark and dilated, and curled her legs around him.

She had his attention and he abandoned himself to the electricity arcing between them. She felt him getting lost on heated waves that turned dangerous enough to claim their souls. He plunged further and deeper, and together they unearthed a tempo that bound their bodies into one, soaring higher, higher until melting into each other, until he buried himself deeply inside of her.

But she had already erupted to a susceptibility of sorrow and joy, power and hope, of loss and longing. How would she free herself from the control he had on her? While he would merely be filling a moment of physical desire, she had already allowed him to rip her soul apart. Even when the burning within had ignited a blinding light of replenishing spirit, he had drained her of the solitary confinement and had stripped away her failures.

She wondered if his faults had been demolished the way hers had. Had he known the totality that would replace the poverty they each knew, would he have submitted? Regardless, her barren heart couldn't negate the tranquility that flowed between them before each succumbed to the sleep of denied love.

CHAPTER 18

The mantra cry of a woman woke Mac first. He looked at the window and listened. Ghosts had no creditability but the audible weeping was as clear as the cloudless sky. Did Patriot hear this same sound in his head? It certainly didn't contain any messages of death.

He adjusted himself insignificantly. Katharine lay next to him in peaceful sleep. The stress lines were gone from her face. Her hair flowered the pillow cover. The flaming strands definitely a match to the rising sun. This same woman who had once merely fascinated him now made him feel like King Kong on cocaine. Unlike the drug's addictive power, he felt reenergized. His competency had returned because she figured out a vital element to the case. How could he not love her for that? *The very idea of a relationship with anyone made him feel trapped* he answered himself silently.

Emotion overpowered his silent thought and Mac propped his head up with a hand. He lightly brushed red strays of hair away from her face.

Katharine's eyes popped open and she flinched. "What time is it?"

"Good morning, Princess. It's early Sunday," he murmured, caressing her lips with a kiss. He drank in the morning scent of her bedroom flesh, deliberately relishing the taste of her. She moaned when he branded a path down her neck and across her shoulders.

"Let's go sailing."

"Sailing like last night."

"I'm willing to oblige," he responded, exploring her belly, kissing her navel—

His eyes flew open. Mac looked at her then sat up. Chills crawled along his spine with new excitement.

"Mac, what is it?"

He hadn't fully concentrated on one particular piece of evidence. "The tarp."

She sat up, covering her breasts with the sheet. "What about the tarp?"

"Katharine, at the crime scenes of the seventh and eighth victims we discovered threads of a camouflage tarp. Yet there was no evidence of a tarp anywhere near the Henderson girl or the Green Bay victims. Where would someone buy and store a large tarp around here?"

"Boat covers."

"Camouflaged," he spoke automatically. "So they could hide a boat in the brush."

She touched his shoulder. "Mac, do you realize what you just said?"

He glanced back at her, took her hand and kissed each finger.

"You referred to the killer as *they*. More than one. I know you don't want to consider it, but we have to look at the possibility we might be dealing with two killers, a copycat."

"Believe me I've weighed the idea over and over. The problem I'm having is we never released the type of poison the killers use or the fact that the victims were sixteen and Native American. One of three girls murdered here died from paraquat. No one could have known that poison unless Patriot *is* working with someone."

"Then you think Patriot has an accomplice? That there's not a copycat, but one is killing with the abrin and one with paraquat?"

"I'm not sure what to think."

"Considering that the La Pointe murders don't match the marriage dates of the Cadotte daughters an accomplice might explain the murders taking place here," she said.

"If Patriot killed these last three victims, how do we explain the use of different poisons? Has he really started killing more to feed his insanity? Did he switch the poisons to intentionally throw us off his trail? Without those answers, and the results of the Henderson girl's cause of death, we've got a lot of work left to do."

"With the evidence of the seeds we found, what are the odds that Jessica didn't die from abric acid poisoning?"

Deep in thought, he shrugged. "We're missing something. Besides the abrin, the tarp is a new clue. The other thing that's bugging me is how did the Stewart boys find her when we'd searched everywhere?"

Katharine blinked. "I hadn't considered that point. I don't know. Maybe it's time to check them out."

The faraway look on Mac's face meant his direct attention was elsewhere. "I'm gonna grab a shower before we go sailing."

Mac did a double take and seized her wrist. "Princess, as much as I want to have you on a sailboat this case is my priority."

"I know." She kissed him before she slid out of bed and sauntered toward the bathroom.

"Yup, I was right," he said.

"About what?"

"You definitely have a very nice ass."

"Kiss it, Dobarchon."

"As tempting as that offer is, I'm hungry for food. Breakfast will be ready in twenty."

"Last chance," she flaunted, scooting into the bathroom when he vaulted from the bed and stopping abruptly. "Mac! It's an outdoor shower!"

Chuckling, he said, "Yeah, so?"

"What if it was still raining or someone was watching?"

"Singing in the rain would give a peeping tom a dual show."

"I do not sing in the shower or the rain," she told him, and brushed him away to monkey with the water nozzles.

He chuckled again and located his jeans. Tugging them on, he sprinted downstairs and called his partner at home while he made coffee. Early Sunday morning, Cole would grumble and then he'd listen. Bugged by the limitation of his own suspension, Mac wasn't about to jeopardize the case and Cole was the only way around his predicament.

Cole Gilroy not only griped, he cussed up a storm. After hearing the new information, he agreed to some time off. They decided to keep the captain out of the loop and Cole would arrive on the island in a couple of days. Mac filled a mug with steaming coffee when Katharine bounced down the stairs looking better than he'd seen her since first meeting her.

"Thought you said breakfast would be ready, Dobarchon. Who were you talking to?"

He stepped forward embracing her in his arms. "I want you for breakfast."

"You had your chance. Who was on the phone?"

"My partner. He's coming up here midweek since he's still active."

"Good thinking. But let's still have Gage swear you in."

Her seductive eyes were intoxicating and he kissed her again. "You smell sexy, outdoorsy. Refreshed."

"You're horny."

"What're you gonna do about it?" he asked, placing kisses along her neck.

"Last night was fantastic but I already gave you your second chance. Now, we've got work to do."

"Fantastic, eh?"

"Very," she said. "And you need a shave."

Reluctantly, Mac let her go. "Your ghost woke me up this morning, Princess. Fix breakfast while I grab a shower."

"I don't cook for anyone."

"Do it anyway," he insisted, climbing the stairs two at a time.

"You'll be sorry," she muttered, when he disappeared.

Katharine shuffled through the kitchen cupboards. Opening the fridge, she smiled at Mac's thoughtfulness. He'd mixed up a pitcher of iced tea and she poured herself a glass. Leaning against the counter and sipping, a bizarre thought struck her. Throughout her life, she was obsessed with the need for success. She took charge and handled things responsibly because she couldn't tolerate indecisiveness. She'd learned to figure out ways to cope with life's pressures since the moment her father had announced Gage would eventually replace him. What she hadn't realized was how unworthy she'd felt as a result. It did explain why she spent the next fourteen years proving she could do the job her father had refused her. She had consciously rerouted those painful feelings into strong desires of uplifting humanity and saving the world.

She sighed. Last night the passion she experienced with Mac bulldozed that obsession. He had grounded her with a new foundation and she willingly traded in her heart. Without knowing it, the pain of her own hidden desire had connected her back to Madeline Island, her island, and the one she stubbornly ran from years earlier. Now for the first time in her life, she could acknowledge she needed someone, and that, she admitted, answered her question of what she wanted from Mac. Could he see through the physical desire to fulfill her needs? Probably not.

Katrina's embellished cry filled the early morning air and Katharine gazed through the kitchen window. "I sure hope Sully and Michelle are right," she murmured. "I think I'm falling for him, old girl."

* * *

Katharine and Mac sat in the station's conference room reviewing their approach to re-interview the Stewart Brothers when commotion sounded at the back door. Checking it out, Katharine faced her brother at the office threshold. She would have giggled at the disorderly sight of her intoxicated brother except that his gun belt hung on his shoulder.

She stepped toward him, a prominent odor of alcohol consuming her and cursed under breath. Katharine yanked the belt off his shoulder. "You know better than to mix alcohol and weapons."

"Pis'queak, gimme that!"

"Not on your life, Bro. What did you do last night?"

Smacking his lips, Gage stuttered, "Didn't get lucky like you. Johnnie and me chugged a lug." He wobbled on his feet stuttering some more. "Sis, I really really loves you! And Mac ain't bad neither!"

Before she could catch him, Gage staggered backward and toppled to the office floor.

"Oh, big brother," she whispered, "I love you, too." She

stooped and stroked his scruffy hair lovingly. "Mac, I need help here."

Mac appeared, looking over Katharine's shoulder. "He knock back a few?"

"More than a few. Help me get him to the cot in the other room."

Katharine grabbed his feet and Mac picked Gage up under his shoulders. "Poor sap is flatlined. He's gonna regret this one."

After laying Gage on a cot, Katharine said, "He isn't a big drinker. I've never known him to have more than two beers in one sitting. He said he was with someone named John."

"I couldn't get a hold of the Stewart boys and Del called. He's dropping off the autopsy report shortly."

They left Gage to sleep. "I'll call Josie and find out where the clan is."

"The way those three were tossing back shooters last night, I doubt they're gonna be any better off than Gage. What do you say we go boat hunting?"

Del entered the station, handing over an enveloped file. "I've released the body to her parents. Funeral's gonna be in a couple of days. This was one of the hardest one's I've done. You'll see in the report where I noted traces of poisonous beans were found in her stomach. There's one thing different between our three victims."

Mac had already opened the file and was reading when he looked up at Del. "What's that?"

"Although I didn't find semen present, the Henderson and Martin girls weren't virgins. Both died of heart failure caused from the abrin. Wicket died of respiratory distress and lung failure brought on by the ingestion of paraquat. She *was* a virgin."

"Same as the first six," Mac replied.

"Morning," Gus Rankin said, entering the office. "I wanted to personally deliver the lab's results."

"What've you got?" Mac asked.

"According to the tox screen, the peanuts you found at the scene were mixed with the poisonous seeds abrin. The Johnny Walker liquor did not contain the chemical paraquat. However, we had a hit on the latents found on the bottle."

Holding his breath, Mac finally asked, "Patriot, right?"

"The match came back listed to the alias, Kenneth William Sheldon. The prints we matched show an arrest down in Florida back in January of this year on a felony. You wanna take a shot at what he got caught stealing?"

Katharine piped up, "Plants."

"Not exactly. Apparently, the guy who belongs to our latents placed an order for a hundred abrus precatorius plants. He went to the greenhouse to pick them up and wrote a check, got the plants loaded into a pick-up, went into a nearby store and was nailed for walking out with a carton of cigarettes."

Mac shook his head. "How's a carton of cigarettes amount to a felony?"

"There's more. Our match, who the police later listed with a real name of John Doe, told the locals down there about the plants in his truck and when they checked the parking lot, they found the large amount suspicious. They went in and talked to the clerk at the garden shop who'd rung up the order. The personal check John Doe wrote matched the Florida D-L their guy had on him along with the pick-up's plates. So they left the truck in the parking lot, took John Doe downtown, booked him as Kenneth Sheldon on the petty theft and released him. Later that day, the real Kenneth Sheldon filed a police report for the theft of his pick-up, checks and drivers license he kept in the glove compartment."

"And Patriot was long gone without the locals ever finding out who he really was," Mac snarled. "That would explain why we couldn't find him after December."

"About sums it up," Gus responded. "And he did get away with the plants."

"But it still doesn't connect the paraquat he used on seven of the nine victims."

Katharine added, "Or where Patriot hid the hundred plants and how he got them back here in the winter. Was the pick-up truck ever recovered?"

"Yeah," Gus said. "It never left Florida. Other than the check he used to pay for the plants, the I-D and checkbook were still in the truck. Man with a vicious purpose has a conscience."

"Did you check with the locals down there to see if they've had any murders that match ours?"

"No and I didn't check out how long your perp was there either."

"I'll look into it but I'm betting not long since his apartment rent is paid on time." Mac looked at Katharine. "What did Joe say about the seeds? Something about the pods."

"The poison seeds are inside pods about an inch or so long. Maybe Patriot stripped the plants of their seeds and just mailed the seeds back here."

Mac couldn't dwell on the idea of this case venturing into another state. "All we have to do is figure out to what address. Del, did you find any evidence of a tarp at the Henderson crime scene?"

"Not a trace."

"This tells me he's using the tarp to move the body for discovery. It'd make sense in country like this compared to the city."

"Mac, the wife and I have plans to go out on the lake today. I just wanted to get my findings back to you quickly. If you need anything else, give me a call."

Shaking hands with Gus, he said, "Thanks, we will." Gus left and redirecting his attention, he asked Del. "Was there any evidence of drugs in the Henderson girl?"

"Marijuana and alcohol. I had the liquor analyzed. It's a match with the Johnny Walker Black and was mixed with the ground up seeds and peanuts in her stomach."

"Ground up? We found whole seeds mixed with nuts at the crime scene."

"Somehow he has to break the protective covering to get to the poison. The food content in her stomach was ground up as if done in a blender. She died slowly like the others and the only other difference was early discovery. She'd been dead about four hours evident by rigor—stiffening in the small muscles, eyelids, face, lower jaw and neck. It hadn't spread to the rest of her body."

"Anything else?"

"I've documented precisely how insects provide a method for determining the time of death. There's a universal death scent, which attracts hundreds of insects to a corpse. Within ten minutes the first to arrive are the more common green flies. They feed on flesh and lay their eggs in the olfactory areas. She hadn't been dead twelve hours since those eggs hadn't hatched into maggots that feed off body tissue. The rigidity of the body I mentioned comes just after four hours."

"Okay then. Hopefully, we won't need your services anymore."

"I'll keep my fingers crossed. I know you'll call if you do. Later," Del said, and left the police station.

Mac closed the door behind the medical examiner. "You've got that look, Princess. What's on your mind?"

"The virginity. Why were all but two victims virgins?"

His brow tilted with uncertainty. "Does that mean your doubting your own theory?"

Katharine paced the tiled floor. "I think you may be right. There really are two people that are doing the killing together."

"Let's go back to the conference room and analyze everything we know." They did and Mac pulled the photos from the files and posted them on the board one at a time. "The first homicide, Amelia Rainbird is on July second. Runaway, sixteen, Native American."

Katharine sat down and watched as one by one, Mac put up each photo of the dead victims. Teardrops touched her heart when he hesitated on the sixth. His niece had the same jet-black hair as her uncle. Her innocent eyes were large and brown.

"October eighth we find Emma Coldbath, same stats. Third homicide is Marcia Racine found on December twenty-seventh also same stats as victims one and two. Six months slip by and victim number four dies a few days after her birthday. The same date, July second, as victim one only a year later. She's half Native American. Victim five dies October eighth, her stats match the first three victims. December twenty-seventh we find Clarissa Noma, who disappeared," he hesitated, "or ran the day after her birthday the first week in December. She was half Native American like victim four who'd also been reported missing the day following her sixteenth birthday. Clarissa wasn't found until the week between Christmas and New Years."

He said it like none of the homicides bothered him and Katharine asked, "Are the dates when they actually died or when the victim's were discovered."

"Discovery," he said. "The first six victims didn't know each other and were runaways."

"All six are wearing a hand-made bracelet and died of paraquat poisoning. Left at the scene is an empty Johnny Walker Black liquor bottle."

"The bottles were in one piece and wiped clean." Inhaling deeply, Mac added, "They all had marijuana in their system."

"Did you uncover any other similarities between these six victims?"

"They all went to the same school and had problems at home. Some minor, some not."

"Where did you find each victim?"

"Outside within a mile radius of the same sleazy bar." Mac glanced over his shoulder at Katharine. "Which did not sell our liquor. It's readily available in most off-sales but not very popular. Goes for around thirty-five bucks a liter."

"Any steady boyfriends?"

"None. We interviewed kids they hung with and kids they didn't. Came up empty."

"Where'd you find the print that I-D'd Patriot?"

Mac crossed his arms, held his chin with one hand and began pacing. "On the bottle. The match came back from an O-U-I arrest a few years back in Green Bay."

"O-U-I?"

"Operating under the influence."

"Okay," she replied, knowing it in Minnesota as DUI. "This year, July second rolled by without incident and you take time off. When you arrive here on July twenty-sixth, Joey discovers the seventh victim. Only this time she's dead because of abric acid poisoning and the liquor bottle is broken in pieces. She's not a virgin."

"There's evidence of the body being dragged on a tarp because camouflage threads are discovered at the crime scene. Victim eight is discovered four days later dead from paraquat. Virgin."

Katharine looked up. Mac's back muscles were taut and strained. "And victim nine, Jessica Henderson, is the only victim discovered at the location of death. Death resulted from abrin poisoning for the second time. Mac?"

He turned around to face her. "What?"

"Our second victim was found dead from paraquat just four days after the first one who died from the abrin."

"Yes, I know."

"You're right to be suspicious of the Stewart boys. It's too coincidental they forgot they had a hunting shack."

"Based on the facts of each poison used, there's no way one person could physically kill both girls at the same time either. That shack was too small."

"Maybe Patriot was experimenting with the poisons on victims seven and eight. They were the only two who knew each other and both were Ashland runners. What if he made the Wicket girl watch the slow death of her friend?"

"That's not a bad theory considering the hut was located behind the Upland Cottage Patriot rented. He could have kept her tied up there."

"Yeah," Katharine said, getting a juice out of the fridge. "Experimenting between the two poisons was Joey's idea and it does fall in sync with the rosary pea warding off evil spirits."

"You mean warding off voices in a psychotic's head."

"Let's go roust the Stewart's out of bed. I don't care if they're still drunk. I wanna know if they're involved in anyway."

"Princess, I love the way your lip curls when you're riled." He moved toward her and pulled Katharine into his arms. "First, I want some lunch since you refused to cook breakfast for me."

"Dobarchon, haven't you figured out I don't do what anyone tells me?"

"You were very cooperative last night."

He took her mouth slowly, wanting to pursue more. He also benefited from the contact and the way it inflamed his insides. Desire raced, tongues came together and their breathy sighs and moans were squelched in a prolonged kiss.

"You keep seducing me, Princess, we'll never catch Patriot."

"I'm not the one packing a pistol."

"Pistol?" He grinned at her then gloated. "Sarge is a forty-four and if you'll recall, packs a mighty punch."

Katharine smothered a giggle with the roll of her eyes. "Just what I need. A guy who compares his male engine to a respectable weapon."

Discharging rich laughter, Mac gave her a playful look.

"No time now. Come on, I'll buy lunch. Just don't ever expect me to cook."

"Not ever?" he asked, with a flick to her chin.

"Never. Lemme check on Gage before we leave. I wonder where Joey is today."

"Worked last night. He'll be in this afternoon with Pete and Alesha."

* * *

After lunch at the Tavern, they tracked down Kevin and Mark Stewart. The interviews were somewhat laborious with both were toasted to the gills. Neither fully grasped that they were being questioned as potential suspects. Mark, the youngest, had alibis for all nine murders. Katharine thought it bizarre Mark could remember back two years when Kevin's answers left them with doubts. The drunkard had difficulty remembering what he did last week let alone two years ago. It also took arduous efforts on Katharine's part to remain objective through Kevin's leers at her. Her distrust of him didn't prove anything, but over the course of two hours, Kevin nervously inhaled an entire pack of cigarettes, told them he'd never been to Green Bay and did not know or meet any of the victims except Jessica Henderson.

"You have a serious look, Princess. What's on your mind?"

"It amazes me how much you ask me that question. In the two plus years Steven and I were together, he could've cared less how I felt let alone what I was thinking."

"I see it a lot. And people wonder why relationships don't work. Was he another cop?"

"No. I met him one day when my car broke down. He's a mechanic and owns his own garage. He worked the proverbial day hours. I'm sure in the end that was the hidden meaning behind a majority of our arguments. His bed time was my breakfast and vice versa."

"Did you love him?"

She shrugged. "I thought I once did."

"Is that who you were thinking about just now?"

His tough-boy features didn't disguise the obvious. "Is that jealousy?"

"Princess—"

"Dobarchon, I read you like a book. I was thinking about how much I despise Kevin Stewart and how my personal feelings are running interference. Turn here, Josie and Curt live down that way."

Mac did. "Then you have doubts about what Kevin told us?"

"Some, yes. It's hard to tell through the tragedy of alcohol if he's being truthful. I'm more concerned with the fact that we interviewed them in a drunken state. Will it hold up in court? There it is, on the right. What do you think?"

"I agree with you about Kevin. Mark is a follower and does what he's told. Certain innocence about him separates him from Kevin. As far as holding up in court, neither of them gave us anything we can use for or against them. Later, if necessary, we'll Mirandize them and take a formal statement."

Mac parked in front of the house and both exited his Jeep. A teenager with Josie's blond hair exited the pretentious house.

"Hi, I'm Katharine LeNoir. You must be Clyde. Is your dad home?" Katharine looked past the kid as the screen door swung open and Josie came flying out of the house.

"Katharine, you made quite a splash last night the way you left the party. Kevin already called. He said you'd be coming here. Curt didn't get home until seven this morning and is sleeping now. Gage can come back later and talk to him."

"Josie, wake him up. This is about Jessica's homicide and we have a few more questions to ask Curt."

With her eyes on Mac, she said, "Curt has nothing to say to Gage's assistant."

"Josie. See this," Katharine said, whipping out the badge Gage gave her. She caught Mac's downward smile as he inched backward. Yanking her windbreaker open to expose her nine millimeter, Katharine said, "Now avert your eyes on this before you think about calling me Gage's assistant again."

A Josie gaped at the weapon, Katharine ordered, "Go wake Curt up so *I* can talk to him. Right now."

"Clyde, come with me."

When the kid followed Josie into the house, Katharine said,

"Wipe that smirk off your face, Dobarchon."

"You certainly know how to redirect someone's attention. I doubt she'll give me anymore predatory stares."

Curbing her aggravation, Katharine snarled, "It'd be in the floozy's best interest."

"Careful, Princess. You're gritting your teeth and turning envy green."

"You wish."

Mac propped an elbow on Katharine's shoulder. "Would you like me to tell you what I'm wishing for right now?"

"No."

"I was thinking about last night."

"Liar. You were watching her wiggle that tight ass of hers."

"Princess, she's as splashy as this house and not my type." He kissed the top of her head. "I already told you that."

It was an act of defiance to cross her arms. Katharine didn't know how to justify feelings she didn't understand, but she resisted fueling Mac's ego further with an argument. Minutes later, Curt weaved out through the front door half-dressed in a pair of jeans.

"What's up? Josie said you wanted to talk to me."

"Curt, we want to ask you a few more questions. We've already talked to Kevin and Mark today."

He lit up a cigarette. "No problem. Mind if we stay out here? Josie won't let me smoke in the house and she's getting me coffee. Either of you want anything?"

Mac and Katharine shook their heads.

"Hope you'll forgive me. I'm feeling the aftermath of the party last night. What time did Gage make it in this morning?"

Katharine shot Curt a stunned look. "Gage was with *you* last night?"

"Does that surprise you, Katharine?"

"No. He said he was drinking with some guy named John."

Curt half smiled, squinting under the bright sunlight. "That'd be Johnny Walker Black. As in liquor. We slugged back a bottle of it."

"You did that after drinking shooters?" Mac questioned, with raised eyebrows.

Taking a drag off his cigarette, Curt nodded. "Not the smartest thing I've ever done. You mind if we do this in the shade?"

Katharine and Mac followed Curt behind the house to an awning-covered patio. When they sat down around a glass-top table, Mac began. "Curt, do you and your brothers drink Johnny Black frequently?"

"Shit no. Too expensive."

"As we told your brothers, this will be informal. We need a few more questions answered while conducting our investigation."

"*We're* suspects? You think one of us killed Jess?"

"You're not under arrest or any obligation to answer our questions. You also have the right to retain a lawyer before you say anything to us."

"You just said I haven't been arrested. What the hell do I need a lawyer for?"

"It's your legal right to have representation at any time during a routine police investigation."

"I didn't kill Jess and I don't need a lawyer!"

"Then you're willing to answer our questions?" Mac asked.

Curt shifted uneasily then looked at Katharine. "You don't really believe I had something to do with Jessica's murder, do you?"

"You aren't the only one we're questioning," she replied. "Like Mac said, this is routine. If you want an attorney, you can certainly have one present before you say anything."

"Jesus H. Christ, Katharine! Does Gage think I had something to do with Jess' murder?"

"Curt, this is Mac's case."

Josie exited the house carrying a tray of cups and coffee. She avoided Katharine by going the long way around the table. "Sweetie, they can't be serious to think you killed poor Jessica."

"Baby, don't upset yourself any more than you already are. Go on back inside."

"No. I want to hear what they have to say."

Josie sat next to Curt after pouring him coffee and adding extra sugar. Mac then asked a second time. "Curt, are you willing to answer our questions?"

"Yeah," he blew out.

"Okay. Where were you last Monday night? The night Jessica

Henderson disappeared."

"Clyde had a baseball game in Ashland. I got home late from work, showered and took the ferry back to Bayfield. I met up with Josie at the game. She took Clyde over in her car. After they won the game, the three of us stopped for pizza."

"Every parent at the game can vouch for Curt. In fact," Josie sneered, "Clyde's best friend Matt and his parents went with us for pizza."

"How'd you know about the hut where you and your brothers found Jessica?"

"Is that what this is about?" His eyes shifted from Mac to Katharine. "I thought Mark told you. Gage knows. We made the shack for trapping a few years back. Now we use it mostly for deer hunting. I haven't been there since last fall and Kevin thought we should check it out."

"Did you know either Sherry Martin or Jennifer Wicket?" Mac asked.

Curt slugged back his coffee and refilled his cup a second time. "Nope. How would I? Thought they were from Ashland."

"Then you've never seen or met them?"

"*No*, goddammit!"

"Have you or your brothers ever been to Green Bay, Curt?"

"Green Bay? You think one of us had something to do with *those* killings?"

"It's routine to ask."

He exhaled. "Once, a few years back. Got my hands on Packer tickets."

"That's not easy to do," Mac responded.

"Josie and Clyde went with me and we stayed with her cousin. Kevin, Mark, Clyde and I went to the game. Never been there before and haven't been back since."

"Kevin was with you?" Mac glanced at Katharine as Curt confirmed it with a head nod. "Do you know if Kevin has gone to Green Bay other times?"

"I'm not his keeper," Curt said.

"I visit my cousin in Green Bay several times a year but Curt doesn't go with me," Josie informed them. "He says all we're gonna do is talk girl stuff and since she's not married, he doesn't want to be around us."

"Curt, can you recall where you were within a week of the dates July second, October eighth, and December twenty-seventh the previous two years?"

"Not unless Josie had something going on and marked it on the family calendar. Even then I doubt I'd remember it."

Mac stood, careful not to bump his head on the low end of the awning. "That's it for now."

"For now?"

"For now?" Josie repeated. "This is preposterous! How dare you come into our home and accuse my husband of murder."

"Baby, they've got nothing because I'm innocent." Curt stood. "I did not kill Jess or any of the other girls."

"Then you haven't anything to worry about, do you, Curt? Thanks for your time. We'll find our own way out."

Once seated in the 4x4, Katharine asked, "Why'd you ask him where he was Monday night?"

"Wanted to see his reaction in case Patriot is working with a local here. What do you think? Is he telling the truth?"

"Remember when I told you awhile back how nothing shakes up the Stewart brothers?" He nodded. "Well, Curt was definitely worried, but cooperative. We blindsided him and I don't think he knows a damn thing."

"Unfortunate for us, I agree."

They returned to the station early in the evening. Upon entering, Katharine received another gut-wrenching blow.

"*Steven!*"

"Hey, Kat. Long time."

CHAPTER 19

Katharine loved the innocence of dawn. Right after the shadows of night and the moments before singing birds woke with the rising sun. The minutes where the entire world was at peace were precious. She'd enjoyed the transition on numerous occasions and used the juncture to reduce the stress of dealing with the worst side of life.

A street cop's career was by no means glorious. Too many times their sincerest efforts went unnoticed. Cops had to be doctors and lawyers, psychologists and counselors. As peacemakers of the world, they were damned up and down in the fight against corruption and death. With their soul soaked in human cruelty, the once eager men and women of the police force turned into mechanical robots in order to save themselves. The original purpose, to protect and serve, transformed into one solitary goal. They wanted to go home at the end of a shift to see their loved ones maybe one last time. The last thing any officer wanted was to expose the dirty side of life to the people who meant the most to them.

Sitting on the steps to her parent's backyard, Katharine looked up when robins chirped their universal morning greeting. Her flight back to Madeline was a monumental do-over she thought she'd never survive. When she saw Steven with Gage at the station, the past two years of her life flashed through her eyes. They went outside to talk, and like always, Steven's lip twisted. It was a sign that marked his disapproval of her career. She couldn't recall when the symbol turned verbal but one day he began telling her how much her job interfered with their relationship. She was stunned to see him last night. She was more shocked that he still referred to them in any capacity, let alone together. Their conversation escalated until she finally agreed to meet him for lunch today. He'd been the one to end it with her months ago, but she suspiciously expected he was going to grovel to get her back.

"Hah!" she said sharply to the singing birds. "Steven doesn't grovel."

Yup her life was a do-over and deep down she'd always loved Madeline Island and Lake Superior. She hadn't realized until her return how empty she felt without either as well as without her friends and family. Steven was not part of this do-over. Instinctively, Katharine glanced over her shoulder. Gage stood inside the screen door drinking coffee.

Coming outside, he said, "Morning, Pipsqueak. Care if I join you and you can tell big brother what's on your mind?"

"I'll take your company any day of the week. Do you remember when you fell off the swing-set and broke your arm?"

He swallowed his coffee and nudged her with an elbow. "What I remember is being pushed."

"I didn't push you! Your foot slipped off the bar and I tried to catch you."

"Pipsqueak, you couldn't catch a softball. How were you gonna catch a sixty pound kid?"

"True," she chuckled. "But I did not push you."

Wincing when the sun peaked over the treetops, he taunted, "Did too."

"How's your head feel today?"

"Like I took a nosedive off the cliffs and missed the water. How you doin?"

"I wasn't drinking. I'm fine."

"I meant about this guy showing up last night. Who is he and why did he keep calling you cat?"

"K-A-T," she spelled. "It was a nickname the guys at work gave me. Steven and I lived together briefly. He broke it off early April this year."

"He didn't hurt you, did he?"

Shaking her head, she quietly said, "Not really."

"If he broke it off, how come he wants you back now?"

Katharine gawked at him. "Is that what he told you?"

He shrugged. "Not directly. You want him hanging around?"

Big, brotherly and protective, and Katharine loved him dearly. Mac was right about Gage's protection of her. "I'm not sure of anything other than catching Patriot." Sighing she confessed, "Steven hated my job. We argued daily about it because he wanted me to quit."

"Bet that went over like a lead balloon. What'd you ever see in this guy?"

"I don't know. He was nice at first."

"I don't like him."

"Gage. You didn't like Mac when you first met him either."

"Mac's different."

"How so?"

"Mac's not selfish. He cares about people and he has this way of making my only sister smile. He's also the only one I've ever known who can control you."

Giving him a brotherly slug in the arm, she retorted, "I don't need to be controlled."

"Not the way you think, Pipsqueak. I see the way you and Mac look at each other. You seem satisfied when you're with him."

"Then tell me, dear brother, why you tried to punch out his headlights."

He stretched out on the porch steps. "It's a man thing."

Laughing now, she said, "Men. You're all alike the way you feed off your need to protect us."

"You women love it. Speaking of needs, I'll be right back."

When Gage returned with a coffee refill and plopped alongside her, Katharine studied him for a long moment.

"What?"

"Bro, my love for you runs as far and deep as Superior. But more than your faithful protection, I need you to understand something."

"What's that?"

"Shooting and killing that guy did change my life, but not the way you think. It wasn't what sent me over the edge." Katharine retold the same story she told Mac. "I became more inadequate than Dad ever thought I could be. I was a danger to my officers and myself. I couldn't protect myself let alone the citizens anymore. What I need is for you to be able to trust me even when you have doubts."

Gage set his mug down to wrap his arms around her. He hugged her tight for the longest moment. "Katharine, I trust you more than you think. And silently, I'm thanking God he spared you."

She swallowed with difficulty as her eyes brimmed with tears.

"At first, I was peeved you didn't come to me. Now I know why. It was hard when I found out what happened to you. The pain in your eyes just about killed me. I thought you didn't need me anymore."

"Gage, I'm sorry. I'll always need you. You're the last person I'd ever hurt."

"I'm sorry too, Sis. I'm sorry any of this happened to you. I'd wipe it out of your mind if I knew how."

Half laughing, half crying she used his t-shirt to wipe her eyes. "A lobotomy would do it."

Kissing her temple, he pulled away to look at her. With a grin, he teased, "And give up your independence and free-spirit? I don't think so. Pipsqueak, I love you this way. I wouldn't change a thing about you."

Looking up, she asked, "Nothing?"

"Well, there is one thing."

"What?"

"Stop using my t-shirt to wipe your nose."

"I didn't wipe my nose on your t-shirt."

"Maybe not this time, but I have a bag stuffed full for old-time sake."

"You do—you do not!"

With more oomph, Katharine slugged him in the arm again. "Ouch. That hurt."

"More than Mac's fist?"

Kissing her cheek, Gage taunted, "Not even close. Now let's go catch ourselves a killer."

"Gage, I promised Steven I'd meet him for lunch over in Bayfield."

"I hope with the intention of giving him the boot. I'll say this and then I'll shut up. He doesn't deserve you Katharine and you're definitely more worthy than the credit he gives you."

"Gage, what don't you like about Steven?"

"Too self-centered. He thinks he's better than everyone else. Whaddaya want me to tell Mac?"

"The truth. Tell him the truth. I'll catch up with you guys later."

* * *

When his son stood, Frank shuffled quickly into the living room. He rushed up the stairs as fast as his stubby legs would carry him. The last thing he needed was for his children to see his grief. Tears were unmanly. With some relief, he realized he'd taught both his children well, but until now, he hadn't grasped how wrong he'd been. Katharine wasn't a quitter like he once assumed. He never could stay out of his kid's business and called her lieutenant. Waves of shock riveted through his body when he learned she'd shot and killed a man. God, it was the horror of horrors, and she had survived it. But to hear her tell Gage the real reason she quit her job left a baseball-size lump in the middle of his gut. He had no idea she'd given up her badge because she lost faith in herself. Nor had he realized the impact he'd had on her life.

And his son. Frank still didn't know how to deal with the internal conflict he had about Gage. The boy had his mother's emotional capabilities. He always knew exactly what to say and when to say it, as he just proved. Those *feminine* qualities were the one thing that bugged him the most about Gage. His son was thirty-three and rarely dated. Did it matter if Katharine trusted Gage enough to find solace? He supposed not. But how could Gage float through life on patience and kindness? Why did he always put things off instead of facing the issues head on?

Peeking through the bedroom curtains, both his children were gone now. He'd heard the door slam twice as each left the house. Frank exhaled heavily. Katharine was his first priority. He'd hurt her the most. Somehow he had to figure out way past his own faults enough to let her know he was proud of her.

* * *

Inside the Bayfield Inn restaurant Katharine waited for twenty minutes. Steven finally showed up after she had the desk clerk phone his room. No one seemed to notice Steven the way he galumphed into a room. His nondescript appearance hadn't changed. Why *had* she been attracted to him? What had drawn her attention to him?

He hugged her, and said, "Why are you still wearing your gun? Never mind. The shop called with a problem. I'm glad you agreed to have lunch with me."

Excuses without apologies as if her time had no value, and she'd hated the way he dismissed her answers to his questions. She did the same most of the time and now wondered if she'd picked up the bad habit from Steven. She hadn't noticed his lack of noble qualities either, until today when he ushered her to a table and sat down before she did. Katharine stood there to study him for a long moment.

"What? Sit down, Kat."

She refused. Instead questioned, "Why are you here, Steven?"

"I took ten days off. I thought we could patch things up."

"How'd you know where to find me?"

"I called you at work one night because I wanted to see you again. Someone told me you no longer worked there. It became a process of elimination. Kat, you didn't tell me you were going to quit that job."

She snorted out a half laugh and slid onto the chair. "Gee, the morning you told me you wanted me out, I hadn't killed anyone yet."

"I heard about that. You should've called and told me."

His lack of concern to her life on the job no longer shocked or surprised her. "Why? I didn't decide to resign until four months later."

"You being a cop always ran interference between us, Kat. If you had called me, I would've taken you back."

She leaned back in the chair, betraying nothing of her annoyance. "Let me see if I understand you. You're telling me that that horrendous act would have made everything better between *us*. The fact that I killed someone would have fused *us* back together?"

"It was your job causing all the problems between us."

The waitress came over to take their order and Katharine asked for her usual salad with iced tea then waited while Steven mulled over chicken or steak. She couldn't blame him for misunderstanding that her quitting the job wasn't directly related to her shoot. Nor did it matter that she hadn't explained why she quit. Steven missed the entire point. After five minutes of deliberation, the man across from her settled for a well-done hamburger and fries.

When the waitress left, she said, "Steven, the problems we had had nothing to do with my job. You wanted someone forever barefoot and pregnant in *your* kitchen. You wanted to control me in a way no one will ever control me. You tried to turn that fact around by telling me I didn't know how to maintain a relationship."

"Kat, calm down."

"I am calm, Steven. I'm more rational and calm in your company than I've ever been since I met you."

"You know if you would have worked days in a normal job instead of what'd you call it—doesn't matter. If you had worked day hours like normal people, at least then we could have considered starting a family."

There it was, she thought, when the waitress returned with their drinks. She wasn't normal like him. Her life, and what she wanted, didn't matter in the least to him. Katharine deliberately sipped the iced tea slowly. He never even asked how she was doing since he'd found her. He could care less that she took a life in self-defense. He wouldn't want to, much less know how to help her through the aftermath that followed her shoot. He certainly wouldn't trouble himself to ask why she quit a job that he knew meant everything to her. Katharine almost laughed aloud now. Steven would fault her for the panic attacks she had no control over. He would think nothing of it if she were to tell him that she'd almost died in the line of duty.

He couldn't even look at her this moment and she finally replied. "Steven, you always did put the cart before the horse. You never once suggested marriage to me yet you always talked about having kids."

"Kat, you know what I want."

She studied him, shortly. "You're right, but tell me something. Do you have any idea what I want?"

"I know how you shut me out. You'd barely say two words to me in the morning. Do you know how much I hated sleeping alone or coming home to a note you'd left because of court or a recorded message you were working late? Let's not forget about your workouts and going to the range or additional schooling. I put up with the fact that you weren't much of a housekeeper. But the one that really ticked me off was you going to a bar in the morning with the guys instead of coming home. My God! You don't even drink!"

Katharine elbowed her arm on the table and propped her chin in her hand. *What would he think about the night she got plowed with Nicole and Michelle?* She didn't care. Instead, she asked, "And you want me back, why?"

"Now that you've quit that insufferable job, you can stop all this foolishness and come home where you belong."

His words hit her head-on. "I'm working a case here with my brother. I know saving human life isn't on your list of priorities but it's at the top of mine."

In that righteous moment, Katharine stood, dug money out of her pocket and flung the bills on the table. "And one more thing, Steven. You've forgotten that you kicked me out. I'll never come back. Madeline Island is my home. *This* is where I belong."

"Kat, don't do this."

"Go back to the Cities, Steven. Find a sweet little thing willing to cater to your every whim. Someone who doesn't have an ounce of intelligence and needs you to tell her what clothes to put on everyday."

Katharine marched out of the restaurant exonerated. Except for waking up next to Mac yesterday morning, she couldn't recall the last time she felt this good. She practically ran to the ferry dock to buy a ticket. With a wait for the next ferry, she found a vacant bench and basked in the warmth of the sunshine then smiled broadly. Steven had no clue he'd finally done something good for her. He made her understand something she felt but hadn't been able to decipher until this moment. She was really falling in love with another man. A man attentive to her needs. One who had helped her find her way back into life because he cared enough to listen to her. It was so simple. And right now, that man was on Madeline Island sweating bullets over the capture of a murdering parasite.

Anxiously, Katharine watched the Island Queen ferry snake across the water's surface. She stood and headed toward the loading dock eager to return. Cars waited in a long line to board. The glimmering sun reflected off their metallic colors. Then she froze where she stood. Patriot's empty black Chevy was parked in the ferry's lot.

CHAPTER 20

"*Keerist* I feel like shit!"

Owly himself, Mac smirked, "Just a tad crispy are we?"

"Forty-eight hour hangovers suck! Other than recalling the exchange of a bunch of recycled dick jokes, I have no idea what I did Saturday night," Gage said.

"So much for sterling reputations."

"What the hell's eatin' you today?"

His temper erupted and Mac blew out gruffly. "Are you sure Katharine didn't say what time she'd be back?"

"Mac, what I'm sure of is that you have nothing to worry about. Now sit down before you wear out the tile."

Bunching his fists, he reluctantly sat. "Fine. Tell me why you were drinking Johnny Walker Black with Curt Stewart. I'm sure Katharine told you we re-interviewed them all yesterday."

"No, actually the case never came up in our conversation this morning. Why'd you talk to them again?"

"Don't you find it odd they drink Johnny Walker Black and just happened to find the ninth victim in their hunting shack?"

"Frankly, I thought about Curt the day we found the first victim because I know he drinks that crap. I also eliminated him as a suspect the day you walked in here and told us about Patriot. Mark doesn't drink the stuff. He's smarter than the rest of us."

"What about Kevin?"

Gage popped a couple of aspirin slugging them back with

coffee. "Don't trust him as far as I can throw him. He's a drunk and I doubt smart enough to keep his mouth shut when he's in that condition. The other thing you should know is that every man who's got a shack within fifty miles is checking it. If they find anything, they'll call us. I've got Joe working with Tom on it."

Grunting, Mac decided Green Bay PD suspending him made him impatiently irritable. Katharine meeting that toad for lunch today made him downright cynical and he lacked what it took to restrain the emotions gobbling up his insides. "Gage, there's another problem."

"Wha's that?"

"I've been suspended." Mac subsequently explained the entire situation. "I called my partner and he'll be here this week so nothing is jeopardized on this case. Katharine thought you should swear me in. I'm not sure I agree with her."

"Mac, I'm really sorry. I never would've plastered Patriot's picture all over La Pointe and Bayfield. Why didn't you just tell me about your niece?"

He exhaled a long breath, stood and started pacing again. "Who knows? Probably the same reason I didn't think before I went ballistic on the mayor."

"I just happen to have a tin here with your name on it." Gage opened a desk drawer and tossed it across the desk.

Mac turned and stared at the shield.

"It was mine when I was sergeant under my dad."

"You sure you wanna do this?"

"Never been more sure. Mac, I also trust Katharine's judgment. We both can't be wrong about you."

"You trust me?"

"I've always trusted your expertise. My doubts were with your motive regarding my sister."

"*Were?*"

"Past tense. Don't ever hurt her. Now, tell me why you think there's another person involved."

Mac detailed everything he and Katharine had discussed. "Gage, I don't think we're dealing with a copycat. If anything, Patriot's been working with someone all along. I'm sure now, it was an accident he left his print at the crime scene of the sixth victim."

"You really believe one of the Stewart brothers is involved?"

He picked up the badge, fingering it. "If I had to choose one it would be Kevin. I need backgrounds on all of them."

"I'll call Joe in and have him get started."

"We need to link them to the Green Bay homicides. Curt told us they'd all been to a Packers game a few years back. He also has an alibi for the night the Henderson girl disappeared. Kevin on the other hand said he's never been to Green Bay. Considering his state of mind, it doesn't surprise me he can't remember. Mark claims to know where he was at the time of each murder. We need his alibis checked out as well."

"Okay, but I've got a question regarding your theory."

"What's that?"

"Didn't Katharine see Patriot basically take Jess last Monday?"

"Yeah."

"Then why do you think Patriot is working with someone?"

"The evidence suggests it. The switch of poison and a tarp used on two of nine victims."

"The dirtbag is psychotic. I'm by no means an expert but even your profiler pointed out he'd start killing more because of inadequate feelings. The fact that he's alternating between two poisons suggests the craziness of the inadequacy he feels. He's indecisive. Just think for a minute. What if the voices he hears in his head are telling him to switch?"

"That's possible. I'll get in touch with the profiler and check it out."

"I've also been giving some thought to where Patriot might be hiding. Outer Island would be my first pick."

"You mentioned that before. Why that one?"

"It's about seven miles long. It's also the furthest and least visited by tourists. There's a boat landing on the south end, lighthouse on the north end. It's secluded. I'll call Tom and we can organize a search with his men."

"Patriot needs a boat."

"Look around you, Mac. They're all over the place."

"You think he'd risk getting caught renting one?"

"He might under an alias."

"Katharine and I figured the thread evidence found at the two crime scenes came from a boat cover. I'd be more inclined to think Patriot has both hidden somewhere."

Gage started to respond when the phone rang. He listened to the excited voice and spoke. "We're on our way."

"On our way where?"

"That was Katharine," he said, dialing a number. "She found Patriot's vacant Chevy in the parking lot at the Bayfield ferry landing."

"We need a police hold and to have the lab boys go over it."

"I'm calling Gus right to meet us there."

* * *

With the Chevy secured in a sea of yellow police tape, Katharine halted ferry boarding of passengers and cars until Mac and Gage arrived. She advised Bayfield PD to block the entrance to keep vehicles from leaving and new ones from entering the lot. She then went to question gift shop employees who sold ferryboat tickets and discovered a boat skipper for the Island Cruises in the quaint shop had observed the Chevy upon arriving at work mid-morning. Unfortunately, no one caught the driver of the car, and nobody had seen David Patriot.

Katharine glanced at her watch at one-thirty and returned to the parking lot. Bayfield police had run the Wisconsin license plate, which told them the vehicle was clear stolen checks. The plate also belonged on the eighty-five black Chevy and showed the owner was David Patriot with a Green Bay address. The State computer disclosed expired tabs on the license plate, but the displayed tabs were current. A Bayfield officer was waiting for sales and owner info of the current tabs from his dispatcher. Gage and Mac arrived and docked, and Gus Rankin arrived moments later.

She told the three men, "I made a decision to stop the ferry because I figured we'd want to check the vehicles for Patriot. Bayfield agreed to help."

Gage scanned the long lines of people and cars. "Mac, how do you wanna handle this?"

"Gus, do your thing on the Chevy. You Bayfield guys talk to the walk-on passengers with Katharine. Gage and I will check vehicles. Find out if anyone recognizes the Chevy or saw who was driving it. Let's get to work. The sooner we get through the lines, the less likely tempers will rise."

Their excitement wasn't false. They had Patriot's ride. Nevertheless, their addictive enthusiasm mingled with their continuing fear. The dread their fugitive had escaped. The latter didn't stop them from working expeditiously to question each person and search every vehicle. Nor did it change the tone of angry passengers when they were finally allowed to board the ferry. An hour later, Mac slammed the trunk of the last car. "It was worth a try. Most of these people aren't from around here. Gus, you find anything?"

"Plenty. A cooler, three unopened bottles of Johnny Walker Black and two boxes of seeds that I'm betting next week's pay are poisonous. The boxes are marked with Florida postage. This guy has future plans to kill."

"What address were they mailed to?" Mac asked.

"P.O. box in Green Bay."

"You find any bracelets or evidence of the chemical paraquat?"

"Nope, but he's definitely living out of his car evidenced by fast food garbage. I've called for a tow to our forensic garage. It'll take a couple of days for tests and analysis on everything."

A Bayfield officer returned telling them, "We just got the info back on the tabs. They were stolen off a ninety-six, four-door Chrysler and registered to a guy named Hunter in Green Bay with October expiration. The owner didn't know his tabs had been stolen until he was stopped a few months ago for expired registration. He's since had them replaced."

"Damn. Natalie Hunter was our fifth victim," Mac said. "Write up a statement with your findings and get it to me ASAP. Gus, check for receipts on the fast food. There aren't any locally and I wanna know where he's buying his meals."

Gus wiped the sweat from his brow with the back of his arm. "Mac, I just found something else in the trunk?"

"A tarp?"

"No, a box of .38 Specials with a receipt from a gun shop in Ashland dated this past Friday. Six cartridges are missing."

"Is there a sales time stamped on that receipt?"

"Yeah, six at night. Why?"

"We'd already found the Henderson girl by that time. If Patriot returned to the shack and saw us processing the crime scene, he knows we're close. He's suddenly developed a need for self-protection."

CHAPTER 21

It might have been a perfect sunrise. The bright orange ball rose and filled the bluish sky with blaze. It set fire to the unruffled waters. The gentle winds blew at will within the rich and pleasing scenery. It was a morning in paradise, and God, how without fail it reminded him of her hair. Silky smooth and sweetly sexy, the vibrant reddish-orange was a faultless union.

Mac tried to forget the nirvana he'd felt Sunday morning upon waking up next to Katharine. He put forth efforts to walk away from her yesterday after they hooked and towed the black Chevy. Every breath she inhaled and every move she made distracted him. It left him panicked and destitute. He was a loner and too stubborn to consider he might not be able to walk away and forget her existence. The minute Patriot was in custody, he'd go back to Green Bay. Besides, Katharine didn't belong to him. He had no claim on her and couldn't assume she wouldn't go back to the toad. She'd told him she thought she once loved him. What was to stop her from going back a second time? With desperate frustration, Mac decided the toad had to be a damn fool to let her go at all.

He'd worked into the wee hours again last night fighting fatigue against his feigned indifference. They were another step closer thanks to Katharine, and so he didn't care what she did. All that mattered was Patriot's capture. Thanks to her, they knew Patriot had changed his hair color. They held Patriot's only form of mainland transportation because of her sharp observation. All the new leads were because of Katharine. *Shit!* He *did* care and needed to shove his destitute spirits into his subconscious.

After returning to the station yesterday, he tried to contact Cole. He wanted him to check the post office box in Green Bay where the rosary peas had been shipped. Patriot's name on the PO Box would establish the connection they needed. True the poisonous seeds inside the vehicle proved possession. Unfortunately, no one had possession of the vehicle at the time of seizure. Loopholes and unturned stones were unacceptable, and he'd missed making contact with his partner at home. Cole should have made it to Bayfield late last night. He probably stayed in a motel until the ferry ran this morning.

Presently stuck in a wait-and-see process, Gage had Joe running backgrounds on the Stewart brothers. Gus needed a couple of days to analyze the contents of the Chevy, but they had learned Miami knew of no murders with Patriot's M-O. Checking all airlines within the week before and after Patriot's Miami arrest, the names Cannon, Patriot and Sheldon weren't on any airline passenger lists. Patriot either paid cash or used another alias with plundered ID and matching credit cards to purchase a ticket.

The cartridges found in the Chevy produced new concerns. The dirtbag was now armed. He and Gage had tossed around the idea of foot searches on the islands, but searching each island would burn up valuable time. With tourists invading half of them, the plan was also risky.

A grating squawk diverted Mac's focus and he looked to the water's edge. With labored flight, a crop of blue herons noisily lifted their large bodies. The fiery shell of the sun had converted into full energy of vibrating yellow. It climbed briskly between the cloudless sky and vast body of water. No matter how many times Mac watched the sunrise, it had a way of seducing and mesmerizing him. It was nature's magic casting a spell and in that potent moment, he saw her. Her reddish-gold strands flapped carelessly as she jogged near the shore.

When he should have withdrawn back inside the Carriage House, Mac set his mug on the wood deck ledge and sprinted toward the shoreline. He watched her. The exercise appeared effortless the way every ounce of her flesh and muscle moved in natural fluidity with the waves rolling onto the sandy beach. Her wild beauty was a natural gift to the surrounding scenery. Her presence added intense power and strength to the setting. Whether Mac wanted to fight it or not, he knew, Madeline Island was where Katharine belonged.

She jogged with her eyes cast down and hadn't noticed him yet. He tucked his fingers into the front pockets of his jeans and waited until she finally glanced up. The corners of her mouth curved upward and her face brightened at the sight of him. She picked up her pace then came to a stop in front of him.

"Hi," she panted out.

Barely worked up in a sweat, Katharine walked in circles. Mac gave her a minute to cool down then asked, "Exercise or stress reliever?"

"Both."

"I'm debating over renting a sailboat for a few hours. You wanna go out with me?"

She stopped and faced him. "Mac, Jessica's funeral is at ten. Everything on the island is closed until afterward."

The idea of attending a funeral bit hard in his gut. Sharp lines lacerated in Linda's grief-filled face vividly mingled with the guilt in his mind. The parents and mourners would remind him of the loss—*of his mistake*. "Are you going?"

"The service, yes. Are you?"

The bite in his gut contracted into a tight ball. He couldn't face the parents when he'd been responsible for their suffering. "Cole's on his way. He'll probably be on the first ferry over here this morning. I'll need to brief him."

"You can't face it yet, can you?"

He shrugged, knowing if Katharine had the power, she'd release him from the self-blame. She would dispose of the intense emotions that ripped through him. She would again reassure him the murders weren't his fault. He'd never been more positive of anything.

"Mac, we're close," she said, touching his arm. "We'll get him."

His hands slid out of his pockets, slipped up her arms and pulled her close. He hugged her like there was no tomorrow. The sudden urgency clamoring through his veins caught him off guard and he crushed her and took her mouth greedily. Her concealed weapon pressed between them. Katharine cupped the back of his head, pulling him deeply into their kiss. Her reaction was wanting, wild hunger. He forced her mouth open wider and thrust deeply inside. A hot and hungry fire blazed inside of him. The blood pounded in his brain. His body throbbed desperately for her. Hurtled beyond the point of no return, aggressively bending her backward—

"Ouch!"

His eyes flew open and he brought her up. "I'm sorry. Are you okay?"

Giggling now, she nodded. "Guns and sex don't mix."

He twisted her ponytail around his hand and spoke hoarsely. "I know how to remedy that, Princess."

She sighed, leaning into him. "Funerals and partners, Mac."

* * *

He felt the renewed terror and removed the .38 Specials from the two-inch Colt revolver. The Smith and Wesson was purchased in a Green Bay pawnshop. He never believed he would have a need to use it. But things had changed. He spun the empty cylinder, aimed and pulled the trigger.

"Bang, bang. You're dead," he muttered.

He needed to find out who that red-haired sorceress was. She was showing up everywhere. She was a menace to all his plans. Those witch-like eyes could rip him to shreds and destroy him. The moment he saw her on the ferryboat he knew she would cause trouble. She was evil, and stupid, too. She thought he wouldn't recognize her at the beach. She called him Jim, of all the idiotic names. When he returned to the shack to conclude the Divine Creator's ceremony, the she-witch was there, too. She took his betrothed Jessica away from him.

That made his Creator yell and shout. *"Devil spawn! You worthless piece of shit! You screwed up again!"*

He begged forgiveness like he always did, but it wasn't good enough to atone. She was responsible for his painful suffering. His cry of distress came with the many voices. They ran together in blaring screams in his head now. The woman, the girls, the

Creator—he couldn't tell them apart anymore. It was the witch's fault. Her piercing cold eyes had withered him to nothingness, had made him feel the repetitive ineptness.

His body twitched. She'd cast her wicked spell on him and took his car. So he would take her. He would punish the evil witch to free himself of blame. He spun the cylinder once more, aimed at the mental image of her face and dry fired the weapon. He reloaded the Colt with six cartridges then tucked a new box of .38 Specials into his jacket. They all thought he was insane, psychotic. Probably thought he was doped up on drugs, too. The media informed of that much. It was time for all to learn precisely how smart he was. He knew exactly how and where to take care of the redheaded bitch.

* * *

When Katharine and Gage arrived at the historic Catholic Church, folding chairs, the metal kind, were being setup outside front. An outpouring of Island residents as well as Bayfield and the surrounding community residents had crammed themselves into the sanctuary to pay their final respects. The rest were huddled outside in small circles away from the ancient cemetery exchanging their disgruntled opinions. Katharine spotted Michelle in a dress suit alongside Nicole attired in a sophisticated A-line classic. Nicole wore a pair of expensive-looking shades, most likely to conceal tear-stained eyes from crying over the loss.

Depleted from exhaustion, Katharine forced herself out of the vehicle. She hadn't missed the handful of La Pointe's residents nudging each other and nodding at Gage as he drove up. Their angry faces were set in gypsum. Gage glanced at her across the car's roof.

"The natives are getting restless," he said.

She nodded when a handful of men marched toward them. Katharine recognized Josie's father, Bert Hanson, leading the pack. Was he still the God-fearing individual he once used to be? Ted Evans, owner of the Red Rock Tavern marched a close second behind. Ben McEvoy, owner of the Upland Cottage, where Patriot had been staying, followed Ted. Carter Taylor from the Town Board was alongside Ben. Each exposed varying degrees of hostility the way they paraded toward them in authoritative fashion. Katharine recognized the outright terror that lay hidden behind their rage, and though justified, this wasn't the place to express it. She also observed their father near the church entrance watching the situation skeptically.

Before the men reached her and Gage, she whispered, "Tell them you're calling a town meeting tonight."

"Are you nuts?"

"Trust me on this and just do it."

Bert was the first to articulate their misgivings. "Chief, these murders are outrageous. This predator is preying on young girls and we want to know how many more have to die before you make an arrest?"

"Bert, this isn't the time or—"

"Bullshit!" Carter Taylor blurted, stepping forward.

"Carter, the victim's funeral is not the time to discuss this. Now back off."

"It's as good a time as any."

"Fine. Besides myself, I have one full time, two seasonal officers and two homicide detectives who are refusing pay to work this case. Green Bay PD sent another member of their Task Force up here to help us out. Tom Coville's men and Bayfield PD are also working with us and we're all operating around the clock. If that's not good enough then maybe you need to open your pocketbooks and hire me additional help."

"Why hasn't the FBI been called in? How can you possibly suspect the Stewart brothers in this mess?"

"Carter, this is an active investigation and I'm calling the shots. I'm not about to disclose anything to you or anyone else."

"Gage, we voted unanimously for you to fill your dad's shoes. We can easily reverse that decision if it becomes necessary."

"Knock yourself out, Carter. Just remember this. You interfere with this case now and you'll kick it back to square one. Then where will you all be?"

Gage stepped around the speechless men and marched away. Katharine followed her brother realizing he didn't panic easily under fire. Unmistakably, he'd made his point. Gage took a seat in the back row and she hunkered down next to him as mournful people stole looks at them.

She leaned left toward Gage and murmured, "Good job, Bro. But why didn't you do what I said?"

"All they wanna hear is he's been arrested. I can't tell 'em that, yet."

Michelle and Nicole walked over and sat on Katharine's right. Nicole lifted her sunglasses briefly, giving Gage a supportive look as Michelle reached across Katharine and touched his hand reassuringly. The sun seemed to blaze down on the crowd that had gathered for the funeral.

"Murder is not God's will ...,"

Katharine recognized Father Napoli's voice over the loudspeaker. She could visualize his apple green eyes watching over a fear-filled congregation from the lectern inside the church. Nicole shifted, Michelle coughed and Katharine's mind drifted reluctantly as she recalled several other funerals. A member of the department's Honor Guard, she'd been part of too many twenty-one gun salutes. The blaring bagpipes from men in kilt skirts and the echoing drown from a shiny brass trumpet as a uniform blew out taps were ingrained in her memory forever. She'd never forget even one. Senseless death caused in the fight to protect communities from crime and evil. She'd acquired coldness to the concept of death and used it as a shield for self-protection.

Guilt swelled and consumed inside of her, believing she'd given up too easily. Katharine wiped her brow with the back of her hand. The heat made sitting here difficult. She felt dizzy, weak and found it harder to keep her head up. Her breath quickened.

The child's voice screamed loudly in ears then several loud cracks penetrated the air—your sister is a failure sang verse repeatedly in her ears.

Katharine's heartbeat raced. The sun beat down hotly upon them. Sweat beaded her temples. Her throat closed and cut off the air into her lungs.

"... Jessica is in God's hands ...,"

Her chest tightening, she gasped harder for air to reach her lungs, clenched her fingers tightly to stop the visible shaking. Her vision suddenly blurred and blackness fell around her.

"Get down, Sarge!" Kat heard her officers, but she couldn't move. Her hand was frozen on her right hip. The shots rang out, flying in all directions. The end in sight, she was going down. It was too late to make up with her

father. Screams cut the air. Clouds and treetops swirled around numerous sparkling white lights. The gasps, shrieks and voices blurred together.

"Sarge!"

"Omigod!"

"Kat!"

"Pipsqueak! Everyone get down!"

CHAPTER 22

Mac wondered how many times he could read the same reports and come up empty. Joe's backgrounds on the Stewart tribe showed no connection to Patriot. Grunting, he pilfered a cup of fresh coffee before brewing had finished. He glanced at his wristwatch and decided the funeral must have taken longer than an hour. The station was directly across from the church and one of them was supposed to call the bungalow since he didn't want to be anywhere near mourners. Almost noon, he brooded over Cole's lateness. Yawning, one of them pounded on the door and he went over to it.

"Hey, partner."

"Where the hell have you been, Gilroy?"

"You didn't tell me I'd have a problem getting to the island."

"Huh?"

"I arrived in Bayfield last night too late to catch the last ferry over and every motel was full. I debated over sleeping in the car or driving back to Ashland. Got up early and returned to Bayfield then couldn't get a ferry over here. The lines were ridiculously long."

"The funeral," Mac grunted.

"Yeah, I saw it."

His sandy-brown haired partner of eight years was energized and the fresh blood they needed right now. Mac didn't know why the good cop/bad cop routine they used on suspects came back to him either. A few years older, a flashy grin with deep-set dimples, Cole Gilroy gave the appearance of the good cop. Mac always teased him that his dimples made him look charming when his partner was actually as vicious as a dog in heat. He'd become a bit too cocky since developing his new cynicism, too, and that made Mac worry most days. The transformation came after Cole shot and killed a man.

"I'm sure everything's booked on the island, too," Mac said. "You can bunk with me."

"You look like walking death, Mac."

"I feel worse. Want some coffee?"

"Of course."

Cole pulled out a pack of cigarettes from his windbreaker and lit up. Mac filled a mug and handed it over.

"What'd you tell Sanders?"

"The captain knew what we were up to the minute I told him I was taking time off."

"He say anything?"

"He handed me one of his grumpy glares and blew out his usual rhetoric about manpower. Then he turned his back on me and said 'don't come back here until you catch the bastard'. So, where we at?"

Mac found an empty pop can for Cole to flick his ashes. "We hooked Patriot's ride yesterday. Crime lab is still working on the contents."

He advised Cole on each of the last three deaths, the poisonous seeds they discovered shipped from Florida along with the box of .38 Specials they found in Patriot's car. He made Cole aware of their misgivings on the Stewart brothers and finished with re-telling his and Katharine's thoughts that Patriot has been working with someone all along.

"I checked with the profiler on that. She said it's possible but it would have to be someone he revered in order for him to buddy up. Someone who would fill the loving role of his mother, but more likely someone he could look up to. She said the individual might replace the abusive father he had."

"Well the Stewart brothers certainly don't fit that idealism. Gage calls them the Island's designated drunks. The middle one,

Kevin would have been my choice. Backgrounds on all of them came back zilch."

"Explain who this Gage and Katharine are again?"

"Brother and sister. Gage is the police chief here and his sister was a sergeant in Minneapolis."

With a straight-line look, Cole said, "*Was?*"

Mac didn't know what to say. Cole still had major flashbacks to his justified shooting. "It's a long story."

"You trust her?"

"She's the one who I-D'd Patriot with the new appearance and found his Chevy. She's a witness to seeing Patriot with the ninth victim the night the kid disappeared. She also figured out the reason Patriot is killing sixteen year old Native Americans."

He was playfully ashing out his cigarette on the top of the pop can and stopped. "Dip me in the proverbial you-know-what. What *is* the reason?"

Mac detailed the history behind Madeline Cadotte and the Island along with the wedding dates that all matched the first six murders. He avoided the explanation of *how* Katharine had figured it out. Cole would have him committed if he mentioned he'd been hearing a crying ghost. "I double checked the dates myself. She's dead-on accurate."

"It makes sense especially if this fruitcake is hearing voices." Cole hesitated then said, "Linda called me the other day."

"She okay? What did she want? You didn't tell her anything did you?"

"I told her you'd taken some time off and where you were. She was worried. Said she hadn't heard from you."

"I walked into this unexpectedly. I can't raise her hopes."

"How you holding up?"

"We're so close and yet we're not. Since yesterday, we don't know whether Patriot's on the mainland or has a boat and is on one of the islands. For all we know the bastard has fled again."

"We'll pinch the s-o-b."

"That's what everyone keeps telling me. I told Gage the outcome of my actions. He swore me in against my better judgment. That's why I wanted you here."

"You just miss my damn good expertise."

"Gilroy, take that horn you're always blowing and shove it into those crater-like dimples of yours."

"That one gets me right here," Cole said, punching his chest. "I'm hungry. Where can I grab a burger and fries?"

"You can't. Everything is closed until the funeral's over."

"Are these people allergic to fast food? I haven't seen one since Ashland this morning."

Mac checked the time again. "I wonder where the hell they are. Somebody should've called by now."

"It's only one. Maybe they stayed for the burial."

Mac slugged back cold coffee and filled his mug a second time. "They said—"

The door opened violently and Gage rushed into the bungalow. Red-hot anger and fear filled his face.

"Katharine's been shot!"

His ceramic mug crashed to the floor. Glass and coffee sprayed everywhere. The muscles in his shoulders and forearms hardened. Panic clawed Mac's throat, cutting off his breath. With his heart thumping madly, he'd lost the love of his life.

"He was there!" Gage exclaimed. "Patriot was at the funeral. The service had just ended when bullets flew everywhere. Katharine slid out of the fricking chair right next to me. I yelled at everyone to get down and grabbed her gun. I saw that son-of-a-bitching bastard, but I couldn't get a clear shot. I lost him."

Mac couldn't respond to Gage's words. Sudden silence tightened with tension. Cole's expression told him his own face betrayed his emotions. The words to his questions were stuck inside of him.

Cole shifted and faced Gage. "I'm Mac's partner, Cole Gilroy. You must be Gage. Where'd they take your sister?"

"The EMT guys took Katharine and one other person who'd been hit. The closest hospital is Ashland. Depending on the severity, they'd airlift 'em to Duluth or have another ambulance waiting at the Bayfield ferry landing. I've been at the church until now."

"How bad is she?" Mac finally managed in a voice like an echo from an empty tomb.

"I dunno," Gage said. "Ted Evans is the other victim. I don't know how bad either is. I chased Patriot and lost him. I left my dad doing chaos patrol. Gus is processing the scene right now. Mac, I want you there as well. Let's go."

CHAPTER 23

A strange voice and flaming pain in her left arm brought Katharine to a semiconscious state. She remembered being at Jessica's funeral and feeling the onset of another panic attack. A loud crack of gunfire cut the air and she was instantly back in Minneapolis reliving the incident—her eyes flew open. She jerked and tried to sit up but someone put a gentle hand on her shoulder.

"Take it easy. You're gonna be okay."

She didn't recognize the calm voice and focused on the man huddled over her through fuzzy vision. "Where am I? What happened?"

"You're at the Emergency Services building in La Pointe. You were shot in the arm. It's a flesh wound but you're gonna be okay."

Her breath quickened, her pulse roared in her ears and her words came out high and hysterical. "Nicole! Michelle! Are they okay? What about my brother?"

"They're all okay. Can you tell me your name?"

She shivered then realized she'd been disrobed of her shirt and jacket.

"What's your name?"

"*Katharine!* My name is Katharine LeNoir. Where's my gun?"

"She's gonna be okay, Frank. She needs to rest."

Frank was her father. *He was here? With her?* Katharine tried to sit up a second time, but the man held her down.

"Lie still. I'm gonna bandage your arm."

She needed to talk to her father. "Where's my dad?"

"How many fingers am I holding up?"

"Two. Now let me see my dad!"

"I'm right here, Pumpkin," he said, touching her right hand. "Just lay still 'til Don finishes."

"Where's my gun?" she asked, clutching her father's hand tightly.

"Gage has it."

Her dad smoothed her hair and studied her with guilt-filled eyes. Her thoughts before she passed out had veered to the broken fence between them. Here was her second chance. She swallowed hard to bite back the tears but broke out with a cry. "Daddy, I-I'm sorry. P-please don't be mad at me."

"Don, you 'bout done here?"

"Yep. All done. Take her home, Frank, and make sure she rests. She was out cold when I got to her. I suspect partially from exhaustion."

"Thanks, Don."

With shaky hands, her dad pulled a blanket up to cover her. His pale face was haggard with worry. His Adams apple bobbed with hard swallows. When she heard a door close, Katharine asked, "W-where's Mom?"

"She's waiting outside with Nicole and Michelle," he answered, his voice hitching. "You know ... your mother never could stand the sight of blood. I always had to bandage your scraped knees and elbows."

His facial muscles twitched nervously. Shifting and reshifting his feet, he shoved his hands into his pants pockets where he jangled change. Katharine waited.

"I'm not mad at you."

He'd whispered the words in a lifeless voice so quiet she barely heard them.

"Katharine," he said clearing his throat. "I'm sorry for everything I've done to you. I'm sorry for what happened to you in—"

"Oh, Daddy."

He held up his hand. "I never deserved the pedestal you kept me on. I didn't realize how much influence I had on you until your mother told me why you decided on your career. I was afraid of losing you forever when you decided ... went away ... I thought I'd never see you again."

"You thought I'd die protecting others."

He turned away to smother a sob in his throat. It was difficult for him to accept her accuracy. He inhaled a deep breath and turned back to her.

"Katharine, Gage is my first born. He's *my* son. I've made mistakes with him as well. But, you." He stared into her eyes. "You were always my ray of sunshine. From the moment you came into this world, you and I had a special bond between us. I knew the minute I saw that shock of red fuzz on your head you were gonna be stubborn like your old man. You were always fussy. Mother never could get you to stop squawking. You definitely acquired my disposition. You wanted things your own way and I'd have to hold you in my arms to calm you until you curled up against me and settled down."

Tears welled in her eyes. Katharine felt the hope he'd hung onto. She felt the pain and happiness he'd experienced through her. It was a complexity of delight, anger, joy and yes, the worry parents feel through their children. He turned away from her again. Would she ever feel this depth of affection for one of her own?

"I knew you wanted to work with me," he spoke, solemnly. "It was the one thing I couldn't give you."

"Why not?"

He shifted. Sorrow etched his face.

"Pumpkin, your old man is old-fashioned. I didn't want my baby girl doing a man's job. I should have seen it. Hell, I did see it, but I never thought you'd go off and find it somewhere else. I couldn't accept—I didn't want to—I didn't want you to die."

"Oh, Daddy," she cried again and struggled to sit up. When she managed it, Katharine grabbed hold of his hand, bringing it up to her cheek. "You taught me well. I knew the risks. I love you so much I wanted to be like you. All I ever wanted was for you to be proud of me."

He took a quick breath then broke down and cried. She was

speechless for a moment then reached and wrapped her arms around his neck. He responded and snuggled her tightly the way he used to do. His chest was heaving against hers. Deep sobs racked up inside of her and the ache to her throat hurt worse than the graze to her arm.

"I am proud of you, Pumpkin. I love you more than anything."

"I love you too, Daddy."

After several minutes, Katharine leaned back, pulling the blanket to cover up. "Are we okay now?"

"Yeah, Pumpkin. We're good."

"Then tell me what happened out there?"

"Don was right. I saw your head bobbing around. You'd already started sliding out of the chair when the gunfire rang out. Thankfully, it's what saved your life. Your brother reacted quickly and grabbed your gun because he wasn't wearing his. He yelled over to me that you'd been hit—I died a thousand deaths inside. Then he took off running."

"It was Patriot, wasn't it? Did Gage catch him?"

"He saw Patriot, but lost him in all the bedlam."

"Dad we towed his car yesterday over in Bayfield. We found a box of .38 Specials with six missing. Mac said he'd never used a weapon before. Was anyone else hurt?"

"Ted Evans was hit. They rushed him to the hospital."

"How bad is he?"

"I don't know."

"Dad, I'm gonna catch him if it's the last thing I do."

"Katharine, it almost was the last thing you did. You're coming home with me. You need your rest."

She slid off the gurney. "I'm fine. I'm going to chase this piece of slime relentlessly. He's killed nine girls, one of which was Mac's niece. He is not getting any more."

She found her shirt and tugged it on carefully over her head. "You can help by taking me to Gage's location."

It was too automatic to shake his head and frown at her, but he answered, "All right, just promise me you'll be careful."

"Deal." Katharine hugged her father again. "Promise, I'll start wearing my vest too. Now let's get out of here."

When they went outside, frantic cries greeted them. Meeting

her mother and her two best friends half way, Katharine let them hug her. She winced when they squeezed her arm but kept silent—she was still alive, and geared up emotionally to kick back harder than ever.

Her father drove her to the station and parked in the lot across from the Catholic Church. Katharine saw Mac immediately. He was with a stranger with their backs to the parking lot. The entire church and surround yard was cordoned off with crime scene tape. Chairs were scattered and tipped. She waited for her dad to stop the car.

"Pumpkin, Nicole told me to send everyone to the Tavern when they finish here. She'll have a meal ready."

Katharine loved hearing her dad use the pet name for her again. She also felt his frustration with his lack of involvement in this case. "Thanks, Dad. I'll tell them. Would you find out what you can on Ted Evans' condition and get back to us?"

"I'll call the hospital and let you know."

"Dad, if he survived, we're gonna need his statement. Would you like to drive over and take it for us?"

"You sure?" he said with surprise in his voice.

"Yes, I'm sure. You can take the recorder and tapes from the station."

"You and Gage be careful."

Katharine opened the passenger door, exited and stood outside of the car as Mac turned around. His eyes brightened at the sight of her then quickly switched to a black, piercing glare. He wasted little time burning a trail in her direction.

"What the hell are you doing here?"

"Nice to know you care, Dobarchon. No hello or glad you're still alive?"

"*Obviously*, I can see you're still alive. *That* bloody hole on your jacket says you should be home in bed!"

The brown haired stranger, a tad shorter than Mac, leaned against the fender of her dad's car. He crossed his arms and a curious smile exposed the most amazing dimples Katharine had ever seen. She averted her eyes to Mac and glared at him.

"Get back in that car right now and get home in bed where you belong!"

Katharine squared her chin. "I'm going after Patriot with or without you, Dobarchon!" Then she slammed the car door shut and stomped away.

"Katharine!" Mac yelled, following her.

Frank slid out of the vehicle and came around the car to stand with the stranger. "Hi, Frank LeNoir. I'm that little spitfire's father."

"Cole Gilroy," he replied, shaking hands. "I'm partners with the pigheaded one."

Leaning against the car, Frank said, "Well, Cole. I'm pretty sure the pigheaded one's gonna discover real fast nobody tells the spitfire what to do."

Mac grabbed Katharine's injured arm and she slugged him with her good one. "Let go of me you big dumb jerk!"

He did, insisting, "Let me see it."

She narrowed her eyes with disgust. She wanted to cross her arms out of spite, but her fist smarted, her arm ached and her feelings stung. "Why?"

"Princess, I'm sorry. I've been crazy since Gage told us what happened. I was dumbfounded when I saw you get out of the car. I didn't know what to think."

"It's just a flesh wound," she said testily.

"I wanna see it."

She rolled her eyes but complied by removing her jacket with his help. She glanced at the wound herself. It had blossomed colorfully. Bruising had spread beyond the outskirts of the squared bandage. Orangish-colored antiseptic surrounded the wound. "It's ... there's ... when I—I needed you to hold me," she blurt.

"Does it hurt?"

"Of course it hurts," she snapped.

"My little warrior," he said, pulling her close and hugging her.

She dissolved in his arms. The ache of inner longing replaced the throbbing pain of her wound. After several long moments, she leaned back. "I'm *really* pissed off right now. I can't wimp out and go home to bed."

"Did they give you anything for the pain?"

"No. I'd have to get a prescription from a doctor. I'll take Tylenol or something if it gets too bad."

He hugged her tighter and murmured into her hair. "Katharine, I thought I lost you."

"It'll take more than being grazed by a thirty-eight to stop me but at least now we know Patriot's on the island and needs a boat to get off."

He studied her for a long moment. His mouth tightened with the thought. "This is a helluva way to learn his whereabouts. We sent Joe over to keep the marina closed. Pete and Alesha are cruising the shoreline looking for boats."

"What about the ferry?"

"We couldn't stop it from running. Too many people had to go back after the funeral. Others left for good. We did the next best thing and posted copies of his photo. If anyone sees him, we'll hear about it."

Mac leaned and kissed her. Because he had to.

It was deep and slow, melting her down like butter until he brought her exhausted senses to life. They parted a few inches and she pulled away from him. "Is that your partner with my Dad?"

"I saw the way you looked at him. I'm not sure I want to introduce the two of you."

"Too late, partner," he said coming up behind Mac. "I've already met the father, who by the way invited me to a meal."

Mac grimaced and said, "Katharine, meet my partner the bottomless pit, Cole Gilroy."

"I've never known anyone to cramp Mac's style the way you just did, Katharine."

"His style could use a little cramping," she said.

"She's got your number, partner."

"Katharine, are you okay?" Gage yelled, rushing toward them. "What are you doing here?"

"Not again," she grumbled shifting to face her brother. "The bullet just nicked my arm."

Encircling her in his arms, Gage said, "Sis, this scared me shitless. You sure you're okay?"

"Yes. I'm fine. I asked Dad to find out about Ted Evans for us."

"Good idea. Dad, let us know."

"I'll call you." Frank then left.

"We found six spent cartridges and four bullet holes in the church's outer wall," Gage told them. "I called Tom Coville. He has his men cruising around Madeline. If Patriot tries to get off the Island, they'll find him. Mac, this is your case. How do you wanna handle it?"

"Has anyone given any thought to why this shit zeroed in on Katharine?" Cole asked.

The three men tossed their ideas back and forth while Katharine considered Cole's point. Distracted by her panic attacks, this time she stepped closer to death than the last. She squelched the fear and anger tearing up her insides to offer, "I'm the only one who's seen him four times. I can I-D him."

"Ginger and Sadie can also I-D him," Gage said.

Mac informed Cole who the two girls were.

"All the same, his M-O has changed," Cole said. "Because he knows where they live, we need to get those kids off the island"

"I'll get on it," Gage said. "What about Katharine? Her life is still in jeopardy."

"He missed the first time and he won't get a second," she replied.

"He didn't miss!" they responded in unison.

"You were lucky," Mac told her.

"I will not let him hold me prisoner. Gage, give me my gun." When he handed over her weapon, she said, "If you're all done here, I'm starving. The Tavern is open and Nicole told us to come over. We can plan our strategy while we eat."

When they entered the nearby Tavern, the last person Katharine expected to see was Steven.

"Kat! You're covered with blood!"

She glanced at her stained shirt and made introductions instead of explaining. Steven's eyes glided over the men without word.

"Kat, I came over on the ferry. I've been looking for you. Can we go somewhere to talk privately?"

She turned to the others. "Would you excuse me for a minute, please?"

Steven didn't wait for their response, but gripped her arm and steered.

"Let go of my arm!" she yelped, yanking it from his grasp. He was half way through the exit and stopped to look at her. She regarded him impassively. "What are you doing here, Steven?"

"This can't end between us."

"It already has."

He reached for her and she stepped back. "Don't touch my arm again!"

"Calm down, Kat. I just want to talk to you."

Clenching her teeth, her bitchy side came out and she ripped off her jacket, thrust her wound in his face and threw words at him like stones. "Take a good look! A madman shot me! Now, go home! Get the hell out of my life and leave me alone!"

Steven's eyes expanded to big circles. Vivid scarlet colored his face before he paled. When he gulped for air, Katharine cussed under breath, aware of what was coming. His head swayed and he was going down when Mac came up behind her and grabbed hold of Steven, guiding him to a chair.

"Get him a glass of water."

"Here ya go," Cole said, handing over a glass filled with gold-colored liquid. "Mac, you got it under control?"

"Got it."

"Good, cuz I'm starving. Katharine, come with us."

"But—"

"Mac'll take care of him," Cole reassured.

"That's what I'm afraid of," she muttered.

They entered the dining room and sat down at a quiet corner table. Nicole came over with Mac handing out menus. "Everything's on the house tonight. Whatever you want."

"How you doing, girlfriend?" Katharine asked, taking hold of Nicole's hand.

"Hon, I should be asking you that question. What in God's name are you doing here anyway?"

"I'm fine. How's Michelle?"

"Shaken up. She's debating about starting up with the smokes again. We're spending the night together."

"I might be joining you. But first I want one of those drinks you made me the other night."

"One Long Island Iced Tea coming up."

"Nicole, this is Mac's partner, Cole Gilroy and that's Gus

Rankin."

"Nice to meet you both. What can I get you gentleman?"

Gus requested a beer, Gage ordered a large Coke and Mac asked for a double scotch. Then Cole asked, "Are all the ladies on this island as pretty as you two?"

"Not in the least. Nor do they always recognize a come on," Nicole said with a smile. "Now, what would you like to drink?"

"A dry martini."

"I'll have Hayden make your drinks and be right back."

While the conversation rambled between the men, Katharine listened and gulped down her first drink. She requested a second alongside a burger and generous portion of fries when Nicole returned to take their meal order. Her own thoughts drowned out the discussion as the day's events played themselves out in her mind. It started with a jog and a kiss to die for—*no, she didn't mean that.* When Nicole delivered their meals, Katharine ordered a third drink. She devoured the burger and fries, thinking the only good thing about the entire sucky day was making up with her father. Why had Steven come looking for her she silently wondered, ordering another Long Island Iced Tea. Hadn't she made herself clear? She swallowed a big gulp and realized the pain in her arm had lessened. Mac leaned over and placed his arm on the back of her chair after the others momentarily excused themselves.

"Helluva way to get your appetite back, Princess. You keep slugging back those drinks and I'm gonna have to carry you out if here."

Katharine hiccupped then giggled. Staring into his jet-black eyes, she smacked her lips. "T-take me, Dobarchon! I'm yours. D-did you know I almost died today?"

"Okay, sweetheart. That's enough for you."

He slid the glass out of her hand setting it on the table. Mac then muttered something to Cole who returned from wherever he went.

"I'm taking you home, Warrior Princess."

"I-I'm s-staying with Nic-cole and Mi-Michelle."

"No you're not."

Katharine pushed herself up, stumbled and grabbed the table. Cole took one arm and Mac had the left one.

"Does the ... do the roooms always spin vi-violently after drinking?"

Mac ushered Katharine out of the Tavern and when her wobbly legs refused to cooperate, he scooped her into his arms. By the time he reached his Jeep, she was out cold. Somewhere between her showing up at the crime scene and dinner, he had decided he couldn't let her out of his sight and told Cole to sleep in the back room at the station.

Now seven at night, the day had been a roller coaster of emotions and events. He didn't know he loved Katharine let alone how much until Gage burst through the door of the bungalow with the news of her being shot. He'd forced himself not to consider the L word, but outside the church, a wad of love and hate churned inside of him with anger and passion. Why else would he have been enraged with her if not because he loved her? Her inflexibility constantly provoked him though it was her determination that he found attractive.

Purposely, he hung back to listen at the Tavern's entrance. He needed to hear what Katharine said to the man he was starting to despise. He came unglued when the toad grabbed her arm then he had to hold back laughing when the guy turned pasty white after his little warrior ripped her jacket off to expose her wound. She'd ordered him to go home and leave her alone. That's all he needed to hear to make his heart soar.

He parked the jeep at the Carriage House. His mind and body had separated. He watched Katharine sleep and chuckled quietly. She didn't look nearly as stubborn as she did in the verbal slaying with him at the church. Her iron-willed jaw had relaxed, and yeah, she was right. She *could* read him like a book. The toad made him jealous. Whether he wanted to believe it or not, he needed this woman for the rest of his life.

In one fluid motion, Mac slid out of the Jeep, walked around and carefully lifted his ragged warrior out. She moaned slightly and wrapped her arms around his neck.

"Are we home?"

"Yeah, Princess, we're home. You're safe."

Her mouth curved into a faint smile. Smugness consumed him and just as quickly, his confidence took a nosedive. How could he consider asking her to leave the one place he knew she belonged?

CHAPTER 24

He slapped the side of his head repeatedly. Did it to stop the ribald shouts and screams. They were playing with his mind. He didn't know how to unravel the different voices. Men sounding like women, all sounding like the Divine Creator. Their hair colors were a mass of confusion—too many dark colors mixing with light and that red-hot fire. Clutching his head with both hands, the killer had to stop the agony. This fiasco was her fault. That destructive witch had caused this new torment. Because of her, the voices bellowed angrily at him. Called him worthless slime and devil spawn. Blamed him.

He choked on his own sniveling breath now as the pain and suffering rooted unmercifully inside the center of his brain. Everything was going amuck. He couldn't fall into the dark pit of despair again. He needed the preaching of his Divine Creator. He needed prayer to end the throbbing inside his chest. The Creator's voice always eased his aching heart. He can't feel weak. He must feel safe. Then he would continue. He must do as the Supreme Being—*NO*—he must do as the Divine Creator commands.

As his head cleared and his thoughts became organized, he understood what must be done. He sat upright. He knew the red-haired enchantress had magical powers that were a great deal mightier than the Divine Creator. She was trouble. She had caused this trouble. She'd annoyed and taunted him and it was time to get rid of her for good. He would try again. Those magical powers of hers were strong, but he was stronger. No one would destroy him. He would destroy her.

After he expunged her from earth, he would then satisfy *his* needs. He would eliminate the heavy burdens, dispose of those spiked emotions, his conflict between love and hate. He would eradicate all affliction and turmoil, escape every feeling by acting out the ceremony that filled his empty cavity and finally disposed of his lonely impotence.

This time he would not miss and she would burn in hell. He knew where she was and she had to die in order for him to live.

* * *

The aroma of coffee, bacon and pancakes woke Katharine. She recognized the loft bedroom, but couldn't remember how she got here. Lifting her wrist to check the time, pain shot up, down and sideways. Her head felt pounded upon with a hammer. The events from the previous day mixed with her haunting dreams and she groaned. How many Long Island Iced Teas had she drunk? *Now there's a fitting word.*

She nudged upward slowly to the edge of the bed, dangling her feet over the side. She decided that if she kept drinking at this pace, she'd be an alcoholic by the end of next month. And if that didn't take her down, they'd have to cart her off to a nuthouse from the nightmares. She glanced at the unfamiliar baggie t-shirt she wore and scanned the bedroom for her clothes. Her weapon was on the nightstand, but her clothes had disappeared.

Oh damn.

Katharine slid off the mattress and stumbled into the bathroom. Her arm didn't just hurt it throbbed unmercifully. A significant headache grated against her temples and eyeballs. Slowly, she went downstairs where Mac stood in the kitchen preparing breakfast. His muscles moved with ease beneath the tautness of tan flesh. Though he hid the inner turmoil of the monster called failure, she knew it lay bedded in him deeply.

What *did* she think of this man who had made a difference in her life? She loved his strength of mind and courage. He cared sincerely about people. Gage was right. He did make her smile and that was something she hadn't done in years. She couldn't remember the last time anyone cared enough to listen to her or ask about how she felt on anything. Nor could she recall the last time she hadn't been the caretaker for someone else. He patiently sat through the hearing of events leading up to her resignation then said the right words that made her understand the emotional mayhem she'd struggled weeks with.

Oh, yeah, she was definitely falling for him.

Regardless of the relationship outcome, she owed him. She'd go to the corners of the globe to bring in Patriot, if she could just get both feet planted on the ground and feed the arm and head some pain killers.

Bracing her good hand on the wall, Katharine stepped down cautiously. "Good morning."

Mac whirled around. "Well, good morning, Princess."

"What time is it?"

"Nine-thirty. You've been asleep since seven last night. I didn't have the heart to wake you up. Are you hungry?"

"I'd rather have some heavy duty pain killers. You got any?" He set the pan down, shut the burner off and walked over to kiss her.

"Let's have a look at that arm first. The bandage needs to be changed. Then I'd enjoy it if you had breakfast with me."

Guiding her to the table, she moved with slow deliberate steps and willingly sat. Mac rolled up the sleeve to his shirt.

"Does it hurt a lot?"

"A little."

"How's your head feel?"

"Like God used it for a bowling ball. Mac, how bad was I last night?"

He stopped what he was doing and looked at her. "What do you mean?"

"I don't remember anything after the first drink."

"You don't remember the hot passionate sex between us either?"

His black eyes gleamed. His grin was broad and menacing. "Dobarchon!"

"You were a perfect angel. In a happy stupor but a perfect angel. Nothing happened here, at least not until I undressed you."

She knew better and refused to egg him on with a response as he removed the dressing.

"This looks pretty good."

Katharine watched him cleanse the injury and apply a new bandage. She hadn't forgotten about Steven last night, didn't care, but asked anyway. "What happened to Steven?"

"The toad?"

She half laughed as Mac tugged her off the chair, switched places and pulled her into his lap. This time his kiss was long and thoughtful.

"He won't bother you anymore."

"What did you do to him?"

"Helped him regain his composure before he left. I washed out your shirt and jacket. They're hanging outside."

"My, aren't you the domestic creature."

He shrugged. "I doubt you'll be wearing your blue shirt anymore. I'm afraid it's seen its last day."

Katharine stood. "I need a shower."

"Hun-uh. Can't get the wound wet and you need to eat for strength." He stood himself. "Sit here and I'll get breakfast for us."

"Do you have orange juice?"

He laid two pills on the table.

"What are those?"

"Aspirin. They'll alleviate some of the pain."

"One's enough."

Mac poured a glass of juice and coffee then filled two plates and brought them to the table. He sat opposite Katharine the same way he sat in the bedroom watching her sleep all night. On the edge of his chair every time she tossed violently between the sheets from nightmares. He soothed and calmed and watched the torture rooted in her subconscious sneak out repeatedly to taunt her. The four drinks she consumed at the Tavern had kept her buried there. While he sat in darkness, he worried about the number of days in past months she went without sleep or eating a decent meal. He carefully calculated what he would say, knowing she would argue and fight him every step of the way. Waking early this morning, he dwelled on the exact words he would use to convince her when he had to soothe away another bad dream. Finally he decided the only way to handle her was to yank her chain out from under her. The earlier phone conversation replayed in his mind. *"Two should keep her down most of the day and night."*

Mac watched her swallow one pill and dig into the pancakes. It might not be fair, but he had toyed with the idea until three in the morning. The arrangement done, Alesha would arrive any minute.

"Katharine, we need to talk."

"Mac, if this is about my arm it's not on the table for discussion."

"I had a feeling you might say that."

"Then ... what's ... to discuss?"

Damn, Cole was right about the sleeping pills. Katharine's lids drooped and fluttered. "I'm sorry, Princess, but this is for your own good."

"W-what have you done to me?"

He felt a whopping punch to his gut when disbelief filled Katharine's eyes. Her fork clunked the table and Mac moved quickly to keep her from falling forward. He lifted her off the chair and carried her upstairs to bed. Smoothing her hair, he covered her with a blanket. "Princess, I'm sorry, but I can't let anything else happen to you. I love you too much to risk losing you."

Though she was out, he said it as if he thought she'd respond. "My little warrior, it'll be over by this time tomorrow and I'll explain then. Sweet dreams."

He leaned over and kissed her forehead.

* * *

Gage was inside the station watching people horde and circle the building. A steady stream of calls poured in with sightings of Patriot. The more folks gathered outside, the more they demanded resolution. Others decided to form search parties to scour the island.

Mac arrived and wedged his way through those who channeled their anger with shouts. Tom Coville was inside. Frank and Garret LeNoir, fresh out of retirement, were packing iron on their hips. Joe, Pete and Cole sat waiting.

"How's Katharine?" Gage asked.

"Sleeping like a baby. Alesha will get a hold of us on her portable if there's any problem. I told her we'd check in every hour."

"Mac, you realize my sister's gonna be hell bent on skinning us alive when she wakes up and finds out what we did to her."

"At least we know she'll wake up."

"Gus called," Gage then told him. "He didn't find anything in the car that would lead us to a location. Patriot's prints are all over the inside and its contents. We've had a hundred plus calls with sightings here on the island. Tom has five boats in the water to prevent him from getting off."

"Any sightings proved worthy?"

"Not yet," Cole said. "We've been discussing how to handle the search. Unless Patriot has another vehicle, there's no way he's making it from one end to the other as the calls indicate. We figured it'd be best to break the island into four sections. Frank will screen calls from the office and maintain contact with us and check in with Alesha."

"You think it's wise we each go out alone?"

"There's several men my Dad and I trust to help us," Gage said. "We figured if each of us took two or three we improve the odds of finding Patriot. Some are gonna do their own manhunt whether we let them help us or not."

"How's this other guy doing that was shot?"

"He's gonna make it. Took a clean hit in the shoulder. Dad dropped off the slug they pulled out of Ted with ballistics this morning. He couldn't get a statement because of medication."

Mac looked at Cole. "What's your gut reaction to this?"

"Partner, they know these people better than we do. I say we run with it. We can also call in the FBI and wait for 'em to get here."

Mac studied the citizens through the station's window. The angry shouts had increased and it appeared so had the crowd. They couldn't afford to wait for the FBI. "Gage, will these extras be carrying guns?"

"Yeah."

"Tom, can you pull a couple of your guys inland?"

"Sure. What're you thinking?"

"We can't risk harm to this case by citizens holding a grudge. How many men in your boats?"

"Got two in each."

"Let's close the station and break the island into three sections instead of four. Tom, call in one boat and use those men to cover the west side. Pete you know the island and can go with Tom and his men. Let's keep one boat at the marina and the other three circling the island. Cole, Garrett and Gage cover the town. Frank, Joe and I will cover the east. We'll start with the most recent sightings in each sector and advise by radio after each location has been checked. Any questions or concerns?"

All shook their heads.

"Everybody know what Patriot looks like?"

When each nodded, Mac said, "Good, let's do it. Check your portables, weapons and extra ammo and don't let this guy get the drop on you."

Frank drove Mac's Jeep while he and Pete walked the roads and driveways leading into wooded areas. They knocked on doors to every rental beginning at the southeast point of Madeline Island and slowly worked their way to the north. They checked every car, vehicle and camper inside and out. Tom's men, covering the marina and the shores, reported in each time they stopped a boat to no avail. As each hour slipped away, one by one, the reported sightings proved futile. They were coming up empty handed and Patriot was nowhere.

At four in the afternoon, Gage's voice came across the portable. They had searched every building and vehicle in town, talked to hundreds of people and came up empty. Tom's last radio transmission reported they were arriving at the last three rentals on the north side of Madeline. Mac's group arrived at the Carriage House, the eleventh rental they'd checked besides the campgrounds. With seven rentals left to search on the east side of the island, Mac's group would meet with Tom's in between. Mac hurriedly ran inside his rented bungalow to check on Alesha and Katharine. Katharine still slept.

They moved onto the next rental as mosquitoes and flies held a feeding frenzy. The air was hot and mucky away from the shore and the sun blazed down with intense warmth. Their shirts were soaked from sweat and clung like soggy toilet paper against their heated flesh. Mac's eyes burned dryly from fatigue. He felt drained and hollow. The air in his lungs exited sharply while the sound of his panting echoed loudly in his ears.

As each cabin was checked and found secured, Mac presumed the tourists who had chosen to finish out their vacations were out doing their thing. Through his examination of the backwoods behind the rentals, his subconscious thoughts began to surface. Since the first day he'd laid eyes on Katharine, her feminine mystique had aroused him. It actually frightened the hell out of him until yesterday when he believed he'd lost her. This morning he said those three little words but honestly didn't know if he could repeat them to her when she was fully awake and alert. Joe yelling pulled him out of his musings.

Scrambling through brush to the front of the cabin, Mac shouted. "Where ya at, Joe?"

He came around the corner of the fifth cabin they'd checked since leaving the Carriage House and observed a middle-aged woman with Joe.

"Mac, this is Mary Norton. She's positive she saw our man about an hour ago walking southbound that way."

Joe pointed back the way they had just come. "An hour ago? Are you sure?"

"Yes. I remember because I had just put a roast in for the family. My husband took the kids to the lagoon today. They were going to rent a paddleboat. I came outside to relax and read a book since we've been running all week."

"He was walking?" Mac asked.

"Yes."

"Do you remember what he was wearing?"

Mrs. Norton thought it over and brushed a free strand of hair back. "A pair of faded jeans and a white t-shirt with one of those black fannypaks everyone uses. I know because we all have one. He's the one who's been killing those poor girls, isn't he?"

"Mrs. Norton when will your husband be back with the kids?"

She glanced at her watch. "Any minute now. Should I be concerned?"

Mac stepped away as Joe told Mrs. Norton not to worry. He radioed Gage and Tom with the new info. Both advised they'd proceed immediately to Mac's location. "We're doubling back southbound. Tom, catch up to us. Gage, keep your eyes open in case he's coming at you—"

"Fire!"

It was Frank yelling and Mac turned, looked in the direction Frank was pointing from the Jeep. Clouds of heavy black smoke swelled over the treetops. A gob of panic stuck in his throat. The black smoke pooled into the sky. He shouted into his portable radio for Gage to start fire and ambulance. He then radioed Alesha, getting no response. He called her again and still no answer. That's when he yelled, "It's the Carriage House!"

CHAPTER 25

A woman's voice cried out to her, pleading for help, yelling and begging Kat to save the child. Many attempts to breathe life into the baby failed while a second cry echoed distantly. The sound came out of the dead child she was unable to revive. More wailing, yelling, screaming, shouting, the voices all forewarned of danger. Officers were shouting over the roar of gunshots, yelling her name in warning but she stood there traumatized.

The shooting wouldn't stop, ra-ta-ta-tat, ra-ta-ta-tat. She felt sharp pain as she sent down, thought it was a flying bullet and kept dropping, falling into an endless hole. Nicole screamed, the mother cried, the dead child stared at her, Michelle in distress, each calling out to her for help but she couldn't reach any of them. She couldn't save any of them as she plunged deeply into the hole. Her father's expression appeared and he took her hand, holding her face, soothing her soul, but even that dwindled to nothing as her body floated further from his touch until his features had faded away. "Come back. Daddy, please come back. I need you, please come back."

Another man appeared replacing the image of her father. No identity only murky shadows. More cries and screams followed, alternating between the child, the dead girls, the woman, Nicole, and Michelle. Each cry a haunting expression of grief until the man who had saved her from her own demons emerged. She called out desperately to him when he started to walk away. But he just turned, smiled then waved goodbye. He would never know she loved him.

Death had exhausted her, the fight had depleted her soul, an unmerciful wind swept away her sorrowful tears ...

Katharine's eyes flew open. She struggled through the cobwebs of her nightmare, shook her head trying to focus. Her throat burned, her lungs were charred and smarting. She was coughing, gasping for air. Her entire body throbbed in pain as she strained to sit up silently cursing the ghost. *"Katharine! Wake up!"*

But Katrina had never *screamed* her name, never called out in audible words. Thought her mind reeled, Katharine quickly grasped the woman shouting her name was real. A roar in her ears muffled sounds of a struggle. The room darkened around her with gray-blue smoky swirls. Her lungs were taking in less and less air, fear and terror knotted inside of her as she realized the place was full of smoke. Mac's rental was on fire!

Katharine called out but the words came out a hoarse whisper. The thought of Mac in trouble tore at her insides. She had to find him. Gasping the smoky air, panting on fear, she rolled off the bed and dropped to the floor beneath the cloud. Feeling for and finding the bedside nightstand, she reached and clutched her weapon tightly in her right hand. She groped the floor through the darkness and crept toward her way out on all four. It seemed to take a lifetime to find the door and open it.

Big mistake.

Smoke and heat whooshed into the bedroom forcing her to her belly. Hugging the floor, her determination faltered and sheer fright swept through her. She forced herself to settle down, forbade herself to tremble and inched her body along the floor. The fire crackled and snapped in competition with shrilling tones from a smoke alert. Massive amounts of smoke had consumed the downstairs living area. A wave of apprehension swept through now, gnawing away more of her determination and confidence.

Locating the edge of the stairs, she came to an abrupt stop. Her heart pounded in her chest. The room was blacker than the ace of spades and the heat was rising. Katharine felt for the steps, shifted her body and slid down one at a time. Impossible to see, a burden to breathe, sweat oozed out of her pores with the rising temperature. Wheezing and choking, her lung were ready to give up. She yanked her shirt over her face and called out. "Mac! Where are you? Mac!"

Gun in hand she crawled as best she could in search of Mac,

avoiding hot spots. She couldn't see shit and bumped into the sofa, a chair, and a broken end table. Feeling her way around each piece, she discovered his head near the back of the sofa, felt the rest of his body for the wet red stuff. He wasn't moving and her old friend fear curled around her. Sweat covered her face. The fire was stealing the oxygen and she didn't think she'd last much longer.

Katharine reached and turned Mac's lifeless body over, gulped back a frightened sob. It was Alesha and she was unresponsive. She still hadn't found Mac, her lungs couldn't take much more, and her brain was fogging up fast. All of a sudden, windowpanes shattered blowing shards of glass in all directions. Katharine ducked, covered her head. She waited a beat and looked up at light now seeping in through the smoke. She wiped her eyes with her shirttail.

"Witch, you're going to die!"

She stiffened right up, rolled over immediately onto her back and a skinny figure parted the graying haze. That familiar prickle tightened in her stomach with the threat of death, and he stood there, his deep-set eyes fixed with evil, watching her.

"You're dead witch!" David Patriot said coming closer.

He reached inside the fannypak around his waist, lunging at her. Katharine rolled away from Alesha and Patriot landed with a thud, cussing and swearing in difficult breaths. She kept rolling until she hit a wall. Her tearing eyes burned, her lungs sated and short of breath, she listened through the roaring flames and the alarm. Patriot was close, gasping for air himself.

She would never give up without fight. She wasn't going to die and balanced on her knees. Gripping her nine with both hands, she aimed, watched and waited.

"Die witch!"

Prepared, trained, her finger on the trigger, Patriot charged. She barely made out the small weapon in his hand the moment she discharged her weapon, the rounds hitting his torso. She fired more, watching him balk with each hit, but she kept firing until the magazine was empty and his body fell to the floor. She scrambled to his body, searching for the thirty-eight, found it underneath him and stuffed the weapon inside her pants.

The bungalow was engulfed with thick, black smoke and unbearable heat stealing the oxygen but Katharine crawled back to Alesha ... had to save her, had to save Mac. She had to find him ... had get to Alesha ... had to go on ... her body refused.

* * *

Mac, Frank and Joe arrived in front of a fully inflamed rental. The crack of eight gunshots rang out as Frank slammed the Jeep into park. Sirens wailed in the distance. Mac jumped out.

"I'm going in!"

Before either man could stop Mac, he ran to the rental. Booting the door, flames leaped out singeing his skin and forcing him backward. "Joe, the back," he yelled, and took off running around the burning structure.

Booting at the back door, the hinges caved on the third try. Smoke billowed out solidly as Joe came around the corner. "Wait here," Mac said.

Using his t-shirt to cover his mouth, he went in crouched low. The beating of his heart roared in his ears as loudly as the flames burning in front. He had no idea who he'd find dead of gunshots or smoke inhalation and prepared himself for the worst.

The sirens rose in volume and stopped. A faint glare of flashing red lights could be seen beyond the smoke and flames. Mac coughed and choked on the heavy fumes then came upon Patriot's body. Flipping him over, he couldn't tell if he was dead or alive. He wasn't moving. Mac kept crawling until he reached two more bodies. Katharine was humped over Alesha with her gun still clenched in her right hand. He shoved it into the waistband of his jeans. He rolled her over, scooped Katharine into his arms, turned and bumped into Joe.

"Told you to wait outside!"

"Shut the hell up!" Joe grabbed Alesha and flung her over his shoulder then both men fled out the back door. Gage and Cole came sprinting around the opposite corner when Mac laid Katharine down in the brush.

"Patriot's still inside. I'm going back in. Somebody check Katharine."

Mac didn't give either time to rebuttal, inhaled a deep breath of fresh air and darted back inside through the smoke, dodging the blaze. Feeling someone behind him, Mac pulled his weapon, swung rapidly and aimed until he recognized Cole.

"Christ, Mac!"

"Over here, against the wall," he yelled. Groping his way to the location where he'd spotted Patriot's body, several drops of water sprayed over his head. The fire department was dousing the flames from the front. The smoke blackened, Mac choked and the flames leaped higher. He held his breath, grabbed Patriot and flung him over his left shoulder. His body teetered and he stepped back to brace the added weight, hitting his foot against a piece of furniture. He fell backward with Patriot landing hard on top of him. Smoke swirled and what little light there was quickly went black.

"I need help in here," Cole shouted.

The ambulance arrived in front just as Pete, Tom and his men were stomping around to the back of the bungalow. Joe was working solo on Katharine and Alesha.

"Where's the goddamn ambulance?"

"They're here now. Where are the others?"

Joe gasped, "These two are unconscious. Mac and Cole went back in after Patriot. I heard one of them yell something and Gage went in."

Two Emergency Medical Technicians arrived and took over. With assistance from Tom's men, they carried both women around to the front of the building. Tom and Joe hung back waiting outside for Mac, Cole and Gage to exit with Patriot. Flames snarled and soared from the roof, threatening trees that surrounded the Carriage House.

Tom looked at Joe. "This place is gonna go any minute. We gotta get 'em outta there!"

Seconds later Gage exited the house first, sucking in short breaths and carrying Mac over his shoulders. Behind him, Cole followed out of breath and hauling Patriot. Tom assisted Gage with Mac as Joe relieved Cole.

Gagging and spitting, Cole panted angrily. "When my partner comes to I swear I'm gonna shoot him with his own fricking gun."

"Katharine ...," Gage sputtered and choked. "Is she ... gonna be all right?"

"EMT's took her and Alesha," Joe said. "This place is coming down! Let's get the hell outta here!"

Gage and Tom picked up Mac. Joe and Cole lifted Patriot's body as they scrambled backward trudging briskly along the edge of the forest. With a boisterous whoosh, the bungalow collapsed delegating sparks in all directions. The blast of hot air forced them further into a wooded area of thick underbrush and shrubs. Each conscious man hissed out an array of vulgar language.

Mac came to with arms flailing and coughing up phlegm. "Katharine!"

Gage grabbed him. "She's out! Mac, you got both her and Alesha out."

"What about Patriot?"

Cole sprang off the body, puffing hotly. "You stupid son-of-a-bitch! You went back into that inferno to save a dead man!"

"She got him? We got Patriot?"

Cole grinned, coughed harshly and spit off to the side again. "Yeah, partner, we finally got him. I don't know which one nailed him, but they turned him into a sponge. Take a look."

CHAPTER 26

Katharine opened her eyes to bright sunlight filtering in through the hospital window. Glancing around the room, flowers decorated a shelf and tables. A large bouquet of red and white carnations came from Nicole and Michelle who'd been by every day to visit. Bayfield residents had sent her a small colorful basket of flowers nicely arranged. She had no idea what they were but thought them pretty. A larger bouquet of unknown blossoms came from Madeline's Islanders. A scribbled note said 'Thank you, come home soon'. Uncle Garrett and Aunt Suzanne sent her a green vine-type plant wishing her well. A smaller arrangement of beautiful peach colored something or other came from Iola and Wilbur Tibbs, and Gage and Joey brought her yellow roses.

Alesha was in a room down the hall recovering with a mild concussion and had received just as many bouquets of flowers. They'd all been in and out to see how she was doing except the one person she wanted to see the most. Mac. The only thing she knew was he had returned to Green Bay. She assumed to wrap up the case with Cole.

During one of Gage's solo visits, he tape-recorded her statement then told her how they'd plotted against her the morning after the shooting. Mac had given her sleeping pills instead of aspirin. None of them believed she was strong enough to survive the manhunt they'd discussed in detail the night before at the Tavern. It was a moot point. She couldn't be angry. Officers involved in shootings were automatically put on a three-day leave of absence. And she certainly couldn't remember any part of that night's conversation either. Since she'd set her mind on forgetting that entire day, she'd slugged back too many of Nicole's drinks. Gage then informed her, the Carriage House had burned to the ground and Mac had saved her and Alesha.

With a clear mind and thoughts now, and try as she might to forget, she remembered every detail at the Carriage House. She'd had plenty of time to think about all of it. The dreams were straight in her mind. She remembered Patriot coming at her. That's when she shot and killed another man for the second time in her life—to save her and Alesha—to stop the murders. Everything was vivid in her mind, right up to passing out. Her last thoughts were of wanting to live. Death was a high price to pay but she'd done the job she was trained to do. She stopped another from killing more.

Alesha filled in the rest telling her how Patriot burst through the door, whacked her over the head and set fire to the stove. There was a struggle. They fell to the floor in a scramble until he finally punched out her lights she'd said. Alesha never had a chance to call out her name. She truly believed it was Katrina who had woke her up. So, if she was supposed to live, where was Mac? Without Mac, her life wouldn't matter. None of what she'd done would matter.

The indecisiveness that had confronted her since Easter wouldn't matter either. It went with the job she'd chosen. In the end, she did what training had taught her. Coming out alive and surviving is what counted. *Right?* No panic attacks in four days either. She and her father had rectified a fourteen-year-old dispute. He enjoyed bragging about her heroics alongside catching up on lost time.

Katharine forced a smile and blew out her breath. If she lost Mac, so what. If he lacked feelings for her, too bad. Tears leaked out of the corners of her eyes and down the sides of her cheeks. It had been a little over a month since he'd weaseled his way into her life. The memory brought a twisted smile to her face. She sighed heavily. She was too stubborn to follow him to Green Bay. If he didn't want her, she refused to chase him. Besides, La Pointe and

Madeline were home and she never wanted to leave again. He'd helped her figure out that much. She'd just have to carry her love for him deep inside forever.

He was your life preserver the voice inside her head told her.

At least she still had the portrait she'd drawn of him the day he sailed up on the beach. The single rose he gave her the first time they had dinner was another keepsake. Sighing again, keepsakes were sentimental rubbish. Mac never indicated a future. He made his goal clear.

Glancing through the room's window, sketching pictures for Iola's gift shop wasn't a bad thing. Maybe Iola would sell out before next year's tourist season. Katharine had pensions she could cash in to help pay for the shop. She'd find a place to live. Though her parents would insist she stay at home, it wouldn't feel right living there the way Gage did. Nicole or Michelle might let her pay rent to stay with them until she found a place. Whatever came of the rest of her life, she did owe people—big time.

Go home and start anew the voice said.

If the doctor wouldn't release her today, she'd get up and walk out on her own. After four days, she felt fine. Hell, her arm didn't even hurt anymore and her lungs were working. The door opened and Dr. Edelstein walked in.

"How are we feeling today, Katharine."

"*We* are feeling fine," she grumbled. "I wanna go home."

"Why don't we listen in on those lungs and we'll see."

"Doc, you got a turd in your pocket or what? You keep saying *we* like you went through this with me."

Ignoring her exasperation, he told her to sit up as he slipped the stethoscope under her gown. "Take a deep breath."

Katharine did each time he said the words, checking her from the front and back.

"They sound better. Let's have a look at your arm."

She rolled up the baggie sleeve and let the doc do his thing convinced the words let's and we went along with his bedside manner. After several minutes, she said, "Well?"

"Katharine, I doubt you'll let me keep you here another day. Promise me you'll go home and take it easy for at least a week."

"You got it. Just let me outta here."

"Call someone to come and get you and I'll sign the release for you."

She shot him a devious grin. "I already did. They're are on their way."

Dr. Edelstein smiled. "I'll have the nurse get your papers ready. It'll take about an hour. I mean it, Katharine. You take it easy."

"Thanks, Doc. I will."

She took a long hot shower after he left. Her mother, who brought clean clothes for her to wear, must've taken Mac's t-shirt home to wash. The nurse came in with papers to sign, which Katharine did eagerly then sat on the edge of the hospital bed combing her wet hair. With the TV on, the news stations continued to broadcast Patriot's demise and the heroic acts of the police. Katharine sighed with relief having escaped the media scrutiny.

Someone knocked and she looked at the closed door. Nicole never knocked on doors before entering. "Come in," she said, wondering why the saucy twit started announcing herself now. When the door opened, Katharine dropped her comb. All she could do was gape at him. A breeze had ruffled his hair. His beautiful black eyes gleamed simultaneously with an easy smile.

"Hello, Princess."

"Mac, you came. They're letting me go home. Nicole and Michelle are supposed to be here."

"I know."

She slid off the bed and bent to pick up the comb. She pulled it through her hair nervously, then fidgeted and dropped the comb a second time. Her fingers trembled slightly as she retrieved the plastic object once more. She straightened and studied him. He just stood there, smiling at her. Eagerness consumed her and she cleared her throat.

"I must say, Princess. I'm glad you handle a weapon better than you do your comb."

"What did you mean you know?"

"Your girlfriends are smarter than you think. Michelle called me."

She needed to pace and recalled Michelle's words the night of Aunt Suzanne's party. "They're not coming?"

"Does it bother you they sent me instead of coming themselves?"

She shook her head. Then each took a step and Mac pulled her into his arms. Her head came up, his mouth swooped down and they buried their lips in a frenzied kiss.

CHAPTER 27

Early morning, Katharine sat in her mother's backyard sipping orange juice. Birds chirped merrily and Superior's waves rolled serenely to shore beyond the cliff. The sun beamed brightly out of a vivid blue sky. All was right in the world. Iola told her to take as much time as she needed to rest before coming back to her job.

A week ago, when Mac showed up at the hospital and brought her home to Madeline Island he explained he went back to Green Bay to finish the case then went to see his sister to tell her about Patriot's capture. Katharine's heart cracked in two when Mac detailed how the two of them went to Clarissa's gravesite and both cried. There was emotional relief in his voice. More importantly, he believed in himself once again. Linda had never blamed him for Clarissa's death.

Since bringing her home from the hospital, they had spent every day together. Katharine exposed all her favorite spots in the Apostles and they shared dinners in the evening. Today Mac was taking her sailing for the first time. He told her last night he had a surprise for her. She lost sleep dwelling on it and jumping to only one conclusion. He and Cole were heroes and Green Bay PD was going to unsuspend him. Mac had been avoiding the subject, and she didn't ask, wanting nothing to interfere with her contentment.

She stood up from the porch step when the black Jeep pulled up out front. Rushing through the house, Katharine swung the door open. His exuberant grin greeted her under a Packers bill cap. It shaded the details of the inherent strength in his face, but she'd already memorized every line.

"What're you looking at?"

"Nothing."

"Doesn't look like nothing to me. You ready to go?"

"You betcha." She pushed the screen door open and he instantly pulled her into his arms. His mouth covered hers hungrily in a spicy kiss. Those demanding lips caressed hers as hot tongues swirled and twisted. Pulsating shivers raced through her veins, like always, until he placed kisses in a ticklish hollow at the base of her neck. The gesture always made her giggle. Mac said it was the only way he knew how to control her.

Her father coughed behind them and Katharine abruptly broke their embrace. Her face flamed hot and Mac's infectious laugh became a full-hearted sound making her blush even deeper.

"She's priceless, Frank."

Her father chuckled as he shook his head and ambled toward the kitchen to start his morning ritual.

"I can't believe you just said that."

"I can," he responded, grinning at her.

* * *

Katharine thought they were floating on angel halo clouds until the sailboat caught the wake of a motorboat zipping by. Perched near the bow, she braced her body against the cabin until the waves settled. Early evening, the sun began dipping in the west. They'd sailed to Raspberry Island for the day where Mac was out-of-control with his camera. He snapped off a roll of film on the lighthouse, several rolls of her in front of it and everything else he saw. After hiking for a couple of hours, they returned to the sailboat to eat the lunch she'd packed. Mac had other ideas. And eagerly, they made wild passionate love inside the boat's cabin. It was the first time they'd done it on a sailboat. She savored every moment of it, feeling as though it might all be over soon. He still hadn't divulged his surprise. Now she didn't want to know.

To avoid the inevitable, she thought about the other subject they'd been avoiding. All week she asked questions about the case but each time she brought them up, he said later. It seemed as good a time to ask once more. Katharine inched her way back and sat opposite Mac.

"Your wheels are spinning, Princess. What's on your mind?"

"Mac, how did you eliminate the Stewart brothers as suspects?"

"We did backgrounds on all of them and double checked their alibis. Curt showed us the ticket stubs from the one time he claimed they'd all been to a Packers game. Everything else checked out as well."

"You never found the tarp or any paraquat did you?"

Those two points bothered him. He shook his head. "Sanders told me to let it go since Patriot's dead and nobody cares."

"Mac, you read my statement."

He nodded, and she asked, "Why do you think he was after me?"

"Other than he was insane, I don't know."

"The fact he's dead means we'll never have all the answers. I remember firing at him until he dropped. How many rounds did I put in him?"

"Seven out of eight. We found eight spent casings after the fire cooled and seven slugs were in his chest. We found the eighth slug in the area that would have been a wall across from where I found Patriot before the bungalow collapsed. There were six left in your weapon."

He smiled at her to lighten the moment. "Princess, you never told me you were *that* good with a gun. I'll have to remember that in the future."

"Literally, heat of the moment. Mac, I'm sorry."

The wind had dwindled and the sailboat sat motionless. She moved across the deck in front of him. "For what?"

"I wanted answers just like you did. I'm sorry for killing him because now we'll never know."

"Katharine, you did what you had to do. There's not a cop on the face of the planet that would question it. You had his thirty-eight Colt when I found you."

"Yeah. But that's not what bothers me."

"Then what?"

She had to tell him what she'd been thinking. "Mac, what if there were others that we haven't found yet?"

He reached for her hands and pulled her into his lap to kiss her.

"Princess, you worry too much. We won't find others. Now, how about we lower the sails and I rev up the motor on this thing. I have a surprise for you."

She wrapped her arms around his neck. "I know that look, Dobarchon. You're just as uneasy about this as I am. You believe there's someone else who's involved in this don't you?"

"It doesn't matter what I believe or what I think. Sanders and the FBI are convinced you shot and killed the Green Bay Serial Killer. End of story. Case closed. It's time to get back."

It was pointless to push when they had nothing other than speculation to go on, but she knew as well as he did cases weren't over until all the questions had answers. Pressing her lips to his, she whispered, "Tell me what the surprise is?"

Obliging her hungry mouth, he kissed her back. "Red, the sooner we lower the sails, the sooner you'll find out."

"Red!"

When he cut loose with laughter, she said, "You're a slave driver."

"I tried to tell you you wouldn't be sitting on your butt on my sailboat."

"That's not all you told me," she said with laughter.

An hour later Mac parked the Jeep in front of the burned down Carriage House. The rubble and debris had been cleared away and the hole filled with dirt. A *For Sale* sign posted on the property already had a sold marker, Katharine observed, somewhat surprised. Oddly, looking at the vacant piece of land, it was like the door had closed on her mind and the past.

"Come on; let's go for a walk along the water."

Katharine hopped out and both headed toward the shore hunkering down in the sand instead. Snuggling side by side, they silently watched gulls dive into the water trapping their last meal for the day.

"Katharine, I resigned from the Department."

Rage almost choked her. The tone of her voice was sharp. "You mean they still wanted your badge after everything that happened?"

Taking her hands and kissing each, Mac said, "On the contrary, Princess, just the opposite."

Contemplating his words and the depth of his eyes, she hesitated. "I don't understand."

"Do you remember the last morning you were jogging along the shore here?"

"Doubt I'll forget it since it was the same day I acquired this scar in my arm. What about it?"

"That's the day I realized I'd fallen in love with you."

She just looked at him, her expression betraying her. "I didn't want to, but I did. It's the same day I sat up there," Mac turned to point. "Where there was once a house."

Confused, she would have paced a hole in the sand if she'd been standing. She was speechless.

"I'd been sitting here mesmerized by a sunrise that reminded me of you. Your hair is what first caught my attention. But by God, those piercing blue eyes of yours are what nailed me. Anyway, I saw you running that morning and as I watched you, I realized this island is your home and you belong here. I think old Sully might be right about his ghost Katrina and the missing jewels."

Gaping at him, she spoke hoarsely. "You've gone completely mad."

"Oh hell," he muttered. "I've botched it. Lemme see if I can fix it. All your life you've been powerless to understand that La Pointe and Madeline Island are where you belong. They're your real home, Katharine. Those precious beautiful eyes of yours are the real jewels that Sully rambles on about in his ghost story. Until you're capable of seeing this island is your home and that your eyes are the jewels of Lake Superior, Sully's ghost is gonna keep on crying."

"Okay, Dobarchon, now I know you've flipped."

"Isn't this where you wanna spend the rest of your life?"

She nodded slowly.

"You're part of all of this beauty. I saw it immediately. And somehow, you've embedded yourself into my soul. I know every moment I've spent here since returning isn't a mistake. I can't leave, Princess."

"Mac—"

"Katharine, I'm flapping around like a fish outta water because

I've never told another woman I loved her. I can't live without you. I also can't take you away from something that means everything to you. I could never ask you to marry me until I had a place for us either. That's just the kind of guy I am. I've spent the entire week tying up loose ends and it's a done deal. This hunk a land we're sitting on is mine ... I bought it. I mean it's ours ... to build a home together ... if you'll say yes. Katharine, I love you. Marry me."

As she stared at him with a befuddled express, Mac said something he never dreamt possible. "I need you."

Her fingers trembled, her throat went dry and a cry broke from her lips. Tears spilled over dumping down her cheeks. "Mac ...," she started and unable to speak, bobbed her head up and down.

"Is that a yes?"

"I thought—I didn't—you left." She finally shrieked, "Yes! Yes, Mac! I've been in love with you since the night we talked in your Jeep. Yes! I need you, too. I love you, too."

Laughing now, he said, "Are you sure?" She nodded again when he cupped her face. "You gave me back the belief in myself, Princess."

As her tears flowed out, he slowly kissed them away then touched her lips, caressing them tenderly. "You gave me back my life," she told him.

They looked up at the evening sky then at each other. Katrina's elated cry rippled through the air. They sat in silence and listened. After several moments, Katharine said, "If Sully's right, we won't be hearing her anymore. I think I'll miss her."

Who was he to mess with a ghost of fate? "Come on, I'll give you a preview of our new home."

He stood and pulled her into his arms. She locked hers around him, nuzzling her nose against his chest. Nothing ever felt better. "Mac?"

"What?"

"Are you absolutely sure?"

"Never been more sure of anything. I love you, Katharine."

"But how are we going to afford this?"

"Before you start agonizing over it allow me to explain. I used the money I've been saving for a sailboat as a down payment on the land."

Her head came up. "No way! You're giving up your dream to own a sailboat?"

It didn't feel nearly as bad as her words sounded. He'd never been in love and wanted her more than any cruise down the East Coast. "Dreams change, Princess. The case spiked a new interest for Joe. He gave notice. Enrolled in some college starting next month to study forensics. Anyway, Gage offered me his job and Joe's letting me rent his place until the house is built."

"Mac, I have some money put away. I was gonna use it to buy Iola's gift shop if she decides to sell. But I'd rather put it into our house."

"Nada. You're using that for the shop. I sold the house in Green Bay for a tidy profit. We'll probably end up broke but happy. Let's walk through, figure out what we want, then I'll ravish you."

Walking hand in hand, he asked, "Princess, how soon can we get married?"

Her face lit up and she leapt into his arms. Sliding her fingers through his hair, she planted a deep kiss on him. "I'll go rough up Father Napoli to do it right now."

He grinned. "My, Warrior Princess. Me thinks I'll be doing the child rearing."

~ Madeline's Jewel ~

Barb Dimich's all new Apostle Islands Trilogy continues with the loves and losses of three best friends. . .

A short, abusive marriage stripped Michelle Callihan of self-respect and nearly bankrupted her business. Now, while she's battling against a determined architect and the return of her violent ex, the ongoing murders are about to destroy Michelle's mask of security.

ABOUT THE AUTHOR

Barb Dimich once took 911 calls about real-life tragedies for the Minneapolis Police Department. Now she's turned her experience into fiction, and her stories take you inside the crime scene tape. Barb resides in Minnesota between the BWCA and the "big" lake.